The BLACK FLOWER

For Dada, who taught me to listen.
For Mama.
For all of the boys.

The BLACK FLOWER

A Novel _of_ the Civil War

_by_

HOWARD BAHR

The Nautical & Aviation Publishing Company of America
Charleston, South Carolina

Published by The Nautical & Aviation Publishing Company of
America, Inc. 845A Low Country Blvd. Mount Pleasant, SC
29464.

Printed in the United States of America

This paperback edition first published in:
January 2012.

ISBN: 978-1-877853-74-6

Cover and map design by William Allport
Back cover photograph by Deanna Vanderver

Library of Congress Cataloging-in-Publication Data
Bahr, Howard 1946-
The Black Flower: A Novel of the Civil War / by Howard Bahr.

p.   cm.
ISBN: 1-877853-74-6

1. United States-History-Civil War, 1861-1865-Fiction. I.
Title.
PS3552.A3613B53   2012   97-1029

PART ONE

THE BAND PLAYED
"ANNIE LAURIE"

This day baptized into the Family of Christ Bushrod Pegues Carter aged 11 mos. The 2nd issue of Thomas Joseph and Jane Pegues Carter of this Parish— "of such is the Kingdom of Heaven."

—Register of Holy Cross Parish
Cumberland, Mississippi
September 6, 1839

J. Bishop, B.P. Carter, R.K. Cross and J. McMillan, Seniors, suspension of seven days for drinking, blacking their faces, building a fence across a Public Road, and acting riotously otherwise.

—Faculty Minutes
The University of Mississippi
November 16, 1859

*And for bonny Annie Laurie,
I'd Lay me down and die.*

—Old Song

CHAPTER ONE

Bushrod Carter dreamed of snow, of big, round flakes drifting like sycamore leaves from heaven. The snow settled over trees and fences, over artillery and the rumps of horses, over the men moving in column up the narrow road. A snowflake, light and dry as a lace doily, lit on the crown of Bushrod's hat; when he made to brush it away, he found it was not snow at all but a hoe cake dripping with molasses. All the snowflakes were turning into hoe cakes the minute they hit the ground. The road and the field were covered in them, but nobody else seemed to notice. The boys went on marching as if nothing had happened.

Bushrod broke ranks, clambered over a rail fence, and knelt in a drift of hoe cakes. He scooped up a handful and breathed deep of the smell of them. He was just about to bite into one when he noticed the wink of a lantern among the distant trees. Reluctantly, he dropped the hoe cake and moved toward the light. Suddenly, he was in the nave of the Church of the Holy Cross, the lantern now a sacristy candle gleaming redly by the altar. All was exactly as he had last seen it, only that had been in springtime and now a winter sun fell in wine-colored ribbons of light through the windows. Bushrod walked slowly up the nave, the broad pine boards of the floor creaking underfoot. He knelt at the altar rail. A priest in humble linen chasuble was consecrating the elements. Bushrod crossed himself and waited. When the priest turned at last, it was General Patrick Cleburne. "I am glad to see you, General," said Bushrod.

The Irishman regarded Bushrod with his dark eyes. He turned again, and Bushrod followed him across a broad wooden stage that rang hollow with their passage. There were fires burning, between which the darkness lay whole and impenetrable. The General passed into one of these dark spaces and Bushrod did not follow. Instead he sat down on a balustrade and waited. Presently, his cousin Remy appeared bearing a great ham on a silver platter. It was a beautiful ham glazed with molasses, the marrow in the round bone still bubbling with heat. Bushrod breathed deep of the smell of it.

"Take, eat," Remy said, and cut off a golden slab of the ham with a bowie knife and laid it in Bushrod's upturned hands and he was about to bite into it when he awoke.

"Well, dammit," he said aloud, and the sound of his own voice startled him.

He had gone to sleep standing up, leaning on his musket. Hunger gnawed at him, and he watched regretfully as the dream of hoe cakes and ham and molasses faded away. However, he was glad to see that it wasn't really snowing—that was something, anyway. Like a fool, he had obeyed orders and left his blanket roll with the brigade trains down below Duck River; now he would have to steal another one from the Strangers who waited up ahead. There had been some bitter snow coming up from the Tennessee crossing, but the winter was young and fickle yet, and this November afternoon was such as old bird hunters love to dream on: cool and dry, the brittle grass and broomsage brown in the fields, shadows blue in the fence corners. The air was hazy with wood-smoke and the dust of a multitude's passing. There was the smell of sycamore leaves.

Bushrod rubbed his eyes and tried to remember what day it was. He counted backward toward the afternoon they crossed the long pontoon bridge over the Tennessee. He tried to picture every sunrise in his mind, but they all ran together in a swirl of snow and rain. There were ten, he thought—perhaps eleven—so it was either Tuesday or Wednesday. It didn't matter in any case, he supposed.

Then he remembered. Early last evening when they had formed line of battle, somebody remarked that it was too bad because he liked to keep his Tuesdays free. So it must be Wednesday now.

Last night was worse than any coon hunt. They had stumbled around in the dark, running into trees and tripping over old cotton rows, trying to keep their alignment, trying to catch the Strangers when it was all they could do to keep up with themselves. At last, around midnight, the regiment had gone into a cold bivouac, sleeping on their arms, and way off in the night Bushrod had wakened to the sound of troops passing on the Nashville road. He figured it was the Strangers slipping past them in the dark, and he was right. The stars were still out when the First Sergeant came and prodded them awake. All this livelong day they had hurried north up the same Nashville road in the footsteps of the retreating enemy, and now they were in line of battle again on a broad plain with the hills to their backs and a little village in the curve of a river up ahead. They were in line of battle.....the realization came to Bushrod with a jolt, and the last rags of sleep blew away.

He wished he had some coffee. He looked hopefully, but nobody was making any fires. That was a bad sign, he thought.

4

On this November afternoon, Bushrod Carter was barely twenty-six, but his greasy hair and mustache were already shot with gray. The grime of the long campaign from Atlanta was etched in the lines of his face and in the cracked knuckles of his hands; crammed under his fingernails was a paste of black powder, bacon grease, and the soil of three Confederate states. Though he was a veteran of all the campaigns of the Army of Tennessee since Shiloh, the fortunes of war had left him still a private of the line, carrying a musket in the ranks of the regiment he had joined more than three years before. True, he had been a Corporal once on the march up into Kentucky, but he had lost his stripes (symbolically, for he hadn't sewn any on) in the confusion over a pitcher of buttermilk stolen from the officers' mess. It was just as well with him, for he really possessed no military ambition. In fact, he was sure he no longer possessed ambition of any kind.

He had never been wounded, never been very sick, never been kicked by any of the multitude of horses that always surrounded them (though he'd been stepped on twice), never broken a limb nor fallen from a wagon nor gotten hold of any whiskey he would call bad. All this singular good fortune he credited to the Saint Michael medal that dangled from his watch chain, a parting gift from Mister Denby Garrison, Rector of the Church of the Holy Cross. On the medal the archangel with drawn sword was in combat with a dragon; around the struggling figures were the words: St. Michael Protect Us in Battle.

Bushrod wore a brown felt hat, misshapen by many rains, with a brass star pinned to the crown of it. He wore his gray roundabout jacket unbuttoned, but arranged so that the Masonic device sewn to the breast was clearly visible beneath his cartridge box strap. He wore checkered wool trousers stained with mud in gradations from the cuffs, and shoes on the Jefferson pattern purchased with Illinois state bank notes from a man in Florence, Alabama, just before they'd crossed the river. Bushrod was glad to be rid of the wrinkled, blood-speckled bills which, until they were translated into shoes, bore the animus of the Recently Departed Stranger from whose pants pockets he had taken them.

Bushrod had taken—on loan, as he saw it—other things from the Strangers during his army career, and many of these he was wearing now. He had a Federal bull's-eye canteen covered in dark blue wool, a Federal cap box on a Federal belt (though the buckle was his own: a brass oval with a star), a Federal tarred haversack with a good linen liner, and a Federal cartridge box still bearing the "U.S." plate crammed with fifty rounds of .577 ball cartridge taken from a waylaid United States Quartermaster wagon just over the Duck River crossing. Back with the trains was his excellent Federal wool blanket rolled in a waterproof gum blanket, also Federal, neither of which he ever expected to see again.

His own side—that is, the Confederate States of America, which existed for Bushrod only as a vague and distant, and rarely generous, entity—had provided him a first-rate Enfield rifle with blued barrel and a rich, oily walnut stock into which he had carved his initials. The blueing was nearly all rubbed off now, and the lands and grooves of the rifling so worn that he imagined the ball wobbled on its outbound trip, but he had carried the piece too long to want to give it up. Besides, he was not a sharpshooter; Bushrod preferred to leave his targets to chance. For this rifle the Confederate States had given Bushrod a bayonet (currently affixed), a bayonet frog and scabbard, and a nipple-protector on a brass chain which he'd thrown away long ago. Finally his government had sent him over the years a series of stylish gray roundabout jackets, on the Army of Tennessee pattern, which he thought were flattering to his rangy frame. His current jacket was stained, tattered at the cuffs, and comfortable. For these, and for all things, he was grateful.

Bushrod also wore a light gray civilian waistcoat; in its pocket, at the other end of the chain from the Saint Michael's medal, lay a gold watch he'd won for declamation as a senior at the University of Mississippi. The watch was thin and fragile and should not have lasted this long, but it ticked on faithfully, wheels turning, balance swinging, and no doubt the time it measured owned some meaning somewhere.

Thus accoutred, Bushrod Carter stood in the melancholy sunlight, wishing for coffee and waiting for something to happen.

❧

When the regiment came into line that afternoon, they were given the command to rest almost at once. They did not stack arms, however, which was always a bad sign. Now most of the boys were sitting or lying in place on the ground so that it did not seem to be a line at all but a vast, untidy mob of lounging vagrants, some talking quietly, some playing cards, a few reading letters or writing them. Many lay with their hats over their eyes, wandering through restless dreams of their own. Bushrod, even tired as he was, did not feel like lying down. He stood with his musket between his feet, idly thumbing the socket ring of his bayonet, and looked at the sky.

In the southwest, the sun was sinking lower and lower. Across the blue interval of the heavens, a quarter-moon was rising in the southeast. Moon and sun all at once, vaguely disturbing, portentous, maybe a bad sign though it could be a good one. Bushrod didn't know. He only knew that, in the narrowing interval between that moment and darkness, something was bound to happen.

Ordinarily, Bushrod tried not to think too much in the time before a battle. Long ago he had learned to close his mind to speculation, fixing his eyes on the crossed straps or blanket roll of the man to his front or, if he was in the front rank (as he was now), the ground at his feet. He never, never, never looked up at the enemy, not since the first charge on the sunken road at Shiloh when the sight of the bristling blue ranks and the waiting guns double-shotted with canister nearly froze his heart. When a fight was joined in earnest, Bushrod did not think at all. The roar of his own blood consumed all thought and drove him deep into the marrow dark, where he huddled in supplication while Another in his shape loaded and fired the musket, swung it at the heads of Strangers, and waded through the shambles. Only afterward—when the mortal spark, having survived once more, crept upward and looked timidly about—did Bushrod dare to think again. He would look at his hands or at some humble element of earth—a rock, a cloud, a blade of grass—and gradually all the scattered atoms of his being would draw together like particles of quicksilver into one Bushrod Carter again. At such times, he could remember almost nothing of what he had done in the battle. The remembering came later, like magic lantern slides, at unexpected times and places, but most often as he was about to drift into sleep. Then he would watch as scene after scene unfolded, with himself at the center of each, and whatever of terror and outrage and violence he'd missed before would return undiminished in fatal clarity and no effort of will would make it stop until it was played out to the end—Bushrod all the while telling himself *That could not be me* but knowing all the while that it was.

So Bushrod went to great lengths not to think before a fight, knowing there would be plenty of time for that later. On this afternoon, however, he could not seem to keep from thinking, could no more stop thinking than he could check the movement of the sun and moon. He even began to think about this time tomorrow, something he rarely allowed himself at any time. He pictured himself walking out alone by the little river that curled around the village like a protecting arm. There, among the willows, he would sit in the cold twilight and smoke and write in his book. He imagined a kingfisher darting down the tunnel of barren trees. He saw the dimple and swirl of fish in the shallows. What was about to happen now would be all over with then. *I wish it was this time tomorrow,* he thought.

Then he risked a look at the prospect ahead where the Strangers were waiting for him, and immediately wished he hadn't. A line of trees marked the river, and there were the spires and rooftops of the town, all elements of a world to which he had no access at the moment. Instead, clearly and painfully visible, like new-turned furrows in a field, were the mysterious works of the enemy; these alone, in the prospect ahead, were of his life and of his comrades' lives. Between Bushrod and those works was a good mile or more of treeless plain which he personally would have to cross to get at the Strangers, and he knew that the gunners over there had long since laid their pieces to sow every yard of it with shell and canister. Over there, too, were the long bayonetted Springfields soon to be levelled at him by men he did not know, with whom he had no personal quarrel, whose lives he could not imagine—but who would, if they could, send him straightway to join the long ranks of the Departed.

An unwelcome, but not unfamiliar, thought arrived in Bushrod's mind. If only those boys over there could get to know him for a while—if only they could learn what a charming, what a really extraordinary fellow he was—perhaps they would not be so keen to erase all the possibilities he represented. Then he thought how, among all the minions of the enemy, there was really only one who needed to know him—the one whose every living step since birth had been toward the moment when he would raise his musket or pull the lanyard of his gun or aim his pistol and drop death like a stone into the heart of Bushrod Carter. But which one was it? And even if he knew—For a moment, Bushrod stopped breathing. It was like being underwater, the green world only a circle of light too far above. How could they want to kill him? How could they dare? It was not fair that all his dreams (he had none at present, but no doubt some would appear at their appointed time) were at the mercy of a total stranger, a man to whom he had never been introduced but who, in an instant, could be wed to him so intimately and rob him of all that God Himself had promised—

His breath came back in a long, ragged sob. He looked wildly about, every nerve vibrating against the air. He did not want to think about these things. He did not want to remember what it was like to walk across the open ground in good order under the flags—

Look at you said a voice in his head, disapproving and cold, speaking from somewhere in the marrow dark. It was a voice Bushrod had heard many times before; he believed it belonged to that other Bushrod Carter with whom he swapped places now and then and who rarely saw things as he did. *All a-tremble over things that ain't happened yet, that might not happen atall. I won't have this, won't have it. Now, listen. Listen—*

Bushrod shut his eyes tight, and in the dark behind his eyes arose a vision: the battlefield, the tangled breastworks of the enemy floating closer and closer, what had been life's endless prospect shrunken to a few yards of brittle grass. And the Departed! The Departed rising from the earth like blackbirds, by the hundreds, by the thousands, groaning and chattering, disappearing forever into the smoke—

No, you don't the voice commanded. *Listen!* So Bushrod set his heart against the vision and listened. What he heard was the murmur of living men, his comrades, and beyond that the sullen utterance of the great army spread around him, that lay under the press of something even greater still. The dark necessity, somebody had called it. *That was Hawthorne* said the voice. *Remember what he said. The black flower. Let the black flower blossom as it may—*

Slowly, for the second time that afternoon, Bushrod Carter began to awaken. It was as if he had not awakened at all until just now. He passed little by little out of the shadow and his breathing settled into the regular, unconscious rhythm of life. *All right*, he thought. *All right, I can stand it.* And he remembered at last the truth he'd had to remind himself of time and again over the years: he was a soldier after all. He was an old soldier and he could stand anything, even the certainty that something was about to happen to him that had not happened before.

He touched the medal on his watch chain. "Protect us in war and tumults," he said into the gathering dark, "and support us in the day of battle."

"You look like you swallowed a eel," said a living voice beside him. Bushrod opened his eyes and looked into the gaunted, bestubbled face of his friend Jack Bishop, who himself had just risen from sleep and was brushing the grass from the front of his jacket. The pale autumn sky gleamed in Bishop's spectacles; behind them, the eyes were red and listless. Bishop uncorked his canteen and took a long swallow. "Ah, me," he said, "I am gettin too old for this business." He stoppered the tin drum, picked up his rifle, and ran the tip of his finger around the inside of the muzzle.

He inspected the finger critically, then wiped it on his pants. "What's the matter with you anyhow?" he asked.

Bushrod hesitated before replying. In the interlude before a battle, when the imponderables of life and death teetered in delicate balance, a man had to be careful about what he revealed of himself. It was part of the complex, unspoken old-soldier's code, a rubric a man could learn only by violating it, as every man did who was new at the trade. Bushrod had learned it long ago, as Jack Bishop himself had learned it, and all the boys who had come this far with them. So when Bushrod spoke at last, he said only, "Oh, nothin atall. I reckon I was wishin it was this time tomorrow."

Bishop laughed. "Me, too," he said. Then, as the code allowed, Bishop opened the way for further discussion. "You know," he said, "I am not the least bit comfortable with the way this affair is shapin up. What you reckon that old peg-leg son of a bitch has in his head to commence this thing so late in the day?"

The reference was to their commander, General John Bell Hood, who'd lost his leg at Chickamauga. Hood was an old Indian fighter and apparently thought he could fight the Strangers in the same way. Bishop, who studied generals as he might some species of exotic bird, despised the man, and always referred to him as a peg-leg son of a bitch.

"No tellin," said Bushrod. "No doubt he knows what's best."

"Shit," said Jack Bishop, and spat.

Bushrod had known Jack Bishop for all their twenty-six years, yet sometimes wondered if he knew the man at all. Long ago, Bushrod had accepted the fact that his friend was insane, though it was only after the winter battle at Murfreesboro—called Stones River by some—that Bushrod knew it once and for all.

The night of a big battle was always bad, but Stones River remained in Bushrod's memory as one of the worst. In the freezing rain of that awful night, for reasons never adequately clear, Jack Bishop had divested himself of everything but his spectacles and his hat. In the bulk of his uniform and accoutrements, Bishop looked like every other private of the line, but Bishop naked was so scrawny as to invite attention even in that pinched and rawboned army. Naked, Bishop prowled the line at Stones River, scaring the pickets and leaving a trail of incoherent reports still current in the folklore of the army. Finally he materialized out of the frigid dark at a little fire where Colonel Ike Stone and his staff (in defiance of the order forbidding fires) were trying to boil some coffee. Colonel Stone was Bishop's godfather.

"Jerusalem!" cried Colonel Stone when the apparition appeared at his fire. The Colonel and five staff officers and a mounted orderly reached for their pistols.

"Aw, Uncle Ike," said Jack Bishop. "I am only out for a stroll."

"Goddammit," said Colonel Stone. "Mister Clark, fetch a blanket, will you? Goddammit, he used to be such a good boy."

Now almost two years later Colonel Stone was buried and at rest, and Jack Bishop stood twisting his thin, grimy hands around the muzzle of his rifle. He, too, was looking toward the village and the long, empty plain before it.

"This is all folly," Bishop went on, "and I for one am inclined to forego the whole thing. See those trees yonder?" He swept his arm toward the river. "They will make this whole end of the line bunch up toward the center, and it'll be a fine day for hog killin, won't it Bushrod, old pard?"

Bushrod knew it would happen just as Bishop said. Somewhere out there they would have to wheel under fire, and the whole line would be caught in enfilade. He had seen it happen before on divers fields, to them and the Strangers both, and it occurred to him, as it often had, that if he, Bushrod Carter, a humble private of the line, could predict such a thing.....

"You would think the General could see it, too," he said, completing the thought. "I mean, him bein a General and all. Maybe he is just tryin to get em to run again."

"Hah!" Bishop snorted. "The gallant Hood is mad because they stole a march on him last night and made him look the fool. Now he's caught em, he ain't about to let em get away. Don't tell *me!*"

"Nevertheless," said Bushrod.

"Well," Bishop said, "you can 'nevertheless' all you want to, but it don't take Napoleon to see we fixin to get our ass in a fight."

"Nevertheless," said Bushrod stubbornly. He looked back toward the hills whence they had come, as if he might find proof there of a guiding hand, wise and benevolent. But there were only the barren trees, deep in the shadow now, rising gently toward the sky. The sight troubled him.

"Well, anyway," Bushrod said, "the whole army must be up. Just look out yonder." He indicated with his hand the great tattered host spread out upon the plain.

"Yes, indeedy," said Bishop. "That's a real comfort. Say, you got any more of that good tobacco?"

The two friends filled their pipes from Bushrod's poke, and Bishop produced a box of Lucifer matches made in Cincinnati, Ohio. They smoked in silence, contemplating the ground before them.

They were not cowardly, nor weak, nor faint of heart. Any who had been these things had long since given up, or their bones lay bleaching in the woods and shallow graves along the road behind. Bushrod knew that when the order came, he and Jack would step out smartly with the rest and follow the colors into the great Mystery awaiting them in the twilight.

He knew just as surely they would run like rabbits if they thought it meet.

For they had come a long way, as memory measures such things, from the sunlit fields of their youth, and they no longer had any illusions about themselves. Valor or cowardice, glory or shame: they heard the generals offer these as paths a man might actually choose—when in fact, at this late hour, they were all of a piece, and nobody but generals and newspaper correspondents gave any weight to them at all.

In his haversack, Bushrod carried a little clothbound book—a commonplace book, they called it then—where for all his soldiering he had put down things the boys had said, and things he had out of books, and thoughts that came to him in the quiet watches when the mystery of the world possessed him. On the flyleaf, written by candlelight one vanished evening, was the single line:

Act well your part; there all the honor lies.

When he'd copied it from a newspaper, Bushrod thought he remembered that it was from *Hamlet*. When he learned it was Alexander Pope, it made no difference, for Bushrod loved young Hamlet and thought he should have said it even if he didn't. It was Hamlet anyway, not Pope with his hobby-horse couplets, who spoke over the cloudy reaches of time to the last soldiers of the Army of Tennessee. Hamlet might have stood for them all, Bushrod thought: exiled from peace, muttered at by ghosts, melancholy, driven by his own inner voices toward a moment from which there could be no turning. Hamlet played it out the best way he could, and Bushrod supposed they would also, and in the end that was all that mattered. Bushrod smiled to himself. *Act well your parts, my lads*, he thought— *and flights of angels sing thee to thy rest.*

Thus it was that Bushrod Carter could look away toward the distant trees and feel no less a man for being afraid.

Throughout the cluttered sprawl of infantry, men were beginning to rise stiffly to their feet as if some unseen herald had passed among them. Talk was growing thin, and there was little laughter. Some were already absorbed in the arrangement of their clothing, tugging at crotches and galluses, buttoning and unbuttoning and rebuttoning their short gray jackets. After this came the labored drawing-on of accoutrements, accompanied by the clatter of tin cups and boilers and canteens and bayonets and frying pans hung on blanket rolls that had wisely not been left behind, and no little cussing and grunting and tightening like the harnessing of so many mules. There was nothing chivalric or grand about it, any more than the harnessing of mules was chivalric or grand—except that these were men preparing for battle, many of whom would soon be torn, eviscerated, or blown into a fine red mist before the muzzles of the guns. With that as a possibility, even buttoning a fly assumed the dignity of a final act.

Among the last to stir was Virgil C. Johnson, whose place in the line was at Bushrod's left shoulder. Virgil C. was encouraged to rise by the prodding foot of First Sergeant William ap William Williams, whom everyone called Bill. The First Sergeant was a Welshman who had served nearly twenty years out west in the Indian-fighting army; he was the only enlisted man Bushrod ever heard of who quit the old Regular Army to join the Confederate one, though plenty of their officers had done so. No one knew why William Williams had joined the rebels, unless it was simply because he was Welsh, and had waited all those twenty years for a hopeless cause to throw in with—so the common wisdom ran, anyway. It was known that if old Bill were captured and recognized he would be shot as a deserter, no questions asked, and buried in an unmarked grave, and the grave marched over by troops until every trace of it had vanished. Officers, on the other hand, were allowed to resign their commissions in the old Regular Army—if *they* were captured, they were received by their former peers not as deserters but as wayward fraternity brothers fallen temporarily from the fold. The First Sergeant relished this bitter distinction; its chief effect was to stimulate his ardor in battle—God help the Stranger who tried to take him prisoner. And yet, on this November afternoon, even this accomplished warrior could inspire Virgil C. Johnson to rise no further than a sitting position.

"Goddammit, Virgil C., get up!" snarled the First Sergeant, whose natural Old Army instinct was to draw back his foot and deliver a comprehensive blow to the ribs on Virgil C. Johnson.

"Oh, the nation, Bill," said Jack Bishop. "Now see what you've done—you've gone and woke him up, and he has not had his sugar-tit." Bishop gave his musket to Bushrod and went about gathering up Virgil C.'s scattered equipment. He shook out the soiled wad of Virgil C.'s jacket and hung it over the man's sloped shoulders. Meanwhile, Virgil C. scratched himself and peered groggily about. "Where are we now?" he said.

"You see?" said Bishop, retrieving his musket. "Now he is good to go."

"Jesus Christ deliver me," said the First Sergeant.

"No doubt Virgil C. will get up in a minute," said Bushrod hopefully.

The First Sergeant spat a stream of ambure into the grass and leaned on his musket. He was looking past them toward the distant Federal works. "I expect he will," said the First Sergeant. Then he seemed to forget them all. He narrowed his eyes and stared across the open plain.

Two gentlemen approached, ambling along in quiet conversation. They were Tom Jenkins, the company's Second Lieutenant, and Mister Sam Hook, their Brigade chaplain. At their feet trotted Old Hundred The Marvelous Dog, who belonged to the Chaplain.

"Hey, fellers," said Tom Jenkins.

Bushrod saw the First Sergeant's jaw tighten. In old Bill's mind, officers did not greet enlisted men with "Hey, fellers." It was a breach of decorum that threatened the very fabric of the Republic—or, in this case, the Confederacy. But the First Sergeant said nothing; he only shook his head and went on looking across the plain as if (Bushrod thought) he expected to see a war party of Comanches sortie from the village.

Tom Jenkins had been with the Cumberland Rifles (the name was one they had given the company in the old, innocent days—in these latter times it was only invoked in moments of irony) since the beginning. At home he owned a cavernous, dingy, chaotic mercantile on the west side of the square—that is, everyone thought he still owned it. None of the old Cumberland men knew that the town had been burned in October by marauding Federal cavalrymen operating out of LaGrange, Tennessee. Now Tom Jenkins stood grinning, rocking on his heels, hands thrust deep in his breeches pockets, in his tattered frock coat and slouch hat. He had left his sword belt somewhere and were it not for the rusty gold bars on his collar facings he might have been crossing the square on his way to the barber shop. "What's goin on?" said Tom Jenkins.

"Why, Tom, we're glad to see you," said Bishop. "We been discussin tactics, Bushrod and I."

"Tactics," nodded Tom Jenkins. "Well, that's mighty good. I am glad to hear it. What did you decide?"

"We decided we gone get our ass whupped," said Bishop.

"Now, wait a minute—" began Bushrod.

"That don't seem like much of a tactic to me," said Tom Jenkins. "I thought tactics was where you studied how to whup the *other* feller's ass."

First Sergeant William ap William Williams grinned in spite of himself. Next to Captain Byron Sullivan, Tom Jenkins had developed into one of the best line officers in the whole regiment. Since he had no use for army politics, he'd risen no higher than the second-lieutenancy of his rifle company—but even the First Sergeant had to admit that Tom Jenkins had a natural talent for soldiering. He was the kind of volunteer officer who drove the Old Army brass to distraction.

"No, no, no, Tom," said Jack Bishop. "You are confusin the tactics of *this* army with somebody else's. In *this* army, you run around in the woods all night, then march like hell all day, then about sundown you fix bayonets and charge across two miles of prairie calculatin to run the other fellows out of trenches *they've* spent all day diggin—that's tactics. Why, Tom, it lays over any tactics I ever saw—just thinkin about it makes me proud to be a soldier of the Sovereign South. Now, you take those trees yonder—"

"Say, Sammy," said Bushrod, wanting to change the subject. "Has Old Hundred bit anybody of note lately?"

The Chaplain gazed with affection on The Marvelous Dog, who at the moment was gnawing on his private parts. Old Hundred was a terrier cur the Chaplain had picked up during the Atlanta campaign. He was hateful and ill-tempered and had no use for anyone, not even the Chaplain. His coat was like a wire brush; he had a grotesque overbite and forever swarmed with fleas and with ticks that, once safely aboard, swelled overnight to the size of pistol-balls. In camp, Old Hundred prowled from fire to fire begging scraps, and was not above stealing saltpork out of the very frying pan. In battle he waxed hysterical, tangling himself in the feet of the soldiers and biting at their ankles and snarling, though no one had ever seen him close with the enemy. In all, he was the most offensive dog Bushrod Carter had ever seen.

"Well," said Sam Hook, "in answer to your question, I can't say that he has. He took a piece out of Squire Chevis over in Company E last night—or this mornin, whenever it was—but that ought not to be a surprise to anybody—there's always been bad blood between them two. He is a noble creature if you allow for his faults—Old Hundred, I mean."

"Well, well," said Bushrod, not knowing what else to say.

In the old times, Sam Hook was a lawyer in Cumberland. His clientele were exclusive: the poor, the hopeless, the friendless; peckerwoods barefoot and gallused, and clay-eaters whose childrens' bellies swelled with hookworms; murderers, the insane, women whose husbands used them badly, prostitutes from the Devil's Elbow up at Wyatt's Crossing—That Sort Of Thing, as Bushrod's old-maid aunt always phrased it. It was *pro bono* as vocation, or rather avocation, since the money that fueled Sam's interests came from eight hundred acres of river-bottom cotton land—and, it was said, certain shrewd investments he'd made in the steamboat trade as a youth. He had an office over Frye's Tavern that opened onto a broad gallery, and in good weather, when court was not in session, Sam Hook could usually be found with his heels up on the railing, holding court of his own. His auditors were anyone, of whatever color or age or rank, who could talk about sporting—about guns and horses and dogs and gamecocks—who liked whiskey, and who could laugh. For years, Sam Hook was known as the best wing shot in Cumberland County, and owned the champion rat-killing dog and a pair of the best fighting chickens in that part of Mississippi. In addition to these credentials, he was an ordained Methodist.

Sam had the little congregation out in the Yellow Leaf community, four miles in the county from Cumberland. Every Sunday morning he saddled his sleek, long-legged racer and rode out there to call down thunder and lightning on the Faithful, many of whom had seen him perform in just that way in the courtroom. Then, after dinner, Sam rode back to Cumberland again, always in time to take his accustomed seat in the legendary card game that had been held every Sunday evening at Frye's since before the War with Mexico.

In the first spring of the current war, the company known as the Cumberland Rifles was formed at Frye's, and Sam Hook was called down from his office and informed he'd been elected the company's chaplain. He told them he would prefer to be a general; they replied to the effect that there were no openings for generals in a company of infantry. Sam declined participation then, saying he was a Union man anyway and they could all go to hell. There followed much argument and rhetoric, during which Byron Sullivan, Captain-elect, delivered his third (and some said his best) blood-curdling war speech of the afternoon. Also, Mister Frye opened the bar. In an hour or so, Sam Hook was converted to secession, willing to compromise with the rank of Captain.

Three long years later, Sam Hook was Chaplain for the whole of Adams' Brigade, and had been since they were over in Cleburne's. It was, according to Sam Hook, a position of such oppressive responsibility that God Himself would expect no less than a general to discharge it. He had once petitioned President Jefferson Davis on that subject, but the President's secretary replied, in a curt note, that no one in any authority knew of any chaplains who were generals. There the matter rested.

Sam Hook had been with the boys in all their fights—cursing, exhorting, driving them on, seeming to be everywhere at once. He even led the old Cumberland Rifles in the Chickamauga battle when Captain Sullivan was down with the shingles—led them in charge after charge with a walking cane and a dragoon pistol borrowed of a staff officer. In every action, he would have the boys understand that God, who would take no side but who was not adverse to going in with the infantry, was walking with them—no easy task amid the smoke and noise and the ample evidence of mortality. The same God stood beside him at church call every Sunday, fair weather or foul, when Sam Hook—no matter how bad his hangover—flung his profane, eloquent sermons over deeply flawed men who walked always along the chilly margins of death.

Now here was Sam Hook in the autumn afternoon, watching with his comrades across the open plain. He wore a Mexican War forage cap, and for a uniform the old Knight's-Templar frock coat with crosses on the collars that he'd worn in lodge in Cumberland. At his feet, The Marvelous Dog curled up in a wiry ball and began to snore.

"Well, Sammy," persisted Jack Bishop, "these fellows don't want to hear about tactics from me—but I judge we are goin in by and by and I want a learned opinion. What do *you* think, a man of the cloth, a warrior monk and so forth?"

Sam Hook's eyes narrowed in thought, he thumbed his cap to the back of his head. "Bill," he said to the First Sergeant, "what do you see yonder?"

The First Sergeant spat again. "It is a damn long ways over there, Chaplain," he said.

"It is that, now," agreed Tom Jenkins. "A long ways to walk, and no place to run."

"Hmmm," said Sam Hook.

"Oh, you boys are killin me with your tactics," said Bushrod in exasperation. He watched them, their little group, as if he were hovering somewhere above—among the blackbirds, perhaps, that were streaming toward their roost in the river trees. Bushrod wished he were a blackbird, free to fly wherever he chose. He would go South, all the way to the big water, perhaps even to the far and fabled islands where there were no men.

"So, what do you think, Sammy?" asked Bishop.

"I say fuck it," said Sam Hook. "Let's go. I'd as lief try it now as have to try it tomorrow."

"That ain't what I asked," said Jack Bishop.

"Hmmm," said Sam Hook. "No—no, I guess it ain't." He knelt and scratched the tattered ear of Old Hundred and the dog groaned in his sleep. Sam Hook looked at Bishop, at Bushrod, at Tom Jenkins and the First Sergeant, at Virgil C. where he sat upon the ground. "Ain't it curious," he said. "How we do, I mean. Always wantin to know how a thing will turn out, when it will turn out just the same anyway." He smiled and looked off toward the Federal works. Something glinted over there—a rifle barrel, perhaps, or a bayonet, or a belt plate. There was movement, too—a restless undulation like a swarm of dark bees. They were shifting troops. Sam Hook turned his eyes away. "I have loved you boys," he said.

Bishop nodded. "Well, I reckon that is a good answer," he said.

"Yes, I reckon it is," said Bushrod.

Virgil C. Johnson yawned and scratched himself. "Say," he said, "has any of you all seen my coat?"

※

In that other, forgotten life before the Shiloh battle, Virgil C. Johnson was a fiddler. His people had traveled from upper Missouri in the forties seeking a warmer climate where the land grew something besides rocks and abolitionists; Virgil C. was born on the way, in the shanty of a flatboat riding the high spring flood of the Mississippi. In Virgil C.'s recollection, the first sound he ever heard was his Uncle Ham's fiddle sawing out "The House Carpenter."

"Now, how the nation could you know that if you was only just borned?" Jack Bishop asked when Virgil C. first made that revelation. The three boys were sitting on a rise near the Yellow Leaf Church, listening to old Relbue Carter's dogs run a coon in the Leaf River bottoms. Bushrod and Jack were fifteen, Virgil C. two years their junior. The full Wolf Moon of January spread over the familiar valley below in glittering illusion, and the clapboard church, empty and silent, gleamed like marble. The black squares of its windows stared out on the burying ground where dark cones of cedars huddled among the graves.

Virgil C. was smoking kinnikinnick in a dingy corncob pipe. He exhaled a rank cloud of smoke and said, "Well, Jack, I reckon I know that song when I hear it."

"But how could you know it *then*," said Bushrod, "when you was just born?"

"Well, because that's what the song was," said Virgil C.

"Virgil C., you are a damned lie," said Bishop. "Your mama told you about it."

"She didn't," Virgil C. said. "You a damn lie your ownself."

"She did!" said Bishop.

"She didn't!" said Virgil C.

"Look!" said Bushrod, pointing.

The shadow of an owl, skimming low, flicked across the valley. They watched it strike. There was a rustle in the broomsage, a shrill piercing scream, then silence. Then the owl, beating hard against the dead weight of the rabbit, rose again in the silver night and glided with its prize toward the dark line of the trees.

"Great God," Bushrod began, "did you see—" But Virgil C. caught his arm.

"Hush," he said. "Look yonder, by the church."

The way he said it made Bushrod shiver. He did not want to look at the church. It was too silent, too empty, too bony white in the cold moon, and if you looked too long and too hard the dark clumps of cedars in the burying ground would start to move. You couldn't actually see them move, but if you looked away and then looked back, they would have shifted. Some of them would be closer, you would swear to it. Bushrod knew in his heart that it was only a trick of the shadows, but still—

Bushrod hated the night. He was afraid of it, especially when the moonlight lay like a shroud over the land and nothing looked like it was supposed to. He thought what a damn fool thing it was to run coons anyhow. Some boys drew pleasure from it—he knew Jack and Virgil C. loved the high solitude away from lamps and houses. But Bushrod believed Man to be a creature of the day, who ought to have sense enough to hunt his hole when the sun went down.

"I don't see nothin," Jack said. "Don't spook us that way, Virgil C."

"Hush," Virgil C. said again. "I can see him. In the big shadow hard by the church house."

The three boys peered across the moonlit valley. The church flung out a long shadow, black as pitch, over the west yard. In that dark pool was a darker shape, still and quiet, like a piece of the vast night itself.

"It's a man a-horseback," whispered Virgil C.

"You fulla shit," said Jack, but he, too, was whispering now.

This time Bushrod felt the hairs rise on the back of his neck. He felt a cold deeper than the January night. He believed he could see it too: a man on a big horse, watching from the shadow of the church. It moved just a little, as a horse will when it's restless, and the cedars did a little dance. They had not heard the horseman come, like they should have in the cold clear air.

"It's just your uncle tryin to scare us," whispered Jack hopefully.

"No, it ain't Uncle Relbue," Bushrod said. "He's up on Tallyrand tonight, remember?" Tallyrand was a gelding white as milk; you could not hide him in a shadow. "Who do you think it is, Virgil C.?"

But Virgil C. didn't answer. Instead, he stood up, and without a word began to walk down the slope into the valley.

"Virgil C. Johnson, you get back here!" hissed Jack Bishop, but the other boy went on. They could hear his feet whisper in the broomsage. They watched him cross the broad slope, his long-legged shadow flung out beside him. Bushrod thought he heard the muffled *clump-clump* of an impatient hoof. Virgil C. crossed the valley. He was the only thing moving in all that pale silence. His shadow slanted as he began to climb the far slope toward the church and the huddling cedars and the pool of shadow; he did not slow or falter as the distance closed. Then, just as the dogs set up a mad chorus in the river bottom, the shadow swallowed him up.

Bushrod and Jack waited in breathless silence, but the only sound was the beating of their own hearts and the distant ghostly yelping of the dogs. Jack stood it as long as he could; before Bushrod could stop him, he stood up and cupped his hands and sent his voice across the valley: "Vir-gil Ceeeee!" Bushrod thought it the loudest sound he'd ever heard, but it brought no answer save the ringing echo in the hills. When these died away, Jack Bishop said, "Well, we got to go over there."

"The hell you say," said Bushrod. "What you want to do that for?"

"It ain't a matter of wantin to," said Jack. "He'd do the same if it was us, you know dern well he would."

Bushrod looked out across the valley. "Well, I suppose," he said. "Let's get it over with, then. Damn Virgil C. to hell anyhow."

The boys unfolded their long legs and started together down the slope. Gravity and fear took over at once, and before they knew it they were running. The cold burned their lungs as they plunged down into the valley, the dry, brittle earth slipping away easily beneath them. As they raced down the hill and up the far slope, Bushrod fanned desperately at the cold ashes of his courage. The Yellow Leaf Church was getting closer and closer, looming before them in icy solitude. Bushrod could not see the shadow now but knew it was there all right, lying in wait with all its secrets, and if something didn't happen pretty soon he was going to faint dead out. Then, at the last moment, a flame sprang up in Bushrod's heart; it leapt and flared as they tilted around the headstones; it was roaring when they rounded the corner of the church, and suddenly at its center was the shape of one Bushrod didn't recognize, but whom he knew somehow to be himself. For the first time he relinquished everything and withdrew to a place he'd never been before, and from that secret chamber watched the Other outrun Jack Bishop in the dark—

And there, squatting against the weatherboards of the church, hands dangling between his knees, the corncob pipe clamped in his jaw, was Virgil C. Johnson himself. He was alone. "Howdy, boys," he said.

Jack and Bushrod stood speechless, drawing deep, raling draughts of the bitter air. It seemed infinitely colder here. Bushrod looked up: over the roofline he could see a glittering sprinkle of stars. Then Jack Bishop spoke, his voice coming in angry gasps: "Damn you.....Virgil C. Johnson.....damn you....."

"Hush your mouth," said Virgil C. He pointed at Jack Bishop with the stem of his pipe. "You don't know everything. He was here all right. I know he was."

"Who was here, dammit?" said Jack Bishop. "*Who* was?"

But Virgil C. didn't answer, and Bushrod looked down at his hands and tasted ashes, cold and dead, in his mouth.

***

Tom Jenkins and the Chaplain and Old Hundred were gone, Virgil C. had risen to his feet at last, and the First Sergeant was making ready to continue down the line. That gentleman's patience, never substantial at any time, had spun out to the breaking place, and he regarded Virgil C. with malice. Virgil C., meanwhile, was struggling to get his arms through the sleeves of his jacket. He smiled earnestly at the First Sergeant. Old Bill took a step toward Virgil C., the muscles of his jaw quivering. Bushrod and Jack tensed, ready to step in should old Bill forget that he was in the Confederate army now where privates were not manhandled at will by their officers. Bill remembered this, though it would seem to be just in time. With hand outstretched he stopped, paused, and everything in him seemed to relax at once. Old Bill cradled his musket in the crook of his arm. Carefully, almost tenderly, he buttoned the single surviving button on Virgil C.'s jacket and smoothed the wrinkles down the front. He lay his hand in a grandfatherly way on Virgil C.'s shoulder. "Virgil C. Johnson," said the First Sergeant softly, "surely there is a God, and as surely He will make a soldier even of you in this hour of our death." Virgil C. smiled and nodded. The First Sergeant scowled once at Bushrod and Jack and passed on down the line. When he was out of earshot, Virgil C. spoke. "What do you reckon he meant by that?" he asked.

Behind the line, the brigade band were shouldering their instruments. A courier rode by, swollen with mysterious import, his horse's hooves throwing up little clods of dirt. In front of the regiment, a cabal of officers broke up, each hurrying importantly away, his hand on the hilt of his sword. Bushrod knew from long experience these were bad signs, that something was fixing to happen soon. Overhead, the chittering blackbirds still passed in their uncounted thousands.

Bushrod wondered if, somewhere down in the company, Uncle Ham Johnson was making one of his apocalyptic appeals to Deity. The old man was nearly seventy, brown and hard and wrinkled as last year's pecans, with a long white beard he kept tucked under the strap of his cartridge box. But he was still with them, one of the oldest men in the army. He was given to praying long, impromptu, tedious prayers whenever he was excited, and he always went into battle singing hardshell Baptist hymns at the top of his voice. It was spooky in a fight to hear him down there, bellowing about the Blood of the Lamb or some such thing—Virgil C. always said he only did it to alert the Almighty that Uncle Ham Johnson, the greatest fiddler in the Army of Tennessee, might be on his way to glory, just in case the Powers and Principalities wanted to get up something particular for him. Bushrod did not doubt that this was so. He smiled at the thought, and bent to tuck the stiff, mud-crusted cuffs of his trousers into his socks.

Along the line, lieutenants in their swords and frock coats were fussing like hens. "Fall in," they admonished cheerfully. "Look sharp, boys, and fall in!"

When Uncle Ham and Virgil C. enlisted, they naturally brought their fiddles with them. In the early days, when it was all a lark and soldiering seemed like a big barbecue under the stars, the Johnson boys made things lively around the fire of a night.

Virgil C. was a first-rate fiddler, for he'd been playing from a time when he was still too short to reach the plow handles. Still, he was humble about his gift and always waited to be asked to play. Then, once petitioned, he would always tell how, when anybody in Cumberland held a dance or a wedding or a funeral, they would hire him *not* to play, and having told it he would move slowly into the circle of firelight, and tuck his fiddle under his chin, and look at the bow as if he'd never seen one in his life—all the boys watching meanwhile with the firelight shining on their faces. Then Virgil C. Johnson would touch the bow to the strings and wring from his instrument a single experimental note so heartbreakingly pure that, for however long he chose to sustain it, the boys could believe that what they were living was not a dream, but was connected to all they had ever known, and all they had lost. Then Virgil C. would dip, and launch into "The House Carpenter," the tune he always started with, and for a little while the dark woods would reel and the very stars seemed to dance.

But the old gay times, like the fiddles themselves, were fragile. They were more delicate even than Bushrod's watch.

On the night of the Shiloh battle, the company and the regiment were spread out all over the woods, and Virgil C. was missing. Bushrod and Jack joined the throngs of men who prowled the field, searching for lost companions in the dark. Wordlessly, in growing terror and disbelief, they toured the nightmare landscape of their first engagement. The woods were lit by fires smoky and fitful in the drenching rain. The Departed were everywhere, in heaps and piles and windrows. They were tucked into thickets where they had crawled to die alone, they were even in the branches of the shattered trees. There were so many, and their faces so awful to look into, that the boys soon lost all hope of ever finding Virgil C. They wandered aimlessly through the wreckage of the battlefield. Now and then a hand would claw at their trouser legs. Voices rose from the shadows, disembodied like voices in dreams. Some demanded relief, others begged; they asked for water or for a surgeon, they asked for mothers and sisters, these voices. Some begged to be shot. From all these the boys shrank in guilty horror.

Bushrod and Jack still wore the little narrow-billed caps of the early war, so the rain drove in their faces and blinded them. They stumbled and swore. They dodged the shells sent over by the Federal gunboats moored in the Tennessee—big shells that crashed to earth with random malice. They were fired upon more than once by pickets, whether their own or the Strangers' it was impossible to say. In time they lost all sense of direction. There were no landmarks, only the tangled underbrush and the fires and the rain. They had no idea where their regiment was.

At last Bishop stopped. He snatched off his useless cap and flung it down. "I am done with this," he said. "I vote we try to find the rear, if there is any such thing, then go to the rear of *that* and lay low 'til daylight. I believe south is over that way, though it may not be. Shit, who knows—"

Bushrod took off his own cap and wrung the water from it as he would a rag. "What about Virgil C.?" he asked. He was trying to keep his voice from quivering.

"God in the mornin," said Jack. "We could hunt til the Kingdom comes and never find Virgil C. in this goddamned mess. Time to fall back—tomorrow's another day."

"Tomorrow's another day," said Bushrod. "Have you ever seen the ocean?"

"What the hell kind of question is that?"

"Well, I mean, if we're to fall back, I vote we try for the Gulf of Mexico. I never seen the ocean myself. My Uncle Jarvis was a sailor in his day—crossed the line lots of times, to Brazil or someplace—said they's fish down there would swallow up a cow if one should happen to fall in. Imagine a fish that big, imagine a cow in the ocean, that's pretty funny, ain't it? Ain't it, Jack? Great God—"

Bushrod fell silent and looked at his hands. Jack Bishop regarded his friend through fogged spectacles. After a moment, he said quietly, "It's all right, boy. Come on. I wish this dern rain would stop."

Bishop turned, took a step, tripped and fell headlong onto the body of a Recently Departed who lay in his path. The thing was black with rain, but there was a beard, there were teeth; it heaved a moist sigh and closed its arms around Jack like a lover.

"Son of a bitch!" cried Jack and clawed frantically away, retching and spluttering.

"This is worse than hell, worse than anything," sobbed Bushrod.

A big Dahlgren shell from the gunboats plowed through the trees and exploded with a deafening roar, filling the air with humming fragments.

The boys hugged the ground under a shower of dirt and branches, then ran for their lives. They had not gone fifty yards before they found Virgil C.

He was propped against a big gum log that glowed with foxfire. He was soaking wet, and his blackened, swollen face reminded Bushrod of Luther Falls, a strange, unhappy boy who had tied an anvil to his leg and jumped in the deep turn hole of Little Spring Creek. After two days, the search party thought of the turn hole. It was Bushrod who dove to the bottom and found him, his eyes wide open, his hair waving in the slow current like grass. Now someone must have dragged Virgil C. out of the dark waters of the battle and sat him up against the gum log. Across his knees, like the dismantled skeleton of some small animal, lay his broken fiddle. Jack Bishop took off his glasses and rubbed his eyes. "Well goddamn," he said.

Bushrod felt a knot rise in his throat. Before this day he had thought of death in battle as a romance that he and his comrades flirted with. By association, death would make them all wise, thoughtful, mysterious; it would give them dark memories that they would only talk about if pressed, though they might write poems about it. However, death was expected to be a thing that happened only to people they did not know— and now here it was, sordid and wet and personal, like Luther Falls after two days in the turn hole. "No!" Bushrod choked, as if someone had struck him in the chest. "No, that can't be Virgil C., that can't be—"

At the mention of its name, the Departed fluttered an eyelid and groaned. Jack and Bushrod jumped as if bitten. Then the eyes popped open. "Oh, howdy boys," said Virgil C.

Before Bushrod could stop him, Jack Bishop dove for the grimy neck of Virgil C. Johnson. "Damn your soul!" cried Jack. "Goddamn you to hell!" He was shrieking now, and hammering Virgil C.'s head against the mushy wood of the log.

"Whoa, Jack!" cried Virgil C. "You gone bust my goddamn fiddle!"

Then Jack Bishop sat down against the log himself and laughed for a long time, great tears cutting furrows in the powder grime on his cheeks. "Damn you, Virgil C. Johnson," he said over and over. "Oh damn you anyhow."

They found a bloody shelter-half and a blanket and made a place for themselves against the big log. They huddled together, shivering with cold and exhaustion, ignoring the ghostly shapes still shuffling through the coiling smoke around them, calling the names of men who would never answer. They ignored the rain, the shells, the picket firing, even the crying of the wounded in the dark. They ignored, as best they could, the thought that tomorrow was another day. They only wanted to sleep, and tomorrow was far away, and maybe with luck it would never come at all. As Bushrod began to drift among the phantoms of sleep, he heard, as if at a great distance, the voice of Virgil C. Johnson: "Oh, I ought to of left this fiddle back in Corinth. I wisht I'd never brung it now. I didn't know it'd be this way, did you? My, what a circus. I got lost. I saw a man that was blowed in two, half over here, and half over there. Say, you think this fiddle is broke, or do you think—"

"Goddammit, Virgil C., shut up," said Jack Bishop. "Just please won't you shut up?"

"Well, all right, then," said Virgil C.

Bushrod thought he heard a horseman pass. He heard the hooves scuff in the leaves, pause, and move on. Then he slept.

"It's times like these," Jack Bishop was saying, "that a man's confronted by his own mortality." It was the same remark that he made before every action, large or small, and it drew the usual response from Virgil C.

"If you are killed," said Virgil C., "can I have your watch?"

"No!" said Bishop. "I have told you a hundred times, that watch was give to me by my mother, and I intend to carry it even unto the grave."

"What you care what time it is down there?" asked Virgil C. "What about us that is left to bear the sorrow? You and Bushrod always had a watch, and I have forever had to ask what time it is. You would think—"

"Bushrod Carter," Jack said, "I charge you to make sure that should I fall this man don't prowl among my remains."

"Oh, hell, Jack," said Bushrod. "That watch of yours ain't anything but a piece of junk. It makes more racket than a sawmill engine—I can hear it tickin away out here. And besides, Virgil C. can't tell time anyhow, can you, Virgil C.?"

"Yes, I can," said Virgil C.

"My mama give me that watch," said Jack. "It hurts me you should talk about it in that way."

"Oh, your granny," said Bushrod.

"You just try me, see if I can't tell time," said Virgil C.

The company, the regiment, the brigade were formed up now. Beyond them were other companies, regiments, brigades: thousands upon thousands of men all confronted by their mortality. Across the way, the great host of Strangers, similarly confronted, waited in the autumn twilight for something to happen. Bushrod could not remember when his army had last been arrayed like this, where he could see nearly all of it at once. It seemed an enormous living thing, breathing and moving, possessed of instinct and intelligence and malevolence all its own. Bushrod knew it was the sum of many parts, that those parts were individual men, each one the result of a complex personal history and each one convinced that he stood at the very center of the universe. But to look at it like this, to see the long lines flung out in diminishing perspective over the folds and wrinkles of the land—to see it thus, a vast patchwork quilt of color, all the faces and hands blurred by distance—then the individual was completely absorbed, lives were poured and blended into the one great Life, and Bushrod felt as he did when he contemplated the enormity of the stars. *How else could we ever do this thing?* he thought.

With the Strangers over there, the effect was even greater. They presented a creature—dark blue above, light blue below—whose aspect changed only at certain times in winter when they wore their dashing, much-coveted sky blue overcoats. It was Jack Bishop who once devised a figure for their seasonal mutation: "They are like so many mushrats," he said. "The meat's no-account, but the pelt is prime." Even the individuality of their hats and blanket rolls did not mar the impression, from a distance, that the Strangers' army had been stamped out by some mill in Pennsylvania. This made them easy to kill, from a distance, like so many mushrats. Up close, it was another matter. Up close, the Strangers seemed uncomfortably like themselves, and for this reason Bushrod hated any contact face-to-face. When prisoners were taken, Bushrod hung back. When opposing pickets traded for coffee and tobacco, Bushrod stayed by the fire. Most of all, Bushrod Carter hated hand-to-hand fighting. He left that to the Other who, in rare, unhappy times when they actually grappled with the enemy ("crossing bayonets" was the way the popular journals phrased it), seemed to have no scruples about the individual life.

Lastly there were the Departed, who were in a class by themselves. No group Bushrod had ever known were so jealous of their anonymity. Having surrendered everything to the great Mystery, they had nothing left to offer those who had not. The color of their uniforms made no difference.

Today, Bushrod was trying very hard to lose himself in the greater whole. He wanted desperately to forget himself and be absorbed into that abstract, faceless swarm from which fear and injury and death emerged as mere numbers on the First Sergeant's morning report. But it was all very theoretical and, try as he might, Bushrod kept coming back to a lonely, corporeal fact: that here he was, Bushrod Carter, standing at the center of the universe with ashes in his mouth.

Then, with a great tin-plated crash, the band of Adams' Brigade, stationed immediately to the company's rear, erupted in song. For once, Bushrod was grateful: he had been thinking too much, and in the presence of that band, philosophy and introspection could not live.

Because he loved music, Bushrod hated all military bands. The rigors of the field kept the instruments perpetually out of tune; the bandsmen played too fast, they used up rations, and the glittering bells of their horns drew fire from the Strangers' artillery. Moreover, these Confederate bands seemed to know only one song really well: "The Bonnie Blue Flag," which the Brigade Band was playing even now.

Bushrod despised "The Bonnie Blue Flag" with all his heart. Early in the war, the song had stirred him, awakening in his mind a collection of noble images—pennoned lances, tilted banners, the Holy Rood, and so on. Now, after three years, he had heard it played and sung so often he could not suffer the sound of it. Worse, the merest suggestion of the tune would usher its threadbare lyrics into Bushrod's consciousness, there to chant for hours in maddening iambics:

> We are a band of brothers, native
> to the soil,
> Fighting for our liberty with treasure, blood, and
> toil.....

Bushrod's right foot, shod comfortably in the Jefferson shoe, was already tapping in time. He willed it to stop, but it was useless to resist that inner chorus.

> Hurrah! Hurrah! For Southern
> rights, hurrah!

Bushrod's was the color company of the regiment. A few files to his right, the color guard huddled protectively around their charge, a standard battle flag painted with the names of their most celebrated combats:

Shiloh, Perryville, Murfreesboro, Chickamauga, Missionary Ridge, Atlanta. Like all his comrades, Bushrod felt an almost supernatural affection for that flag. In his mind it existed as the stained and ragged symbol of their stained and ragged selves. Whatever else it might have stood for had long ago been humbled by the terrible names written across it.

Hurrah! for the Bonnie Blue Flag
That bears the single star.

General Loring, their division commander, rode across the regimental front, his staff jingling along behind. The General gravely acknowledged the salutes of the officers in the ranks; some of the soldiers raised their hats, but nobody cheered as they had once cheered for General Cleburne. The men had nothing against Loring, but their hearts were still with Cleburne, in whose division they had once served, and who was now way off to the left somewhere. Besides, the boys seldom cheered for anything these days.

"Attention.....Company!"

At the Captain's command, Bushrod's heart made a practice leap. He forced it down and came reluctantly to attention, his musket pressed against his right thigh. Jack and Virgil C. jostled him on either side as the long line squeezed together, dressing on the colors. They were in the front rank, and Bushrod hated to be in the front rank. He felt naked, exposed, vulnerable. Whoever was behind him would invariably discharge his musket in Bushrod's ear. Still, there was nothing to be done about it now.

We are a band of brothers, native
to the soil.....

Even Jack and Virgil C. had quit their foolishness for the moment. Bushrod wondered if they too, in the moments before a battle, closed down the delicate machinery of thought. *Tomorrow, I will ask them*, Bushrod thought. Tomorrow they would go all three down to the river in the twilight, and Bushrod would ask them about it. He glanced at his friends. Jack was muttering to himself and wiping his spectacles with a filthy handkerchief, his rifle in the crook of his arm. Virgil C. caught Bushrod's eye and grinned faintly but said nothing. Bushrod could smell their rank wool and the indelible reek of wood-smoke that hung about them all.

Hurrah! Hurrah! For Southern
rights, hurrah!
Hurrah! for the
Bonnie Blue Flag.....

"Load and prime! Come to order arms!"

Ah, me, thought Bushrod. He brought his rifle around and planted
the butt between his feet. He fumbled in his cartridge box, extracted a cartridge, and tore off the paper tail with his fingers (no use biting it off this
early in the dance—plenty of time for all that later: the blistered lips the
swollen tongue, the acid taste of black powder and no more spit—). Then,
as he made to pour the powder into the muzzle, his hand began to shake
so badly that all the powder spilled on the ground.

"Load and prime, boys," said the lieutenants walking up and down
behind the line. "Move smartly—keep your muzzles up, there."

Bushrod dropped the torn cartridge and reached for another. This
was bad business; ammunition and water were two things Bushrod was
loathe to waste. He cursed softly as he noted that all the men around him
had charged their pieces and were rattling the long steel ramrods back into
their guides. Bushrod could not even tear the new cartridge. He held it up
in frustration and contemplated the shaking of his hand. Bushrod's eyes
suddenly swam with tears: he could not load his goddamned musket—

Then Jack Bishop lifted the cartridge gently from Bushrod's fingers.
"Here, old pard," said Bishop. He tore the paper, poured in the powder,
and started the ball into the muzzle of Bushrod's rifle, pressing it down
with his thumb. Then he turned away and busied himself scratching under
his hat.

"Much obliged," said Bushrod, his face burning. He dried his eyes on
his coat sleeve, then finished ramming the charge. *Now to prime,* he
thought. He brought the piece up, cocked it, and with finger and thumb
plumbed his cap box for a percussion cap.

Now I guess I will drop the cap, he thought, *and if I do I will by God go in
without one.* But he didn't drop it. In fact, when he brought his hand up, it
was steady. He slipped the cap onto the nipple, lowered the hammer (not
to the regulation half-cock, but all the way down), and came to order
arms. He felt ashamed, as if he'd forgotten his lines in a play.

Hurrah! Hurrah!.....

Bushrod was sure he was the last man in the company to load, but in fact that distinction belonged to another. Nebo Gloster, Virgil C.'s rear-rank man, was only now beginning to prime. Nebo was a conscript, and this would be his first fight. He was barefoot, without uniform or bayonet or accoutrements, only a musket and his civilian rags and an old, grimy quilt draped over his shoulders like a shawl. He was so new, so inept, so miserable that he should have inspired pity. Instead, by the harsh merit system of veteran armies in all ages, he was an object of contempt. Into Nebo Gloster's gangling, malarial frame, the men of the company poured all the disdain they felt for those who, by choice or chance, had not shared in their adventures. Not one of Nebo's comrades-at-arms could tell his history. Not one of them cared that he should never have been sent to the army at all. When they did take notice, it was only to remark that someone, at least, was more wretched than they.

So Nebo Gloster labored on unaided and, for the moment, unnoticed. Now he affixed the percussion cap and was engaged in lowering the hammer. He seemed unable to coordinate thumb and forefinger. His eyes were narrowed in concentration; his lips moved as if he were reciting some mysterious inner catechism. The muzzle of his cocked and loaded rifle wavered two inches from the back of Virgil C. Johnson's head.

At this moment, Bushrod happened to glance to his left. "Great God!" he yelped, and with his hand knocked Nebo's muzzle skyward just as the man's thumb slipped off the hammer. The Enfield discharged with a prodigious roar over the crown of Virgil C.'s hat.

"I am killed!" shrieked Virgil C., and collapsed in a heap.

Nebo flung the rifle away in horror. "What happened! What happened!"

"What happened, hell!" Bushrod cried. "You like to blowed his head off! Damnation, man—how many loads did you have in that thing?"

Nebo began to hop from one bare foot to the other. "I done it just like they tol me," he sobbed. "Bushrod, I done it just like—"

"Shut up, for God's sake," said Bushrod. Men were craning their necks to see what had happened, and Bushrod was as embarrassed as if he'd been the culprit himself. He took Nebo Gloster by the arm. "Just be quiet, will you? And quit that dancin around."

All the company's lieutenants came on the run, their swords rattling. "What happened here?" said Tom Jenkins.

"Why nothin, Tom," said Jack Bishop. "Nebo was just tryin out his musket. Shootin at the moon over yonder, I think."

"That's right," said Bushrod. "He's mighty eager to get into the fray."

Tom Jenkins glared at Nebo. "Didn't nobody teach you how to—"

"Go easy, Tom," said Bushrod. "He's only a conscript, and Virgil C. ain't hurt—just thinks he is."

"Sure," said Jack. "I declare, I never saw Virgil C. so animated."

The other officers and file-sergeants drifted away. Tom Jenkins shook his head. "You fellers be careful," he said, and went on down the line.

The conscript's rifle lay in the grass. Nebo regarded it as he might a venomous snake.

"Might as well pick it up," said Bushrod.

Virgil C. had arisen and was brushing himself off. "Well, I am back from the grave," he said. "My lands—how many loads *did* you have in there, Nebo?"

Nebo Gloster blew his nose on the quilt. "Well," he said, his voice trembling, "I thought two of powder and one of ball. Was that too many?" He held out the extra ball in his hand.

"Jesus and Mary," said Bushrod, and they laughed while the band played "The Bonnie Blue Flag."

Nebo Gloster was not the only conscripted soldier in the company. A dozen or so had come in since the draft law was passed two years before—reluctant citizens smoked out of the thickets and back alleys of the Lower South and sent up to bolster the dwindling line regiments. At least that was the expectation of the Confederate Congress, who naturally understood soldiering only in its broad outlines. It was Bushrod's experience that the conscripts were useless as soldiers. There was, for example, the Portuguese fisherman who had been shanghaied on the levee in New Orleans; he arrived in the company knowing only seventeen words of English, all of them so esoterically vile that only the First Sergeant had heard them before. The Portagee never fired his musket, never even loaded it so far as any of them knew. The night of the Chickamauga battle, he got lost in the woods and was challenged by a nervous picket post and rattled off most of his seventeen words before he was shot to death. He was a good-natured little fellow, though, as Bushrod remembered it.

Another man enjoyed telling, in picturesque detail, how he had gotten his sister with child, then murdered her in a cunning way and never been caught. Bushrod thought the man insane for telling such a thing; no one found it amusing. This conscript's brief career was ended in the fighting at Rockfish Gap. He was discovered riddled with balls and nailed to a pine tree with a bayonet. Around his neck hung a crudely pencilled sign that read:

> The Nakedness of thy Sister
> thou shalt not uncover.

Sam Hook told Bushrod it was a quotation from Leviticus, and whoever came up with it must have known the Book pretty well.

Nebo Gloster himself, when he was treed by a cavalry detachment in the swamps of Wilkinson County, Mississippi, had no idea there was a war in progress. In fact, the whole notion of war—that is, men shooting at one another on a grand scale with the approval, even the applause, of the government—was news to him. Bushrod, try as he might, could never impress upon Nebo the concept of the Enemy—but then, Nebo also believed the world was flat and could not see it otherwise, no matter how many astronomical sketches Bushrod made in the dirt.

And yet, of all the conscripted rabble who made their way into the ranks, none held Bushrod's attention like Simon Rope.

It was in the days last summer when Sherman's mean Western army was driving them back on the city of Atlanta—a bad time, one of the worst. They fought every day among tangled breastworks and pine trees and red clay, under a merciless sun that was, by itself, enough to drive them mad. They simply could not make the Strangers quit. Every man seemed possessed by his own hollow-eyed demon, and killing was all they studied: killing in the thickets, in the briars and pine-barrens—killing the gaunt, ragged Strangers who swarmed at them like fiends out of the smoke. Later they would remember it as the Hundred Days: not once, in all that time, did Bushrod's regiment unfix their bayonets.

One afternoon on the Kenesaw Line, the regiment was burying the Recently Departed to its front. This was done under a rare flag of truce sent out by the Strangers themselves, who no longer wished to attack over ground where their own dead had lain for days in the blistering June sun. The parlaying officers were in agreement: the Departed must be hurried under the soil, the battlefield tidied up. Thus, at the appointed time, the living of both armies laid down their arms and rose from behind their works and straggled timidly onto the field.

The Departed awaited them. The Departed were always a problem, but especially so in hot weather. They were patient enough at first, lying in their heaps and tangles on the field, but after awhile they began to call attention to themselves in ways that moved the nightmare of battle into deeper shades. With luck, the survivors of both armies would move on in advance and retreat, leaving the problem of the dead to burial details and to angry civilians who must watch their cotton patches and backyards turned into cemeteries. On the Kenesaw Line, however, the armies weren't going anywhere for a while, and the problem belonged to the soldiers.

The men assembled on the open ground and moved circumspectly among the hundreds of dead. Bushrod Carter was aghast at the whole business; he felt uncomfortable standing erect in the open, and found himself curiously afraid of the Departed who lay sprawled around him. He did not enjoy the novelty of seeing his own works from the outside. Worst of all, he was surrounded by Strangers. Federals and Confederates alike had removed their jackets and so were practically indistinguishable, and the thought came to Bushrod that if trouble erupted now he would not know whom to flee. He stayed close to Jack and Virgil C., hoping that nothing would happen.

While the common soldiers mingled in solemn courtesy, the opposing officers gathered in congenial little groups, chatting amiably, hands clasped behind their frock coats. Bushrod was amazed at their sense of fraternity, and noted with some satisfaction that the Strangers' officers seemed as superfluous as their own. Finally, after the officers had worn themselves out pointing and discussing and pacing off distances, the work was begun.

A United States Quartermaster wagon, brimming with spades, trundled out of the Federal lines, and the tools were issued to the men.

"Just imagine," said Virgil C. "A whole wagon full of nothin but shovels."

"No doubt we will borrow a few of these," said Bushrod, admiring the shiny new implement in his hand.

A young man at Bushrod's elbow laughed. "Hell," he said, "I never knew a Reb to borry anything he couldn't eat!"

Bushrod realized with a start that the man was a Federal soldier. He was about to step away when the man put out his hand. "Bill Provin of Cairo, Illinois," he said. "What's yer name?"

Bushrod's raising would not suffer him to leave the man's hand dangling in mid-air. "Bushrod Carter," he said. "I am from Cumberland, Mississippi." They shook hands. Bushrod thought it the strangest thing he had ever done.

Under the blazing sun, the men began to dig. The ground had been baked until the whole earth seemed a solid brick; presently a wagonload of picks was sent for, and the soldiers took turns breaking up the ground. They sweated and cursed and fought the millions of flies that rose in black swarms from the dead; they gagged and vomited in the almost liquid cloud of corruption that hung like a fog over the field. No sooner had they begun when other interested parties arrived: buzzards, wheeling by battalions in the sky. The boldest of these lit and hopped clumsily about among the harvest, pecking and tearing until the soldiers drove them off. They never went far, however, and finally a buzzard detail of sunstruck men was put together to at least keep the birds on the move.

As the soldiers worked, their common misery began to effect a fraternity of its own. They traded mild insults and gossip, they complained, they sat in the meager shade of the pine trees and rested together. Now and then a fistfight broke out, and men would gather around and shout and wager until officers came and set them to work again. Beyond these personal eruptions, which Bushrod found oddly moving, there was no trouble.

At the center of it all were the Departed. Officer and man, they all looked alike; faces blackened and puffy and featureless, bodies swollen until the buttons on their stained blue uniforms popped, arms raised (many of them) in the pathetic gestures that bloating imparts to the body. Perversely, the Departed now seemed to resent the attention that was being given them. They showed a common reluctance to being buried in the shallow trenches where the feral hogs would almost certainly be at them after nightfall. Dragged over the ground, they wheezed and belched and sighed in protest; their clothing snagged on the least obstruction; sometimes they simply fell apart and had to be prodded into the trenches with spades. For a while on the Kenesaw Line, the focus of the great war shifted; the living found a common enemy in the dead.

In the hottest part of the afternoon, Bushrod and Jack and Virgil C. and the young Stranger from Cairo were preparing to fill in a section of trench. For the moment they leaned on their spades, blinking in the glare and passing around the Stranger's canteen. It was filled with good, sweet spring water from behind the Federal lines.

Jack Bishop had said very little during the afternoon, and now he stood with his head down, staring blankly at the red earth. He refused the canteen when it was passed to him. Bushrod studied his friend, thinking the sun might be getting to him—several men had already died that way since they'd begun digging, and the soldiers kept watch on one another for the signs. But Bushrod decided that, with Bishop, it would never be anything as simple as that.

"What's the matter, Jack?" asked Bushrod finally. "Are you feelin bad?"

Jack Bishop made no reply. He went on looking at the ground: his eyes (he was not wearing his spectacles—they were only an added torment in the heat) were heavily-lidded, red and swollen from the glare; his face, like all their faces, was drawn and hollow, unshaven, greasy with sweat and powder stain. As Bushrod watched, Bishop moved his hand over the dead men lying in the ditch, as if he were offering some secret benediction. His mouth began to shape words, but no sound came.

"You ought to try some of this good water, Jack," said Bushrod. "Are you feelin all right?"

"Maybe he's fixin to keel over from the heat," said Virgil C.

"Are you fixin to keel over, Jack? Say, are you all right?"

Bishop looked up, slowly, as if it were an effort to raise his head. His eyes moved until they found Bushrod's. *Uh-oh*, thought Bushrod.

"If you ask me that one more time," Jack said, "I will kill you and put you in this hole."

"Such language for a brother in the lodge," muttered Virgil C.

"Sure, Jack," said Bushrod. "Never mind."

"What's the matter with your pard?" asked the Stranger, thumping the cork back into his canteen.

"Best not to inquire," said Virgil C. "Let's just dig."

They turned again, all but Jack, who went on staring at the ground.

Bushrod tried not to think about what they were doing. He could not bear the sound of the dry dirt falling on the bodies, and he tried to close his mind against it, to think about something else, anything else. But it was no use—no memory, no image, no ghost of himself in other days could live long in the terrible heat, among the stink and the flies. So he began to work faster, and in a few minutes' time a furnace was roaring in his head and he could not think at all, and in a few minutes more the fatal red haze began to creep up behind his eyes and he could even quit being afraid of whatever it was Jack Bishop was about to do. So he shoveled and shoveled, the veins pounding in his temples, the red haze creeping higher and higher as he flung the hard dirt viciously into the faces of the Departed *who were moving, shifting, swatting at the clods that struck them—now they were coming out of the trench, shrieking and groaning in protest, clawing at the edge of the trench, some of them were already out, groping blindly. Bushrod shoveled harder and harder—*

"Say, Bushrod—whoa, now!" The Stranger wrapped his arms around Bushrod, held him fast. Bushrod fought against him, made to strike him with the shovel. "Go slow, boy! You gone burst your bilers here!" said the Stranger.

Then Virgil C. had him too, and they scuffled in the red dirt, the dust rising around them, while Jack Bishop watched with his dull eyes. Finally a soldier none of them knew brought a sponge bucket full of water and poured it over Bushrod's head, and Bushrod settled down and let the Stranger hold him while the red haze faded and the dust thinned around them, and at last Bushrod could think again.

"Whew!" said the Stranger. "Now, that's better." He held out his canteen with the sweet water. "Drink. Drink slow."

Bushrod drank, gagged, drank again. "Much obliged," he said.

"Don't mention it," said the Stranger. He put the canteen strap over Bushrod's head, tucked his arm through it. "Keep it," he said.

"Much obliged," said Bushrod.

The Stranger grinned. "You boys is all crazier 'n owl shit."

"Lord, ain't they though?" said Virgil C.

"Damn these flies," said Bushrod vaguely.

"Now, now," said Virgil C. "I'd have no use for a fly that wouldn't come to a melodious odor like this."

The Stranger spoke again: "Whup—look out, boys." They followed his nod and saw two men approaching, one of them a Confederate officer.

"Oh, it's only Cap'n Sullivan," said Virgil C. "He's all right."

"Evenin, boys," said their Company Commander. "I been huntin for you. My, Bushrod, you look a little ragged out."

"The sun got him, but he's good to go now," said Virgil C. Then, nodding at the second man: "Who's that, Cap'n?"

The newcomer had the unsavory look of the Piney Woods, sallow and malarial, with the bad teeth peculiar to that region of Mississippi. He was in civilian clothes—a filthy brown sack coat, jeans trousers baggy at the knees, brogans, a shapeless felt hat turned up in the front. His face was a little oval of flesh in the midst of a great tangled beard; in its center was a bladelike nose flanked by tiny, glittering eyes. He wore an expression of indifference, as if he'd done all this before.

The man's hands were clasped in front, joined at the wrist by iron shackles.

"Ah," said the Captain, as if he had just remembered he was not alone. "This is Mister Simon Rope, just come to us by way of the conscript draft. Say howdy to the boys, Simon."

The man turned his head and spat.

"As you can see," said the Captain, "Mister Rope is a little testy after his long journey."

"Indeed," said Virgil C., and spat himself. "What about those irons?"

The Captain shook his head sadly. "Well, I am told by the provost guard that ever time they take the shackles off, Mister Rope tries to run away. They didn't say why."

"Hmmm," said Virgil C., and tried to spit again, but nothing came this time. "A fresh fish," he said.

"He don't look so fresh to me," said the Stranger.

Then Jack Bishop was among them. He put his hand on Bushrod's shoulder, and Bushrod turned and saw that Bishop's eyes were quick again, a little too quick perhaps. *Oh Jesus and Mary*, thought Bushrod, and knew that something was about to happen.

"Evenin, Cap'n," said Bishop. "Who's the scholar there?"

Patiently the Captain explained again, while Simon Rope gazed contemptuously at the horizon. When the Captain was finished, Bishop nodded gravely. "I see, I see. And he is bad to run away, is he?"

"That's what I am told," said the Captain.

Jack Bishop rubbed his chin and contemplated the new man. "I can fix that," he said.

"Do tell," said the Captain.

"Sure," said Bishop. He stepped forward until his face was inches from Simon Rope's. "I can fix that right away, if you'll just loan me your pistol for a minute."

"Now, Jack," said the Captain. Simon Rope's eyes glittered like chips of coal.

"Take the irons off, Cap'n," said Jack. "I'll give him a good head start. I'll even dig him his own hole, though he'll have to share the bugs—"

Simon Rope held up his manacled hands to the Captain. "Take em off," he said, his eyes on Bishop. "Then give him your pistol."

"I ain't givin anybody a pistol," said the Captain. "Now listen—I am goin to take these shackles off, and you must all go back to work. We must get these poor fellows buried, you know, so we can shoot some more—ah, beg your pardon, young man."

"Never mind, Cap'n," said the Stranger. "It is only a hard truth."

"Well, it is a sad thing," said the Captain. "A very sad thing. Anyhow—Mister Rope, you do as these boys say, and don't be tryin to run off. Understand?"

"Sure," said Simon Rope, and held up his hands again.

While the Captain fished in his several pockets for the key, Bushrod studied Simon Rope. Bushrod, like most of his comrades, had long ago ceased to be afraid of individual men—not out of bravado, but simply because he no longer had any fear to spare. But Bushrod was afraid of Simon Rope. He was more afraid of Simon Rope than all the mysteries he'd encountered in the long war. As Captain Sullivan removed the shackles, an image floated into Bushrod's mind of a fat, boiled spider he had turned up once in a mess of turnip greens. That was Simon Rope. Bushrod shuddered and turned his eyes away.

"All right," said the Captain. "Now, boys, I came to you because I believe nobody can educate Mister Rope like you can. Do I make myself clear, Jack?"

"Sure," said Bishop, holding up his hands. "No hard feelins—we are all a little prickly with the heat."

"Sure," said Simon Rope. His eyes were on Bishop's face. "No hard feelins."

"All right, then," said the Captain, and turned away.

Bushrod did not see the Captain leave. He had fallen asleep on his feet and was already dreaming.

He and his father and old Parson were gone up to the Tallahatchie to meet Cousin Remy on the steamboat. Bushrod watched the little one-armed steamer pop out of the morning fog, feeling for the channel in the overflowed river. When the boat neared the landing, the pilot pulled down on the whistle; a jet of steam leapt skyward and the deep, melancholy chime rolled over the flooded woods, the hills, the landing where the mules and horses shifted restlessly at the sound.....

Then all at once there was another dream on top of that one. In the new dream, Jack Bishop and Simon Rope were standing in the fiery sunlight and everything around them was red and Simon Rope had a big knife of the kind they had all carried when they first went soldiering. He was holding it in Bishop's face with the point just under Bishop's nose.....

Meanwhile the steamboat was gliding up to the landing, her miniature stern-wheel paddling lazily, her single stage run out. The boat's captain was standing by the bell with a hammer in his hand.....

Why, Mister Rope, Jack was saying in the other dream. There ain't any cause to be offended—I was only makin fun, wasn't I, Virgil C.?

Sure, said Virgil C., Jack is always funnin.

No, said Simon Rope, I think you just got a big mouth. Anyway I'm fixin to make another one for you.

As the two dreams drew closer and closer, Bushrod thought: *Well I know what is fixin to happen.* Sure enough, the steamboat captain raised his hammer and Jack said Well, all right then, and the captain brought his hammer down on the bell and Jack Bishop, swinging from the hip, pole-axed Simon Rope with his shovel—

Clang!

Bushrod woke to see Simon Rope windmilling backward. The shovel blade whistled in the air as Jack swung again and missed, and Simon Rope disappeared over the edge of the trench. Bushrod heard him grunt as he landed among the Departed down below.

"Bully!" cried the Stranger. "First-rate! Let's haul him out and do it again!"

But Bishop hadn't stopped. He was already driving his spade into the pile of fill dirt; he brought up an enormous shovelful and flung it down into the trench. He followed it with a half-dozen more while the others watched in astonishment. Finally he stopped and looked at them, breathing hard. "Well, you gone stand there all day?" he said.

"But, Jack," said Virgil C., "don't you reckon we ought to see if he's dead first?"

For an answer, Jack went back to shoveling. The hard dirt rattled in the trench.

"Wish we didn't have to bury him with our men," said the Stranger. "Maybe we could—"

"No!" said Bushrod. They all looked at him. "No! Cover him up! Do it quick, while we got the chance!"

Virgil C. shrugged. The Stranger shook his head. "You boys is somethin else again," he said.

So they all began to shovel, and in no time that portion of the trench was filled. Bushrod worked as hard as the rest; he felt elated, better than he had in days. If they could just get the whole thing finished, maybe pile on a log or two..... And then he saw the Captain hurrying back from wherever he'd been watching and Virgil C. said, "Aw, shit, boys," and they stopped.

"Here, here," said the Captain. "What're you men doin?"

"Why, buryin the dead, Cap'n," panted Virgil C. "God rest their souls."

"Amen," said the Stranger.

"Now, hold on," said the Captain, pointing to the trench. "Is that the new man you have under there?"

They looked at one another. "Well, Cap'n, he might be under there," said Virgil C.

"Now, look here—is he dead?"

"He was feelin pretty low, the last we saw him."

"Mighty low," agreed the Stranger.

"Damn!" said the Captain. "Just dammit anyhow. You must dig him up right away. Bring him to light again."

"But Captain, likely he's dead *now*—"

The officer looked at Bushrod Carter. "Hush, boy," he said gently. "You don't know what you're sayin."

"Yessir," said Bushrod, and ducked his head.

Bushrod Carter did not turn his hand to the job of uncovering Simon Rope. He stood by the Captain and watched, and the Captain left him alone. Presently, Virgil C. and the Stranger got down in the trench and hauled the conscript out. He was a mess, but no one doubted that he would survive. They leaned him against a spindly pine tree and poured a cupful of water over his head and went back to work.

"I suppose you have made an enemy, Jack," said Captain Sullivan. "I'm sorry to have to put that on you."

Jack Bishop shrugged. "Never mind, Byron. Maybe he learned some manners."

"Maybe so. Anyhow, keep him in front of you in a fight. That is, if we should get into one before he runs off again."

Bishop laughed this time, and shook his head. "Godamned peckerwoods. This used to be a respectable army, Byron. What happened?"

The sun was a malevolent copper ball just over the pinetops when they finished. All the many Departed had been hidden, at least for a little while; the living, moving like specters, turned their spades and picks back to the Federal Quartermaster's men, then collapsed on the ground while the officers sorted them out.

The young Stranger from Cairo sat down by Bushrod. "Well, did you keep your shovel?" he asked.

"Shit," said Bushrod. "I don't ever want to see another shovel long as I live."

They shared the last water in the canteen. The officers were prodding the soldiers back to their lines, though nobody was moving very fast.

"Lemme ask you somethin," said the Stranger.

"Sure," said Bushrod.

"You reckon we was really gone bury that fellow alive?"

"I reckon," said Bushrod. "I was anyhow."

The Stranger nodded. "I was too." He thought a moment then, twisting the canteen strap in his hands. "Ain't it curious," he said at last. "What we've all come to, I mean."

"Curious?" said Bushrod. He looked around at the field, the raw trenches, the hollow-eyed men and the frustrated birds still sailing overhead. "Naw," he said.

The Stranger nodded again, and after a moment pushed himself erect. Bushrod rose with him.

"I better go," said the Stranger.

"I better too," said Bushrod.

They stood looking at the ground. Bushrod put out his hand. "Farewell," he said. "Thanks for the good water."

"So long," said the Stranger.

They shook hands, and the Stranger was gone. Bushrod watched him stumble away over the clodded earth.

"Let's move along, boys," said an officer, herding his flock.

"Fix.....bayonets!"

Bushrod's bayonet was already fixed when the command came, so he shut his eyes and listened as thousands of others rattled home on thousands of muzzles. He always shuddered at the sound, so terrible in its finality. They were going to move now, and soon. When Bushrod looked again, he saw that the sun was very low, almost to the trees, and the pale moon was climbing.

Again his breath failed him. There did not seem to be enough air. His heart began to hammer against his breastbone. *Steady,* the Other's voice said. *Steady. We have done this before. It is nothing—only a noise.* Bushrod forced himself to breathe. He smelled the grass, the dust, the evening.

"Well, old pards," said Jack Bishop, "we have come to that moment once again."

"I wish we could do like the Chinee," said Virgil C. "I'm told they fight one another with parasols and firecrackers."

Bishop snorted. "Virgil C., why do you torment us with that rubbish? You know perfectly well—"

"Silence in the ranks, there," said Jeff Hicks, the new Third Lieutenant, in a voice squeaking with excitement and zeal. He was a good boy from one of the best families in Cumberland, but since his appointment to Third Lieutenant he'd been a nuisance to them all, and especially to Jack Bishop, who had raised him in the army like a son.

"My, the young general is snappish today," said Bishop.

They all laughed.

"Hey, I said ya'll quiet'n down!" said Hicks.

Bishop turned his head. "'Hey'?" he queried. "What is this 'Hey,' young Hicks?"

"Well....just ya'll quiet'n down," said the boy. After a moment he added, "You're at attention, y'know."

"Well, goddamn, I am glad to know that," said Bishop. He jabbed Bushrod in the ribs. "Straighten up, Carter—by God we are at attention."

They laughed.

"Remember to keep your dress!" shouted the Captain from the right.

"Keep your dress, boys!" chorused the lieutenants.

"Keep your dress, keep your dress," parroted Bushrod. He turned to Jack. "How many goddamned times—"

But the light had gone out of Jack Bishop's eyes like a snuffed candle. The skin of his face was taut and shiny, he was working hard to breathe, the air whistled in his nose. He was staring to the front.

"What's the matter, pard?" said Bushrod.

"Nothin. Nothin is the matter."

"Take it easy. It ain't really all that far—just a little walk and we'll be done."

"Right-o," said Jack. "Just a little walk. We done it lots of times before."

"Lots of times," said Bushrod.

Jack was breathing easier now. He spat and wiped his mouth and adjusted his spectacles. "Mankind," he said. "I'm like you. I wish 'twere this time tomorrow."

"It will be," said Bushrod.

"When you think they'll let us make supper?" said Virgil C. "I could sure use—"

"Shut *up*, dammit!" thundered the First Lieutenant. "Silence in the godamned ranks!"

This time, the ranks were silent.

The band began to play "Dixie's Land." "Shoulder.....arms! Right-shoulder-shift.....arms!"

Bushrod and Jack and Virgil C. and hosts of other lads with similar names from back-country farms and houses in town and steamboats and offices and narrow, cluttered mercantiles and saloons and universities—all moved without thinking through the old, familiar evolutions, and in an instant the line was transformed into a bristling forest of rifle barrels and bayonets. The color bearers shook out their flags.

"Forward, *quick* time....."

"Oh, shit," said Jack Bishop.

"Easy," said Bushrod. "Let the black flower blossom as it may."

"Let the what?" said Virgil C.

".....march!"

The drums began, the boys stepped out smartly, and Bushrod heard, far down in the company line, Uncle Ham Johnson's voice raised in "On Jordan's Stormy Banks":

Oh, who will come and go with me?
I am bound for the Promised Land!

Bushrod touched his medal, and set his face to the front.

CHAPTER TWO

Early on the afternoon of the Thirtieth of November, while Bushrod and his comrades were still toiling up the Columbia Pike, a Confederate staff officer of Stewart's Corps rode out in advance of the line. He was nervous, for no one knew exactly where the enemy lay—hopefully, they were all up in Franklin digging holes in the citizens' gardens, and the peaceful afternoon through which the staff officer rode would remain peaceful for a little while longer. In any case, there was nothing he could do about it, so he rode on, at a comfortable trot, trying not to think too much but watchful all the same.

He came out through a gap in the hills; here he reined up and sat for a moment in contemplation of the ground before him. Open ground, perhaps a mile and a half of rolling fields drowsing in the autumn sunlight. He could see the village among the distant trees, and between himself and the village he could see the enemy—or part of them at least, a brigade anyway—digging rifle pits in the fields. The officer shook his head, extracted from his coat pocket a thin cigar, and lit it carefully with a Lucifer match. He watched his hands, saw that they were steady, and flicked the match away. "Well, Buck," he said, "I would not want to be those fellows when the army comes off the Pike." The horse nodded as if in answer, the man smiled. "All right, Buck," he said. "Let's walk."

He met a boy ambling along the road. "You seen a mule runnin loose?" asked the boy.

"No," said the officer. "What's he look like?"

"Like a mule," said the boy.

"Well, I ain't seen him. You know the way to McGavock's?"

"Over yonder," said the boy, pointing.

"Much obliged. I see your mule, I'll tie him."

The boy nodded and walked on, and the officer turned into the fields. He rode toward a big patch of oaks, and on the edge of these he discovered a great brick house. "McGavock's," he said, and the horse nodded.

He reined up in the yard, sat and smoked for a while and watched the oaks—a big grove, underbrush, a good place for pickets. Then he saw a pair of crows, they settled in a top branch and began to mutter quietly to themselves. "All right," he said, and relaxed. For the first time in months he felt completely alone and unnoticed, so he sat his horse in the weak sunshine and studied the house before him.

He was raised on a similar place down in Limestone County, Alabama, and it all seemed familiar to him; the quiet yard, the smell of brown grass and wood-smoke and the bitter, dusty smell of the oaks, the shutters needing paint (it seemed all shutters, everywhere, were always needing paint), the dry forlorn tangle of last summer's morning glory vines, the glimpse of a china figurine through a window. A little wooden horse on wheels watched him from the portico. More crows came to settle in the grove, and from the chimney of the kitchen-house a pale feather of smoke rose toward the sky.

The solitude and the sight of the quiet house moved the officer in ways he had not anticipated for this busy afternoon. The instruments of his trade—his pistol, the saber strapped to his saddle, his field glasses case, even his present purpose—seemed to let go of him, to fade away into some other place and time while he remained, touched by a longing he barely recognized—

Jesus Christ, thought the officer—*I am homesick.*

He laughed aloud, and the horse moved restlessly, and the world came back again. But the feeling did not go away; the officer did not know that he even wanted it to go away. There was no pain as there once was—only a calm place, like a pool, where the images of his life gathered and where he could still believe in possibility. He would have to shatter it soon, but not now. For the moment, he would look at the house and let his mind travel where it would—

Now just suppose what if there was a girl lived here—her name is Susan—no, no, let it be Nancy—and here I come ridin been ridin all this time toward this place without ever knowin it and she is here she would talk to me put her hand on my sleeve when I had to go—and what if I promised her—no, what if it was a long time from now, not today, only I promised her today, but it is a long time and I am coming back like I promised and the war—and I am, and the war—and the war is—

"Ah, shit!" said the officer aloud, and pulled the rein so that Buck began to turn in a little circle, turning and turning while the officer thought *You are a goddamned fool, you are*—because it was making him hurt and the war simply was and always would be, and besides, there would be no girl in the house yonder, and if there was she'd be married—they always were. Then Buck got tired of turning and nipped at his boot and the officer stopped. "All right, old pard," he said. "Hell, let's get on with it." He drew once more on the cigar, stubbed it out against the pommel of his saddle, and flicked it away. "Come on, Buck," he said, and together they walked the little way remaining to the house.

He had been in the saddle since daylight, and it was not easy to dismount. He stretched, and the horse nuzzled him in the ribs. "You are a good boy, Buck," he said, rubbing the horse's bony nose. "You stay right here while I go break the news to these good citizens."

The officer straightened out the skirt of his jacket under the pistol belt, turned, and limped stiffly up the steps and across the little portico. He raised his hand to knock, and stopped. He looked around one last time, for it occurred to him that this place would not be the same after this day was done, not ever again. A movement caught his eye—a white hen strutted around the corner of the house and began to peck in the grass. She wouldn't last long with the troops about, he thought. Then he knocked.

Later, the family would recall every detail about the officer but his name. They would remember how he stood before them just inside the door (he declined to come further), caked with mud and smelling of wood-smoke and horses, delivering his message as if he'd memorized it, then forgotten it: General Stewart sends his compliments, who has been informed by a scout who knows the country and therefore yourself, sir— that is, the General asks would Squire McGavock consent to his house— situated as it is, by the fortunes of war, in advantageous relation to the anticipated—consent, that is, with all due regard—that is, with every assurance of—in any event, consent to the use of his home as a hospital for the corps, to receive the inevitable fruits of the battle which even now—

"Battle!" interrupted John McGavock. "In the name of God, does General Hood mean to give battle here?"

The officer was out of breath from his speech. He had tangled it up so badly it was a wonder the gentleman even understood his purpose. He was about to make reply, about to say that, as far as he could tell, both God and General Hood seemed to have that intention, opened his mouth to say it, when he happened to glance toward the hall stairs and see the girl.

It was not fair, of course—that was his first thought. He had only allowed himself a moment's dreaming, had let go only long enough to have a single foolish thought, and now look. The girl stood on the bottom stair, her hand on the banister, watching him.

"Captain?" said McGavock.

"Um, yes, sir," said the officer, finding his voice. "As to that, I can only say, sir, that God—that is, yes, I believe General Hood will, yes. Sir."

She was about his own age, he thought. Not a girl really—it was her slightness that fooled him. He understood that every woman his own age was either married or in eternal possession of her maidenhood. Still, she did not *look* married—

"Very well, then," John McGavock was saying. "Please communicate to the General my willingness—"

The officer tried to listen: the house was at the General's disposal, etc., etc. Indeed, some part of him did listen. The rest of him was thinking: *A governess, that's it* then *No, please not a governess they are always so encumbered with morals* and *What is she lookin at, anyhow?* While Squire McGavock talked of battles and hospitals and death, the officer studied the girl's left hand and even in the dim light of the hall he was sure there was no ring—

"Captain?" This was another voice, a woman's certainly; she had come out of a room off the hall and now stood by the Squire, gripping his arm. Her voice startled the officer, he caught himself and bowed slightly. "Ma'am," he said, thinking that here was a lady sure enough—slight, like the girl, but not old enough to be her mother—maybe her sister. The woman went on in her pleasant voice: "In the press of circumstance we have forgotten our courtesy. We can offer you coffee, or cider if you like, and perhaps something for your horse?"

The officer knew he should decline; he had lingered too long already and Old Straight Stewart would have his ass and he had to get away from the girl on the stairs and her watchful eyes which from this distance certainly did appear to be green—

"Oh, well," he said, "just a cup of water would do me fine, and if you had just a handful of corn—"

"Surely," said the lady. "John, do make this man comfortable while I see to it."

When the lady went, the girl came off the stairs and followed her without looking at him again. He was watching her move away when the Squire took his arm.

"Come," said McGavock. "Time is pressing."

The Squire led him back to the portico where they stood together by the steps. The officer felt like a suitor on his first call. McGavock was looking off toward the south, his hands clasped behind him, as if he were about to ask what the young man's prospects were, or what he thought of the last cotton crop. Instead, the older man inclined his chin toward the woods and said, "The army will come from there, I suppose."

"I expect they will, sir," said the officer.

McGavock turned to him, his face suddenly serious, his voice urgent. "Between the railway and the Lewisburg Pike, the enemy's line bends to the north. You must tell your general that."

The officer was sobered by the tone in the other's voice. He took out a greasy memorandum book and the stub of a pencil and began to write.

"Say to him also that he must be prepared for the hedges."

The officer looked up. "The hedges?"

"Osage orange," said the Squire. "They have been growing for thirty years, so thick a field mouse couldn't get through. They are all along the enemy's left, nearly to the Carter gin house. Say to General Stewart that he must be prepared for them."

"Very good, sir," said the officer, scribbling. "Anything else you might think of?"

McGavock looked to the south again. "Yes," he said, after a moment. "Tell him.....tell him the works are very strong, and I do not see how—" He stopped himself, fell silent.

The officer closed his book. "I will tell him, sir."

McGavock turned on him again. "You must go *now*," he said. "You must not delay, sir. There is—"

But at that moment a young negro came out carrying a tin pail full of corn. "Hey, Marse John," he grinned, and crossed the portico and went out to old Buck, who greeted him like an eager child. The officer felt a pang; he was glad for Buck, but ashamed he'd asked for corn in these hard times. It was all the girl's doing, she—

"Here is your water," said the girl, and offered the cup.

The officer was astonished. He had expected the lady, or a servant— was she a servant? Ridiculous. Her eyes were very green, and she watched him in a sidelong way that made him uncomfortable. He felt the blood rise in his face. "I am.....my name is....."

The girl lifted an eyebrow, waiting. The officer stammered on. "Patrick Tanner.....that is my name—of Limestone County, Alabama. We haven't, that is *I* haven't.....been introduced. Let me ask you, your name— it, um, it wouldn't be Nancy, would it?"

"No," said the girl, "it wouldn't."

"Ah," said the officer. "No, of course it wouldn't." He looked down at his boots. They were caked with mud.

"Your water?" said the girl.

"Oh, yes," he said. He took the cup, searched for a clever thing to say, found one. "'A sweeter draught from a fairer hand was never quaffed,'" he said. "Whittier."

"I know," said the girl.

She was intolerable. He struggled to get past her eyes, decided she wasn't all that pretty anyhow, searched for another clever thing to say and found nothing.

"Captain," said John McGavock, "it is already late in the day."

The officer smiled then. "Yes, sir," he said, still looking at the girl. "It most always is."

He drank the water quickly; it was clear and sweet, the first in memory that didn't taste like the rust in his canteen. When he returned the cup, he looked at the girl's hands. They were small, of course, and ringless, and they were shaking, and young Patrick Tanner suddenly realized what he had done.

He turned and fled. It was only a few steps to his horse, but he felt he would never reach the saddle. The sky seemed darker, the woods yonder full of malignant promise—beyond them lay the army that would soon sweep down on this house, on the girl and the gentleman and lady, on the negro boy, the little white hen, the chinaberry trees, the child—wherever he was—whose wooden horse watched him go with its glass eyes. And after that the long and terrible night that he, Patrick Tanner, had brought down on them, and it was no wonder the girl looked at him as she did and no wonder at all that her hands were shaking.

He gained the stirrup at last and swung himself up, and it was all he could do to look back again at the people gathered on the portico. The lady lifted her hand. "God be with you," she said, "and with all of you this day."

The officer felt he might cry, he did not trust himself to speak. He still held his cap, where he had removed it in the hall; he waved it, gallantly he hoped, and bowed in the saddle, and was about to turn away when the girl stepped off the portico. He watched her cross the little way between them and stop at the horse's head. She touched the rein, not exactly looking at him, but not looking away either. "It is Anna," she said.

"I.....I beg pardon? I—"

"My name," she said. "It's Anna, not Nancy."

"Anna," said the officer. He struggled to make the words come. "Miss Anna, you got to understand—if it was up to me, we'd all quit and go home. I didn't mean to—"

The girl nodded. "I know," she said. "I know you didn't."

"Ah, my God," said the officer.

"Go!" broke in John McGavock. "Say to the General we will be ready."

Anna dropped the rein. The officer looked at her a last time. "It was sweet water," he said, and smiled, pulled Buck around and cantered away. He did not look back.

He was still at the canter as he passed through the woods, Buck's hooves making a good sound in the dry leaves, the shadows of branches flickering. Beyond, in the fields again, he pulled Buck down to a trot, then a walk, and at last stopped. He sat a moment, then turned the horse's head back toward the house. He couldn't see it, but he felt it there, strong and solid in the waning light. *Maybe it will be all right*, he thought. *Maybe we are stronger than any of us think*—

Horse and rider stood absolutely still, like an equestrian statue in the field. Again there was no pain, only the calm place, and the officer thought *When I come again, I will make sure to ride over this very field—I will remember that rock yonder, and that hickory with the busted limb, and I will say how glad I am it is that day and not this*— He closed his eyes and watched him and Buck ride through the little wood and across the yard toward the house warm in the spring sun, all the windows open and the curtains billowing out in the breeze, white and fair, and the white clouds poised overhead. And there was Anna in the yard, watching him come with her hand shading her eyes—

Young Patrick Tanner smiled, shaping in his mind the words he would say, trying to get them right, almost had them when a Federal sharpshooter lurking among the rocks of the field shot him once through the body. It was an easy shot: the man had a telescopic sight, the range was less that sixty yards and almost no wind. The officer fell backward over his horse's rump and landed face-down, his arms flung out before him. Buck shied and trotted away a few paces, looked back at the man, waited for him to rise. When he didn't, the horse walked back, nudged him once. In a little while, he lowered his head and began to crop the brittle grass.

Time passed, and the people in the great brick house made ready for what was to come. They watched the sun, and they saw the moonrise, and when they had done all they could, they waited.

Late in the afternoon, Caroline McGavock found herself in the parlor. It was empty, everything moveable or breakable had been carried to the attic—all but the clock. She had told them to leave the clock, for she took comfort in the simple movement of the hands across the cracked and yellowed face. She would point to it a hundred times in the coming night as proof that even suffering could not last forever.

The room seemed larger now, and colder than she had ever known it, though already there was a fire in the hearth. In the vacancy, she heard the actual tick of the clock for the first time in years. Anna, who had come to close the shutters, was standing at the window, gazing off toward the south, and Caroline came to stand beside her. There was not much to see: only the slope of the yard, the barren woodline and the sky. It all seemed so familiar, so beguiling, as if nothing at all was going to happen, as if there were no great armies poised for battle, no men about to die.

Caroline McGavock put her arm around her cousin's slight shoulders, the other inclined her head so that she stood close beside. They breathed the cool smoky air and let the thin sunlight fall on their faces. Outside, in the dying afternoon, long shadows reached toward the house.

"Well, cousin," said Caroline McGavock after a while, "did you ever think, when you came to visit, that we'd be in such a fix?"

"No, cousin," said Anna, smiling. "But if I had thought it, I reckon I'd have come just the same."

"Me, too," said Caroline. "Though I'd of rather had a frolic and a pig-roast."

"Lord—for all these folks?"

"Two pigs, then."

"I suppose you'd have the Yankees too?"

"Oh, by all means," said Caroline. "I am told they have some excellent bands."

They laughed. "Well, cousin John would never stand for it," Anna said. "Why, he'd have—"

Caroline cocked her head. "Wait—listen."

Anna listened. "Musketry," she whispered. "Is that what it is?"

Caroline nodded.

"It is begun, then."

"Yes," said Caroline. "It is begun."

Anna pressed her hand against the window glass. "All right, then," she said. "Let em come if they're comin, and make an end of it. That's what I—"

A gun discharged in the Federal line; even at that distance the concussion rattled the window in their faces and the women jumped back, startled, and Anna threw up her hands. Caroline saw that they were shaking, and took them fast in her own. "Anna," she said.

"Oh, my God," said Anna. "It's nothin—only fear, and there is plenty of that to go around, don't you think?"

Caroline McGavock drew her cousin to her in the twilight. Beyond the trees to the south, they could hear the measured cadence of many drums.

"Well, little one," said Caroline, "we best close the shutters. They are coming now."

CHAPTER THREE

They were moving forward, their feet whispering in the grass.

"That jaybird back there better pull in his feathers," Jack Bishop was saying. "If I hear 'dress it up' one more time, I'll haul his freight."

"You mean young Jeff Hicks?" asked Bushrod.

"The little general himself," said Jack. "He has gotten forevermore too big for his breeches."

"I guess he is only tryin to do right," said Bushrod. "No doubt he's nervous."

"Say, Jeff!" shouted Virgil C. over his shoulder. "Your Uncle Jack thinks you are too big for your breeches!"

"By God, Virgil C. Johnson, for bein such a smart-ass I will haul your freight as well," said Jack.

"Your granny," said Virgil C.

"Quiet, you men!" bellowed the First Lieutenant.

They laughed.

It was not so bad, now that they were moving. They were swinging along, scaring up rabbits and quail, ignoring the band and taking their time from the field music.

The fortunes of war had pared the regimental field music to three drummers. There had been a brace of fifers once, who announced every evolution from reveille to retreat with their absurd tweedling and marched men into battle with warbling tunes that set Bushrod's teeth on edge. He was grateful when the idiot fifers were reduced to the ranks. But the drummers remained; three gaunt Presbyterians from the hills of North Mississippi, who kept to themselves and rarely spoke and never laughed. They had come down to Cumberland in rusty black clawhammer frock coats and breeches that ended well above their ankles, bearing fat carpet bags and well-thumbed Testaments, and offered themselves to the recruiting officer with the proviso that they would not, under any circumstances, take the life of another man. So they were instructed in the drum by an old drum-major of militia, and ever since they had been the field music for Bushrod's regiment. They had outlasted the fifers, outlasted a fat bass drummer who deserted, outlasted a succession of pink-cheeked drummer boys whose legs could not match the ground-eating stride of the Western army. They had woven black crepe into the ropes of their drums so that each resembled a catafalque; they wore black crepe rosettes in the lapels of the frock coats they had never relinquished. They drove men into battle soberly, implacably, the funereal drums bouncing on their thighs, drag ropes swinging. Their drums spoke a frightening magic, older than fear, older than death, and Bushrod regarded them with no little awe.

They had three cadences, these spectral drummers, which they called First Kings, Second Kings, and Revelation. Going into a fight, they went from one cadence to another with no apparent signal until the officers began to shout commands and men began to fall. Then the drummers began a solemn drill beat that Bushrod believed would be the muttering undertone of every nightmare he would ever have.

The drummers were beating Revelation now as the regiment stepped along, and Bushrod Carter raised his eyes and looked about. What he saw filled him with wonder and dread.

The long, mottled lines of Confederate infantry were emerging in perfect order onto the plain, bands playing, drums beating, bayonets gleaming in the sun. The great Life of which they were all a part had surged into movement, pressing forward in bristling waves and bearing them along to some purpose they could but dimly perceive. For the first time in all Bushrod's soldiering, the sight of his army arrayed for battle drove fear, reluctance, even the sacred knowledge of death itself from his mind, and in their place burned a single, incandescent idea: that here, on this field, he was witness to a scene that would never be played again, and whatever the balance of his life, he would measure it from the moment now unfolding around him.

Jack Bishop felt it, too. "Mankind," he murmured. "Look at that, would you? If that don't make the cheese-eaters run, then I'm your granny."

"They won't run," said Bushrod.

"I bet I would if it was me," said Virgil C. "Hell, it's all I can do to keep from runnin now."

"For God's sake, keep your dress, boys!" shouted the Captain. "Guide center! Don't let the line bow out!"

"Guide center, boys!" echoed the lieutenants.

"Dress it up!" said young Jeff Hicks.

All the flags of the army were loosed now. They spread and blossomed in the breeze and marked every regiment with a bright splash of color. Bushrod glimpsed, far to the left, the fabled blue flags of Cleburne's men and the flutter of blue guidons on the bayonets of their company guides. His own regiment's flag flapped lazily around its tilted staff, and he thought of their first company flag sewn by the Ladies of Cumberland and lost at Perryville, and of Mister Denby Garrison who had blessed it, saying We will rejoice in thy salvation, and in the name of God we will set up our banners.....*Oh Lord God of Hosts*, Bushrod thought—*make us an army terrible with banners and support us in the day of battle.*

Along the division front, skirmishers trotted out in a thin double line. From a distance they seemed almost casual, like bird hunters. Bushrod knew better. He had been there before and knew that to be on the skirmish line was the lonesomest, nakedest feeling in the world. He was glad he was not out there now. He was glad, too, that he was a private soldier and not one of the field officers on their nervous mounts, nor among the couriers who cantered back and forth before the lines. He welcomed the press of his friends' shoulders, the reassuring clank and rattle of the ranks, the bristle of bayonets and the dark, compelling music of the drums.

"Too-ra-loo," said Jack. "See the artillery over yonder!"

Sure enough, the Strangers across the way were already trying their guns: first a blossom of white smoke snatched away by the breeze, then a dull report and the curious, hollow whine of the arcing shell, then the *pum-pum!* of the aerial burst over the heads of the troops—for all the world, Bushrod thought, like a battle picture in *Leslie's Illustrated*.

"Where the hell's *our* guns at?" asked Virgil C. He was breathing hard now and soaked with sweat. "I bet they are strung out all the way back to Spring Hill."

"Naw, there's some around here somewheres," said Bushrod. As if in confirmation, a Confederate gun far to the left ripped off a shot toward the Strangers. "See there?" said Bushrod. A second gun fired, its report echoing across the fields. Bushrod saw the shell erupt in front of the first line of works. Still, Bushrod admitted, it wasn't much of a show. Like all infantrymen, Bushrod was scornful of anyone who did not belong to that arm of the service—especially the gunners, those curiously un-accoutred specialists perched upright on their limbers like little dolls. But if he had to go into a fight, Bushrod liked to pass through the smoke of his own guns on the slim chance that they had prepared a way for him. There would be no such comfort now.

Another blossom of smoke rose from the Strangers' works. Bishop began: "Boys, I am inclined to think—"

The shell exploded directly above them like a thunder clap. It was case shot, spraying musket balls and fragments in all directions, a lucky shot for the gunners over there. Someone cried out in pain and surprise, Bishop was knocked sprawling, the colors dipped and rose again and unfurled in defiance, and the line swept on.

Someone was yelling. "Oh, sweet Jesus! Oh, sweet Jesus!"

"Close it up!" the officers cried. "Close it up there, boys!"

Meanwhile, great cathedral bells were tolling and clanging in Bushrod Carter's ears. The concussion of the shell had staggered him. He nearly fell, righted himself, stumbled on dimly aware that some bad things had happened: Bishop was gone, somebody was hurt, the officers were shouting, the horizon was tilting. Bushrod heard the band—a remote, infuriating blur of brass and percussion across which moved the thin, keening wail of a human voice—

Then he was sinking, down and down into a tangle of weeds and green water and liquid bars of sunlight to find Luther Falls again with his cloudy eyes and his long brown hair waving in the current of Little Spring Creek—

"Bushrod!"

He heard the voice, but it was Luther's face he saw. It was swollen, tattered where the little fish had pecked it—

"Bushrod!"

His lungs were bursting now and he shot upward toward the little circle of light far above, broke out into the bright sunlight and the good air full of dust and milkweed and the chattering of blackbirds—

"Hurrah!" he cried. "Drive the sons of bitches!"

"Bushrod!" Virgil C. cried again.

But Bushrod Carter was swept up in the red joy of life. His chest was swelling with it, his muscles aching with the power of it. He fairly danced with the desire to get his hands on something—a fat blue gunner, a general, a bandsman. The drums surged in his blood, beating in counterpoint to his pounding heart, and he might have broken into the charge then and there had not Virgil C. taken him by the arm and shaken him like an errant child.

"Goddammit, Bushrod, what is the matter with you and where is Jack?"

"Great God!" cried Bushrod. He looked about, saw Handsome Bob Wheeler to his right instead of Jack. "Great God! Is Jack killed?"

Handsome Bob was about to reply when a familiar voice broke behind them: "Out of my way, you peckerwoods!"

Handsome Bob grinned. "No, here is ol' Jack now," he said.

Jack Bishop shouldered his way back into the line. He had lost his spectacles and his hat, a thin ribbon of blood ran down his temple and disappeared under the collar of his jacket. He was carrying his Enfield by the first band, dragging the butt along the ground. Bushrod took the piece while Jack adjusted his accoutrements.

"By God," said Jack, "I have lost my damn spectacles—blowed clean off me. Now what'll I do?"

"You'll have to squinch up, I guess," said Bushrod.

"Bushrod Carter, you—"

"Here," said Virgil C. "Wipe your face 'fore your mama sees you." He reached across Bushrod with the rag of a handkerchief even filthier than Jack's own. Bishop took it and daubed at the trickle of blood.

The bells had ceased in Bushrod's head, but enough of the joy remained so that, for the moment at least, he did not have to be afraid. When Jack had shouldered his rifle again, Bushrod asked, "How is it with you? Is it a bad hurt?" He knew it was not, but asked just the same.

"Mortal, I fear," said Jack. "Tragic, ain't it?"

"Can I have your watch?" said Virgil C.

Without thinking, they had fallen in step with the drum cadence again. The line moved forward, creaking and clanking, the tips of their bayonets bobbing in time, as if nothing at all had happened.

They passed over the body of a young officer lying on his face, his hands flung out before him. There was a big hole in the back of the man's shell jacket; from its tattered edges spread a wide stain glistening with flies that swarmed testily when the troops passed. Bushrod, careful though he was, nudged the man's leg in passing and found it stiff, and the blood on his coat was old. Bushrod wondered what the man was doing out here, and when he might have been shot.

"One of those staff fellows," said Virgil C., as if in answer to his thoughts. "Bet he was scoutin about and a sharpshooter got him."

The man's horse had been grazing near the body; now it trotted off a little distance and looked back expectantly. The line opened and passed around it. Bushrod had little use for staff officers, but there was something about this one—the way his hair was ruffling in the breeze, perhaps, or the lonely manner of his death—that touched him. Bushrod was glad he couldn't see the man's face.

Now a rabbit leapt up from under Bushrod's feet and bounded away, showing his heels to the Confederate army. "Bang!" said Virgil C., pointing his finger at the rabbit like a pistol. Up ahead loomed a great brick house and an oak grove; the skirmishers were already dueling with the Strangers for the yard.

The joy that had possessed Bushrod's heart was steadily leaking away. He couldn't shake the image of the dead staff officer; he kept thinking about the man lying by himself in the field while his mount waited patiently for him to rise. Then another thought came to him.

"Jack, how many was lost back yonder?"

"Only one, that I saw."

"Who was it?"

Bishop did not answer right away. He walked on, balling Virgil C.'s handkerchief in his hand. Then he pressed his fist tight against his teeth and bit, hard. That, Bushrod knew, was his answer.

"The little general," said Bushrod.

Bishop nodded.

They went on. The skirmishers had disappeared into the oak grove, from the sound of it they were having a sharp fight in there.

"Dammit!" said Jack suddenly. "I wish I hadn't—"

Bushrod waited for his friend to continue, though he knew he wouldn't. Young Jeff Hicks was gone for good, and taken all his nineteen years with him, and nobody could undo it with words that had no need for speaking. Wherever the boy had gone, he would already have plenty of company, and was likely to have plenty more before this time tomorrow, and there was nothing to do but let him go. So Jack Bishop shook his head, and passed the handkerchief back to Virgil C., and the line moved on.

Bushrod looked at the ground and watched the grass pass under his feet. The dead staff officer and young Jeff Hicks passed with it: two more left behind among so many.

Out of the corner of his eye Bushrod saw the regimental flag, its stars and saltier and the names of their battles painted on. He thought of the days when each company had a flag of its own, when a regimental line looked like something out of King Arthur with all the gay banners whisking silkily around their varnished staffs. It might as well have been in King Arthur's time, so long ago it seemed now. When they went into the fight at Perryville, they were still carrying their beautiful Cumberland Rifles flag—there it was stolen from the dead hand of young Silas Kessler by a Federal cavalryman, and borne away never to return. Bushrod wondered where it was now. Perhaps it hung in one of the Strangers' state houses, or among ranks of trophies in the hall of an emporium: an object of curiosity, marvelled at by the citizens. They would not know about the Ladies of Cumberland who made the flag, nor about young Silas whose mother lost all three of her boys on the Kentucky campaign. They would not know that nearly all of the original Cumberland Rifles were dead or maimed or vanished now.

So many gone. Some were home, hobbling the plank sidewalks of Cumberland with pinned-up sleeves or trouser legs, or lying in bed watching the darkness fall. Others had gone to prison camps, some had joined the cavalry, at least one had fled to Mexico. But most of them were dead, and Bushrod wondered what they were doing this afternoon. Were they watching? Did they know what was going to happen?

The line was taking more fire now, plunging fire coming from somewhere across the river. A shell erupted in their front, spewing dirt and rocks and iron fragments—no field artillery, that. They walked through the smoke of it.

Well, Bushrod thought, the dead were dead. They were gone, and took with them their faces and voices and whether they drank coffee or not and whether they believed in infant baptism or not and who they liked and who they didn't—gone with all their years and all the baggage they carried: tintypes and handkerchiefs and luck charms, pocket knives and Testaments and playing cards and rheumatism and all the half-remembered images of their short and uncompleted lives—all flown up like blackbirds into that undiscovered country from whose bourn they would not return, not today nor tomorrow nor the next day, forever and ever, amen—

Another big round shot struck the ground undetonated and bounded toward them like a ball; the boys parted to make way for it, and it bounced off toward the rear. No question now, the Strangers had guns across the river, too. Well, well, there was never any end to the troubles. But by this time tomorrow *all* the guns would be silenced and they could go down to the river and build a good fire and make some coffee: Bushrod and Jack and Virgil C.—and Uncle Ham too, Bushrod decided. In fact, he might go through the camp tomorrow and gather up all the old boys from Cumberland and they would all reunion down by the river among the willows. There would not be many; they would not need more than one fire.

What a long way they had come since Cumberland, and all of it, save for that first larking trip to Corinth on the cars, had been afoot. Bushrod wondered how many miles they had walked all told, counting drilling and marching and charging and retreating; counting sentry and foraging and scouting and pacing up and down before the fire, nights; counting strolling with girls and going for water and hunting for comrades after a fight. Bushrod supposed they could have walked to California and back by now, though none of them had ever had any clear idea what it was they were walking toward. Victory, they had thought, once upon a time—more likely it was only the little river waiting up ahead, or some river beyond that. Well, there was no time to look back now. They were pressing on, to the urging of the immortal drummers, hurrying toward whatever destination each man carried in his fate. For Bushrod, the river would do for now. Perhaps tomorrow they could rest a while and consider the long way they had come and rehearse what they would say about it to children in the distant, unimaginable years.

For the last time, Bushrod looked up to see his army spread out across the plain. What he could see of the brigades and grand divisions still advanced in order; had there been no Strangers, no fatal purpose, no guns or muskets across the way, they might have marched on forever under their bright banners and gleaming bayonets. But already behind the ordered lines the fields were dotted with rags of the Departed, and the smoke was rising, the white smoke that soon would hide them all. Bushrod knew it was only the smoke of the guns, but for a moment it seemed as if it might have risen from the long way itself, like the mysterious fogs that crept from the ditches and hollows in the lonely country nights, that were cold on the face and made saddle horses run wild. Well, no matter. The smoke was rising; into the smoke the long lines passed, and Bushrod knew he would see them no more. "Goodbye," he said aloud. "Goodbye, goodbye."

The great brick house was close now; Bushrod figured they would stop soon and realign before beginning the attack. He entertained the hope, as he always did, that Adams' Brigade would go in reserve.

The band was still playing; Bushrod noted the fact with irritation, though at least they had found another song. "Listen to the Mockingbird," it seemed to be, though it might have been anything. Bushrod allowed himself to wonder about the band and what zeal had possessed them to follow the brigade so close under the guns of the Strangers. He thought about the only member of the band he knew personally: Calvin Jones, once a professor of music at the Cumberland Female Academy, who had

joined them just before (or after—Bushrod couldn't remember) the fall of
Atlanta. Bushrod recalled an extraordinary fact about Professor Jones. It
was known widely in Cumberland that the Professor, in times of distress,
came under the influence of an unusual delusion. Bushrod did not pretend
to know what distress could enter the life of a professor of music, but at
such times Calvin Jones ceased to be Calvin Jones and became, for reasons
known only to himself, the Archbishop of Canterbury. Fortunately, the
Professor lived with an old-maid sister who nursed him through these fits,
calling him Your Grace and Your Eminence and bringing him tea until he
recovered, which he always did. Now the Professor was back there in the
band, and Bushrod had to smile at the thought. You could hardly top a battle for distressful times, and Bushrod wondered what His Eminence would
think to find himself going into the fray blowing a saxhorn.

"Prepare to halt!"

The command was passed from brigade to regiment to company, and
the men tensed as they always did before a command of execution. "Oh,
hell," said Virgil C. "I hate to stop once we commence."

"You are never satisfied with anything," said Jack.

"Halt!"

The line swayed to a halt, and the band ceased.

The regimental adjutant, a boyish major in a butternut frock coat too
big for him, stepped out in front and gave the commands that brought them
down to order arms, and the men once more planted their brass butt-
plates on the soil of Tennessee. Bushrod thought it might be a good sign. "I
bet we are going in reserve," he said.

No one answered.

"*I* bet we are going in reserve," he said again.

"Mister Carter?"

Bushrod Carter turned to the man behind him—Eugene Pitcock,
once a Tennessee River steamboat pilot, who still clung to the dream of his
former life, as if any moment he might be called upon to spar a great
packet over the Muscle Shoals. Eugene was particular in his habits. He
called everyone "Mister." His hat was a fine beaver that he still kept
brushed; in his haversack (Bushrod had seen them) were a pair of white
gloves and an ivory toothpick case. But the fortunes of war had begun to
have their way with Eugene Pitcock. Lately he had been grounding harder
and harder on a dark shoal all his own. He spoke very little now, ate almost
nothing, and slept nearly all the time. In camp, when he was awake, he had
taken to wandering off by himself; Bushrod had found him once sitting

under a pine tree, stroking the white gloves and talking to them. Bushrod had always liked him, used to seek him out to talk about boats and the river. Now he made Bushrod nervous, like a piece of unexploded ordnance.

"Hey, 'Gene," said Bushrod cautiously. "How is it with you?"

"Why do you ask?"

"Well, didn't you say my name?"

"I did, but that don't mean there's anything the matter."

"Well, 'Gene, I only—"

"But I will tell you anyhow," said Eugene Pitcock. He inclined his narrow, finely-sculpted face toward the man on his left, Nebo Gloster. "You might better see to this orphan," Eugene Pitcock said. "I have tried and tried myself, but.....well, you can see how it is."

Bushrod could indeed see how it was. Nebo Gloster was still standing rigidly at right-shoulder-shift, the knuckles of his hand white where they gripped the musket butt. He was pouring sweat, talking to himself and nodding in reply.

"Nebo?" said Bushrod.

The gaunt face whipped around. "I ain't done nothin!"

"Nebo, we are at order arms now."

Nebo Gloster clawed his musket down to order arms. His eyes darted fearfully to Eugene Pitcock, but that gentleman had fallen asleep on his feet. Nebo looked at Bushrod. He spoke in a harsh whisper, as if his throat were closing. "Bushrod, can I tell you somethin?"

"Yes, indeed," said Bushrod.

"You won't tell?"

Bushrod did not see how they could share a secret standing cheek-to-jowl with the entire army, and especially with Virgil C. Johnson already taking in every word. But he said, "I won't tell, honor bright I won't."

"You won't sure enough?"

"Honor bright."

Nebo looked around, edged closer. He smelled like moldy leaves. "All right," he said. "Bushrod?"

"Yes, Nebo?"

"Bushrod, I can't remember if my gun is loaded or not."

Jesus and Mary, thought Bushrod, and at once a brilliant sarcasm leapt to his tongue, a little gem to make the boys laugh. Bushrod opened his mouth, drew the very breath to speak—

But he did not speak. The *bon mot* withered, and its paltry soul fluttered away, and Bushrod Carter thought how, of all the sights he had seen in the long war, few had been so dreadful as the look on Nebo Gloster's face. It was pale, of course—that long, unhappy face was always pale—but now it glowed with a fear that Bushrod understood completely because it was his own. Nebo's smoke-reddened eyes were looking far into an unknown country, into the great Mystery which no heart could comprehend, and he thought that Bushrod Carter, of all people, could explain it, could shape words around a thing more intricate and impossible than the riddle of the soul itself.

So Bushrod was ashamed, and looked away. He felt transparent, as if he had no more substance than water in a gourd, and the knowledge came to him that even Nebo Gloster believed he stood at the center of the universe. When Bushrod finally spoke, he said gently, "Well, never mind, old fellow. It happens to everybody. Run your ramrod down the bore—you can tell that way."

"Thank ye," said Nebo. "Thank ye kindly."

Bushrod nodded and turned his face to the front.

Virgil C. nudged Bushrod in the ribs. "That clay-eater beats all I ever seen," he said. "Can't he do anything for himself? Why, a little thing like—"

"Now, Virgil C.," said Bushrod. "We all get tangled up now and then. Who was it loaded his rifle all the way up to the muzzle during that fight at—"

"I believe that was you," said Virgil C.

"Well, nevertheless," said Bushrod. "You see my point."

"I know, I know," said Virgil C. "I didn't say it to be mean. It's just—well that fellow ain't got any business up here soldierin."

"Who does?" said Bushrod.

They waited for something to happen. Down the line, Handsome Bob Wheeler was telling a story about a fat girl, and Eugene Pitcock was snoring, and Nebo was fiddling with his ramrod. Virgil C. began to fret. He tugged at the cloth under all his straps and belts. His blunt fingers moved aimlessly over his chest. Finally he wiped the sweat from his face with the grimy sleeve of his jacket and said, "I swear to God I am freezin to death up here, Bushrod. Wish I hadn't lost all these buttons on my coat. Say, pard, would you sew some more on for me after while?"

Bushrod, who did all the sewing for the company, said, "I will if you promise not to pull em off again."

"What you mean, pull em off?"

"You know damn good and well—"

"Whoa!" said Virgil C. "There goes Jack again."

Jack Bishop was quietly, modestly, vomiting between his feet, taking care to avoid splashing the stock of his rifle which he held out before him for support. There was not much on his stomach to come up: water, a little coffee, some bacon, the biscuit a woman had given him on the march from Spring Hill.

"Great God, Jack," said Bushrod. He could never get used to the fact that Bishop did this every single time before a fight.

"It is nothin," said Jack, waving his hand. "Just lemme alone, goddammit."

"The word 'snappish' comes to mind again," said Virgil C.

"You are lookin a little peaked, Jack," said Bushrod. "Is your hurt botherin you?"

Bishop tilted his canteen, swished water in his mouth, and spat on the ground. "I have a headache," he said. "Otherwise, I am havin just a wonderful goddamn time."

"All right, Jack," said Bushrod.

The regiment stood fast in the midst of great confusion. The grounds of the big house were full of soldiers, interrupted in their passage like water boiling against a jam. Beneath the disinterested gaze of the house, Loring's Division boiled against the jam of Time, seeking desperately to arrange itself for a swift run to the sea. A steady murmur of voices rose in the twilight; across that restless susurration the officers' sharp commands broke like the cries of birds. Always the rustling, always the dull metallic clamor as troops shifted back and forth under their gliding bayonets, their drummers beating *tick-tick-tickticktick* on the dented rims of the swinging drums. From the shadows of the oak grove, where exploratory tendrils of smoke wove among the branches, the skirmishers were returning with worried faces, their minds working over what they had seen, their mouths black with powder. Beyond the grove, the noise of the battle was swelling to an incoherent roar, pierced by the weird, falsetto chorus of Pat Cleburne's men going in on the run. It would not be long now. An Alabama regiment knelt to pray.

Byron Sullivan, the Captain of Bushrod's company, stepped out in front of the ranks, plucking nervously at the frayed French-blue cuffs of his frock coat. A regiment was passing in column behind him, their feet whispering in the grass; the dust they raised trapped a wandering spear of sunlight and suddenly Captain Sullivan seemed to stand in the glow of a great lamp. He faced the men whom he had led for nearly three years. They watched him in expectant silence. The Captain removed his hat and studied the inside of the crown. He had the look of a man who had forgotten what he wanted to say. Bushrod felt for him; he wanted to tell the Captain not to worry, that there was nothing he could tell them they did not already know. Finally the Captain looked up, not at them but at a point above their heads where the cold stars waited for night. "Now, boys," he said, "we are fixin to go in, and.....and you must make a good fight of it. Just keep your dress and look to the colors. We will all meet—"

A crash of musketry beyond the trees blew the Captain's words away like smoke. He stood a moment more with his hat in his hand, looking at the faces of the men. Then he turned and walked away.

Now we will never know the meeting-place, thought Bushrod. He felt Virgil C.'s elbow in his ribs again. "What'd he say? I couldn't hear him for all this racket."

"He said we fixin to get our ass in a fight," said Bushrod.

Virgil C. did not reply. He was worrying the last button on his jacket, pulled it off at last, and stood turning it in his fingers. He was staring off toward the trees. After a moment, he said, "Bushrod, look at him out yonder."

Bushrod followed his friend's gaze. He saw many men against the trees beyond. "Look at who?" he asked.

But Virgil C. only squinted toward the trees, turning the button in his fingers. In a moment it dropped to the ground and Virgil C. closed his hand.

Bushrod shook his head. He stooped and recovered the button and put it in his pants pocket and a sadness drifted through his heart. He had noticed lately that the boys all seemed to have secret rooms they passed into from time to time, each one alone. Bushrod believed Virgil C. was in such a room now, and nobody could follow him there.

The thought of rooms made Bushrod recall the great house, and for the first time he turned his attention to it. The windows were shuttered tight, the doors secure; Bushrod wondered if the folks were still in there, cowering in the gloomy shadows of the drawing room or huddled like mice in the cellar, waiting, like all of them, for something to happen. Perhaps they were watching through the shutters—what would they think of all this madness?

The house itself seemed indifferent. It stood serene above the clamor in the yard: old-fashioned, melancholy, the white portico still holding the afternoon's light. It was built of brick like so many of these Tennessee houses, and it seemed to have stood there since the creation of the world. Bushrod thought how it would still be rooted in time long, long after they were gone, when all that was left of all these boys would be a half-seen shadow among the oaks, a voice mistaken for the wind, a button or a belt buckle turned up by the garden plow. For a moment, Bushrod regarded the house with shame and yearning. He had done so much, come so far— if only he could quit for a little while, slip away somehow and hide himself among those quiet rooms until morning, when all this would be over and done and he could start afresh. He was tired, and he wished for the first time in his life that he could save himself from being forgotten.

He could actually do it, he thought—any old soldier could. He could slip away, hide from the battle, then tomorrow show up in camp and lie through his teeth about all his night's adventures. He considered it, and felt a guilty elation. Why not just this once? He had stepped off into the Mystery so many times—was it not reasonable that he be given this little respite from honor? Did he not, after all, stand at the very center of the universe?

Fool, said the voice he knew so well.

Bushrod smiled. Fool, indeed. Even after all this time, he could still catch himself believing that he walked into the smoke by choice, and could remove himself by choice. In fact, he had no choice at all—too many things conspired to make sure Bushrod Carter acted well his part. The shelter offered by the great brick house was illusory—within the hour it would be crawling with wounded and with officers and surgeons and stragglers blown out of the hurricane that awaited them, and there would be no peace there. Then there was Jack, and there was Virgil C.; there was the eye of God; there were the irresistible waters gathering themselves to sweep him along—

All right, all right, he thought—*But for God's sake, let us get it over with—*

A staff officer came plunging out of nowhere on a lathered horse and passed so close that a fleck of foam lit on Bushrod's cheek. He brushed it away in disgust. Why could these popinjays never control their mounts?

"It's gettin colder, don't you think?" asked Virgil C.

It was indeed, now that the sun was nearly gone, and the thought of winter crossed Bushrod's mind. Soon they would be cold all the time, hurting all the time, stiff from the stupid mockery of sleep, their chests raling, their eyes swollen from the smoky fires—the cold, lashing rain and the damned, eternal, everlasting, imperishable nights when men died of heart failure and froze to death in their blankets—Cold Moon, Wolf Moon, Snow Moon sliding reluctantly, each in its turn, toward another bitter spring—

"Do you see him now?" asked Virgil C.

"See *who*, dammit!" said Bushrod.

"He's right up there amongst the trees. You could see him if you'd just look."

"All I *see* are the goddamned trees, Virgil C.—them and about five thousand fuckin troops. You tell me which one you want me to look at and I'll—"

"Never mind," said Virgil C. "It don't make any difference now."

Bushrod gave up. They ought to all be in the lunatic asylum, he thought—every last one of them, himself included. He started thinking about that, how they might all go together and have a big time, when the unmistakable hum of a stray round passed overhead. Somebody shooting high over there, beginning to lose his nerve, about ready to run *Wait a minute*, thought Bushrod—*Hold on a minute, here!* And suddenly he knew that Virgil C. had been right about one thing: it didn't make any difference now. Time was run out.

Damn, thought Bushrod. *What have I been doin?* He looked around in alarm. The staff officer had wrestled his horse to a dramatic halt before the regiment's colonel, gestured wildly toward the Strangers, and was now galloping back across their front. The rider seemed to pull a cold wind behind him that stirred in the regiment's bones, and the men began to tug at their cartridge boxes, loosen their ramrods, push down on their hats. Officers checked the loads in their pistols, the Colonel called for the Adjutant, the Captain for the First Sergeant. These were signs Bushrod knew well—they were the last, the worst of all, and they meant that whatever was going to happen would happen quick now. But they had come before he was ready. He had been thinking too much, not paying attention, he should have asked Virgil C. once and for all who he saw in the trees up ahead but it was too late—the battle smoke was rolling in now, darkening the sky, and suddenly there was no more sun or moon or clouds or streaming blackbirds, only the smoke and the sound of the guns as the black flower opened before them—

"Too-ra-loo," said Jack Bishop. "Get your ass in the wagon, boys—we goin into town!"

It was all happening fast now, time was broken and the waters were rushing down. The lead brigades were already in motion, passing into the smoke, their flags and bayonets swallowed up and gone. Now officers were shouting up and down the line of Adams' Brigade; the forest of bayonets sprang up again and the colors blossomed and shook loose and trailed the smoke like pennants. "Attention, Company!" shouted Captain Sullivan in a high, cracked voice that did not sound like his voice at all. "Right-shoulder-shift! Right-shoulder-shift, boys!" A shell burst in the oak grove, bright orange flashed among the ghostly trees—

And in the field of trampled grass, amid the false twilight and the rush of living water, Bushrod Carter looked at his hands. He was not afraid now—the worst of that was over, back at the foot of the hills when they could see the long plain stretching out before them and the works where the Strangers waited. He was not afraid, he just wasn't ready, and he knew that if he had a hundred years he would be unready still. Too many things to say, too many thoughts he hadn't shaped yet, too much life. So he looked at his hands, and through them he offered up all that he was and ever had been: all things he had made, good and bad, all the faces he had touched, all the bright threads that had passed through his fingers in his little time. It was the best he could do, it would have to be enough.

The band was playing now, a song Bushrod recognized but couldn't put a name to. It seemed important to think of it, so he listened, trying to remember, looking at his hands. What was it? Something remembered, like a face half-seen in a passing coach but never forgotten: his cousin Remy sitting at the hopeless, wheezing parlor organ his father had packed in from Virginia—

Then it struck him. *"Annie Laurie,"* he thought, *and us goin into a fight*— But it didn't matter, it was all right, better than all right, the band playing the old song and there was Remy watching him, rolling her eyes in mock distress, and the organ groaning and him and his papa both laughing like schoolboys—

"Bushrod!" It was Jack, shouting over the noise. "Bushrod, come on! We fixin to go!"

Bushrod turned, blinking in the smoke. Jack had shouldered his rifle, was supporting it with his left hand, thrust his right at Bushrod. "Once more, old pard!" he said.

Bushrod blinked again, looked at the outstretched hand, then took it in his own, squeezing hard. "Too-ra-loo," said Bushrod. "Care for a stroll?"

Then Virgil C. was jabbing him in the ribs, grinning. "Come on, boy, get your rifle up, we fixin to start the ball!"

"What?"

"Shoulder your piece, ass-hole!" shouted Jack, grinning too.

Bushrod realized he was still at order arms. He dropped Jack's hand, brought his musket up and shoved it hard against his shoulder. It felt good riding there, the old Enfield, worn out like himself. He was all right now, doing what he did best, whether he liked it or not no matter. He looked up at the bayonet. *Damn soldierin*, he thought, and remembered the Other and hoped he would come when he needed him. But it was all right for now. *"Annie Laurie,"* he thought. *Carry me home to die.*

The big guns across the river were firing smartly now, engaging the lead brigades. The smoke rolled over the trees, over the great brick house, over the men of Adams' Brigade straining like race horses—

Bishop put his mouth to Bushrod's ear and shouted: "Listen! When the charge commences, you get on t'other side of Virgil C. and we'll go in like that!"

"All right!" said Bushrod.

"And if you or me get the chance, whack that goddamned conscript in the head before he hurts somebody!"

"All right!"

"I mean, don't knock his brains out or anything, you understand!"

"No, no," said Bushrod, "just hinder him some!"

"Right-o!" said Jack. "Now, come on, boys, let's drive these square-headed sons of bitches!"

Bushrod laughed. "Where you want to drive em, Jack?"

"Hell, it don't matter, long as it's someplace we can't chase em!"

"Amen!" said Bushrod. "Then let's quit and go home!"

"Hell, let's just go home now," said Virgil C. "Save all that trouble!"

They laughed, and again Bushrod felt the red joy of life burst in his heart like a Congreve rocket. He wanted to get on with it, wanted to be moving, driven by the drums and carried along on the rushing water, on the long swinging stride of the Army of Tennessee, raising the old yell in the smoke and the hurricane—

He heard the band again, and he thought they had never played so well and that made him laugh and think *You are asylum-bound for sure*, when all at once Jack Bishop began to sing at the top of his voice, not "Annie Laurie" but another song from another time:

> Well met, well met, my own true love,
> Well met, well met, said he—

Bushrod looked at Jack in amazement; he never knew Jack could sing at all, yet here was the boy's clear tenor voice singing:

> I've come from far across the sea,
> And it's all for the love of thee—

"Listen to that, Virgil C.!" shouted Bushrod. "You hear? It's 'The House Carpenter'!" And Bushrod turned laughing to his friend just as Nebo Gloster, still trying to decide if his rifle was loaded or not, fired his ramrod and a .577 caliber ball into the back of Virgil C. Johnson's head—

PART TWO

NIGHT WATCHES

Some times I do not think I shall live to be very old—but should it be God's will for me and any come to me and ask how it was in the old War times, I will say—that there was really no victory, and no defeat. There were only brave men.

—Bushrod Carter's Commonplace Book
Florence, Alabama
November 16, 1864

CHAPTER FOUR

A soldier's candle lantern stood on a table in the hall of the great brick house. The taper was short, and the flame, feeding on the pooling wax, leapt and threw fantastic shadows on the wall. The shadows were of men, blown out of the hurricane.

Other lanterns and the fires roaring on the hearths added figures to the dance. The shutters of the house were thrown open now, light spilling out onto the broad back gallery and the yard. Beyond was the night, where smoky fires and torches burned.

Out there, in the night, the earth crawled with struggling apparitions. These, too, were men. They moved among the glare of the fires, searching. The air they breathed was heavy with death and terrible with the birdlike cries of wounded men. Many weary of the dark were drawn like ponderous, wingless moths to the light, to the great house gleaming in the oaks. But these men brought the night in on their clothes, it clung to them like the smell of death itself, and so there was really no escape: what they had thought to be light was only a different, crueler darkness. They fled again, many of them, but others remained. Perhaps it was the comfort of walls that held them, or the nearness of simple things—patterned wallpaper, a rug bunched in a corner, the indefinite memory of life. For whatever reason, they stayed, holding to the light that mocked them. They stood about, hollow-eyed and mute, always in the way, oblivious to the wounded and even to the whicker of bone saws, which alone was enough to drive some men back into the dark. At first the bloody-aproned surgeons cursed them, the provost's men drove them out the door with musket butts. But after a while they drifted back, one by one, to stand forlornly in the shadows, and in time they were forgotten.

Meanwhile the great brick house, no longer serene, suffered through the night. Men died on its polished floors, slipping away unnoticed like diffident guests. Others cried in their pain or muttered private incantations of home. Some waited in terror for their turn at the table when men would pin their arms and the lancet would make its first exquisite penetration and they would try not to scream, even when the surgeon picked up the saw and wiped it on his apron and began to cut. They hoped they would not have to scream. Maybe somebody would come with some morphine or chloroform before their turn came. Maybe they would pass out at the first touch of the knife and not have to hear the sawing. They communicated these hopes to Anna Hereford when she passed, and Anna would say, "Be easy. It will be all right. God is here, He will look after you," and so on. Stupid words, Anna knew, but the only words she had.

Anna Margaret Hereford was twenty-four years old, unmarried and likely to remain so, small of build with dark hair cut short and green eyes that seemed, at first glance, too keen, too watchful, and too old for her face. Her eyes were what boys and men noticed first about her, and what women envied most, and it was her eyes that kept them all at whatever distance Anna chose. Her face was thin, a little long of jaw, still a girl's face though it wouldn't be for long, and not a hard face yet, though it might be one day. On her right cheek, just across the ridge of her cheekbone, lay an inch-long crescent scar where a pony had kicked her years before; it was a scar, but no man who'd gotten past her eyes had ever thought of it as a flaw.

Anna was from Lincoln County, ninety miles to the south on the Tennessee line, where she lived with her father (her sister was long married) in a house on the Mulberry Pike. When the Confederate army began its eastward march from Atlanta, Mister James Hereford had sent Anna to her cousins McGavock in Franklin, promising to come himself by and by, though he had no intention of doing so and Anna knew it and there was much heated debate before Anna finally packed her trunks and set out up the muddy roads with an escort of Union cavalry that happened to be going to join Thomas in Nashville. She had come then to her cousins' great brick house, worried about her immovable papa but glad to see her kinsmen, glad to see the quiet fields and the little river that curled around the village, and glad most of all to be with her cousin Caroline whom she had loved all her days. And now here she was, and if she had felt like smiling she might have smiled at her papa, who had argued that the Rebels were headed for Memphis and the safest place Anna could be in the whole world was the village of Franklin, Tennessee.

Anna crossed the smoky, dim-lit parlor, weaving among the men crowded there, and gained one of the windows that looked out on the south lawn. She pressed her fingers to the glass, saw her reflection there and points of light that were candles in the room, and the moving shadows of men. This afternoon she had watched through the shutters here as the soldiers formed up in the yard, their tattered flags stirring in the breeze that came with twilight. She had seen them march away rank by rank into the smoke, drums beating, one of their bands playing "Annie Laurie." And now they were back, but no flags now, and no music. They had been coming in since long before dark, first one then another, then more and more, until they were coming in now by the wagonload it seemed, and there were too many and still they came. There were at least fifty men in this room, and more in the other rooms and on the porch and in the yard and on into the darkness clear to the ends of the earth, and it was easy to imagine the whole earth carpeted with suffering men, piled high with the dead, a vast charnel place lit by fires and dripping torches, where the night itself must go on and on and there would never be another dawn.

Anna pressed the heels of her hands against her temples and wondered what time it was, and no sooner had she thought it than the parlor clock struck twice. How many hours did that make now? All that time she had followed her cousin Caroline, trying to do as she did, trying to be as strong and as tireless and as gentle—Caroline, who moved among the wreckage with water and bandages, with kindness and infinite patience, touching each man's life with her hands, her voice, until they began to call for her by name. Only once had Anna seen her cousin fail. A boy had asked her to pull his blanket down, wanted her to tell if it was bad or not as they so often did. Caroline pulled back the blanket, Anna watching, and when her cousin saw what the artillery had done she cried aloud, caught her retching with her own hand, rose and fled while the boy shrieked at the sight of himself, Anna saying over and over "It's all right it's all right it's all right—" When her cousin returned, the boy was dead. Caroline knelt beside him, took his hand, and Anna left her there. Now she was in the parlor, pressing her hands against the hurting in her head, knowing she would not be much use before long.

As if she had ever been much use, really. It was not the blood, though there was plenty of that—on the floor, on the walls, on the fringes of the drapes, on her own garments, on her hands. It was not the suffering or the sight of wounds or the white ends of shattered bones—she had become used to these things, or numb to them, almost at once, even before she had time to think about it. But she couldn't do as her cousin did. Watching herself, Anna saw a thing that frightened her more than all the terrible revelations of the night: her own face, cold and graceless, mouthing words she did not believe, wanting to shout Yes, they'll have to cut—Yes, it'll hurt—No, I can't fix it—Oh, God is here all right but all He can do is grieve and suffer too and anyway He won't listen to me I have tried—

A bright spear of pain struck her, blinded her for an instant, and when it passed she found herself on the sticky floor beside a boy whose hair was the color of straw. She watched him gather the hem of her dress in his hand. "Go ahead," she said. The boy looked at her, started to speak. "No," she said. "We are all in hell, all of us." Then she leaned her head against the plaster of the parlor wall and began to cry. In a little while, her cousin Caroline found her there, the boy still clinging to the hem of her dress.

Shortly after two o'clock, a party of musicians from the band of Adams' Brigade followed the scouts probing the abandoned Federal line. The musicians had been working the field all night as litter bearers and were worn to the edge of madness. They had long since emptied their stomachs, their minds were unwinding like neglected clocks, their bodies were turned to stone. None of them could remember how many men they had borne rearward to the great brick house: a procession of ashen faces, clenched hands, clotted beards, stretching all the way back to sundown when the band was withdrawn from the line and ordered to take up litters. Some of their own had been left very near the point of farthest advance— dead men absurdly clutching their dented brass instruments—and it was these the bandsmen sought now as they followed the scouts forward through the ruins of the army.

One of those bandsmen who had made it to the Federal works would never be found—not by this party of used up musicians, not the burial details that would come later, nor the crows and vultures, nor even the beetles that were the last and finest gleaners of all.

Calvin Jones, Professor of Music at the Cumberland Female Academy, was a man born for dim recital halls where dust floated in the twilight and young girls frowned at the fingerboards of their violins. From his youth, Calvin Jones had moved in a world smelling of cork grease, of ink and resin, of the vague, indefinable odor that clings to the inside of instrument cases. Unmarried and unmarriageable, he walked through life in rumpled frock coats and soiled collars, collecting dust, listening for pitch and key even in the songs of birds and the hum of telegraph wires. Calvin

Jones had sublimated his whole being to a single illumination: Music, the divine utterance that raised the dark, imperfect souls of men to unimaginable realms, among whose clouds every mean and common thing was transformed. For the Professor, music alone gave order to the universe and shaped, as words could never do, the infinite variations of the soul. Before this cosmic truth the Professor stood in humility and awe. It was the only truth he knew, and the only one he needed—so he thought.

But the world offers too much for any single truth to suffice. For every archangel there is a dragon, and the true artist is one who can embrace them both. Calvin Jones was never prepared for dragons.

In the spring of the Professor's fifty-second year, the war arrived. It came as a complete surprise to him; even more surprising was the fact that everyone expected him to have an opinion about it. He formed one soon enough, and it was simple in the extreme: the war had nothing whatever to do with him.

The events of that first spring and summer of the war seemed to confirm his opinion. His finishing students performed as always on the lawn of the Academy, received their diplomas under the elms, and went away into the world. In June, following his usual custom, Professor Jones went to New Orleans by steamboat and heard the symphony. That September the Academy opened to fewer students but opened nevertheless, and the Professor once again moved with his baton and sheet music among the bright faces. The winter passed, as it always did, and spring came again.

It was an April afternoon of almost unbearable softness. The tall windows of the music room were thrown open to the air, to the white blur of dogwoods and the breath of the warming earth. Professor Jones was lecturing on vocal combinations, particularly the pact duets in Verdi. His audience, ten young ladies of good family, ignored him; it was spring, their minds were full of other things. If the Professor understood this, he gave no sign. Then the Sexton knocked timidly on the door: Headmaster sends his compliments, Sir, and would the Professor kindly suspend his class and bring them out to the Oxford road?

The girls fled rejoicing into the sunlight. Professor Jones was puzzled; it was an extraordinary request, and at the very moment when he was about to make a point about *La Forza del Destino* that would weigh heavily on the final examination. He followed the girls outside, his lecture notes still in his hand.

The fenced greensward of the Academy bordered the Oxford road for the space of a hundred yards. Professor Jones was astonished to find the entire population of the school gathered along the fence: the girls, demure in their spring frocks, chattering like robins and bending to admire the yellow daffodils in the grass; the faculty in a somber cavil of clawhammer coats and beards and watch chains. In the road young Prince Rupert, the Headmaster's negro boy, was dancing a pigeon-wing to the time of his uncle the groundskeeper's jews-harp. Singular indeed, thought the Professor. There was nothing else in the road but the sunshine and the dust raised by the negro's bare feet.

"What is all this?" asked the Professor of young Fitter, a mathematics instructor whose enthusiasms always made the Professor uneasy. Fitter laughed. His hat was pushed back on his sandy head and a daffodil nodded in his buttonhole. "Ah, Professor, you are too much by half," the young man said. "Perhaps you are the only white man in the state don't know we have had a great battle up in Tennessee and emerged victorious."

"We?" the Professor queried. "*We* have?"

"Well, yes," said the young man. "Who else do you suppose? But look—yonder they come!" With that, Fitter ran to the fence, where everyone was waving handkerchiefs and talking at once. The Professor, left alone on the green, turned and peered up the road.

A band of horsemen was approaching in column-of-fours, the van, so the Professor surmised, of the army come from the late victory in Tennessee. He observed that they sat their horses with an easy arrogance; he noted an interesting atonal quality in the clank and jingle of their accoutrements. But the Professor, whose vision of an army had been formed years before while observing Her Majesty's Household Cavalry in review, could not reconcile the appearance of these men. If these were light horse (a term he recalled from a news dispatch out of the Crimea; remembered it because it had a pleasing sound), then why, he asked himself—for there was no one else to ask—did they so resemble a band of farmers? And why, if victorious, were they moving south when the enemy, as he understood it, was at the north?

The very fact that he was moved to wonder these things disturbed him. His thoughts drifted back to the empty music room where, only moments before, the world had stood in perfect order. He felt an unsettling nostalgia for the place, as if it already belonged to the unattainable past. Ridiculous, he chided himself. Reality lay there, not here; this foolishness on the road was ephemeral, a momentary distraction that would last only so long as it took the dust to settle on the roadside leaves. Let the young men laugh, let the girls wave their handkerchiefs in the sunlight.

For himself, Calvin Jones would make his place among reliable truths, and there he would await them. The Professor took a last look up the road, shook his head, and turned back to the Academy. He was a little way across the green when the people began to cheer.

The sound grabbed him, held him fast. The April afternoon leapt upward on those jubilant voices, high above the long procession of afternoons that made the life of Calvin Jones, and through the bars of sunlight in the elms the Professor caught a glimpse of something outside himself, terrible and exhilarating and divine. He opened his hands, his lecture notes floated down to the grass like leaves.

Then he was at the fence with the others among the voices and waving hats and fluttering handkerchiefs. The horsemen were abreast of the Academy gates now and the Professor could see them clearly, and all at once a strange sympathy grew in his heart. He gripped the fence rail, watching.

Young men they were, with brown, lean faces, and they laughed at the girls among the daffodils who stretched their white arms toward the horses' necks. The boys turned in their saddles, bowed, doffed their hats, while their mean-looking horses danced with excitement and fought their martingales. They did indeed look like farmers, in their slouch hats and short brown jackets (some in their shirtsleeves), and their boots and jeans trousers, and it might have been a fox hunt, not a battle, they'd been to. But these were no farmers. They were caked and spattered with dried mud, even to their blanket rolls and saddlebags, and powdered with the dust of the road. Some carried cut-down shotguns, some carbines in slings or held with the butt pressed against a thigh; all bristled with revolvers, each had a saber strapped to his saddle skirt. Confederate light horse they were—filthy, raffish, and dangerous—and they filled the bright afternoon with the stink of violence and death, and if the girls loved them it was because they did not know. But the Professor knew, and was drawn to them still. He found himself wanting to touch the horses' necks, wanting to go out in the road and press his hands against the horses' sweaty flanks and touch the boots of the boys who rode them and follow down the long road to whatever mystery awaited them.

As the last of the cavalrymen passed on toward the Cumberland square, Professor Jones bowed his head in shame and wonder. It took an effort of will to loose his hands from the fence rail and turn away. Then, having turned, he could not think of where to go. He looked about, as if there lay hidden in the sunlight and the elms and the buildings of the

Academy some compass that would guide him—but there was nothing. Then he caught a glimpse of memory, like a bright light behind a half-open door:

At twilight on Ash Wednesday, the huddled bells awoke; they pealed and clamored over the town, sending vast flocks of pigeons aloft to reel against the sky. Inside Canterbury the bells echoed in powerful resonation like the voice of God, and the young Calvin Jones made his way to the altar rail where the Archbishop waited, and the ashes—

Then it was gone—the image, the memory, whatever it was—and Professor Jones stood on the green of the Academy and thought *Ridiculous, ridiculous, that was too long ago* and took out his handkerchief and mopped his face while the young people chattered behind him. The young, how lucky they were, how little they knew of what it meant to be alone, to be poor, to be afraid—

"Bah!" he spat, and shoved his handkerchief angrily into his sleeve. Professor Jones had been trained at the Royal Academy, it was where he first shaped the truths that guided him, and if he had been poor and lonely and afraid what had that to do with the spring of his fifty-second year and a band of armed children passing in the road? Hah—the remote absurdity of youth. He was glad to be rid of it, to be never again beguiled by spring. He laughed, and was laughing when he felt the tug.

It was just that: a tug, a pull, as if someone had yanked on the tails of his coat. He glanced about, but no one was near. A prank, he thought. Young people were like lambs in spring. Then he looked toward the road again.

He blinked. A solitary horseman—a man, not a boy—sat in the middle of the road, the dust settling around him. He rode a big sorrel mare, her flanks sweaty and caked with dust; she was restless, but the rider checked her with a tight rein and she backed a little, pawing at the road. The people were craning over the fence to see what was coming next, but none of them seemed to notice the rider in the road. The rider, in his turn, seemed unaware of them all; his gaze was fixed toward the south, toward the Presbyterian spire, just visible over the greening trees, that marked the town of Cumberland. Yet the Professor had the impression that the man was not seeing anything at all, that he was lost in some contemplation that not even his fractious mount could disturb.

Timidly, the Professor approached the fence. There was something familiar about the man—

After mass young Calvin Jones found himself in the cloister, the cross of ashes still cool on his forehead. With the ashes were the words, still playing in his mind: Remember that thou art dust, and to dust thou shalt return. The boy rubbed the ashes away with the back of his hand, but the words remained.

The light was gone now, and with it the pigeons that had risen to praise God with the bells. But in the cloister there were lanterns and people moving among the arches. Dust they were, all dust.

It was cold. The boy sat in an archway and listened as the people passed over the damp flagstones, their voices soft, remote. Dust they were, or like the candles in the lanterns burning themselves into nothing: light for a little while, then dark forever. The boy shivered in the cold, and he was dust too. He began to weep, afraid, in the cold dark with the ashes smeared on the back of his hand—

The Professor moved through remembering, among images he did not know he remembered. Close now, he looked hard at the rider's face, was about to speak when the mare made a violent side-step that brought her nearly to the fence. The Professor shrank away as the rider, shaken out of his reverie, tightened the reins and spoke softly to the horse. She calmed immediately and stood with all four feet planted firmly in the road, nodding her head and blowing. When she was still, the horseman turned his head and looked at the Professor for the first time—

My boy, said a voice above him. Why do you weep so? Young Calvin Jones looked up to see the Archbishop himself, who had marked him with the ashes, who had said that he was dust. The boy shrank away, even as he heard himself speak—

Dust? said the Archbishop. He was in a plain black cassock and shawl; he gathered his skirts and sat down beside the boy on the cold stones. Ah, me, he said—

"I know you," said the Professor.

The horseman nodded.

"But where? I—"

The horseman turned in his saddle, his gloved hand on the cantle, and looked back down the road. The Professor sensed that something was approaching, looked himself, saw nothing. "What is it?" he said, and turned again to the horseman, but the road was empty. There was only the silver dust hanging in the air.

The Professor gripped the fence rail and stared at his hands. He heard a wren, loud and insistent, calling in the trees. From the town, half a mile away, floated the chimes of the courthouse bell: two o'clock.

Dust? the Archbishop said again? He took the boy's hand in his own—

Then something changed. The Professor looked up, feeling it, like the drop in temperature before a summer storm. The people were silent now, staring down the road with their handkerchiefs limp in their hands. They stood with expectant faces, hands draped over the fence, watching. Presently there came a creaking, groaning, a jingle of trace chains. The Professor looked down the road, saw a wagon approaching drawn by a pair of weary mules, their heads nodding. The ungreased axles popped in the soft air. Behind this wagon was another, and behind that, as far as the Professor could see, were still others. They came slowly, and the people watched.

Soon the first wagon was abreast. The driver was a jaundiced country man in a ludicrous stovepipe hat. His jaws worked around an enormous plug of tobacco. When he saw the Academy girls, his face opened in a brown-toothed grin. "Hidy!" he said. When he got no response, the driver laughed and spat a long stream of ambure over the brake-handle. He slapped the reins, the mules jerked, and from the wagon bed rose a howl. "'At's right, boys," said the driver over his shoulder. "Yuns wake up—we comin into town. Hey, Gully—somebody out here wants to see yo' face!"

The Professor stiffened. Something was about to happen, he knew it—

Feel my hand, said the Archbishop. Is it dust?

No, said the boy.

You are afraid of the dark, aren't you?

Yes, said the boy.

Ah, said the Archbishop. So am I, sometimes.

You? said the boy.

A thing rose above the wagon box and draped its arms over the side, and for an instant the Professor thought it was some giant, ungainly bird until the dark and blistered face took shape and the Professor saw that it was a man who had no jaw. Where the jaw had been was a moist vacancy rimmed by the upper teeth from which the tongue dangled like an iris beard. The man shook his head and the tongue waggled; a girl shrieked hysterically and young Fitter fainted dead away and the driver laughed: "How 'bout that, ladies? Ever see a thing like that before?"

The young ladies of Cumberland Academy dropped away from the fence like leaves from a vine. They turned and fled, sobbing, or backed away slowly, eyes alight with a terrible understanding. The men shook their fists in outrage at the driver, who laughed again and slapped the mule with the reins.

84

Meanwhile, the Professor stared in shock at the jawless man. He could not have imagined that such a thing was possible. The wagon passed and another took its place, groaning and creaking like the first, and the Professor went on staring—

The Archbishop touched the boy's forehead. Do you remember how I marked you here? So you would remember death?

Yes, said the boy. Yes, you—

Now watch, said the Archbishop. He took the boy's hand and with it made the sign of the cross on his breast. Now I mark you here, said the Archbishop, so that you will remember the light. Between these two signs lies the truth. Can you understand that?

The Professor raised his hand and with it made the sign of the cross on his breast—

Remember me when the dark comes and you are afraid. Remember me, and through me remember the One whose sign has marked you forever. It will be we three: you and I, and the One before whom no darkness can last. We three, always. Do you understand?

Yes, said the boy, and he understood.

Will you remember?

Yes. Yes, I will remember.

The wagons passed, and the men. Some sat on the tailgates with their bare feet dangling, watching across the sunlit afternoon at the girls fleeing over the green. Others walked beside the wagons, tottering like old men, their eyes fixed on some distant place. The dust rose about them all. And by the fence, the Archbishop of Canterbury spread his arms, loving them, while from his heart bright birds arose to wheel above them, offering praise, offering grace and humility and love. The Archbishop wept, and the young men saw and believed.

All afternoon the wagons passed, bearing the wounded from the great battle of Shiloh, and all afternoon the Archbishop moved among them. Prince Rupert followed with a cedar bucket of spring water; the Archbishop dipped cup after cup for the thirsty men, bathed their faces, their feet, their hands, and spoke to them—not of God's will but of His suffering, as if God Himself were lying in the reeking straw of the wagon beds—and the young men listened and believed. And when the people saw the thing which the Archbishop had begun, they returned to the road— girls, matrons, the bearded faculty, all—bringing water and food from the kitchen, and coffee, and fresh bandages torn from sheets. All that afternoon and night they labored as the wagons passed, and the young men were grateful.

Next morning, the Archbishop made his way home. He climbed the steps, fumbled at the door, then stood blinking in the gloom of the hall. From the back of the house a woman appeared, wringing her hands in her apron. "Calvin!" she cried when she saw him. "Oh, Calvin, for God's sake where have you been? Have you heard—" Then she stopped, and for a moment watched him where he stood smiling wearily in the hall, his hat in his hand. "Calvin?" she said at last.

"Ah, Mrs. Wexford," he said. "It has been a long night indeed."

Agnes Jones' shoulders fell. She came to her brother, took his arm. "No doubt it has, Your Grace," she said. "Would you like a cup of tea?"

That summer of 1862 Calvin Jones, once Professor of Music at the Cumberland Female Academy, enrolled in the Confederate army as a bandsman. When it was done, he went home and told his sister.

"You are an old fool," said Agnes Jones. "What business have you marching around in the hot sun like a militiaman? And what if they shoot you, eh? What then?"

The Professor shrugged. "Well, it is music anyhow," he said.

He was sent to Mobile where, among the sand fleas and mosquitos of Fort Morgan, Bandsman Jones learned the mysteries and evolutions of military life. By and by he caught a fever, and was in hospital. Then he was felled by sunstroke and was in hospital again. He practiced the saxhorn, wrote his sister, and studied the cries of the gulls that wheeled over the refuse dump. He waited for the war to discover him.

Then at last, just before the Battle of Mobile Bay, the Professor was sent north with a draft of older men to join the Army of Tennessee. They traveled by the cars and arrived, like tardy guests, among the confusing backwaters of the Fall of Atlanta where they were immediately captured *en masse* by a regiment of Indiana cavalry, only to be recaptured by Confederate infantry that same afternoon. Presently the Professor became separated from his comrades and, having discovered that no one really cared what he did, wandered through the army until he found Adams' Brigade of Loring's Division of Stewart's Corps, in which he had heard there were some Cumberland men. He reported to the Principal Musician, told some picturesque lies about his travels, and was taken into the band. With Adams'

Brigade, then, he set off on the Nashville campaign under the gallant Hood, and on Thanksgiving day wrote his sister from the muddy banks of the Tennessee at Florence, Alabama:

> Mister T.J. Carter's boy Bushrod is here and young Jefferson Hicks, Jack Bishop, and two or three others I do not know. There are not so many as there once was, of the Cumberland men, I mean. They are kind to me—they think me a curiosity, no doubt—though as a general rule they do not entertain a very high opinion of the Band. In that, I cannot fault them, as I have no high regard for it myself.

> Tomorrow, or the next day, we are to cross the River if the Pontoons come up. It is all a great Mystery to me, over there. Pray for us, dear Agnes. Pray for me, an old fool.

So it was that Calvin Jones crossed the broad, slate-colored river into Tennessee, and eleven days later stood with his new comrades behind the line of Adams' Brigade in the yard of the great brick house at Franklin.

They had been playing music all afternoon, ever since the army had formed up at the foot of the hills. They had gone through "Listen to the Mockingbird," "Ben Bolt," "Dixie's Land," "Here's Your Mule," "The British Grenadier," and, of course, "The Bonnie Blue Flag," a tune Professor Jones often heard in his sleep. It was well that they had been so busy for, surrounded by the bleating and thumping of the band, Professor Jones had been able to keep himself inside a bubble of music—fragile, to be sure, but sufficient to keep at bay the reality that was rapidly taking shape around him. Even the explosion of the first shell and the body of young Jefferson Hicks (around which the band had to open files) had registered as little more than the dim reverberation of something that was happening elsewhere. But now, in the yard of the great brick house, they had been ordered to cease their playing so the commands of the officers could be heard, and for the first time Calvin Jones was forced to acknowledge that the war had discovered him at last.

The Principal Musician had gone to confer with the Brigade commander. The bandsmen were at ease, their instruments lay about like strange metallic flowers in the grass. A cornetist, the veteran of many campaigns, said, "Well, I guess this is as far as we go, and damned if *I* ain't satisfied."

Professor Jones looked off toward the gathering smoke. "Am I to assume, then, that the band don't follow the troops into battle?"

"Follow, hell," said the cornetist. "We already *in* the goddamn battle. Didn't you see them dead men back yonder?"

The Professor nodded. "I had supposed—" he began, but at that moment the Principal Musician returned and the men gathered around to hear the news.

The Principal Musician was fidgeting with excitement, which the men took to be a bad sign. They regarded their leader with suspicion, and groaned when he ordered them to fall in. He was the only member of the band to have a regulation dark-gray frock coat with musician's bars across the front—the rest of them looked like farmers. Professor Jones thought the Principal Musician's uniform made him look vaguely skeletal.

"Gentlemen," the Principal Musician said, "General Adams has informed me that the band is to follow closely behind the brigade as it advances....."

"Damn," muttered the cornetist.

"We are to play, to use his word, 'lustily,' to keep up the spirit of the troops as they—"

"Who gone keep *our* spirit up?" asked the cornetist.

"Quiet!" said the Principal Musician. "I expect every man to do his duty. I should not have to remind you that the fate of the Confederacy, not to mention the honor of this band, hangs in the balance—"

Several of the men laughed, including the Professor, though he could not have said why.

"Take your instruments!" snapped their leader. "Let me hear a 'C'."

Beyond the Principal Musician, troops were moving and shifting in unfathomable evolutions. The band picked up their instruments and joined in blowing a "C" note. It was not unmelodious, though the fortunes of war had caused most of the horns to go flat, and the effect reminded Professor Jones of the foghorns of steamships along the Dover coast. Nevertheless, Professor Jones concentrated on warming his horn and tried not to think about the fact that he was here at all.

The wall of men to their front began to move into the smoke. The Principal Musician raised his baton, the bandsmen lifted their instruments.

"'Annie Laurie'," the Principal Musician shouted over the growing din. "*One* two and —"

What! thought the Professor, turning frantically through his part book—*"Annie Laurie"! Ridiculous!* Give them a march, a quickstep—*this* was no song for a battle, but for summer evenings when the lamps were lit. *Voice and piano*, the Professor thought—*perhaps a viola*. Yes, and a young tenor, preferably one in love with the pianist. Absurd that anyone would want to manhandle "Annie Laurie" with brasses in the middle of a broom-sage field. *One* two and.....the band was well into the fourth measure when the Professor brought the mouthpiece to his lips.

There was a gunshot nearby, and men shouting, but the band was already marching across the yard, through the oaks, into the fields beyond, following the Brigade into the fight. Because the bells of the band's instruments pointed backward, the Professor had difficulty hearing the balance of sound—but what he could hear was not really so bad. Needed a little more bottom perhaps, but the bass saxhornist had been invalided with measles, so he was told, and there was no help for it now. The Professor surrounded himself in his bright, fragile bubble of sound.

The ground was rough, it was impossible to keep in step, the smoke was vile. The Professor considered that he ought to be afraid, felt mildly puzzled that he was not. He concentrated on his part-book, noted the rise and fall of the Principal Musician's baton, kept his time—nothing to it, really. Lots of noise, smoke, shouting, but so far it was all a blur and seemed to have nothing to do with him. And surely it would be over soon: how long did a battle last, anyway?

They played through "Annie Laurie" three times and the Professor was getting weary of the tune and almost wished something would happen, then he stumbled and bruised his lips on the mouthpiece of his horn. He turned his head to spit, and when he looked again the Principal Musician, almost frantic with excitement, had turned to face them and was walking backward, his baton held horizontally over his head—

Like on parade, the Professor thought, as the band ceased playing and the drums began to beat cadence. *It's just like he was on parade—*

Their leader opened his mouth, said something that none of them could hear, opened his mouth again, shouted, "'Dixie's Land'! Give them 'Dixie,' boys!" and lowered his baton. The band began to play the quick-step; the Principal Musician seized his baton by the ball end, threw it up in the air, turned with a flourish as the baton twirled above him; the Principal Musician put out his gloved hand and made a perfect catch and evaporated in a blinding flash of light, in a spray of blood and bone and flesh that spattered the men in the front rank even as the concussion of the shell knocked them sprawling and the rest marched through the empty place where the Principal Musician had been—

That is not possible, thought the Professor—*A man cannot simply disappear*—

The band bunched up on itself, cursing and faltering now but still playing "Dixie's Land" as they had been told to do. A heavy bank of smoke rolled over them and they passed over a carpet of dead and wounded men and a riderless horse, wild-eyed, stirrups flapping, ran across their front and was swallowed up by the smoke and the Professor rubbed his eyes and lost his place in the score. He listened, trying to hear the others, but the fragile bubble had burst and there were only ragged shards of music around him as each man played on his own. The Professor blindly fingered the keys of his horn, trying to find his place, but there was no place—

The Brigade to their front began to execute a left wheel but the movement was only a blur in the smoke so the band marched straight on for a time and ended up on the far right of the line, and it was then that the Professor found himself alone. He had no idea where he was or where his comrades had gone, he could not think what to do so he stumbled on, walking blindly into the smoke and the angry hum of balls and somewhere up ahead the *click-clack* of bayonets and a sound like rending wood. The chaos of the battle possessed him; the noise was a solid wall now, a seamless roar of musketry and bellow of guns and the mad snarling and crying of men. The Professor had never heard such sound before; some part of him was captivated by the density of it, he could feel it on his face, had to push against it as if he were in a tower where great bells tolled, the great huddled bells waking—

Suddenly he tripped, fell headlong, his instrument went flying and he jarred against the earth. For a moment he was stunned, his face pressed to the ground; he smelled the grass, considered the rocks, the gravelly soil, the line of ants that marched busily under his nose—*Ants!* he thought, astonished by that detail, almost offended by it; they seemed to mock him, going about their business while he—

Then the noise crashed around him again and he struggled to his hands and knees and looked for his horn and found instead the thing that had tripped him: a man, impossibly old, with a grotesque beard, lying on the thick, ropy coils of his own bowels that spilled out beneath him. The Professor cried out, tried to scuttle away, but the man grasped his trouser leg, held him fast. "Get away!" shouted the Professor and kicked at the gray face and still the wounded man held him. "What!" shouted the Professor. "What do you want!"

90

The old man's mouth moved in his beard. His eyes were yellow globes. "Yes, yes, all right!" the Professor said. He forced the man on his back, fumbled at the gritty entrails, tried to stuff them back. They slipped through his fingers like eels.

"Impossible!" shouted the Professor into the old man's face, but the old man burned him with his eyes and drew the Professor's shirtfront into the knot of his hand and his lips moved and the Professor bent down to hear—

Let darkness and the shadow of death stain it croaked the old man—

"No!" cried the Professor.

Let a cloud dwell upon it—

The Professor grasped the hand that held him, it was cold like a wet stone and strong, he could not move it and the eyes held him even as the light died and the old man said *Let the blackness.....let the blackness.....*

The Professor cried out again but there were no words now and the old man loosed his hand and reached up and touched him once on the forehead and died—

The Professor watched the hand drop away. He rose to his knees, watching, the smoke and the hurricane all around him but no matter for the old man's eyes were on him and he was at peace. He took the old man's hand again, folded it in his own, pressed it to his own breast and with it made the sign, and Calvin Jones was gone. Gone forever now, and no one to regret, no one to say goodbye. Gone without a trace, without even a feather drifting earthward through the smoke.

The party of musicians, led by the Archbishop of Canterbury, at a little after two o'clock on the morning of December first, followed the scouts all the way to the Federal line. The works were abandoned, the enemy was gone. Then began the business of the night.

CHAPTER FIVE

Simon Rope was having a big time, even though he had lost one of his ears. Something—he never knew what—had come along and sliced it off and now it burned like fire, all because he'd been too eager to get among the spoils. Well, he'd been cut a good deal worse in his time, and he wouldn't make that mistake again.

Simon Rope had not participated in the great Battle of Franklin. He managed to drop out of the regimental column just before they reached the gap in the hills where the Columbia Pike cut through. Lying by the roadside, feigning exhaustion, he edged into the brush and waited until the army had passed and was arraying itself on the plain beyond. Then he moved, with great stealth and cunning, up through the woods and behind the place where General Hood had established his headquarters. He actually saw Hood and his officers through the trees and thought how easy it would be to shoot the General in the head right then and wondered what it would be like to shoot a general—but he had left his musket behind, and anyway there were too many soldiers around, so General Hood lived to fight another day.

Simon Rope traveled a long way through the brush until he found a place where no troops were ever likely to be; there he settled down and waited for something to happen.

In time, from his hiding place, he could see the long lines moving forward to the attack. He was impressed by the spectacle; he watched it as a racoon or a weasel might, simply noting the fact without drawing any conclusions or feeling any connection to what was going on below.

He waited a long time. He relieved himself in the bushes and noted with disgust that his leavings were meager and hard—he would get something to eat by and by, down there where the village was. He sat on a log and whittled with his knife and listened to the sound of the fight. He thought about many things, and among them was Jack Bishop.

In all the months since the Kenesaw line, Simon Rope had enjoyed thinking about Bishop and how he would die. Simon Rope made pictures in his mind of how he would do it, where he would make every cut, what he would talk about while he was skinning the son of a bitch alive. He had many plans, but all of them required more privacy than army life had provided so far. He had watched, been patient, been ready to take advantage of the least opportunity, all for nothing. Of course, it would have been simple to shoot the man in the middle of a fight, but that wouldn't answer. For one thing, Simon Rope had avoided every fight the regiment had been in since he'd joined it—a considerable task that took all his energy. For another thing, Simon Rope wanted to take his time with Bishop. He wanted the bastard to know who killed him and to have plenty of time to think about it while it was happening. But now it was too late. Bishop was going into a fight down there from which he was unlikely to return, and Simon Rope had missed his chance.

But then again, maybe Bishop would only be wounded. Simon Rope was cheered by the thought of Bishop lying down there in the dark, just waiting for Luck and Providence to bring them together again. Unlikely, but it was something to think about.

So Simon Rope waited, and after dark, when he believed the battle to be dying down, he began the long trek across the plain below. Only he hadn't been patient enough. He suddenly found himself in the middle of a night action on the Confederate left, and it was here that something came humming out of the dark and sliced off his ear.

But the battle was over for good. There was no more shooting, the field was chock full of dead and helpless wounded, and Simon Rope was having a big time. He found supper in an abandoned cabin: a pot of peas in the ashes of a cold fire, which he ate with his hands. There was bacon grease, too, for his ear. Then he went foraging, and after a few hours the watches and rings and the thick wad of greenbacks he'd collected made a gratifying weight in his haversack. It was simply astonishing what these yahoos carried—he'd even found a diamond stickpin on the body of a Confederate officer. That was funny: the officer had no head, but he had a diamond stickpin. Simon Rope thought if he could only find a lantern—but no, that was too dicey. He had learned not to be greedy.

He was moving to the right, taking his time, avoiding the little knots of living men who made their way onto the field. When he could not avoid them, he simply became one of them—just another poor soldier boy out looking for his pards. Once he even helped pull some bodies out of a rifle-pit; they were mostly Yankees, and it was on one of them that he found the greenbacks.

As he went along, he kept his eyes peeled for Bishop—and for Bushrod Carter and the Captain and the First Sergeant and the Sergeant-Major and a few others. He had plans for them all. He didn't really expect to find them—he had no idea where the regiment had gone in—but he kept hoping anyway.

A little after two o'clock in the morning, long after moon-set, Simon Rope was working around a house on the edge of town, a handsome little place in a cluster of outbuildings. The Yankees had breastworks here, and the piles of dead in the yard and in the trench beat anything Simon Rope had ever seen. He didn't want to get too close to the house, so he was working the fringes of the yard when someone spoke to him out of the dark.

"Oh, please—help me, won't you?"

"Sure," said Simon Rope. He moved toward the voice, taking his time, being careful.

"Here—over here."

He found the soldier lying in a tangle of dead men. In the starlight, Simon Rope judged him to be not much above fourteen years, just a pup. Both his legs were gone at the knees. "What's the matter?" said Simon Rope.

The boy looked at him with wide, grateful eyes. "Friend," he said. "I knowed somebody'd find me, thank God."

"Sure, sure," said Simon Rope, squatting by the boy. "What's your trouble?"

"Christ, don't you see? I am all blowed to pieces! Look at me!"

"Well, you're a mess all right," said Simon Rope.

The boy struggled to rise; Simon Rope watched him until he fell back, panting. The boy rolled his eyes. "I can't get up, Lord, I don't know what.....what to do. Listen, am I gone die, you think? You could take me back to the surgeons, you could—"

"Oh, I don't know," said Simon Rope. "What'll you give me if I do?"

The expression on the boy's face made Simon Rope grin. "Give you?" said the boy. "Well, I.....I ain't got anything to give you. I got a pocketknife—I got some money, five dollars, I—"

"Naw," said Simon Rope. "You'll jes have to go on and die, I guess."

"Don't tell me that!" cried the boy. He clutched at the front of Simon Rope's shirt and Simon Rope knocked his hand away and rose to his feet.

"Shit, boy, you got your goddamn legs blowed off, both of em. You gone die no matter what. Now, lemme see that 'ere haversack."

The boy's haversack lay under his body. Simon Rope bent and pulled it out and cut the strap with his knife. Then he held the knife up so the boy could see it. "You fixin to die all right, and I'm gone help you along in jes a minute. You see this knife? You think about it while I look in here."

The boy whimpered, his eyes were glassy and round in the starlight. Simon Rope talked to him while he examined the haversack. "You know, I seen lots of em cross over, and never a one of em could believe it. You ever think you was gone die? Naw, 'course you didn't. And scared? Oh, they was all scared. I bet you scared, ain't you? Sure you are. What you reckon it's like over there? Dark, I bet, and cold. Man, I'd be scared too." He threw the haversack away in disgust. "Well, you wasn't lyin—there ain't nothin in there worth *my* trouble. Now, then."

He squatted on his haunches again, just by the boy's head. "You get away from me," whispered the boy.

"Oh, I'll go directly," said Simon Rope. He looked around, waved the knife at the darkness. "You know, it's funny to think about, ain't it?— how things go right on when you're dead. Now, jes think—it'll be mornin pretty soon, somewhere your mama's gone be gettin up, prob'ly make some biscuits, fry up some ham, set the table—goddamn, it'd be good to be there, wouldn't it? Only you ain't. You lyin out here in the dark with your legs blowed off and your mama don't even know it. Hell, jes about the time she's gettin up, they'll be throwin you in a ditch yonder—won't nobody even know your name—"

"No! It's.....it's....."

"What?" said Simon Rope. "Speak up, boy, you ain't got but a minute."

The boy coughed, spit blood, tried to rise again. "It's Dan'l.....my name—"

"Well, Dan'l," said Simon Rope, "I'd like to stay and hold your hand, but I got to be movin along. 'Fore I do, though, I'm gone kill you with this knife."

"You *ain't*! Say you—"

"Sure I am," said Simon Rope, and wrapped his hand in the boy's hair and pulled his head back and drew the knife with one quick motion across the throat that seemed too white and slender even for a boy's.....

The party of musicians found their comrades, five in all, spread out along the line of the advance. They gathered them together and laid them out in a row, heels together, hands crossed on their breasts. Each held in his hands a page torn out of a part-book; on the page was written the man's name so the burial detail would know what name to put on the shingle, if there was a shingle. When everything was arranged, the living bent their heads for a moment while the Archbishop prayed quietly, then they shuffled off a little way and sat upon the cold ground. Seven bandsmen, sitting in a circle around a bull's-eye lantern, in the groaning night.

"Well, I reckon that does it," said the cornetist at last. He looked around at the others, who were all staring at the lantern.

"I reckon it does, too," said a short, sallow man who once played the piccolo. "I reckon it does, by God."

"I reckon we have done our part," said the cornetist. "Who's to say we can't slip off? They's bound to be a corn crib or somethin we can hold up in. I'm give out."

"Me, too," said the piccolo player.

The others said nothing. They raised their faces and looked at the cornetist. Then they looked at the Archbishop. "Yes," said the Archbishop. "We are all tired."

The cornetist stood up and stretched himself. "I b'lieve I'll hunt a hole. Who's with me?"

"You know I am, Jim," said the piccolo player.

"I know you are, Delmar," said the cornetist.

The Archbishop stood up then, his face was lost in the dark outside the lantern light. "You all go on," he said. "I think I will stay a little while." Then he turned and moved away. They could hear him walking through the grass.

The others sat a moment longer, not looking at one another. "Aw, well, shit," one of them said at last, and rose, and walked off in the direction the Archbishop had gone. One by one the others followed, gathering up the bloody litters, taking the lantern with them. The cornetist and the piccolo player were left in the dark.

"Well, the damn fools," said the piccolo player. "C'mon, Jim, lets us go."

The cornetist rubbed his eyes and looked off into the dark. He sighed. "No, I guess not," he said.

"What?"

"Come along, Delmar," said the cornetist. "Be a man for once." The cornetist moved away, following the Archbishop. The other man stood astonished, suddenly alone in the darkness. Then, with a curse, he, too, followed in the way.

The musicians, together again, moved in the dim circle of the lantern. Their intermittent shadows were flung across the faces of dead men, they stumbled and tripped over the soft, yielding bodies under their feet. They tried not to step on faces, but sometimes they did. Finally, they came to the ditch along the enemy's works at the cotton gin, and here they stopped.

Others were there before them, and others were coming up from behind. With torches and lanterns they came, some of them talking quietly, some laughing even—but at the ditch they all stopped, and the talking and the laughter stopped, and they stood quietly and wished they had not come at all.

They were young men, most of them, but veterans of a long, vicious war; they were strong, dangerous men, cynical about death, even their own, which they had long ago accepted as inevitable. They had seen other battlefields, other helpless dead, and thought that nothing could ever surprise or grieve or frighten them again. Even so, they found nothing in all their bitter days to prepare them for the scene that confronted them now. They stood in silence, listening to their own heartbeats, understanding all at once that, whatever their experience, they had not exhausted the possibilities for horror.

The empty breastworks, stretching left and right before the shadowy bulk of the gin house, were a tangle of torn earth, displaced headlogs, sharpened stakes; they were strewn with equipment, with broken muskets, gun rammers, hand spikes, jackets, overcoats, hats and caps, bits of anonymous cloth and paper, tin cups, sardine tins—the ground was white with cotton lint and cartridge paper save at the embrasures where the guns had been: there the earth was scorched and blackened by the muzzle blasts. It was pitch dark behind the breastworks, a frightening dark as if some unknown and unimaginable enemy lurked there, and the silent gin house loomed against the stars.

But there was no enemy. The works belonged only to the dead, and neither the dead nor the victorious living had any use for them now.

In the starlight, and in the torchlight as far as it carried, the dead possessed the violated earth. They were draped all over the parapet, festooned in the osage orange hedges, blown back from the embrasures in meaty fragments. In the ditch before the works they lay in geologic strata of regiments and brigades, piled six and eight and ten deep: an inextricable mass of gray and brown, a tangle of accoutrements and muskets, a blur of faces and claw-like hands. Some were almost naked, torn to shreds by canister and rifle fire, the clothes ripped from their bodies; others lay whole and peaceful, dreaming among their comrades. Here and there, dead men who'd had no room to fall stood upright in the pile, still holding their rifles, their faces still set toward the memory of a vanished foe.

Some of the dead were busy. They twitched and jerked from the violence of their passing, they heaved stubbornly as still-living men tried to push up from underneath. The surface layer of wounded writhed and groaned and implored; the whole pile crawled with movement. Steam rose from the fragments, from open skulls and blue piles of entrails. The smell hung close to the ground in the damp night.

There were too many. Too many to believe.

"Jesus Christ," whispered the cornetist.

Yes, thought the Archbishop. *Jesus Christ.*

The Archbishop knelt by the clotted ditch. He knelt as low as he could, until his forehead pressed against the earth. He thought he should pray, but the words would not come. Then it occurred to him that perhaps he was not supposed to pray. *Yes*, he thought—*sometimes I am just supposed to listen.*

So the Archbishop listened, and overhead the sky was full of stars that spread in a vast, luminous cloud from horizon to horizon. Meanwhile the earth turned on its ancient axis, half light and half dark, always morning and evening somewhere. The morning spread across the world's face; it was out there now, making its way toward them, while the night fell westward with the stars. They, too, were moving, these mortals. They moved in a dream of their own making, whether toward the night or morning the Archbishop could not say—he only knew that he was moving with them. He listened, and in a little while the words came that he needed, and he sent them up toward the infinite dark that lay between the stars: *Oh God, Father of all memories, forgive us this victory if You can—*

The Archbishop arose and stood unsteadily on the edge of the ditch, an old man dizzy in starlight. The cornetist took his arm. "Here, now—you all right?"

"Oh, yes," the Archbishop said. "It's been a long night, is all."

Presently some officers arrived and set them all to work. They found muskets with fixed bayonets and, using the trigger guards of other muskets, bent the bayonets into hooks; with these they began to drag the bodies from the ditch. They worked blindly, without feeling or thought. They built fires of boards and headlogs and broken ammunition boxes; the fires gleamed in their eyes and in the eyes of the dead. The smoke swirled around them.

The Archbishop made his way among the ruins. He tried to close his mind to everything—to the stars, the world, God, everything that lay outside the glow of his bull's-eye lantern. There would be ample time for thinking tomorrow and the next day and in all the days and nights he would ever live; tonight he wanted only to be useful, and not to think at all.

But he was tired, and his mind kept drifting into places he wished it wouldn't go. Once he thought the dead were speaking to him, whispering of their lives. The whole field seemed to be alive with whispers as the dead men turned their faces toward the lantern. *I was* they seemed to say. They were insistent. *I was. I was.* And once the Archbishop thought he saw a horseman riding on the breastworks. He heard the scuffling hooves, the trickle of dislodged earth down the face of the parapet. The rider himself was featureless, only a darker shape against the stars. The Archbishop rubbed his eyes, and when he looked again he saw that there was indeed a horse, but it was dead. It lay draped over the works on its belly, shot in mid-leap. There was no rider.

The Archbishop shook his head. *I am too old for this business*, he thought.

The men had uncovered a layer of soldiers from the assault of Adams' Brigade and the Archbishop felt strangely drawn to them. "Who are these?" he asked of a soldier.

"Well, somebody said they's Adams' men," said the soldier. "They said that was his horse yonder on the works. These boys right here is Miss'sippi troops, you can tell by they buttons. Look—that 'un's still alive."

The man pointed, and the Archbishop saw a soldier buried to his shoulders in the dead. He made his way to the man, peered carefully into his face. "I think I know him," said the Archbishop. "He looks.....like a boy I knew once, somewhere."

"Well, shit-fire, let's fetch him outen there," said the other, and together they cleared away the dead men and pulled the soldier from the ditch.

The Archbishop knelt and looked again at the boy's face. It was smashed and bloody, but death was not in it.

"Taken a lick to the head, looks like," said the helpful soldier. "There—his finger's shot away too, but he be awright if the surgeons don't get holt of him."

The soldier went on his way, and the Archbishop looked down at the wounded man's face. Presently, he looked up to see the cornetist standing there.

"Who's that?" asked the cornetist. "Damned if I don't know him somehow."

The Archbishop nodded. "Yes, I had the same thought, but I can't seem to remember."

The cornetist bent closer. "Uh-huh, I know him all right. He's from one of them damn Miss'ssippi regiments." The cornetist's face cracked a smile, remembering. "Over in Georgia, him and some other boys used to chunk pine cones at us when we was practicin."

"My," said the Archbishop.

"His own mama wouldn't know him now."

"No, she wouldn't," agreed the Archbishop.

"Well, let us get these traps off him," said the cornetist. "You, Delmar! Bring that litter, sir!"

While the two men untangled the soldier's accoutrements, the piccolo player slouched up dragging a Saterlee Patent litter. He dropped it on the ground and began to walk away.

"Whoa, now," said the cornetist. "Where you goin? We got to accommodate this here man."

"Like hell," said the other, but he came back and straightened out the litter. Meanwhile, the soldier began to groan amd mutter. The Archbishop tried to give him some water, but he retched violently. Finally they arranged him on the litter and the Archbishop put the man's haversack and canteen on his chest and crossed his arms over them. The man pushed them off. The cornetist bent to retrieve them and the soldier sneezed in his face. Several men laughed at that; their laughter was like the croaking of ravens.

"Bedamned," said the cornetist, wiping the fine red mist of the soldier's sneeze from his face.

"Oh, my God," said the wounded soldier in a voice made thin and reedy from his smashed nose. "Alas, poor Hiram!"

The cornetist looked at the soldier in surprise.

"What'd he say?" asked the piccolo player. "Alas who?"

"Never mind," said the cornetist. "The boy's had his brains bashed out, for God's sake." He bent again and with his long fingers traced the embroidered square-and-compasses on the soldier's jacket. Then he straightened. "Delmar," he said, "do you take the head end, and I the foot."

"Like hell," said the piccolo player.

"I'll take it," said the Archbishop.

"No," said the cornetist gently. "Why don't you carry his traps—Delmar, I'm sure, will take the head."

"I ain't totin no goddamned litter," said the piccolo player. "I done toted all the litters I mean to in *this* life."

"You may very well be right," said the cornetist, "if you don't by God pick up them handles."

"We are all tired," said the Archbishop. But the piccolo player bent to the handles; they raised the wounded man from the earth and the Archbishop shouldered his haversack and canteen. "Well, boys," said the cornetist, "as we used to say in the olden days: 'Forward, for Cleburne's knows no other.'"

"Aw, kiss my rosy ass, you and Cleburne both," said the piccolo player. Then, with the soldier muttering between them, they started off toward the rear.

The Archbishop carried the lantern, and by its feeble light the dead watched them pass. They stumbled over rocks, over corpses, over discarded equipment; men clutched at their legs and cried and implored. Again and again the Archbishop stopped to give comfort. He collected canteens from the dead and gave them to the living; he spoke to the living and dead both, covered them with blankets, arranged their clothing, pressed their Testaments into their hands. Now and then the cornetist had to call him to fetch the lantern.

Once a Confederate battery came blundering out of the dark, drivers shouting, guns and limbers bouncing, horses galloping madly as if they had not been told the battle was over. Wounded men screamed as the wheels rolled over them; others, the cornetist among them, cursed with vain fury as the guns clattered by, frantic to reach a front that was no longer there.

"Where was them sons of bitches this afternoon?" asked the cornetist.

"Must've been a fish fry somewheres," said the piccolo player.

Many civilians were about the field now, wandering dazed and unbelieving through the shambles. Everywhere there were torches, fires, moving lanterns, but between these points of light was a tangible dark into which men vanished like ghosts. Across the field men were calling for their comrades, calling for each other, their voices sharp and unsettling above the monotonous crying of the wounded.

The soldier on the litter moved his hands and talked constantly. Once he tried to sit up and nearly fell out of the litter; they had to stop and calm him down.

"I declare, this boy is a trial," said the cornetist.

"Why'nt we jes leave the son bitch?" said the piccolo player.

"Delmar—" began the cornetist.

"Let us all rest a moment," said the Archbishop. So they lowered the stretcher, and the Archbishop moved off with the lantern and a cluster of canteens. The cornetist watched him go, then shook his head and stretched out on the ground next to the wounded man. The piccolo player began to edge away.

"Where you off to, Delmar?" asked the cornetist.

"For God's sake, Jim," came the other's voice from the darkness. "Can't a feller take a leak on his own time?"

"Sure," said the cornetist. "You go right on." He closed his eyes—oh, it felt so good to do that. Maybe the old man wouldn't be able to find them again and he and this boy could just lay here all night and sleep and sleep. But, no—that wouldn't do; directly he would have to go and hunt for the old man if he didn't show. Then he grinned, listening to the piccolo player slip away into the night. Old Delmar. With any luck he'd make Spring Hill by daylight and some farmer would fill his ass with bird shot.

The cornetist rubbed his eyes, trying to remember when he'd last slept. Maybe, when they got this boy back, the old man would listen to reason and they could go hunt a hole and sleep—though little enough of the night remained for sleeping. Already there was a copper taint of morning in the air. He could sleep right now, the cornetist thought—even on this cold earth with a rock in his back and the damp crawling through him like a worm.

"Well, it's all over," he said aloud to the soldier and the stars that wheeled above them. "I wonder why we done it anyhow?"

"Nevertheless," the soldier said. The stars burned coldly.

The cornetist ached in every fiber. His muscles were twitching, drawing up, and he knew that if he laid here much longer he would cramp. He'd seen men tied into knots from just this sort of thing. Still, it was good to lie quiet for a while, to tempt sleep and wander on the edge of dreams. He dozed and listened to the wounded man talking—from what he was saying, the boy thought he was back at the big dance in Murfreesboro, just before the Stones River fight. My, that seemed like a long time ago. It *was* a long time ago, ages and ages. They had a good band then, used to be called upon to serenade General Braxton Bragg himself. The cornetist remembered the soldiers' dance at Murfreesboro very well; it was a long time since he'd thought of it, and now here was this boy bringing it all back again. There was a young widow there, just a girl; she was dressed in mourning from combs to slippers for her husband who was killed off in the east somewhere. They must have been infants when they were married—and to go so far so quickly. But widow or not, she'd danced with all the boys and scandalized the old folks. The cornetist grinned at the memory. What was her name, anyhow? He wished he could remember it. He searched awhile among the moments of that vanished night, seeing the girl's face as clearly as if it were before him now, but her name was lost to him. Then suddenly he didn't want to think about it any more, for the face of that girl was not something he wanted to carry into sleep—

No, musn't sleep. He made himself rise on one elbow, looked at the wounded man who lay beside him. The boy was having trouble breathing, his hands fluttered nervously. "Well, brother, you are forevermore a mess," said the cornetist. "I hope to hell you are satisfied."

"Alas, poor Hiram," said the soldier.

"I know, I know," said the cornetist, and patted the boy's arm. He sighed, and lay down again and closed his eyes. What *was* that girl's name—

They lay in a low place where the morning mist had begun to form. The tendrils of mist and the smoke from the fires moved over them. The wounded man put out his hands as if he were dancing. The cornetist snored and dreamed of winter gardens where dark figures wept among the trees.

Meanwhile, through the black fields beyond, a man was approaching. When the soldier spoke again, the man in the field stopped, listening.

"Remy, you musn't go," said the wounded soldier. "It is rainin—don't you see it's rainin?"

The visitor moved across a distant fire, like a refugee from the cornetist's dream. He began to circle, closer and closer through the mist and smoke and the bitter hint of dawn. He came shyly, bending and bowing, whispering to himself. When the soldier spoke, the visitor stopped to listen. Then he came on again.

"I never seen such rain," said the soldier. "See how high the river is?"

The visitor lurched out of the dark, into the low place where the soldier and the cornetist lay. He was shivering under his ragged quilt; he was barefoot, and blood seeped through the wet mud on his feet. He bent over the litter and peered into the soldier's face. "Shhh," he whispered, putting a finger to his lips. "We got to be real quiet."

"Rain, rain, rain."

"Rain, rain, rain," echoed the visitor. With a tentative finger, he touched the wounded soldier on the nose—they boy groaned, the visitor backed away, waving his hands. "I didn't do nothin, I didn't do nothin," he said. He watched, and after a moment approached again, cautiously. He knelt beside the litter, and whispered into the soldier's face. "Say, you could help me. I am a-huntin my ramrod. You seen it?"

The soldier frowned, his good eye open, moving in the starlight. "What? What?"

"Bushrod," said the visitor. "I knowed that was you."

The soldier tried to rise, fell back on the litter. "Nebo?" he said. "That ain't Nebo—he's dead."

The other bobbed his head up and down like a bird. "Oh, yes. Yes, indeedy. *Been* dead—only don't tell em."

"They all dead," said the soldier. "All the boys are dead."

"Yes, yes," said the visitor. His thin fingers began to move down the soldier's body, plucking at the cloth. "You ain't seen it, have you? Won't tell em I lost it?"

"All dead," said the soldier.

"All dead, yes, indeedy."

Somewhere in Franklin a clock struck three. The visitor cocked his head and listened, then bent again to his work. His fingers reached the soldier's shoes, he bobbed with sudden excitement and began to untie the laces. In a moment, he had both shoes and socks off the soldier's feet. "These'll be good," he said.

The cornetist spoke in his sleep, a woman's name. The visitor looked up. "No, you don't," he said. "I ain't done nothin." Then, quick as a rat, he scuttled off into the darkness again, the soldier's shoes clutched tightly to his breast.

"I guess you have to go," said the soldier.

The cornetist sat bolt upright. "What?" he said, and looked groggily about, trying to climb out of sleep, not knowing for the instant where he was—the dark, the sound of movement. "Delmar?" he said.

"Nebo," said the soldier.

"Ah, shit." The cornetist came to himself, felt the dark world falling into place around him. He sat for a moment more, rocking back and forth, hurting in his joints like he had known he would but hurting inside too, as if the dark had gotten down in there and he would never get it out again—

He looked up: somebody coming, a lantern bobbing along. *Now what*, he thought, but it was the Archbishop, returning through the broomsage, all his canteens gone. "Over here!" he called.

The Archbishop was out of breath. "I am so sorry, didn't mean to be gone so long. I found—" He stopped, looked at the soldier on the litter. He raised the lantern. "I declare," said the Archbishop. "What become of his shoes?"

The cornetist stared, then shook his head. "In the name of Jesus," he said, "but this boy is a trial."

It took the two of them nearly an hour to find the great brick house. It loomed suddenly before them; men moved across the light of fires and lanterns, the windows themselves gleamed dully with lantern-light. When he saw the house, the cornetist's legs began to quiver.

"This is all the far I can go," he said.

"Yes," said the Archbishop. "Soon we can rest."

They carried the litter through the wounded and stragglers in the yard. No one paid them any mind. The broad porch was full of stiffening dead; they crossed it and entered the hall and stopped, blinking in the light.

"For God's sake, move out the way, can't you?" said a hospital orderly. He was carrying a bone-white leg that had been cut off at the knee.

"Here's a hurt man," said the Archbishop.

"Well, ain't *that* a novelty," said the orderly. He gestured with the leg toward an empty place at the foot of the staircase. "Jes put him down over there—we'll get to him 'bout Tuesday."

"But this boy—" began the Archbishop. He was cut off by a piercing scream from the parlor where the surgeons were working. When the Archbishop found his voice again, the orderly was gone. The cornetist was staring after him. "Where do you reckon he was goin with that leg?" he asked.

"With what?" asked the Archbishop.

"God only knows," said the cornetist, shaking his head.

The heat and the smell were making the Archbishop dizzy. Vague images passed across his mind: a room full of music, a house in bright sunlight, a horseman waiting in the road. "I know you," he said.

"What's that?" asked the cornetist.

"Nothing, nothing," said the Archbishop. The pictures faded, the hall of the great brick house took shape again. He looked down at the boy on the litter. "Just us three," he said.

"Don't I know it," said the cornetist. "Come along now—let's do as that fellow said. Somebody'll come and see to this boy pretty soon."

They propped the soldier against the wall so that his feet would not be in the way of the traffic in the hall. The boy was quiet now, his head fallen forward on his breast. A bright trickle of fresh blood flowed over his mustache, down his chin and into the high collar of his waistcoat. The cornetist arranged the boy's haversack and canteen beside him, then knelt and with his hand wiped away the blood, and with his bloody fingers touched again the emblem on the boy's jacket. "Few days and full of trouble," he said, and wiped the boy's nose again, and stood. He found the Archbishop staring down the hall toward the dark rectangle of the front door. "Say, you gone be all right?" he said.

"Oh, yes," said the other. "I just want to rest now."

"Well, come on," said the cornetist. "I reckon it is all over anyhow."

"Yes," said the Archbishop.

The cornetist took the old man's arm; they moved off together, out the front door and into the pitch-dark morning beyond.

❦

The parlor clock struck four. In the hall, a fresh taper burned in the candle lantern. Though the night was cold, the house—full of candles and lanterns and with a fire on every hearth—was sweltering. The heat rose up the flume of the staircase to the upper rooms where, behind the wall and window facings, a multitude of red wasps stirred in their winter sleep. The heat awakened them, and hundreds over the long night groped toward the unexpected warmth. They thrust their wedge-shaped faces into the light, then, one by one, tried the air with their delicate paper wings. The air bore them up; they circled lazily over the heads of men, they lit on hands and faces and in the gaum of wounds, they died underfoot. They were swatted, and they stung in return.

One of their number joined those that ventured out into the stairwell. He lit on the banister. Below, in the downstairs hall, the candle lantern flickered and danced. The wasp tilted his head at the melancholy flame; after a moment he went aloft and glided in perfect linear flight down the stairs. He found the lantern and, after the manner of his kind, began to tap his head against the glass. It made a hard sound: *Tink. Tink. Tink.* Again and again: *Tink. Tink. Tink.*

But of all the house, the hall was the coldest place. The heat passed up the stairs and drew the cold night in through the open doors. The wasp grew sleepy again; he lit on the wall and wandered in aimless circles, groggy and cold. In time his legs failed him, he lost his hold and fell, straight down, like a dropped match.

He landed in a pool of blood, and there he struggled for a while, waving his legs, making a blur of his wings. At last he pulled free and began to stumble across the hall, drawing a thin line of blood on the floor with the sharp pen of his body. He moved slowly, tacking left and right as he went, sensing but never seeing the enormous shapes that moved above him.

Finally he met an obstacle: a soldier lying against the wall at the bottom of the stairs. The wasp bumped against one of the soldier's bare feet, pushed against it, made to go around it, at last began to examine the foot with his front legs and the jointed wands of his antenna. The skin was cold, white, taut, and shriveled, but it offered good purchase. The wasp began to climb. He went slowly, taking his time, until he reached the pinnacle of the big toe; there he stopped and preened himself of the clinging blood, stretching his legs, stretching his wings. When he was done, he arched his body and trembled. There on the splintered nail of the man's big toe, the wasp sensed he was at a high place and made ready to fly again. He gathered his legs, whirred his wings—and nothing happened. He turned once on the axis of his body and tried again. Nothing. He could not fly. So he picked his way down the slope of the man's instep, through the thin hairs that grew there, and began to climb again.

The soldier's clothing was entirely of wool so that, wherever the wasp traveled, he had to struggle against the nap. Again and again he stopped to free the barbs of his legs from the wool. Climb, stop, pull. Climb, stop, pull. In this way, he moved up the man's trouser leg.

While the wasp climbed, the man began to grow restless. He jerked and trembled, began to whimper. He was drenched in blood, though most of it was not his own—it belonged to the men under whom he'd been buried for hours during the battle. It had come from their mouths, their ears, their multiple gunshot wounds; it was freighted with fecal matter, urine, microscopic bits of cloth and leather and flesh, stomach bile—not to mention personalities, histories, dreams, memories. The man was soaked in his comrades' lives down to the very bolsters of his pocketknife, and while this excited the grayback lice huddling in the seams of the man's clothing, it distressed the wasp. Such a smell it was, mingled with the smells of powder and sweat and wood-smoke, that the wasp pushed his body up and walked on the stilts of his legs.

At the thigh, he met a new obstacle. The man's left hand lay there, fingers trembling; one of the fingers had been shot away at the second joint, and upon it sat a fat, sleepy housefly. The wasp backed away, tried to lift himself off again, but it was no use. He whirred his wings. The housefly circled lazily aloft when the man curled his fingers. Then the hand dropped away, and the wasp moved on.

He clambered over hills and valleys of cloth. For a moment he disappeared under the man's waistcoat; it was warm in there, but the stink was so powerful that he backed out again. Then he was on the waistcoat itself. A gold chain, caked with blood, looped across the man's chest. The wasp followed the chain; in a little while it disappeared into a buttonhole and the wasp moved on. Climb, stop, pull. Climb, stop, pull. From time to time he rested and preened himself.

He was perched atop a button, resting, when there came a sudden heave and tremor under his feet. He braced himself. The man sneezed, and the wasp was nearly dislodged from the button by a fine red mist of blood.

Much cleaning this time: head, antennae, body, legs. It was some time before he moved again, up on the shoulder now, then the high collar of the man's waistcoat, then the cheek itself.

The beard stubble was rough, but there was no more catching of legs. The wasp avoided the open mouth where the man breathed and made noises. He examined the mustache; it was damp with blood, he tried to find a way around it and at last clambered over it and mounted the smashed bridge of the nose.

The man's nose had been broken by the steel buttplate of a Springfield rifle, in a wild melee at the top of the Federal breastworks. It had been only a glancing blow, else there would have been no need to carry this soldier to the hall of the great brick house. A second blow, delivered as the assailant himself was going down, had blackened one eye and nearly broken the cheekbone and sent all the soldier's intellect spinning toward the stars. But to the wasp, the flattened bridge of the nose represented only the last possible opportunity for flight. He could go no higher.

The wasp poised himself exactly between the man's eyes, and for a moment he rested. The man's good eye was partly open, but only the white showed. The eyelid fluttered, but the wasp ignored it. Then he was ready. He turned and aligned himself with the glow of the lantern across the hall. He raised the front of his body and pressed his abdomen against the man's nose. He flexed his wings, then whirred them. One by one his legs lifted off. He was flying. He flew in perfect linear flight to the lantern again and began to knock his head against the glass. *Tink. Tink. Tink.* After a while he fell, straight down, like a dropped match.

CHAPTER SIX

66 It's cousin Anna," whispered the boy, standing tip-toe beside the bed in his linsey-woolsey trousers.

The room was airless and hot and lit by a single candle burning on the dressing table. The grate was heaped with glowing ashes from which a little tongue of flame licked upward now and then toward the dark maw of the chimney. In the corner, a girl sat upon a rumpled pallet, rubbing her fists in her eyes.

"Yes, it is," said the girl. "Mama brought her up here a while ago and don't you go wakin her up either."

"Who said I was gone wake her up?"

"Well, you will if you don't hush," said the girl in a fierce whisper. "Now you get on back here and lay down."

But the boy went on looking at Anna's face. "She looks mad to me," he said. "Can you be mad and sleepin at the same time?"

"You about to find out," said the girl.

"Oh, hush your own self, Hattie. I was only askin."

Anna lay on the counterpane, still in her stained blue cotton dress; her cousin Caroline had covered her with a shawl, but in her restless sleep she had thrown it off. Her legs and her feet were bare.

"She don't have any stockins on," mused the boy.

"Winder McGavock, that ain't any of your business," said the girl. "And anyway Mama took em off. Now you—"

On the mantel, an ancient clock gathered itself for the hour. It did not always chime, but when it did no one could predict how long it would go. The hands said four o'clock.

"Oh, no!" said the girl when she heard the clock. "Of all the times—"

"I believe that's the first I ever saw cousin Anna's feet," said the boy.

The clock began to whir deep in its machinery.

"Hush! Hush, old clock!" said the girl, waving her hands. But the clock began to chime. It chimed and chimed. Then there was another sound, it came from outside on the landing where the soldiers were. Hattie and Winder turned toward the door and listened and the sound came again under the clock's chiming: a sound like a hurt thing crying, and a dry sound like something moving across the floor. Then the clock went quiet and the children listened in the strange, suspended after-chime, and something bumped against the door.

"Sister?" said the boy.

Hattie rose from the pallet and went to the boy and put her arms around him. She was nine years old, her brother seven but nearly as tall. "It is only the poor soldiers," she said, but whispering now.

"They won't hurt us," said the boy.

They listened. Soon they heard a man's voice; they could not make out the words, but it was a real voice and it was steady and somehow that was better. Then it was quiet again.

Hattie looked at their cousin's face. "Well, she is still sleepin anyhow," she said.

"She would not mind if we got in the bed," said the boy.

The bed was tall and the children had to struggle to climb in. The ropes groaned and creaked under the mattress.

"Be *careful*," whispered Hattie.

"You just mind your own self," said the boy.

The girl crawled gingerly across her cousin's body. Anna sighed and fisted her hands under her chin.

"She is frownin, all right," said Hattie.

Winder did not answer. He lay down and burrowed his face into the hollow of Anna's shoulder. Hattie did the same on the other side, pulling the shawl over them all. The mantel clock ticked away; it was the loudest sound now.

"This room is full of wasps," Hattie murmured.

"My, don't she have such little feet?" Winder said.

In a moment, they were asleep.

All the boys are dead, said Bushrod into the dark.

Tink. Tink. Tink. came the reply, and the little sound reached him in the deep place where he had gone. He looked up—far above his head was a circle of light.

Tink. Tink. Tink.

He was rising then, floating upward toward the light. Pretty soon he could make out shapes around him and it was like the picket line at first break of the day when the stump you've been watching for hours turns out to be only a stump after all. He was floating, and it was the easiest thing in the world.

He passed young Jeff Hicks. The boy was trying to sew up a tear in the sleeve of his jacket and Bushrod said *I'll do that for you* but the boy never looked up. He went on pulling the needle through the cloth, his mouth twisted in concentration.

Bushrod heard a girl's voice. *Remy?* he said, but there was no one. He smelled dry grass and sycamores, like in the fall of the year.

Virgil C. Johnson was standing with his hands in his pockets, chewing on a straw. *Hey, Bushrod, where you goin?* he asked.

Hey, Virgil C. said Bushrod. *Well, I am goin—* But he didn't know where he was going. *You come on and go with me* he said.

Aw, I can't said Virgil C.

How come? asked Bushrod, but it was already too late. He was much higher now. He watched his friend's upturned face until he couldn't see it anymore.

He passed the three drummers. They were sitting on their drum-shells, eating peaches from tins with the tops curled back. *Hey, boys* said Bushrod and the three men looked at him and tapped their forks on the tins *Tink. Tink. Tink.* and passed away beneath.

The circle of light grew nearer. It had been greenish at first, but now it was yellowish-white like a lantern in the woods. Now and then something, a shadow, moved across the light.

Eugene Pitcock and First Sergeant William ap William Williams were brewing coffee in the lee of a stone wall. Their accoutrements hung nearby in the limbs of a sweetgum tree. The First Sergeant offered Bushrod a steaming cup of coffee; Bushrod put out his hand to take it but it was already out of reach. *It's all right, Bill* said Bushrod, *I'll get some directly—*

The light was much brighter now, and something was happening. Bushrod felt it in his face, a fire spreading outward toward his cheekbones. His hand was on fire, too. He held it up—something was wrong with it, he couldn't tell what. Then he began to feel sick at his stomach. *It is all this damned floating*, he thought.

He passed through a place where everything was in confusion. Men were yelling and firing and the smoke was so thick he could hardly see. Then in a clear space he saw a man in a dark-blue frock coat with corporal's chevrons and the man was yelling at him.

So—you are the one Bushrod said.

The man was yelling, but there were no words. He had his musket in the "blow to the front" position.

I am really not a bad fellow—began Bushrod, but the man developed the stroke and Bushrod saw very clearly the single screw in the steel buttplate, and he was about to parry the blow when the man disappeared in a bright flash and Bushrod Carter burst out into the light and the pain—

In all the great brick house, only one room had been left intact; only one would have no bloodstains on the floor, nor any ghosts of ragged strangers to prowl the twilights of unborn years. Yet not even that room—the McGavock's bedroom on the second floor—would altogether escape the hours. There would be other ghosts there: ghosts of dreams and restless sleep, of the little candle that burned on the dressing table, of the fire and the dark, looming bed—ghosts, too, of disembodied cries, unseen footsteps, noises on the landing and on the gallery outside. All these things would engrave themselves forever on the memory of that room, to wake again from time to time when the house stirred in its sleep.

In that room, in the dark hours before daylight, Anna and Hattie and Winder slept a little while. Elsewhere the noise and the suffering went on, but for that little while Anna and the children heard none of it. They listened only to their dreams.

Anna frowned. In her dream, birds rose croaking from a dark and pathless wood. They swirled against the yellow sky and settled one by one in the branches over her head. She waved her arms and shouted, but they would not go away. Their droppings pattered in the mould and they squawked at her: *Haw. Haw-haw.* Presently a young officer, a Rebel by his short gray jacket, came riding through the wood. Anna did not know about the Rebels, only that they were coming. She turned, but there was no place to go. The officer walked his horse around so that she had to look at him. *What is your name?* he asked. *Nancy* she said. *No, it ain't* he said and he spoke her name Anna and the birds swirled upward in a cloud and he rode away with her name like he would a locket or a scarf—only he wasn't supposed to have it. Then children she didn't know were gathered around her and she was old, in a rusty black dress, and she was telling them the story of this day, and she told them *I did not want to be in his heart, I did not belong there.* Then one of the children asked *But who do you belong to then?* and there was a soldier she did not know, sitting in the sunlight, drinking coffee from a tin cup. *Nobody* she said, and the soldier grinned. *Nobody* she said again. *Not ever. Not ever*—and the birds swept over her and fanned their wings in her face and shrieked in her ear—sleep exploded in black fragments around her and she sat straight up in the bed.

Hattie, too, bolted upright when Winder screamed. "Mama!" she cried, and scrambled to her knees, her eyes round as dollars.

Winder was crying, his face jammed into the pillow.

For a moment, Anna was completely lost. She saw Hattie's face. "What are you doin here?" she asked. "You are supposed to be upstairs."

"We *are* upstairs," said the girl.

Anna looked around, blinking the dream away.

"We was all asleep," said Hattie, rubbing her eyes. "Now Winder has woke us up."

Upstairs. The familiar room took shape in the candlelight and Anna remembered. Caroline had brought her here, put her to bed like a child, took off her stockings—

"Cousin Anna?"

"It's all right," Anna said. She touched the girl's face. "I was dreamin, is all."

"Winder had a dream," said Hattie.

Anna turned to the boy. His face was still pressed into the pillow but he was not crying now. His hair was soaking wet. Anna lay her hand at the nape of the boy's neck. He moved closer to her. She petted him for a moment, and when he seemed quiet she lay back again. Her pillow was filled with pine needles and smelled like Christmas, and she thought how sweet it was to be there in the bed, in the quiet, with the pine smell and the children around her, and she wanted to sleep for a thousand years—

But the boy was crying again. Anna propped herself on an elbow, touched the back of his neck again, petted him. "Winder," she said, "what was your dream about?"

The boy shook his head.

"I have a notion," Anna said. "Would you care to hear it?"

"What is it?" said Hattie, but the boy was silent.

"Well, my notion is this," said Anna. "Dreams are the broad sea, and the bed is a ship, and Winder McGavock is the captain."

"I *ain't*," Winder said, his voice muffled in the pillow.

"Oh, yes you are," said Anna. She stroked the boy's hair. "I know all about these things. The captain steers the ship, did you know that?"

The boy raised his head and watched her out of his dark eyes. Anna dried his face with the back of her hand. "Now, what are dreams, Winder?"

The boy thought a moment. "Um, what you have when you are sleepin?"

"Fooey," said Anna, and poked him. "Dreams are the sea we are sailin on, dark and troublesome. But the ship is safe—a gallant ship and a brave captain. We are not afraid of the sea, so long as we have the ship under us—are we, Hattie?"

"No, indeed, not us," said the girl.

"But I am the captain," said the boy.

"Yes, you are. Now look yonder." Anna pointed to the candle guttering on the dressing table. "That's a lighthouse, see?" The boy turned his head to look.

"That's a lighthouse, Winder," said Hattie.

"That's right," said Anna. "Now look up there." She pointed toward the ceiling where a squadron of wasps were stumbling and buzzing about. "What do you think those are?"

The boy looked sleepily upward. "Wasts," he said.

"Don't say '*wasts*'!" said Hattie.

"Well anyhow," said Anna, "they are not wasps right now. They are seagulls and pelicans. You know what that means?"

"If they come down here they will sting the fire out of us," said the boy.

"Well, *play* like they're gulls and pelicans, blame it," said Anna. "What do you think it means?"

The boy looked at her, his face gathering itself to cry again. "Oh, my," said Anna. "All right. All right." She drew the boy to her, rocking him, petting him. "It means we are nearly to the shore," she whispered. Hattie nestled against her back; she put out her hand and touched the girl's leg.

"I want to be captain next," said Hattie.

In a little while, when the children were asleep again, Anna gently untangled herself from their arms and legs and sat up on the edge of the bed. Watching her cousins, she wondered if she had launched them on dark and troublesome waters again. But, no—it was better they sleep, dreams or not.

She glanced at the mantel clock and sighed. Four-thirty. She had been asleep a little over two hours, and it was still two hours to sunrise.

God in heaven, she thought—*will we never get to the end of this night?* There was supposed to be an *end* to night, it ought not to just go on and on.

At least the hurting in her head was gone. In its place was a soreness that was almost a pleasure by comparison, like the healing socket of a tooth. But now that the children were asleep and she had no one to talk to, her mind began to gray with confusion and slide back toward the dark sea. She ran her fingers through her hair—like Winder's, it was soaked with sweat. *Why is it so hot in here?* she wondered dully. She looked at her hands: they were grimy with soot and dried blood rimmed the fingernails and the lines of her knuckles. What would the young men think of her hands now? And her feet: what were they doing bare? And why couldn't she breathe? It was not enough that time had stopped; now the very air itself had thickened like a stagnant pool.

Then she saw the fire, or rather the sullen mountain of coals where the fire had been. It glowed and sputtered, and Anna understood that the reason she couldn't breathe the air was that there wasn't any—the fire had eaten it all. She knew a sweet girl once who had died when the stove had eaten all the air in her room and she went to sleep and woke up in the arms of God—Anna nodded and thought *I will open those shutters by and by* but she was looking at the floor and her eyes began to trace the pattern in the rug. It meandered here and there—*vines*, she thought, but she was too tired to study much about it. Her eyes grew heavy and a little pendulum in her mind began to swing in time to the clock's slow ticking, and it all seemed to match the rug's pattern in an interesting way—

She saw a horseman in a green wood and she was moving toward him and her heart was beating very fast, so fast she could hardly breathe. *I knew you would come* he said, and swung his booted leg over the bare back of the horse and dropped to the ground. He stood with his legs a little apart and watched her, smiling, his hand out, and when she drew near he began to back away. She followed, wanting him to stop *Wait* she said. Deeper and deeper into the wood he led her, through the slanting sunlight, and he laughed and teased when she stumbled or when the branches lashed her *Please wait* she said, over and over again. Then he turned and ran away, and Anna stopped. She was angry and felt foolish and was about to turn back toward the house when she heard him call her name and everything flew out of her but the sound of his voice *I'm comin* she said, and ran, and found him at last in an open sunlit glade carpeted with spring clover. His riding coat was spread out on the ground. *Anna* he laughed. *Anna.* He held out his hands.

She walked out into the glade; she came slowly, her heart beating fast, she smelled the sweet clover and the hot, rank grass. Crows were talking to one another in trees somewhere. *Haw* they said. *Haw-haw.*

She came to him. She could see the little beads of sweat on his upper lip and the damp curls of his hair. *Anna* he said. He touched her cheek and traced down it with the tips of his fingers. *Don't do that, don't* she said. *Now, Anna* he said.

The crows were talking in the trees; she heard the dinner bell ringing at home—it seemed miles and miles away though it was just across the wood—and smelled the smoke from the cookhouse. *I better not* she said, but the boy took her hard by the shoulders, pulled her to him. He bent his face to kiss her but she turned her face away *Don't do that* she said and the boy said *What are you afraid of?* and turned her face and kissed her hard on the mouth. *What are you afraid of, Anna?* and brought the flat of his hand down to her breast and the breath nearly left her—no boy had ever touched her there. She tried to pull away but he held her, began to whisper in her ear words she had never heard before, never imagined, but she knew what they meant and the blood rose in her and not all of it shame. She felt his mouth on the curve of her neck *What are you afraid of?* and his hand was on her face and he was talking about her eyes, her mouth. She tried to tell him *No—it is not supposed to be like this* and tried to tell him *But I love you* but his hand clamped hard on her mouth and with a single powerful movement pushed her down onto his coat in the sweet-smelling clover and he was saying her name over and over—the crows, every single leaf in the trees overhead and the sound of the dinner bell a long way off, and somewhere there was pain and a momentary gasp of pleasure to which she almost surrendered, then the hot jetting seed that consumed, in a single wasteful flame, every dream she would have forever—

"Stop it!" Anna cried, and for the second time that night sleep burst in fragments like black glass around her and she was standing in the middle of the room, her legs pressed so tight together that the muscles were cramping—

Oh damn, she thought, and felt her way blindly back to the bed and pulled herself up and sat with her bare feet dangling, her hands pressed hard against her temples. *Oh damn, damn, damn*, she thought. *You are dead. Leave me alone. You are dead*—and she told herself over and over again that he was dead, she knew it, been dead nearly two years on a cavalry raid in Mississippi—she heard it told about one morning by the old men around the stove in her papa's office: what a shame it was, they said—such a good boy, full of promise, lost in the war. One of the old men looked at her and saw her face and said, Why, Miss Anna, didn't you know? and she ran so they couldn't see her face.

But they didn't know everything, those old men tapping their canes on the puncheon floor telling how bravely he died. They didn't know what he'd taken with him, nor about the part of him that hadn't died. Or maybe they *did* know; maybe there were terrible secrets you didn't learn until you were old, maybe there were things you believed all your life until one day you were suddenly old and discovered they were all a lie—like people being gone when they are dead, and the notion that the winter always turns to spring, the night to day—

Then she was choking for air. All at once there was nothing left to breathe and she remembered the girl who had awakened in the arms of God and she thought *all right—I won't breathe then.* All she had to do was lie down and go to sleep, and when she awoke—what? Who would be waiting for *her*?

Then Hattie moved in her sleep and whimpered, and Anna remembered and cursed herself for a fool.

She got down from the bed and felt the floor hot against her feet. She staggered, nearly fell, caught herself, stumbled across the room to the window. She had to struggle with the catch but at last it was free and she raised the window and flung the shutters open with a bang—the air pouring across the gallery was cold and smoky and foul with the taste of lateness, but she breathed deep of it, filled her lungs with it. "You are dead, damn you!" she shouted at the darkness.

"Beg pardon?" said a voice outside.

Anna jumped. She realized all at once that the upper gallery was full of men; they were smoking and leaning their elbows on the balustrade, and now they were all looking at her. She blushed. "Oh, nothin," she said. "Nothin atall, never mind—I, um, I just have to open these windows, there are children sleepin here—"

"Why, that's all right, Missy," said the voice. "We won't be no bother. Jes close the shutters to and you won't even know we're here."

"Thank you," she said, and brought the shutters closed. For a moment she stood with her forehead pressed against them. She could hear the mens' voices now, talking quietly where they stood along the gallery—strangers, waiting for a dawn that wouldn't come. She imagined the dark grove and the fields beyond, and the fires that burned there, and other strangers moving in the night. *These men*, she thought. *They are all in hell, and I am in hell, and cousin Caroline, and Hattie and Winder—*

The thought of the children shocked her. She had almost failed them, and she turned quickly expecting them to be dead anyway, or vanished, or lost somehow. But they were sleeping. Anna found the shawl and pulled it over them. A flame licked brightly in the fireplace, feeding on the new air, and by its sudden light Anna caught a glimpse of herself in the mirror. She stared at the drawn and haggard face as if it were a stranger's, or the face of one she had not seen for a long, long time. Then she shook it off and took up the candle and searched until she found her slippers. She slipped them on, it felt strange to wear them without stockings. A wasp dropped from the ceiling and lit on her arm. She smacked it away, and it began to wander in helpless circles on the floor. She stomped on it with her slippered foot. She stomped it again and again. "*Now* you are dead, you son of a bitch!" she said. Then, knowing it was a lie, she leaned against the dresser and cried.

The clock did not strike at five. It called attention to itself with some vigorous noises, but it did not strike. Anna looked at it without interest. She had cried until the deep well of crying had gone dry, and there was a hollowness in her. She looked at the body of the wasp where it lay on the floor—already it seemed to be disappearing, shriveling away into dust. She was sorry for it now, but she could not bring it back.

She knew she had to go. Her cousin Caroline must still be down there among all that suffering and waste, and Anna, even if she wasn't much use, ought to be with her. She bent once more over the children, careful lest she break the delicate bubble of peace in which they lay. She wanted to touch them, but dare not. "Oh, sleep," she whispered, and closed her eyes and almost prayed, but she caught herself just in time, remembering. There was no use in her praying for anything at all.

She blew out the candle and eased across the patterned rug to the door. When she looked back she could hardly see the bed, the great ship, and the children were only huddled shapes in the dark. But they were all right. They would be all right tomorrow too, if it ever came. Anna thought about the men outside on the gallery. She was glad they were there; finding them smoking and talking quietly had been comforting, it was what men did in the evenings when the work was done. Of course, the work was not done, and she doubted that it ever would be. It would go on and on, even after the house was emptied of strangers, long after the wildflowers had blossomed a hundred times on their graves.

She spoke one last time into the quiet room. "I know You are here," she said. "Are You ready to listen yet?" But there was no answer, and after a moment she passed through the door and closed it softly behind her.

CHAPTER SEVEN

The dawn that Anna feared might never come would appear on
schedule, just as it always had—and after it another and another. And
yesterday would become Last Month, then Last Winter, then Last Year,
then Two and Five and Ten Years Ago, and one day the people would have
to stop and think before they could say how long ago it was that the great
Battle of Franklin was fought. By then the rain would have softened the
rifle pits and breastworks and even the big Federal fort across the river into
smooth, grassy mounds. The vines and creepers would do their work, and
the cedars and oaks, the walnuts and hickories, so that places where men
once fought in the open would vanish in the young woods and underbrush. Older trees, splintered by musketry, would fall to the axe or silently
decay under the rain; these last would glow with foxfire some nights, like
the ghosts of trees. Pistols and rifles and bayonets would sink deeper into
the earth where they would grow into shapeless tubers of rust; buried
shells and round shot would sleep, waiting for the plow to bring them to
light again; discarded jackets would rot away and leave behind clusters of
tarnished buttons, and perhaps a pocketknife, and here and there a watch
frozen at the moment when its wheels and balance had ceased forever.
Boys, after spring rains, would gather minie balls to use for fishing weights,
or to sell to the curious.

Men who found themselves still alive at that first dawning would pass
away from Franklin sooner or later. The wounded, most of them, would be
taken by the advancing Federals in a month or so and sent north to prison,
where many of them would die. The quick would cross the river in time,
and fight at Nashville, and many of these would die. Most, in time, would
find themselves diffused into life again; they would pass into the sunlight of
distant courthouse squares and country crossroads, where they would
spend their days looking backward. The dead, who on that first morning
seemed to possess the earth, would themselves be possessed by the earth,
first in shallow graves and trenches and at last (many of them) under the
grass and clover of the burying ground by the great brick house, where the
McGavocks made a place for them. There would even be stones in time,
and on some of these would be names and the numbers of regiments, and

the names would fade in living memory as the ink faded in the little book where Caroline McGavock recorded them. Other stones would mark the places of men whose names had vanished with their lives, and for these there was a common epitaph: Unknown Confederate Soldier.

Now and then, for a number of years, an occasional squirrel hunter or party of picnickers, or some wandering soul in search of solitude, would discover in the thickets a pitiful collection of bones and rags and buttons and rusted rifle that once was a man. At such times, the people would gather and look quietly down at the thing, while the skull—if the varmints had not carried it off—would stare back at them in mute contemplation. Then, after a while, someone would gather the bones and cloth and buttons and hide them away under the earth, under a new stone with the old epitaph: Unknown Confederate Soldier.

There would come a day when old men would walk among the gray stones and tap them with sticks and say *I knew this one* or *He was of my brigade* or *Were these not Cleburne's men?* These old ones would muse among the graves for a while, then sit in the shade of the trees and smoke (there would be a flask, too, most likely) and try to remember what it was like when they were young and the ground was passing quickly under their feet, and the broomsage rustled, and the flags broke out above them in the smoky afternoon. But too much time intervened, too many seasons, and what they remembered would be as they remembered youth and love: fragmented, lit dimly by the flame of recollected passion but unreachable, and too much lost behind doors that would remain closed forever. Perhaps in their quiet talk they would speak of what it all had meant to them once, and evoke the old proud fictions of Duty and Country and God, knowing all the time that the truth, if there ever had been truth, no longer dwelt among them. Even the old wrathful names of their battles seemed not to ring as they once had—worn out, perhaps, from too much talk. In time the old men would cease talking and merely sit together in the shade, each one thankful for the silence. And they would look out over the stones and the grass and the tranquil bloodless fields and find, each in his turn, the only truth that was left them: that the stones possessed a logic of their own, that it all seemed to make sense once but didn't now, and whatever meaning there once was could no longer be got at by old men drowsing in the sunlight with full bellies and no one to shoot at them. With this, all distinctions blurred—between enemies, between the living and the dead— until the old men arose and knocked out their pipes and walked away, wanting to forgive everyone, starting with themselves.

The women, too, would come and stroll among the graves under the solemn domes of their umbrellas. They, too, had their talk—but of children lost or grown into happiness and success; of remembered weddings and funerals, mutual kin, of what went on last summer at Beersheba or Abita Springs or Pass Christian. Of anything, in short, but what lay at their feet. Meanwhile, among the chatter and gossip and decorum, the women kept a wary eye on their old men yonder lest they should somehow slip away again. For the women had a truth of their own: they had been robbed once, and would be robbed again if they were not careful. The old soldiers smoking in the shade, whose names and children and destinies they bore, had been taken from them once, had journeyed into hell, then returned into the midst of life—only something had not returned. Some part of them abided still, down among the smoke, and liked it there, had to be there, would not choose to return even if it could. This the women could not forgive. Much was taken, too little returned; distinctions blurred, and the hearts that might have lain like picked roses in the women's hands were buried forever under the stones with the dead.

So the women would not forgive. Their passion remained intact, carefully guarded and nurtured by the bitter knowledge of all they had lost, of all that had been stolen from them. For generations they vilified the Yankee race so the thief would have a face, a name, a mysterious country into which he had withdrawn and from which he might venture again. They banded together into a militant freemasonry of remembering, and from that citadel held out against any suggestion that what they had suffered and lost might have been in vain. They created the Lost Cause, and consecrated that proud fiction with the blood of real men. To the Lost Cause they dedicated their own blood, their own lives, and to it they offered books, monographs, songs, acres and acres of bad poetry. They fashioned out of grief and loss an imaginary world in which every Southern church had stabled Yankee horses, every nick in Mama's furniture was made by Yankee spurs, every torn painting was the victim of a Yankee sabre—a world in which paint did not stick to plaster walls because of the precious salt once hidden there; in which bloodstains could not be washed away and every other house had been a hospital.

But their greatest, their supreme and most poignant accomplishment, was the Confederate Soldier. Out of the smoke they plucked him, and set him atop a stone pedestal in the courthouse yard where he stood free at last of hunger and fear and raggedness and madness and violence; where he would never desert nor write home for a substitute, never run, never complain of short rations, never question the sacred Cause of which he was protector, and for which he had marched forth to willing sacrifice. But his musket was always at rest, and not for nothing was he always young, his eyes always soft as he looked backward over the long years. For he really was no soldier at all, but an image created by women, and he was born not of war but of sorrow and of fierce desire.

All these things the women created—and who could blame them? Certainly Anna Hereford never did, as she walked among the quiet stones, remembering.

Anna would never join the United Daughters of the Confederacy, declining their petitions year by year, politely and without excuse, until the petitions ceased. She would submit no elegiac poems to the newspaper, would leave no privately-printed memoir. When the Confederate monument was to be dedicated on the square at Fayetteville, Anna declined to attend, and this time she gave a reason: the face of the statue, she said, reminded her of someone she had once known. She would not say who.

But every year, on the anniversary of the great battle, Anna would return to Franklin. Sometimes the weather was bad and Anna, wrapped in a cloak, would watch the mist-shrouded hills pass almost imperceptibly into night. At such times she would shiver, and look out from under the dripping eaves of her umbrella until the darkness was complete. Then she would return to her cousins' house (or, later, to the boarding house in the village where a room was always waiting for her at the end of November), and there, by the fire on the hearth, she would light a lamp and after a little while take from her Gladstone bag a soiled, clothbound book and open it and trace with her finger the single pencilled line in the flyleaf, saying the words over in her mind until she could hear them just in the way she wanted. Then she would close the book and sit with it under her hand while the lamp burned quietly toward the dawn.

Most years, though, the weather was as it had been when the Army of Tennessee came down through the gap in the hills, and arrayed itself on the plain, and at last slanted its ragged banners toward the enemy in the smoke. On these days, Anna would walk the grounds of the great brick house, and walk in the oak grove (always finding the places she sought there, knowing them even under the vines and the new growth of cedar), and at last she would visit the cemetery. Sometimes a party of veterans would be there, and their ladies walking a little distance apart; with these Anna would pass the time of day, listening to their stories but never telling any of her own, until at last she would take her leave and go up to the family plot and (in time) sit down by her cousin Caroline's stone. There she would look down over the little slope where the soldiers lay, and she would try to understand what it all meant to her.

On such days, beyond the burying ground the woods and fields drowsed in the autumn sunlight as if nothing at all had happened here, as if there could really be no connection between the quiet earth and these men who lay beneath it. Perhaps there wasn't, she thought—at least, not anymore. And yet there *was* something, always: a shape, a movement, imperfectly seen then lost in the light and shadows. At such times, she thought of her old nurse Jeanne, whom her father had gotten from the Ursuline sisters in New Orleans some years before the war. Jeanne said the rosary three times a day in French, and she could see ghosts. She would point to an empty sunlit pasture and say, "You see her, cherie? That young woman there, hurrying along—look quick!" And little Anna would look, and it would seem to her that there *was* something there, like the empty space people leave behind for an instant when they have turned a corner or passed through a door. So it was in the sunny autumn afternoons, when Anna sat by her cousin's grave and looked out over the field of Franklin.

Once little Anna came upon her nurse sitting in the yard, looking south toward where the Elk River lay. Jeanne was still a young woman then, and handsome. Anna sat beside her, and for a while made chains and bracelets out of clover blossoms, then looked at her nurse and said, "Jeanne, *s'il vous plait*, what are ghosts anyhow?"

"Hah," said the other, still looking toward the south.

After a long silence, Anna put out her hand and touched the woman's cheek. It was wet. "Jeanne?" she said.

"I'll tell you what they is," said the woman. "They is rememberin, that's all. Ever now and then the earth turn over in his sleep and remember things, same as we do. Now go 'long with you, and see have Mister James come back from town."

The earth remembers things.

125

On the afternoon of the Battle of Franklin, when the Rebels were going in all along the Federal line, Anna went upstairs to fetch a favorite doll of Hattie's. She found it and was about to go back down, when curiosity drew her to the back gallery. Here, she supposed, was the only battle she would ever be in, and she ought to get a look at it while she could.

One look was enough. In fact, she could see very little: a dense cloud of white smoke boiling skyward was the most dramatic thing in view. But the sound! The sound rose from the battle like a living thing—more palpable, more real than the smoke itself. She had imagined gunshots, vollies, cheers, the heavy report of cannon—but this was a sustained bedlam, not a collection of sounds but a single unimaginable detonation that hung in the air and multiplied upon itself until it seemed the very earth would explode. For the first time she understood why men she had known—Yankee cavalrymen in Fayetteville, paroled Confederates, returned wounded, even men like her papa from the Mexico war, all who had seen this creature—could never seem to describe it. She would never be able to herself; if the words were there, she would never find them, nor ever meet anyone who had.

Then as Anna listened another sound began to rise within the first. It began as a low keening, like the wind in a bottle tree, almost indiscernible amid the guns. Yet it was there, and it grew and grew, gaining strength and timbre until suddenly a new note broke away and was taken up: a high weird quavering like nothing that Anna had ever heard, that peopled the smoke with an army of mourning phantoms. Anna had heard the men talk of this, too—the uncanny demon cry of the Rebel army going into the attack—and now here it was for real, echoing across violence and death for the last time in a wild crescendo that seemed to peak and yet peak again: descanting blood, crying lost youth and the loss of all dreams. One last time it shrilled out of the rolling smoke, then collapsed all at once into a maelstrom of voices—the deep snarling utterance of thousands of men in hell.

Anna fled from the gallery and ran blindly through her cousins' room and across the hall, squeezing the doll as if it were a living child. She gained the stairs and was already in the first turn when she met the General coming up.

He appeared out of nowhere. He was the biggest man Anna had ever seen, and he was taking the stairs two at a time and shaking the whole staircase. He was covered with dust from head to foot; the gold braid and stars on his coat were tarnished to the color of old brass. He creaked and clattered with sabre, canteen, an enormous pistol and a field-glasses case he was fumbling to get into while at the same time trying to hold on to his gauntlets. He was muttering curses through his beard; in his lean face, the black eyes glittered with evangelical fire. The General had the fever of battle in him, and he might have swept past Anna altogether had she not been standing frozen in the middle of the stairs. When he saw her, the General pulled up short and for an instant glared at the girl as if she were some unexpected enemy come suddenly upon him in the dusk.

"Damnation!" he said. "Who is this?"

His manner struck her like an open hand, and a blaze of indignation burst a bright star through her fear and she snapped, "Who! Who, indeed! I belong here, sir—I don't suppose you can say the same?"

"Well, by God—" began the General, but she cut him off.

"Who said you could come in here, using such language and tolling off up the stairs like you owned the place! And take your hat off in Miss Caroline's house—it looks silly anyway!" The General was wearing a broad felt hat with a black ostrich plume nodding from the turned-up side; Anna had never been able to abide a feather in a man's hat, and the sight of it riled her.

"What do you mean?" said the General, sweeping off his hat and looking at it as if for the first time.

"That feather there. It is ridiculous, sir."

The General considered the plume. "Hmmm," he said. "But look here—what is your name?"

"Don't talk to me like a child," said Anna, "and what is it to you anyway?"

The General looked at her. "I stand corrected," he said. "In my haste, I supposed you were a lady."

Anna opened her mouth to speak, but the General held up his hand. "I have acted badly. I passed your missus in the hall without so much as a word, and now I've insulted you. Fact is, I am a difficult man—but I am never rude on purpose. I don't suppose you can say the same?"

Anna looked away. "Oh," she said.

"Let us start over," said the General. "I am Forrest. Perhaps you've heard of me?"

Anna's eyes widened. "You are the *General* Forrest?"

"Just so."

Anna wore a silver Celtic cross on a silver chain about her neck; it had been her mother's, in Ireland, in the old time. She closed her hand on it now, and bit her lip, and said, "Well, I am sorry for bein rude, I would be sorry even if you weren't General Forrest. My name is Anna, and I must hinder you no longer." She stepped back against the wall to let the General pass.

But the General didn't move. He watched her with his black eyes. "I must take a look at the fight, I mean to view it from the gallery yonder— as you just did, I expect?"

"Yes," said Anna, and looked back toward the top of the stairs, her hand tight around the silver cross. "There was nothin to see. Nothin but the smoke."

"Sure, now," said the General, watching her. "Was that all you saw? Just smoke?"

Anna dropped the doll, pressed her back against the wall and felt there the reverberation of the guns and heard again the snarling, like a mad beast turning on itself. "Oh, no," she said, and her voice trembled. "No, that is not all I saw."

"Look at me, Miss Anna."

"General, I—"

"There is not much time. Do me the kindness."

Anna looked, and in the General's face saw the shadow of a weariness that she knew he would never lose, and a dark wisdom she had no desire to own.

"Directly I will be gone," said the General, "and it ain't likely we will meet again in this life—so I will tell you this now, it is all I know, and it will have to answer. What you saw yonder was the last of a great army. You will forget about bein afraid one day, but you will never forget that. Not ever."

Anna nodded, not knowing what to say.

The General picked up the doll. For a moment he peered into its cheerful painted face, then held it up to her. Anna took it and clutched it to her breast. "Thank you, sir," she said.

"Don't mention it," said the General. "And now, one last thing." He tucked his gauntlets under his arm and plucked the ostrich plume from the band of his hat and held it out to her in his grimy fingers. "A remembrance," he said.

"A remembrance," said Anna, and took it from his hand.

The General moved past her on the stairs then, and she felt the strength in him, and smelled the stink of his wool and of horses and woodsmoke and death, and she knew she would not forget. At the landing he stopped, and turned, and looked at her for the last time.

"And anyway," he said, "there ain't any shame in bein afraid. Not ever."

Then he was gone. Anna heard his boots on the landing; she did not see him again.

So Anna did not blame the women of her time for what they had created; it was different only in kind from what she had made herself. And if the old soldiers wanted only to forgive, Anna understood that, too, though in her own memory she could no longer find anything that needed forgiving. In the sunlight by her cousin's grave, she would touch the black ostrich plume in her hat—the plume that, like herself, grew a little older and a little more frayed every year—and think about what all of it meant to her. Down the hill slept the soldiers, and she would visit certain of them in a little while, and the thought of them—their faces, their voices, their particular ways—always made her smile. General Nathan Bedford Forrest himself told her once that she had seen the last of a great army, but he was wrong in that, for they still moved out there in the sunlight, all of them. He was right about one thing though: there was no shame in it, not ever.

CHAPTER EIGHT

W hen Anna closed the bedroom door behind her, it was a little after five on the first day of December, 1864. By the clock it was well into morning, but the sky was not yet graying and the upper hall was as gloomy as it had been all night. There was light from the several hearths, and a few candles in the rooms, and a little glow caught in the stairwell. The effect of these murky flames was worse than darkness.

Anna had no memory of passing this way before, when her cousin had brought her upstairs. Now, as her eyes adjusted to the gloom, she saw that the upper hall was carpeted with the bodies of men; they lay nestled like spoons, they sat with their heads in their hands, even the attic stairs were crowded with dark, huddled shapes as if a flock of enormous birds had come to roost there. Unlike the men on the gallery, these were not smoking and talking quietly; if they made any sound at all it was groaning, and their breathing raled in the stagnant air. Their hands moved restlessly, picking at their clothes, their faces, their wounds. Many were still and silent, and these were dead, Anna supposed. Somehow it seemed only natural that dead men should be lying all over her cousin McGavock's hall.

She wondered how all these had gotten up the stairs, and why they had even tried—there were no surgeons working up here. Anna knew that dogs and cats hunted a place to die when their time came, and she thought perhaps it was the same with men: some inner compass guided them with logic they did not understand themselves, until they reached the one and only place where the dream of life could make an end. Perhaps these men needed a high place, as far as possible from the earth and the worms and beetles that soon must claim them. Well, they had come a long way to die in this dark, smoky hall.

Besides the room where the children slept, there were three bedrooms on the upper floor. These, too, were crowded with men, with the wounded and the dead. There were men everywhere, and it was so hot and close, and the thick air smelled of blood and bodies long unwashed. Before that night, Anna never knew that blood had a smell at all; now she wondered if she would ever smell anything else. And the stink of men. She had smelled men before, but it was always work-sweat or horse-sweat in the hot summertime. This was different, a sour, fetid smell, sickly and vile. Anna took her handkerchief from her sleeve and pressed it to her mouth— the handkerchief was stale with sweat, but at least it was her own.

She knew she ought to open some windows and let in the cool air— but to do that she would have to go into those smoky, murmurous rooms. Alone. The only living thing, the only upright, moving thing. She could not do it. Already she felt eyes watching her through the dark rectangles of the doors, glistening faces turning toward her in the candlelight. The men in the hall, too, were beginning to notice her. *I will send somebody up directly,* she thought, and believed she had spoken it. She shuddered, and began to thread her way toward the stairs.

She had to step carefully among the bodies, at times wedging her feet between them, feeling the clammy flesh or the rough, rancid wool against her ankles. Hands began to pluck at her skirt, hands beckoned from the pile: Over here.....Over this way.....Over here. Voices began to beg for water. She had only gone a little way when she felt a hand close around her ankle; the fingers were cold and dry, the grip strong, and she was held fast. She was trapped in the middle of a carpet of men and, as she watched, it began to move, squirm, like the nest of cottonmouths she'd seen on the Elk River once. She was afraid to pull away, afraid to run, lest they drop on her from the ceiling and coil around her feet and pull her down, and the voices grew louder, more insistent: *Water.....water, please, Missy. Over here. Water, for God's sake.....*

Then, when she didn't answer, didn't move, the voices changed, some of them. *Who are you, anyhow!* cried one. *Why don't you do somethin,* cried another. *Why don't you? Why don't you?*

Leave her be, can't you?

Who said that? Who—

"Stop it!" said Anna.

Hey! Who are you anyhow?

"Stop it!"

What you mean, comin up here like a—

"Shut your mouths, all of you!" Anna shrieked, and in that instant she went blind in a red fog that came from nowhere, that chilled her deeper than any fear until she might have killed them all if she could, rid the house and the land and the earth of all these ragged peckerwood strangers who pulled at her and cried their foul breath at her. She kicked at the face of the man who held her, he loosed his grip and tried to pull away but the press was too close and she kicked him again. "Take your hands off me!" she cried. "Take em off!"

"They off, they off!" wailed the man.

The others were silent, not moving now. The man put his hands in front of his face—it was a plain country face, the kind no one ever remembered long, but Anna would remember. "Damn you," she said, her voice ragged, panting. "What you mean, grabbin hold of me like that?"

"Nothin!" began the man. "I only want—"

"What!" Anna snapped. "What! What! Speak up!"

"A surgeon—"

"You gone need a surgeon, you touch me again," said Anna, and the red fog was fading and she knew she had to get away, down the stairs where there would be somebody to help her, where she wouldn't be alone. She turned. "Get out my way," she said, with the last of her anger. The men parted before her, and in an instant she was gone.

There was a moment of quiet in the hall, then someone spoke out of the gloom. "Holy shit," the voice said. "Warn't she an angel, though?"

Nebo Gloster had been upstairs in the great brick house for more than an hour, waiting for the man by the hearth to die. Nebo was a little put out—he'd come all this way to find the perfect spot, only to discover that someone was there before him. Still, he could be patient. Pretty soon now that fellow would pass, and when he did, Nebo would be right there.

The man was staring at him, which made Nebo uneasy. He just stared and stared, never even blinking. Nebo smiled back and nodded his head as if to say *he* was perfectly satisfied crouching there in the corner—*he* wasn't interested in a spot by the fire. But the man never blinked or smiled or spoke, just lay there with his arm torn off, staring. He probably knew that Nebo really wanted that place.

There were lots of men in the room. They lay around the walls groaning and talking to themselves; the floor was covered with them too, lying every which way. The only light came from the fire, and that was why Nebo had to get close to it. He needed the light to examine his collection. He wished the man would just go ahead and pass if he was going to. Once he selected a ramrod and crawled over and poked the man just to see what he would do. Nothing. He wasn't going to give Nebo the time of day.

In the crook of his arm, Nebo cradled the thick bunch of ramrods he had picked up on the battlefield. A pair of shoes were slung around his neck by the laces. He had found a straw hat, too, and a long gray coat with two bars on the collar. He had traded his old quilt to a man for the coat— it was stiff and crusted with blood and had a big ragged hole in the back, but it was warm. Nebo crouched in the corner and watched the man by the fire—he noticed the man's rib cage was showing, too, just like a side of beef.

After a while, Nebo heard a door open and close. He saw a woman pass across the hall outside; she stopped for a moment and looked right at him, and he shifted uncomfortably and tried to draw back into the shadows. He pulled the straw hat down over his eyes. Then there was a big row out there, and men were shouting and the woman was shouting, and then it was quiet again and Nebo looked and the woman was gone.

The sight of the woman was unsettling; he had not expected to find one up here, and he wondered if it might be a sign. Maybe this wasn't the right place after all, maybe he would have to go back out in the dark again. He looked at the soldier by the fire, but the man was still staring same as ever. Nebo wondered how he could see out of those eyes. A wasp lit on the man's cheek, crawled into his open mouth, crawled out again.

This ain't the right place, Nebo thought—*but it almost is.* He straightened his bundle of ramrods and rose stiffly to his feet. The shoes were heavy around his neck. With a last look at the man by the fire, Nebo began to make his way through the soldiers lying around him. In the hall he stopped and looked carefully about. The woman was gone, sure enough.

Then he saw that of all the rooms upstairs only one had a closed door. The woman had come from there, and she had looked at him. Nebo nodded, he understood the sign now.

He pushed his way through the crowded hall to the door. A hand clutched at him, but he whacked it away with a ramrod. He tried the knob, and the door swung open.

Once inside, Nebo eased the door shut and looked around. It was deathly still, the room was full of furniture and there was a fire banked on the hearth and not a soul about. Nebo nodded again—clearly this was the place and not the other. He went to the fire and poked it until a little flame sprung up, and he was looking at the dancing light when he heard a rustle from the dark loom of the bed—

"Anna?" said a small voice.

Nebo jumped, clutched his bundle of ramrods, two of them slipped out and clattered to the floor. He froze, listening, but there was no more sound. After a moment he lay the ramrods carefully on the hearth. Then he moved toward the bed.

Anna stopped below the turn of the stairs, in the light of the hall and out of reach of the men above. The red fog was gone, and with it the anger that had caused her to despise the wretches on the landing, and she felt half-ashamed. But only half.

She had a cat once, a surly tom that took up residence in the barn, and upon this cat she lavished affection far beyond his deserving, and one afternoon she discovered him returning from personal combat, staggering, panting, his round head (the size and shape of a middling cantaloupe) intersticed with bloody gashes. Filled with pity and grief, Anna swept the old tom up in her arms. It was a mistake. For in the cat's heart still burned a deadly fuse and he turned against Anna's innocent hand with a violence so bitter and mindless that, when she screamed, it was not with the hurt but with the sudden knowledge that something so vicious could be at all.

Such a fuse burned in Anna's heart now.

She found herself panting, as the old cat had done. She tried to compose herself, but the notion only made her stomach knot. *Oh, yes*, she thought—*In the asylum, the lunatics pause to compose themselves.* Her hand tightened on the banister and she remembered that it was just here she had met General Forrest—weeks ago, it seemed—and she wished he were here now, and wondered what effect he would have up above, with his hard face and glittering black eyes. *If I could only be him, just for a minute*—

She thought of the young staff officer whom she had come down these stairs to see before the battle, to whom she had given her name for no reason she could understand. Where was he now, when she needed him?

They were too busy, all these men. Too busy killing themselves, like so many tom cats—

And here came another, limping up the stairs. *No*, she thought, and stepped in front of him.

He was bearded and shaggy, his clothes (he wore no piece of a uniform) little more than rags, and in the pale oval of his face his eyes were like blackened peas, and she could smell the strong stink of him.

"There is no more room up there," Anna said.

The man's little eyes grew even smaller. "So you say."

"Yes, so I say. Get out in the yard where you belong."

She saw the man's stained and broken teeth. He plucked at his clotted beard and cocked his head and his eyes moved over her. Then he passed his fingers over the place where his ear had been and held them up before her. "Look at that—you know what that is?"

Anna brushed his bloody hand away. "Don't you put that in my face," she said. "You're no soldier—get out, or I'll have the provost guard on you."

"Shit," said the man. "I don't give a goddamn for your provost guard."

"You will when they are stickin you like a hog," said Anna. "Now get away from me."

The man studied her for a moment, looked around, then grinned up at her. "Sure thing. I'll jes go right now, never meant a bit of harm." He started to turn, stopped, faced her again. He held up a bloody finger. "'Fore I go, though, I want you to understand somethin, the way things are. You full of sand now, but there might come a time when they ain't no *pro*-vost guard. That bein so, I might want to call again."

"I hope you will," said Anna.

The man laughed. "No, you still don't understand." He licked his fingers, then closed them around the baggy crotch of his trousers. "See?" he said. "Think about it—"

"Get out!" cried Anna. "Provost!"

"I was jes leavin, little puss," he said, and at that moment he reached the bottom and stumbled over the legs of a soldier lying at the foot of the stairs. The man looked down, and laughed again. "Well, I'll be goddamned if it ain't ol' Bushrod! Man, I been lookin all over for you." He kicked the soldier's leg. "Where's Jack? Hey, where's my old pard Jack?" He kicked the man again. "You see him, you tell him—"

"Provost!" Anna shouted again, but the man was gone, limping down the hall and into the dark beyond the door.

Anna was trembling, the fuse guttering out inside her. Her legs had gone weak all at once and she had to cling to the banister to keep from falling. She moved slowly down the stairs and sat on the bottom step near the soldier who was moaning now. She clamped her knees tight together and took the silver cross in her hand. It was cool and she pressed it to her cheek, trying not to think of anything.

"Yew holler for the provost, ma'am?"

Anna looked up. Before her stood a scrawny, barefooted boy with smallpox scars on his face, clutching a bayonetted musket two feet taller than he was.

"Who are you?" said Anna. "*What* are you?"

The boy blushed and rubbed a foot on the shin of his leg.

"You are *not* a provost guard," Anna said.

"Yes'm," mumbled the boy.

Anna put her face in her hands and laughed, and when the tears came they surprised her; she had not thought that any remained in her.

"You-uns is hurt?" asked the boy.

Anna shook her head, brought out her handkerchief again and wiped her eyes. "No, I am not hurt," she said. She sighed. "I need somebody to go down to the cookhouse, guard the biscuits and the ham. You do that for me?"

"Uh-huh. Yes'm."

"Anybody wants to know, you say Miss Anna Hereford said for you to stay down there. Now go along, don't be dawdlin."

"I won't," said the boy. He looked at her for a long moment. "Kin I have a biscuit?" he said at last.

"Tell em I said to give you one. As many as you want."

The boy grinned, slung his musket and went away down the hall.

Men were passing, they looked at her and looked away. Two came by with a litter, the wounded man was groaning and rolling his head back and forth and frothing blood. *That one will be dead soon,* Anna thought. She shut her eyes tight and tried to imagine the world without her in it. It was sweet and peaceful: she was not there, and the world went right along anyhow. For a moment she could almost believe it was true—but then, slowly, like people coming up a road, the voices came again, and the cries, and the little sound of a wasp batting its stupid head against the tin lantern in the hall. *Got to go,* thought Anna, and opened her eyes.

"We got to be quiet," Winder said, "else we'll wake Hattie up, and then we're in for it."

"Ain't it the truth!" said Nebo Gloster. He was busy arranging the ramrods side-by-side on the hearth.

A little while before, Winder had awakened to find Nebo bending over him in the bed. The man had put a finger to his lips and beckoned him to follow. Winder was unafraid; he knew the soldiers would not hurt him, and this man, from the bars on his collar, was a Confederate officer. So the boy crept out of bed, careful not to wake Hattie, and now he and the officer were crouching by the hearth examining the ramrods.

"What you got all them for, anyhow?" asked Winder.

"Got all what for?"

"Well, all those things there. And how come your shoes is around your neck, and it wintertime?"

"I am glad you axed me that," said Nebo. "I was jes comin around to it. But if I tell you, will you not say a thing to a livin soul?"

"Not me," said Winder. "Honor bright."

"All right, then," said Nebo. He beckoned, the boy moved closer. "These here," said Nebo in a whisper, "repersent all the ramrods what was fired durin the great battle. One of em is mine."

The boy waited. After a moment, Nebo touched his sleeve. "One of em is mine," he repeated.

Winder nodded. "Yessir. What else?"

Nebo raised an eyebrow. "What you mean, what else?"

The boy shrugged. "Well, I mean, one of em is yours, and what else about em?"

"Why, there ain't nothin else about em. Don't you want to help me figure out which one?"

"Is that all?" said the boy.

"Well, it's what I come out for," said Nebo.

"But how will we ever tell?"

Nebo stroked his bristled chin. "Derned if I know," he said.

When Simon Rope left the house, he didn't go far, just a little way into the grove where the firelight couldn't reach him. There he settled among the roots of an oak tree to wait for morning, and to think about the woman in the house. He closed his eyes and saw her again in perfect clarity as she stood in the dim light of the hall, and her voice came to him again, and the words, and the way she looked at him. He crossed his arms and huddled against the damp night and played the scene in his mind over and over again, changing nothing, not even trying to think of things he should have said instead of what he did. Then, when he had it all down, he expanded the scene to include Bushrod Carter. Now he smiled. Bushrod was there too, him and the woman, right there in the house together.

It was cold, but Simon Rope did not care about the cold. He shivered and drew his collar tight around his neck. His ear burned with a heatless fire, but no matter. In time he slept, and his sleep was free of dreams.

When Anna Hereford opened her eyes, the first thing she saw was the body of the soldier lying at the foot of the stairs. He did not seem too badly hurt, at least by the rigorous standards of the night—a bruised and bloody face, a bloody hand where his finger had been shot or cut or bitten away. Anna wondered by what blind circumstance he had come to be here, brought out of the night and deposited at her feet as if circumstance expected her to do something about him. She yawned, and brushed at her hair. She ought to wash it soon, she thought, and maybe get Jeanne to cut it. But no, that wouldn't do now. Jeanne was gone, nobody knew where, just gone. Run off with the Yankees, oh, a long time ago. Well, too bad circumstance didn't bring Jeanne here, too, where she could look after Hattie and Winder and keep the ghosts away.

The thought of the children nagged her. She had to get up, go and find somebody to help her straighten out the mess upstairs—she could do that, at least. She yawned again, and rested her chin on her drawn-up knees, blinked her heavy eyes and stared at the soldier while strangers passed in the hall and the wasp knocked against the lantern glass. She would get up in just a minute and go find cousin Caroline, who would know what to do, who would help her.

The soldier looked like a pile of dirty, bloody rags, and he hadn't any shoes. His face might have been pleasant once and his hands, dirty as they were, didn't seem to be a countryman's hands—they were long, slender, almost effeminate, a boy's hands, not a man's. Anna watched as the soldier raised his hands and pressed them to his face—it was a gesture she had seen men do countless times over the long night. He raised one knee then let it fall, and his heel thumped on the floor. He was talking behind his hands, but Anna couldn't hear, didn't much care anyway, wanted only to sleep—

No! she thought—*Wake up. Wake up* and pulled her head up, and at that moment the soldier dropped his hands and looked right at her and said, "Remy Dangerfield!"

"What!" Anna said, and the sound of her own voice made her jump.

Bushrod Carter could not believe what he was seeing. In fact, he could hardly see at all, but there was the girl's face, no doubt about that, so he said her name again: "Remy?"

"Who?" said the girl. "Who did you say?"

So he was not dead, and it was not Remy after all. Bushrod groaned in disappointment and covered his face again. After a moment, he heard the girl's voice closer now, as if she had leaned toward him: "What's the matter with you, anyhow?"

Bushrod looked again and, sure enough, the girl was leaning toward him, watching him over her knees. "Who?" he said.

"You, boy," said the girl. "Who'd you think?"

Bushrod was sick at his stomach. His last memory was a complex and disturbing one: Virgil C. lying face down in the grass, Nebo Gloster running, an officer shooting at him with his pistol. And now he seemed to be inside a house, lying on the floor, and a girl he did not know was talking to him. He was sick, and felt like he might throw up.

"I am fixin to throw up," he said.

"Well, go ahead," said the girl. "Have at it."

So he did, and was ashamed. It was only bile, and not much of that, but the act angered and humiliated him. It was too much. *The very idea— the very fuckin idea—*

"Sorry," he said. "Sorry."

"I don't have time to fool with you," said the girl, but then she was kneeling beside him, wiping his mouth with a rag or a handkerchief, and Bushrod was ashamed and turned his face away.

"Don't then," he said. "Go on."

"Hush," said Anna. She tried to turn his face, but he wouldn't let her. She sat back on her heels and looked at him. "Well, I am only tryin to help you," she said.

The soldier did not reply. He lifted his right hand, the unwounded one, as if to wave her away.

"All right, then, forget it," Anna said, and stood up. "You are not much hurt anyhow."

All right, then how much hurt do you have to be?

The thought came so unexpectedly that at first she believed the soldier had spoken it—but he was staring groggily across the hall, drifting again apparently.

Worse than the one up yonder you treated like a dog?

"That is not fair," Anna said to the soldier. "I don't have time to *fool* with you!" The man turned his face toward her, but Anna didn't think he saw her at all—he seemed to be looking past her at something she really didn't care to know about. She remembered the smoke, the snarling in the twilight. *He was there,* she thought—*In all of that*—

"Ah, damn!" she said. She saw a bloody-aproned figure stumble out of the parlor, like a man drunk or walking in his sleep. "You, sir!" she said. "Are you a doctor?"

Bushrod Carter had been listening to the girl talk, though he did not suppose she was speaking to him. It was a strange music, her voice, and he wished he could sit and talk to her a while. He was thinking about that when a new face swam into his vision: a man, bearded, cheeks glistening with sweat, with the stub of a cigar in his teeth. The smell of the chewed cigar made Bushrod want to throw up again. He heard the girl's voice: "What can you do for him?"

The surgeon had been on his way to answer a call of nature, and he was in fact both drunk and walking in his sleep. He had lost track of the number of arms and legs he'd removed since sundown, and the pounds of lint he'd stuffed into bullet wounds, and the yards of sutures he'd sewn, and the cigars he'd smoked, and the grains of morphine he'd taken, and he was too far gone to want to fool with a man hurt no worse than this one. But the woman who'd waylaid him belonged to the house, and the surgeon had been a man of sensibilities once, and if she wanted him to look at this fellow, well—

The surgeon bent over Bushrod, blue threads of smoke curling from his cigar. His blunt fingers probed various places on Bushrod's head, and he pried open the damaged eye and peered within. Then he settled back on his heels.

"His head ain't broke, God knows why. Took a bad lick on the eye but it's still quick, there ain't any damage, I guess. You might want to wrap up that finger—pour a little whiskey on it first, mebbe, if you got any. It'll mend, most likely."

"How about his nose?" Anna asked. "It looks mashed to me."

"Aw, that ain't nothin," said the surgeon. He grunted and bent forward and took Bushrod's nose between his thumb and forefinger and squeezed. Anna heard the crunch of gristle and winced. Bushrod let out a howl. "Now then, if you'll 'scuse me," said the surgeon, and he rose and staggered away.

"Oh, great God," said Bushrod, his hands hovering around his nose. "Good God in the mornin—"

Anna was kneeling beside him again. "Does it hurt much?" she asked.

"Hurt!" cried Bushrod. "Hell fire and damnation, it hurts like everything!"

"Well, don't be cussin at me, sir," said Anna.

"Well, you asked, and I told you," said Bushrod.

Anna could not argue with that, so she sat on the bottom step again and regarded the soldier. "It seems to me you are makin a big fuss over nothin," she said. "You ought to see some of the boys in here."

"Is this a hospital?" asked Bushrod.

"It is my cousin McGavock's house," Anna said.

"I asked was it a *hospital!*" Bushrod demanded.

Anna clenched her teeth, fought against a sharp reply. "Yes," she said. "They are usin it for that."

"Then I know all about what it looks like," said Bushrod, "and I can't see a thing. Not a damn thing."

Anna had noticed the man's haversack and canteen beside him. She picked up the canteen, shook it, heard water slosh around inside. *No tellin what mud hole this came out of,* she thought. But it was water nevertheless, and she unstoppered the cork and soaked her handkerchief.

"You don't go pullin away again, I will fix it so you can see," she said. She began to wipe the blood and rheum out of Bushrod's eyes. He winced and sucked in his breath.

"Don't be such a baby," she said. When she had unglued his eyes, she took the canteen and poured some of the water over the severed joint of his finger.

"God-*dammit!*" Bushrod wailed.

"I never heard such language," said Anna. "What is your name, anyhow?"

"Oh, mankind," said Bushrod. "What?"

"Your name, sir. So I can write home about you."

"Oh, me. It is......it is Bushrod. Carter. Bushrod Carter."

"That is an odd name," said Anna, and began to wipe his face again. "That truly is an odd name. Where you come from, they would give you a name like that?"

"I need to drink some water, if you please," said Bushrod.

Anna put the pewter spout of the canteen to Bushrod's lips. "You talk like you're from one of those deep-south peckerwood districts," Anna said. "Alabama or one of those, where they would name somebody Bushrod."

Bushrod tilted the canteen and drank greedily until he choked and nearly threw up again. "See there?" said Anna. "If you would just hold your horses—"

"Oh, what makes you so hateful!" Bushrod said.

"That does it!" said Anna. She rammed the cork back in the canteen and stood up. "Call me hateful, and here I am tryin my best to help you. I've half a mind to put you out of this house!"

"Why don't you try it then," said Bushrod.

"Well, I might," said Anna.

"Well, go on and do it then!"

Anna gathered her skirts. "If you keep on, then I will, see if I don't!"

Bushrod was about to speak again, but checked himself. In his view, the conversation was taking a bad turn. He looked at the girl, he could see her better now that she'd wiped his eyes. What he saw convinced him to mind his tongue—she would do it all right, she would put him out in the yard where the cigar-smoking man could get hold of him again. But that was not all. Suddenly he did not want her to go away. He waved his hand as if to brush away all that he had said. "Oh, don't mind me—you are not bein hateful. I have been knocked in the head, is all."

For her part, Anna thought she probably *was* being hateful. She sighed, sank wearily to the bottom step again and tucked her knees under her chin. "No, you are right—I have been hateful to you. I am only tired, I guess." She looked at the soldier, found herself wanting to talk to him about something, anything, as long as it was not about wounds or battle or death. He had a pleasant voice, she was sure it was not always as raspy as it was now. "What's that medal on your watch chain?" she asked.

The soldier looked down, smiled. "Ah, that is good Saint....." He stopped, frowned, touched the medal with his good hand. "I forgot," he said.

"Oh, well, that's—"

"No, I know!" said Bushrod. "It is Saint Michael." He smiled again. "He is on furlough, I reckon."

"Oh," said Anna, though she had no idea what he meant.

There was a silence then, as both of them tried to think of something to say. Finally, Bushrod spoke. "Can I ask you somethin?"

"Proceed, do," said Anna.

"Sometimes I don't remember things," said Bushrod. "What is the name of that village yonder, over by the river?"

"Oh," said Anna, "that is Franklin. Franklin, Tennessee."

"And there was a battle?" asked Bushrod.

Oh, me, thought Anna—*do they never think of anything else?* "Yes, there was a battle," she said. "There was indeed."

"You must tell me what happened."

Anna sighed. "The Yankees were over in Franklin, and you all came across the fields. Now the Yankees are gone, and you all are still here, so you must've won. That is all I know about it." *And all I want to know.*

"Won?" said Bushrod. "We *won* this battle?"

"I suppose you did," said Anna.

Bushrod laughed, and the sound of it struck a nerve in Anna and she flared up in spite of herself. "What do you *want* me to tell you, then? Where you think I been while all this butchery was goin on? You think I was—"

Bushrod lifted his hand. "No, no. Peace, now—it ain't you, Missy. It's just funny how—"

Bushrod was interrupted by a shout from the parlor, and they both turned to look. A man appeared in the parlor door, unraveling a bandage from the stump of his arm. He shook the bandage off and it fluttered to the floor. Then, as they watched, the man struck his fist against the stump again and again until blood sprayed on the wallpaper. Then he saw Bushrod and Anna and lurched toward them. "Look what they done!" he cried, waving the stump. "After I tol' em and tol' em not to do it!"

Bushrod tried to get up but couldn't. "Get away from here, you damn fool," he said.

The man looked wildly about, eyes glittering with pain. He pointed toward the open front door with the thin, bony fingers of his remaining hand. "There!" he told Bushrod and Anna. "It's out there somewheres! I'll find it! See if I don't, by God!" Then he began to sob; he stood above them, swaying and sobbing, until an orderly came and led him away.

When she knew the man was gone, Anna opened her eyes. She had bitten her lower lip so hard it was bleeding. She pressed the wet handkerchief to her mouth.

"My, *he* was a dandy," said Bushrod. "One of the triumphant, no doubt. Reckon what it'd be like around here if we'd lost."

"Oh, shut up, do," said Anna.

"Oh, me," said Bushrod. "Here, you have hurt yourself. Did that fellow scare you?"

"I have seen lots worse tonight," said the girl, but Bushrod could see that her hands were trembling.

"He's gone now," said Bushrod lamely. "But just to make my point—I was about to say how funny it is.....I mean, I am so use to losin, I thought winnin might be different—but it ain't, not so's I can see. Ain't that funny?"

"Oh, I am bowled over," said Anna dryly. She put a hand on the newel post and pulled herself up. "I have to go now and—"

"No, wait!" said Bushrod. "I mean.....don't leave yet. You got to remember, I been knocked in the head—I am pretty agreeable when in my right mind."

"I am sure you are," said Anna. "But I have to find my cousin Caroline McGavock and get somebody to go with me—" She looked up the stairs. "I have to go back up there," she said, as if to herself.

Bushrod squinted up the stairwell. "What's up there?"

"Nothin."

"Then what are you afraid of?"

Anna turned on him. "Why do you say I am afraid?" she demanded.

"Because—" Bushrod began, but his face twisted and he sneezed a dark gout of blood. "Damn," he said. "Oh, damn!"

Anna wiped the blood from his mustache. "Why did you say that.....like that?" she asked.

"Because I can tell," said Bushrod. "Because I am an expert on bein afraid. But never mind that. *I* will go with you."

"What? You?"

"Right as rain," said Bushrod. "I will go up yonder with you, but first you have to get me a biscuit or somethin and some coffee—I am about to die for—"

"Coffee!" said Anna. "You can't even stand up."

"I will practice while you are gone," said Bushrod. "Listen, if there's soldiers around here, there will be some coffee. Then I will help you, honor bright. Ask for First Sergeant Bill Williams and Mister Eugene Pitcock—they are makin some, I saw them—they are down by a stone wall, under a big tree, you must know the place—say to them Bushrod Carter sent you—I mean, *asked* you, if you please—say to them....." Bushrod stopped. He frowned and rubbed his forehead. "No, that can't be right," he said. "I must be thinkin of another time."

Anna shook her head. "You are truly a mess," she said.

"Well, I am feelin pretty low," said Bushrod. "But if you will get me some coffee and somethin to eat, then I will do better. I promise."

Anna had her doubts, yet the boy *did* seem to be coming around, and he *did* seem to have a spark in him, and it wasn't likely she would do any better among this crowd of played-out Rebels. And he was, or appeared to be, a real soldier, whatever that meant. *And maybe it would be nice to have his company.....* Anna shook the thought away. "All right," she said. "I will see about it. By the way, what regiment do you belong to?"

"Do what?" asked Bushrod.

"Your regiment. What is your regiment?"

Bushrod pondered a moment. The number, which he knew to be important, seemed to have drifted away like a skiff in a fog. Then he caught sight of it. "Oh," he said. "It is the Twenty-first."

"The Twenty-first what?" Anna said.

"Hmmm.....oh! It is Mississippi. The Twenty-first Mississippi was my regiment."

"Aha," said Anna. "I *knew* you were a peckerwood."

"Beg pardon?"

"Never mind," said Anna. "I will try to find out what became of them for you, and I will get you some—"

"No, no," said Bushrod, shaking his head. "No, you won't find them. They are all.....they are all....."

"They are all dead," said Anna, flatly, as if she were discussing the weather.

"Yes," said Bushrod. "They are all dead."

"I am sorry. I cannot imagine what.....what it must be like."

Bushrod was silent.

Anna left the bottom stair then and moved into the hall. She looked back at him. "But *you* are not dead."

"No.....no, I suppose not."

"Think on that," said Anna. "I'll be back directly."

"Wait a minute!" said Bushrod. He tilted his face up at her squinting. "What is your name?"

"Anna," she said. "Anna Margaret Hereford of Fayetteville, Tennessee."

"Miss Anna," said Bushrod. "Well, I am pleased to know you."

For reasons she did not have the energy to examine, Anna was glad he spoke her name. She made a small curtsy, something she hadn't done in years. "Mister Carter, the same. Now don't go wanderin off where I have to hunt for you."

"I am riveted to this spot," said Bushrod, and watched her walk away. She moved down the hall, her head up, nodding to the soldiers who stepped aside and swept off their hats in the old deference that not even catastrophe could wean out of them. Then she was gone, out of his line of vision beyond the stairs. Bushrod wondered what such a one as her could possibly have to be afraid of. He glanced up the stairs. Whatever it was, he would find out directly. If she came back. No, she *would* come back. Surely she would.

Slowly, with infinite care, Bushrod tried sitting upright. He supposed that if he were missing any other parts, it would become evident right away. He was relieved when he'd sat up and everything held together. He moved his legs experimentally, noting with irritation that someone had taken his good shoes. Well, he had taken a few pair himself in his time, and would no doubt take another before the night was out.

When he thought he could stand, Bushrod gathered his legs under him, pushed off from the stair, and rose to his feet—too fast. He nearly fell and had to cling dizzily to the newel post while lights spun in his head. Oddly, the spinning lights made him think of the machine at the University they called Barlow's Planetarium, and how the tiny moon swung around the tiny earth and both whirled in harmony around the brass globe of the sun. Bushrod had felt profoundly educated the first time he had observed the device; the feeling lasted for almost an hour, until he left the lecture hall and looked up at the moon. Now, standing shakily on his cold bare feet and gripping the newel post, Bushrod watched the familiar constellations of his life spin away with the feeling that he no longer stood at the center of the universe. The battle had jarred him loose, as if he'd stepped into a blast of double-shotted canister and been scattered in fragments across the night.

Memory played itself out in brief, murky scenes that jumped across time and space. He saw himself in line of battle, saw the girl's face again, watched himself running, his rifle coming down to charge-bayonet; saw Nebo Gloster turning toward him, passed again over the lonely corpse of the staff officer, was in line of battle again.....in line of battle, looking out over the broad open ground, wondering what was going to happen.....

Well, something had happened all right. He had always thought it would be Death, but in that he was mistaken. Death took all the other boys and left him clinging to a newel post, trying to keep from falling. No, it was not Death that had happened to him after all—it was Life. He was alive, and he didn't know what to make of it.

He did know one thing, however: this was his last battle. He was finished, he had acted well his part and now he was through. He had discharged himself, sent himself on permanent furlough. The boys were dead, and the Bonnie Blue Flag was their winding sheet, and Bushrod Carter was done with soldiering forevermore.

Deserter, said the old familiar voice.

"Fuck you," said Bushrod.

He moved his legs, trying to work the stiffness out so he could be useful to the girl when she called on him. For an instant he regretted his promise to her—how much easier it would be just to disappear into the chaotic night. But her face came to him again, and her hands wiping the bile from his mouth, and the glimpse of her bare ankles where she sat on the stair—

He grinned, and shook his head. Around him, men struggled with their various burdens of duty and suffering and grief, but none of that concerned him now. Except the grief, perhaps. He figured that would catch up to him directly, somewhere down the road in a world he could not imagine at the moment. But that was later, when he would really start to remember things. For now, he only hoped the girl Anna would return and bring him a cup of coffee.

CHAPTER NINE

Hattie woke to the voices, low and murmurous though they were. At first she thought she might be dreaming, so she pinched herself, which she had been told was a sure-fire method. It was: she was not dreaming. Then she thought it might be the men outside on the gallery; she vaguely remembered Anna speaking to them out there. Then she heard movement—a rustle of clothing, a clinking on the bricks of the hearth—and she knew with a sudden rush of fear that the voices were in the room with her. Moreover, she discovered she was alone in the bed.

Hattie was so tired of being brave. She had been brave for years and years, it seemed like, and now she was nearing the end of her tether. But Anna was not here, and Mother was not here, and that left her in charge again—she was a McGavock, after all, and McGavocks were brave, after all, and that was all there was to it. So she clasped her hands, made a brief but fervent appeal to the Deity, and rose from her pillow.

The first thing she saw was Winder, his back to her, looking at the fire. Hah! He was messing with the fire, a thing strictly forbidden, and she had caught him at it. "Winder McGavock!" she said. "What are you doin over there?"

Winder threw up his hands. "*Now* we're in for it," he cried. "I *told* you to be quiet!"

But Hattie's relief, and the satisfaction of thwarting her brother in a felony, evaporated when the second figure rose up in the firelight. Now she was done being brave. She screamed.

Winder ran to the bed, fluttering his hands. "Hush!" he said. "Do hush up, sister—it's only a Confedrit officer, old Nebo. We ain't doin anything—"

Nebo Gloster shambled up and stood beside the boy. "Hidy!" he said.

"Mama!" squalled the girl.

"Lord amercy," said Nebo.

Winder crawled up in the bed and bounced on it. "Sister, Hattie, listen—it's all right no foolin we are huntin Nebo's ramrod is all you can help us really you can Mama won't care honest injun. Oh hush up do—"

Winder went on bouncing on the bed, pleading and cajoling while Nebo shifted from foot to foot and grinned hopefully. Finally, when it was apparent that no reinforcements were coming, and that the scarecrow leering down at her was harmless, and that Winder himself was not afraid, Hattie ceased crying. She sniffed resentfully for a moment, then wiped her nose on the shawl and said, "Winder McGavock, who *is* this person?"

"I *told* you. It is old Nebo. He is a Confedrit officer and we—"

"Why, he isn't anything of the kind," said Hattie. "Just look at him in that old straw hat. Look at those shoes around his neck. When did you ever see—"

"Say, I got somethin," said Nebo suddenly. He began to dig in the pocket of his ragged trousers. "You can have it if you want."

"He's an officer," insisted Winder.

"He is not," said Hattie.

"Looka here," said Nebo. He held out his hand; in the palm was an oblong bit of green glass, a lens from a pair of sun goggles. "I got it from a feller down at Alabama, where the big river was that we crossed. I give him a whole dollar for it. It's magic."

"Magic?" said Hattie and Winder together.

"Yep," said Nebo. "The feller said when you hold it up and look through it, whatever you look at turns green. I tried it, and sure enough. Here, you can have it." He pressed the glass into Hattie's hand. "Try it yourself," he said.

Winder laughed. "Why, it turns green because—"

"Hush *up*, Winder," said the girl, fixing him with the sidelong glance she'd learned from Anna. "I *mean* it!" Then she looked at the glass in her hand, turning it over and over. "You really want me to have this?" she asked Nebo.

"Yes'm. It's yourn."

She nodded. She made an "O" of her thumb and forefinger and fitted the glass inside it. She looked at Nebo, then slowly, solemnly, lifted the glass to the firelight. She drew a sharp breath. "Why, you're right!" she said. "It *is* magic, sure enough!"

Anna found her cousin on the back gallery. She was sitting in a straight chair by the door, her head bowed, her hands resting idly in her lap. Beyond her on the gallery lay the soft, muted shapes of dead men, dozens of them, heels together and hands crossed upon their breasts. Anna had the eerie feeling that she had intruded on some intimate communion between Caroline and the dead men, a final moment before the bridge of life and suffering dissolved into the mist between them. Anna wondered what her cousin's thoughts must be, and understood that she could not know them and never would, and how strong her cousin's heart to bear them all.

Anna watched a little while, until her cousin raised her head and brushed at the fall of hair in her eyes. Anna spoke her name, and Caroline McGavock turned on her a face so deep in weariness it should have been past all feeling, but the dark eyes lit in recognition and Caroline McGavock smiled.

"As I live and breathe," Caroline said. She put out her hands, and Anna came and took them. "I had hoped you would sleep and sleep, but here you are."

"I did sleep, cousin," said Anna.

"And why is your lip bleedin so?"

"Oh, I bit it. In my sleep."

"Ah, me," said Caroline, and touched Anna's lip with the tip of her finger. "I am sorry to bring all this on you."

"Hush, darlin," said Anna. "It wasn't you turned the dogs loose."

"Who do you suppose did?" said Caroline.

Anna smiled. "I don't know, but if I ever find him—"

"Now, listen at you."

Anna loosed her cousin's hands and sank, as gracefully as she could, to the rough planks of the gallery. She leaned her head against the balustrade, the cool air felt good on the back of her neck. She told her cousin then about all that had happened since she'd first awakened in the room upstairs, from the dream of the dark birds to the wounded soldier who said he would help her if she'd bring him some coffee. In the telling it all sounded vaguely melodramatic, as if she had made it all up, and she half-expected her cousin to laugh at her—or at the tale anyway. But Caroline didn't laugh. When Anna finished, the older woman simply nodded her head, as if she'd just been told a little light gossip about the neighbors.

"Yes, I saw that bearded fellow," said Caroline. "He was a nosegay, all right—went off toward the grove, going to town I expect. Maybe somebody will shoot him. But you say my little pirates were fine?"

"Oh, they were sleepin when I left them," said Anna. "And no doubt they are safe. Still, it is mighty scary up there, and I will try and fix it if you will only tell me how." She took her cousin's hands again, thinking *Yes, and you might also tell me that everything will be all right and that all of this trouble has only been the old house dreamin and pretty soon it will wake and we will laugh away its dreamin and everything will be just like it was....* She took her cousin's hands and looked at them, the hands she loved, that had petted her all her life; they were twined with her own, and Anna thought it made a pretty picture, never mind the blood and dirt and skinned knuckles, and then all at once Anna realized that she really *was* seeing them—

"The light!" Anna cried, and looked up at her cousin's face.

"Yes," said Caroline. "It seems the night is over at last."

"I didn't think it ever would be. Not ever. I mean, I really did not."

"You, too?" said Caroline. "I thought I was the only one with that notion." She turned her face to the dead men lying on the porch; over them, too, the light was falling. "Do you reckon it really matters? You think it makes a difference if it is light or dark, or the day ever comes at all?"

"Yes," said Anna. "Maybe sometimes I forget it—maybe that's what the night is for, just so's we can know the difference when the light comes again." She waved her hand toward the dead men. "Those yonder, they can't see it—but we can." She laughed. "That don't make any sense."

Caroline looked down at Anna. She leaned forward and touched the girl's face. "That was the right answer," she said.

Together they watched the growing light. It was gray and pale, and where the barren trees rose against it they showed every branch. The fires seemed dimmer now; the smoke lay along the ground in tattered, dingy sheets. They could see the men moving about in the yard, their white shirts glowed like foxfire and their voices were clearer, sharper, suddenly unmysterious. The men stretched and yawned and looked at their watches, no longer shadows but men again. Anna could see the bricks in the wall, the old familiar facing of the door, the little chips of white paint that still clung to the chair in which her cousin sat. The world was emerging, taking shape again. The dawn had come, and with it, out in the oak grove, the thin voice of a single bird.

At last Caroline spoke again. "Now, this boy you told me about—the one by the stairs. Does he seem.....reliable?"

"Well, I only just made his acquaintance," said Anna. "He does have pretty hands, though."

"Hah! Well, that is important, a lofty recommendation. Will you and this paragon go and see to Hattie and Winder for me? That would be a mighty help—and I can make myself useful in the yard."

"Yes, cousin," said Anna. "But I think you ought to take a rest."

"Rest?" said Caroline. "With all these men trompin around the house? Why, I could sooner rest at a gander-pull, whatever that is. Did you ever know what one of them was?"

"I never even heard of one," said Anna.

"Well, anyway, I got things to do. Pretty hands, eh? Well, Anna Margaret, you are a grown woman, I can't be worryin about—Oh, look, yonder goes Major Cross, poor man. He has had the devil's own time with these pitiful provost guards. I will ask him to bring some order to the second floor if he can, and maybe he can chaperone you and Sir Lancelot—"

"Lord, I wished I'd never mentioned it," said Anna, and the two women laughed and men in the yard turned their faces to the sound as they might to unexpected music.

"Well," Caroline said, "I am going to sit here five minutes more—by the watch, mind you—and I might ask you to do one thing for me."

Anna looked up expectantly.

"Down in the cookhouse you will find Mattie Lee and that yellow girl from the widow's—they will likely be arguin about religion or some such thing, but no matter, it is the closest pot of coffee I know anything about. You might drop a tin cup by this chair on your way back. Now, what did you say this boy's name was?"

Anna smiled. "Well, it is Bushrod," she said.

"My lands," laughed Caroline McGavock. "Wherever is he from?"

"Excuse me," said Bushrod Carter. He was just inside the dining room door, about to dispossess an officer of his pistol. The officer was dead, but Bushrod still felt he should be polite. It was always his way when relieving the Departed of their belongings. He moved aside the still-warm hand and slipped the pistol from its holster. He was pleased to find it was a genuine Colt's Navy model. He checked the caps and loads; the blunt gray noses of the balls stared back at him from all six chambers. *Be damned*, thought Bushrod, and looked at the man's sword scabbard. It was empty. "Well, you went in with the blade, didn't you?" said Bushrod. "Lot of good you were." The Departed stared back at him with empty eyes. "Oh, don't mind me, sir," said Bushrod. "I been knocked in the head."

The officer was still wearing his boots, but Bushrod could tell by looking that they were way too big for him, and he didn't care much for boots anyway—too clumsy for walking, and he would have a long way to walk pretty soon. He went back out to the hall and leaned against the newel post again and considered the pistol. No doubt he would need it on the long walk home, and he might pick up a shotgun, too, if he could. He stuck the revolver into the waist of his trousers; the barrel was cold against his leg. Maybe he ought to take the belt and holster, too—

But it was too much to think about right now. He was dizzy again, his head hurt, his left hand throbbed with a dull ache. He held the hand up and pondered it. Amazing! The finger he had known all his life was gone. The severed stump was crusted and brownish, seeping droplets of fresh blood, and there was a white circlet of bone. He wondered why it didn't hurt any worse than it did, and in the same moment realized he'd better quit thinking about it, better get it out of sight. *I got to bind it*, he thought.

He eased back into the dining room where the dead officer lay. He opened the man's coat. There was a big hole in there, just above the belt buckle. "Beg pardon," Bushrod said, and began to prowl through the dead man's pockets. He found a buckeye, two cigars (unfortunately broken), a pencil, a bloody note concerning the issue of rations. Then he found what he was looking for: a silk handkerchief, reasonably clean, monogrammed "HTW." Bushrod took the handkerchief and wrapped it around his finger. "Much obliged," he said.

Back in the hall, Bushrod sat down on the stairs. Bending over the officer's body had made him dizzier than ever. Through the door at the end of the hall, Bushrod could see daylight. Gray and sullen it was, but daylight all the same. Through the years Bushrod had seen the dawn come to many fields, after many hard fights, and it was always a sacred moment to him—proof that the universe was still intact in spite of the blood on the ground, the hosts of Departed beginning their first day in eternity, the dead horses and broken gun carriages and scattered equipment—in spite of all the panoramic ruin of the battlefield so brutal and grotesque that it was a wonder God did not bury it in darkness forever—and with it the guilty living, who crept from their holes or their stiff blankets and looked about with astonishment on what they had done. But God never would bury it. He always seemed to want to start over again, whether out of anger or pity

Bushrod could not say. And now here was another dawn, after another great fight, and once more God had permitted Bushrod Carter to live.

Bushrod sifted reluctantly, cautiously, through the fragments of his memory and decided that yesterday they must have formed up right out there. He could remember that, and he remembered thinking what it would be like to hide out in the great brick house. Well, here he was. He wondered if the girl Anna had been watching from one of these windows. She might have looked him right in the face without knowing it. It was strange to think about. What if she saw Virgil C. get shot?

Bushrod knew that, if he wanted to, he could walk right over to that door and see Virgil C. lying in the yard. He had to be right out there, lying face down in the wet grass, all by himself. The thought made him sick, and he turned from it. He had to wait for Anna—maybe after a while she would go with him out there.

Then he thought about Jack Bishop, and the thought caused a twinge of guilt and resentment all at once.

Should've thought of him before now, said the Other in his old practical way—always mindful of what Bushrod Carter ought to do, or ought not to do, or should have done already—

But I am hurt, Bushrod answered, *and Jack is out there messin around as usual and why ain't he—*

Jack is dead, fool.

"Shut up!" cried Bushrod aloud. He stood up again, too fast, and his head spun like the moon in Barlow's Planetarium and the pistol jammed sideways into his privates.

Jack is dead and you are alive—

Bushrod waved his arm. "Shut up! I got no more business with you!"

A wounded soldier limping by grinned at Bushrod out of his beard. "Hee, Gawd," he laughed, "you crazier 'n a bessie bug, ain't ye?"

"Leave me alone," said Bushrod.

"Aw, that's all right," said the soldier. "I'm crazier 'n dog shit my own self. I kin talk to animals an'—"

Bushrod put his hand on the pistol butt. "You get away from me or I will blow your goddamn brains out right here in this hall."

"I tolt ye," laughed the soldier. "A brass-frame lunatic if ever I see one!" He limped away down the hall, laughing to himself.

"Son of a bitch," muttered Bushrod. "Tell *me* I'm crazy."

He listened for the voice again, but there was only silence from that quarter. "Hey!" Bushrod said into the silence. "Don't you be comin around me no more! Jack and me are goin home—you got somethin to say about it?"

Bushrod clung to the newel post, breathing hard. Men moved past him in the hall, ignoring him. The candle lantern had gone out; the wax of many tapers had overflown onto the fine finish of the table. In the wax were the hard, twisted bodies of wasps.

"Hey!" Bushrod said. "You listenin to me? If you got somethin to say—"

Someone touched his arm and Bushrod squawked and turned so quickly he would have fallen if the girl had not caught him.

"Lord have mercy," said Anna. "Here's your coffee. What's the matter with you now?"

When Bushrod had composed himself, the girl handed him a dented tin boiler of steaming coffee and a big hoe cake—only the Tennessee people, Bushrod had learned, called it a "journey cake."

"Ah," said Bushrod, taking the cup. "'A sweeter draught from a fairer hand....'"

"Oh, please," said Anna, rolling her eyes.

"Well, did you find your aunt?" Bushrod asked. He ate slowly while the coffee cooled; he did not want to get sick again.

"Cousin," said the girl. "It's my cousin. Yes, she is grateful for your help, though skeptical. I assured her you were a gentleman."

"Hmmm," said Bushrod. He held out the remnants of the cake. "Do you want some of this? I should've asked sooner."

"Thank you, no," said the girl. Bushrod noted she had a way of turning her head just a little, watching him out of the corner of her eyes. It made him vaguely uncomfortable.

"Who were you talking to just now?" she asked.

Bushrod chewed the rest of the cake, swallowed, affected a smile. "Just now, you mean?"

The girl watched him.

"Well, to myself, I guess," said Bushrod. "I do that all the time."

"You talk to yourself all the time?"

"Well, some of the time," said Bushrod, taking up the tin boiler. "Don't everybody?"

The girl made no reply. She seemed interested only in asking questions. Bushrod wrapped his hands around the boiler and drank—carefully, letting the coffee cool the rim. It was thin coffee, like the Yankees made, but Bushrod was not about to complain.

"What is that gun for?" asked the girl.

Bushrod had to think: *Gun? Gun?* "Ah, yes," he said. He looked down at the butt of the pistol in his waistband. "Well, that is a good question."

"Well, what do you want it for?" the girl asked.

"Well, it's for.....well, I guess I thought—"

"Where'd you get it? You didn't have one before."

A little red flag unfurled itself in Bushrod's mind. He set the coffee down carefully on the hall table and looked at the girl. "A man gave it to me," he said.

"Why?" asked the girl.

"Why what?"

"Why'd he give it to you?"

"Why, why," said Bushrod, gritting his teeth, wishing he could make himself shut up. "Because he didn't need it no more, that's why."

The girl looked away. "I see. Well, you must do what is best for you. I only thought.....I only thought there has been enough killin for one day."

Now there's a novel observation, thought Bushrod, but he kept himself from saying it just in time. He looked toward the open door where, if he wanted to, he could see Virgil C. lying in the grass. Then he looked at the girl again. She was frowning, turning her silver cross in her fingers. "Anna," he said.

The girl didn't look at him. "Finish your coffee," she said softly. "Then we better go on up, so you can be about your business."

Nebo and Hattie and Winder had moved the pallet near the fire, and now they sat cross-legged on it and pondered the ramrods on the hearth.

"I should like to know," said Hattie, "why you think one of these is yours, and why it makes any difference anyhow."

"Well," said Winder, "any fool ought to know that."

"Very well, smart pants," said Hattie. "Suppose you tell us."

"Well," said Winder. He looked at Nebo.

"I figured as much," said Hattie.

Nebo held up his hand. "There is a tally to be made," he said.

"A what?"

Nebo scratched his long chin; it made a bristly sound that set Hattie's nerves on edge. "That's what he told me—said there had to be a tally soon or late, said I had to find the ramrod, and not just any one would do, he said—"

"Who said?" asked Hattie.

"A man," said Nebo. He turned to Hattie with a puzzled look. "Like.....like when you carry cane to the press, and everything got to be tallied up." Nebo's face brightened suddenly. "We used to go up to Woodville with our cane—was a man there what didn't have any legs, only a plank with wheels on it he used to scoot around on—"

Winder, bored with the ramrod question, found the idea of a man on wheels to be of interest. "How did the man get up on his porch?" he asked.

"Well, he didn't have no porch," said Nebo. "Lived in a bar'l. We boys used to torment him—one time some big boys set him off down a hill, warn't but one hill in Woodville—"

"That was mean," said Hattie.

"I thought so at the time," said Nebo.

"Why do you have to make a tally now?"

Nebo's face went sad again, and he turned once more to the fire. He stared into it a long time while Hattie and Winder waited. Without knowing it, they grew closer together, all three of them huddling in the firelight. Hattie could smell the man's odor. He smelled like a dog that had been out in the rain. Winder smelled like smoke and little-boy sweat. The fire flickered and danced and threw their shadows on the wall; outside, something scraped across the boards of the landing. It came right up to the door and stopped. "Sister....." whispered Winder. The girl was about to reply when Nebo Gloster opened his mouth and screamed.

The sound of it came flapping out of the dark like the sudden swoop of an owl; there were no words but the language was older than words—it was fear, a tongue children understand better than anyone. Nebo howled, flung his hands up while his mouth worked to make the sound and his eyes grew wide. Hattie, her heart pounding, knew what he was seeing: something beyond the fire, something squatting on the other side. She had seen it herself in the nights. Winder pressed against her and hid his face. "Don't," Hattie said, pushing at Nebo's arm. "Stop it! You are scarin us!"

"I seen it all once," said Nebo. His breath was coming in shallow gasps and his eyes glittered wet in the firelight. Hattie realized he was crying, the tears began to roll down his cheeks in big drops like the rain in summer did. "Oh, I seen it happen—it busted his head open an'.....an' I run, I run." His voice dropped then, and he pointed with his long forefinger at whatever he saw across the fire. "I run, run like everything, wanted.....wanted to get somewheres away from where it was. So I run away out into the fields and pretty soon it was all fire out there, fire and smoke, and I run right through it. Then I hid out. Found some little woods—it was a good place, but he found me after dark—"

The children watched him, feeling the dark coming.

"Oh, yes," said Nebo, his voice quieter now. "I hearn his horse comin through the dead leaves—*chuff, chuff, chuff*—and I hearn the creakin of his harness—he was lookin for me. Then I seen him by the light of the stars—seen him turn his head at me, seen his eyes, seen the stars through his head where it was blowed clean away—"

"I want to go, sister," said the boy.

"Hush, Winder," said Hattie.

Nebo's hands shaped something in the air above them. "He told me all about what I done back yonder, said there would have to be a tally for that—but I couldn't remember, it were somethin awful. It weren't my fault." He looked at Hattie. "It weren't my fault, was it?"

"I'm sure not," said Hattie in a whisper.

"What'd you do?" sniffed the boy.

Nebo shook his head. "I never meant to do it—honest injun. Them boys, they was good to me mostly—"

Nebo Gloster began to sob. "I got to find it," he said, and fluttered his hands over the ramrods on the hearth. Winder, too, began to cry, and Hattie wished she could as well, but Mama and Anna were not here and there was no one else, so she patted Nebo's arm and said, "Hush, now. Hush, and we will find it."

"We won't never!" wailed Nebo.

Hattie remembered the little oval of glass in her hand. "Now don't," she said to Nebo. "Hush, hush. You want to look through the glass? You want to look at the fire through the glass?" She held out her hand, nudged the man with it. "See?"

Nebo's crying died away, he whimpered and coughed and finally blew his nose on the tail of his officer's frock. Then he looked shyly at the girl's outstretched hand and the dark glimmer of the lens. "Well, you don't care?" he said.

"'Course not," said Hattie. "Here." She took his hand and pressed the glass into his palm.

Nebo turned the glass over in his hand.

"Go ahead," said Hattie. "It's magic, just like you said."

Nebo's face relaxed. He lifted the glass to the fire. "This is the derndest thing," he said.

Anna followed Bushrod up the stairs. She let him go as slow as he needed; all the way he clung to the banister like an old woman. The treads creaked under his bare feet.

Anna understood that she had probably made a mistake. Down below, when she had asked a simple question about the man's pistol, a dark fire had jumped up in him. Not so much on the outside; he had stopped himself, or seemed to, and backed away from it. But she'd seen it on the inside, licking up into his good eye, the flame like a serpent's tongue out of some deep place she couldn't know about. She ought to have walked away from him then, found somebody sane, or at least a little less mad, just walked away, leave him talking to himself. And she would have too, except he said her name.

Anna, he said. That was all. There was not even the courtly "Miss" that most men tacked onto it, nothing but the name itself, as if there were no distance at all between them. She ought to have been insulted, probably would be one day when time had rebuilt all the fences that people kept around themselves, that the battle and the long night had broken down and scattered. She would be insulted one day, remembering, telling how a strange boy in the ruins of the hall had spoken so freely—

But maybe not. Maybe she would remember it in another way. Maybe she would keep it for herself, and never tell it at all.

However it would be, away off in that other time, right now the boy was alive and toiling ahead of her up the stairs, and no doubt the dark flame was still eating at him, and if that were so, she had probably made a mistake and God might know what was going to happen but it wasn't likely He would tell her, just let her find out for herself. *If I could only cuss,* she thought wearily. *If only I knew the words, and how to use them—*

The soldier stopped, and Anna ran into him. "Oh," she said. "What's the matter?"

The boy didn't answer. He was breathing hard.

"Are you dizzy? You need to rest?"

He turned his face to her. Yes, it was there, still flickering: it was on the outside now, in the lines of his face and in his voice when he spoke.

"Jesus," he said. "You come up here beside me and stay close."

Anna realized then that they had come to the landing. She moved up beside him, took his arm without thinking, not caring now if she'd made a mistake or not as long as he was there to hold on to because if he wasn't there would be no going on.

It was even worse than she remembered. Daylight had found its way here somehow, but it was cheerless and gray and held no promise of anything and it clung to the walls and the shapes of men like a gray scum. It illuminated the silence—no moaning or talk or babble here now, no movement—and the hundreds of eyes in the blackened faces that turned towards them, the dull, resentful, unblinking eyes of dying foxes. Woodsmoke, riven by a single spear of light from a broken shutter, hovered in a cloud on the ceiling. The smoke had run the wasps away, it stung the eyes and choked the breath and hung heavy with the stink of blood. On the other side of the hall, a thousand leagues away, was the closed door behind which Hattie and Winder lay sleeping.

"That door," whispered Anna. "That is where we must go."

But the boy didn't seem to hear. He was looking out over the landing, his breath coming hard, and she felt the muscles in his arm go taut. "Look at em," he said. "I never saw anything like it. Like so many hogs crawled up here to die."

She felt his arm move, looked down, saw him draw the pistol from his waistband. "Wait a minute—" she said.

"Look at em," he said. "Think they can just crawl up here—"

"You don't have to do that," said Anna and she put her hand on the pistol and he jerked it away. His injured eye had come unglued and it stared at her like a red marble. His nose was running blood again, and when he grinned at her she saw that his teeth were rimmed with scarlet.

"You don't know," he said, grinning. "You don't know anything about it."

"Please," she said. "Bushrod. Please."

"Oh, no," he said. He waved the pistol. "Look at em! Look at what they come to! And Virgil C. layin out there in the grass—"

"Who? Bushrod, don't—I just need you to clear a way for me, I just wanted—"

"Oh, yes," said Bushrod Carter. "Oh, I'll clear a way all right, they got to be cleansed of this, they got to be.....they got to know—"

"Don't! Don't!" Anna pleaded, pulling his arm. But he jerked that away too, and suddenly she was standing alone, watching him move out onto the landing, and all she could do was go after him because the mistake was hers and there couldn't be any going back down.

The first man he came to he kicked viciously in the ribs. "Get up!" he said, and kicked the man again and the man cursed him and pushed away and Bushrod cocked the pistol and jammed the muzzle against the man's forehead. "Do you want to die right here? Call *me* a son bitch!" and the man rose to his hands and knees, then to his feet, the pistol following.

"Jesus Christ!" said the man, and lurched toward the stairwell.

"What is the matter with you?" cried Anna. "Don't you see—"

The wounded man collapsed and fell headlong down the stairs and Bushrod watched him, grinning. He shook his head violently, as if to clear it, and drops of blood spattered on Anna's cheek. "We are all in hell," he told her, waving the pistol. "This is the place they told you about—they are all dead, all the boys are dead—"

"No!" said Anna. "They are not all—"

But Bushrod raised the pistol, and for an instant she thought he would strike her and she raised her hands.

"Don't be tellin *me*, goddammit," he said. "But don't you worry—I can raise the dead, I done it lots of times—make em walk again, just like before." He turned again, forgetting her, and shouted into the hall. "How 'bout it boys! You think you could crawl up here and die and all them dead on the works yonder, like soldiers? Well, think again, by God! Rise up, it's Judgment Day!"

He began to kick among the prostrate men, at those who were hurt and those who were not, until voices cried out and the whole mass began to move, writhe, again just like Anna remembered. Bushrod struck with the pistol, kicking and swearing, and Anna followed him toward the closed door and she saw men beginning to rise, shaking their fists and threatening, but afraid of the pistol and the madness, and other men crawling about blindly, moaning, uttering names of ones who might help them if they were only there. And the dead, meanwhile, watched it all with cloudy, indifferent eyes. One of these lay abandoned in Bushrod's path, a middle-aged man who might have been a storekeeper once upon a time, or a bank clerk, or a schoolmaster. Bushrod regarded him with disgust. "Get up, damn you!" he said, and kicked the body, but it only sighed and lay unresisting and Bushrod began to kick it again and again. "Get up, goddamn you! It's the last reveille, by God!" and hammered at the dead face with his heel until something broke.

She could stand no more. With a cry, Anna pushed her way into the hall, it was only a few steps now and in an instant she was at the door, fumbling for the knob; she flung open the door, nearly fell through it, slammed it behind her, and there were Hattie and Winder and—

"Anna!" cried the children, and ran to her and wrapped their arms around her legs, almost knocking her down, and she was looking at a fantastic figure swaying by the fireplace, a man in a straw hat with shoes dangling from his neck—

"Hidy!" said the man.

And she and the children were pushed into the room by the opening door and the fantastic man fell to his knees and put up his hands and wailed, "Not me! I didn't do nothin!" and Bushrod was there beside her, panting, his face wild with recognition—

"Nebo Gloster, you son of a bitch!" howled Bushrod, and raised the pistol.

CHAPTER TEN

"Enough!" cried Anna. "Now that is enough! It is murder, and in front of these children!"

"Oh, call it what you will," said Bushrod. His voice was calm, he held the pistol almost casually in Nebo's face. Nebo himself knelt with his eyes closed, waiting for the last sound he would ever hear.

Anna pushed the children toward the bed, motioning with her hands, but her eyes never left Bushrod's face. She took a step toward him. "Yes," she said. "I will call it what it is—murder and butchery. You are a butcher, just like all the rest."

"You are right," said Bushrod. "Murder and butchery is my trade, and I am damn good at it."

Nebo groaned. "He tolt me there'd be a tally! He said the time would come!"

"Shut up," said Bushrod.

Anna moved another step closer. Bushrod tried to ignore her, but his eyes kept traveling to her face. "Let me alone," he said. "You don't know—"

Anna was close enough to touch him now. "Know what?" she said.

"You don't *know*—"

"Know *what*!" Anna spat the words in Bushrod's face. "I'll tell you what I know! That you are mad, that you are a coward and a murderer! You call yourself a soldier! You are not fit to wear that coat, to be in the same house with—"

"No, *he* is the murderer, goddammit!" cried Bushrod. "*He* is the coward! He shot Virgil C. and run off!"

"Oh, it's a-comin," moaned Nebo Gloster. "It's a-comin all right—"

"Shut up, Nebo," said Bushrod. "Just shut up a minute!"

"Look at him," said Anna. "Look at him, Bushrod. Whoever he is, whatever he did, you cannot kill him and still call yourself a man."

"But—"

"No," said Anna. She put out her hand, closed it over the frame of the pistol, her thumb under the cocked hammer. "There has been enough killin for one day."

Bushrod began to rub his forehead with the back of his injured hand. He sniffed at the blood in his nose. When he exhaled, a bright red bubble popped at his nostril. Then he looked at Anna. "Take your hand away," he said quietly.

"Bushrod—"

"Take your hand away. I got to lower the hammer."

She pulled back her hand and closed it around the silver cross. Bushrod lowered the hammer with the web of his thumb; he regarded the pistol a moment, then dropped it to the floor. Anna watched his face slacken, the tightness around his jaws fall away, the dark flame gutter out at last. He looked around, puzzled, as if he'd just awakened in a strange room. "Where is this place?" he said.

Anna took a step back. "You son of a bitch," she said, and struck him hard, backhanded, across the face.

"God a'mighty!" said Winder from behind the bed.

"Winder McGavock!" said Hattie.

There was an interval of silence then, punctuated by a whir of machinery in the bowels of the mantel clock. The clock struck ten times, and they waited in the tableau until it ceased. Then Bushrod let out his breath. "Oh, me," he said. "I didn't think it was so late."

"That clock hasn't ever worked," Anna said softly.

Nebo Gloster lowered his hands and regarded Bushrod with suspicion. "Say, ain't you gone shoot me?" he asked.

"Jesus Christ," said Bushrod. "No, I ain't gone shoot you. Great God."

Hattie and Winder came out from behind the bed. "You ain't goin to sure enough?" asked Winder.

"Don't say 'ain't'," said Hattie.

The children went to Nebo where he was still kneeling on the floor. Hattie took his bony hand. "It's all right now," she said. "Cousin Anna has saved you."

"I thought you was a goner for sure," said Winder.

"Well," said Nebo. "Say, what become of that glass?"

Meanwhile, Bushrod had moved to the bed and was clinging to the bedpost as he had to the newel post down below.

"Are you feelin dizzy?" said Anna.

"It's hard to tell," said Bushrod. "I feel so compre*hensively* bad that it's hard to pick out just any one thing. Do you know what I would give to be able to crawl in this bed for about a week?"

Anna blushed. "I am sorry I struck you," she said.

"No you ain't," said Bushrod gently.

"Well, maybe a little," said Anna. She drew the handkerchief from her sleeve, it was stiff with blood and she had to shake it out. "Look here," she said, and Bushrod turned and she began to wipe the blood from his mustache, his mouth, his chin. "I do not intend to have to do this again today," she said.

Bushrod winced as she daubed at his nose. "Anyway, I deserved it for bein such an ass. I thought.....well, I thought it would be different. It is a common failin of mine."

"Let it go," said Anna. "It is all over now."

"Yes, I suppose it is. All over. Jesus."

Anna stepped back, twisting the handkerchief in her hands. "Bushrod—" she began, then stopped, composed herself, spoke again: "It is all right to grieve, I would not try to tell you otherwise. Only.....there is no use in blamin yourself."

"You think that's what I'm doin?"

"Yes."

"Why?"

"Because.....because you are alive. Would it fix anything if you were out there with—what's his name?—Virgil C.?"

"Anna," he said, and put out his hand to touch her but she backed away. He smiled and dropped his hand. "All right," he said. "But what you say is true, and I thank you."

Anna looked away. "It is I who ought to be thankin you. For bringin me up here, I mean."

"Oh, me," he said. "I wish I could do it over—"

"You can't do anything over!" said Anna, louder than she meant to. "That's what I'm tellin you, boy!" Then she caught herself, looked down at her hands. "I got to get another handkerchief," she said. "You have about worn this one out."

"Well, here," said Bushrod. He unwound the officer's silk handkerchief from his finger. "Now, take it easy, I won't bite you," he said, and touched the handkerchief to the blood on Anna's cheek, his own blood. Anna stood stiffly while he wiped it away. Then he held the handkerchief out. "Take this," he said.

She took it in her hand.

"It is a memento of the battle," he said, then added: "For the fair."

"What?"

Now it was Bushrod who looked away.

"Oh, you," said Anna, blushing again. *Damn them all and their gallant ways*— "My, it is hot in here!" Anna said. "Do let me open a window."

She moved to the windows and flung back the shutters, the light and air poured in and suddenly the little bedroom looked seedy and rumpled and tired, as rooms will after a long night. "Hattie!" she said. "Leave that poor man alone and come make up this counterpane before Mister Carter bleeds all over it. And you, Winder—take that pallet out on the gallery, and don't be botherin those men out there." She moved about, fussing with candlesticks, plumping up pillows. She found the hearth broom and moved to the fireplace. "What are all these things?" she asked.

Bushrod, too, was looking at the hearth. "Those are ramrods," he said, and looked at Nebo.

Nebo Gloster seemed much smaller than the last time Bushrod had seen him, as if the long night had shriveled him. His eyes under the straw hat were puffy and bloodshot, his hands were trembling, his feet looked as if he'd walked through briars. He lifted one of his long, bloody feet and scratched his shin with it. "Them are mine," he said, "but you can have em if you want."

Bushrod pushed away from the bed and came to Nebo and took the lapels of the officer's frock coat in his hands. The other shrank back, pulled his head into his collar like a turtle.

"Nebo Gloster," said Bushrod, "do you remember killin Virgil C. Johnson?"

Nebo looked away. Bushrod shook him. "*Do you remember killin Virgil C. Johnson!*"

"Bushrod!" said Anna, but Bushrod ignored her.

"Look at me!" said Bushrod, and shook the man again.

"I was tryin to clear my piece," said Nebo. "Like you told me." Then he began to cry.

"Ah, my God," said Bushrod, and let him go. He looked down at the ramrods. "What are you doin with these?"

Nebo wiped at his eyes. "Well," he said, "he told me I had to find mine again. These are all the ones—"

Bushrod looked up. "Who told you?" Then he waved his hands. "No, no, never mind—I don't want to know." He bent over the ramrods, shuffled through them, they clanged and rattled on the hearth. Finally he chose one, held it up. "Here. This one's yours. This is the one. Take it."

Nebo took it, his eyes wide with astonishment. "How'd you know?"

"I just know," said Bushrod. "I know everything there is to know about a ramrod. Now go on, go somewheres. Maybe Miss Anna will take you out on the gallery."

"Well.....I thank ye," said Nebo. "It's a relief."

Bushrod waved him away.

Anna came then, took Nebo by the arm. "Come on," she said gently. She turned him toward the open window.

"Wait a minute!" said Bushrod.

He came to Nebo, lifted one of the shoes that still hung around the man's neck. "Where'd you get these?"

Nebo hunched his shoulders. "Traded a feller for em," he said.

"Well, they look to be about my size," said Bushrod, and lifted the shoes over Nebo's head. Anna shot him a glance. "Oh, peace," said Bushrod. "He ain't ever wore shoes his whole entire life."

"Don't say 'ain't'," said Anna, and led Nebo out to the gallery.

When she returned, Bushrod was sitting on the floor with Winder beside him. He had pulled on the stiff gray socks he'd found in one of the shoes, and he and Winder were contemplating the shoes themselves, which lay before them like two slabs of granite.

"These are my shoes," said Bushrod, shaking his head.

"I suppose you know everything about shoes as well?" said Anna.

"Ol' Nebo stole the shoes right off his feet," said Winder. "While he was layin wounded on the field."

"Hush," said Bushrod. "You don't have to be tellin everything."

Winder motioned to Anna, she came and knelt beside them and Winder took her hand. "Mister Bushrod was in the battle, and he smote em hip and thigh," said the boy.

Hattie was sitting on the bed. "He was struck down in his prime," she told Anna.

"Tragically," said Bushrod. "Don't forget that part."

"Oh, yes—tragical."

Anna shook her head. "Tragical, indeed. Mister Carter, I am gone five minutes and you have already done a day's worth of lyin."

"Well, they wanted to know of my adventures."

"Hmmm." She looked at his hand, remembering what the surgeon had said. "We need to do somethin about that."

"It does throb some," said Bushrod, cradling his arm.

"I have just the thing." Anna rose, went to the wardrobe and opened it, searched for a moment and came out with a little stoppered jug. "Cousin John keeps this for the humors," she explained.

"Now, hold on a minute—"

"Let me see your finger."

So Bushrod held out his hand and Anna poured some of the clear liquid over the shot-away joint.

"Jesus *Christ*," said Bushrod, and pulled his finger away. Winder laughed.

"Bushrod Carter," Anna said, "your language is—"

"Oh, never mind—it is the way old soldiers talk. Let me borrow that jug, if you please."

Anna gave him the jug, he turned it up and took a long swallow. When he brought the jug down, he gagged and shook his head. "Works better from the inside," he said to Winder.

There was a knock at the door. Anna gave Bushrod a fearful look, but he only grinned—the whiskey had washed the blood from the edges of his teeth. "Might as well let em in—it's been pretty dull lately," he said.

Anna went to the door. She opened it, and a man with the collar star of a Confederate Major stepped into the room. When he saw Anna, he smiled and swept off his forage cap. "Well, my goodness," he said.

Bushrod gaped in astonishment. "R.K., as I live and breathe!"

The Major laughed, his tired, congenial eyes crinkling at the corners. "Heard you was up here, Bushrod—knew there couldn't be two fellers with such a name." He turned to Anna. "I am Major R.K. Cross, provost and gentleman, at your service. Your gracious aunt—"

"Cousin," said Anna. She held up the jug. "Would you have a drink?"

An hour later, Bushrod Carter stood on the broad lower gallery, hunting in his waistcoat pocket for a Lucifer match. He was feeling better, had washed his face and hands and gotten his finger properly bound. Winder had followed him down; the boy stood beside him now, Bushrod's haversack and canteen crossed over his narrow shoulders. The haversack nearly dragged the boards.

"I got pipe and tobacco," said Bushrod to the boy. "You keep a watch over these other things 'til I call for em. Can you do that?"

"Yes, sir," said the boy.

"Splendid. Now, go back to Miss Anna and look after her—God knows she needs it. There's a good lad."

The boy saluted. "Forward," he said, "for Clayton's knows no other!"

"*Cleburne's*," said Bushrod. "Like I told you."

The boy saluted again and disappeared into the house.

Bushrod found one of the matches Jack Bishop had left him and lit his pipe. Before him, sitting on the balustrade, his hand draped casually over the hilt of his saber, was Major R.K. Cross of the cavalry. He, too, was smoking. Major Cross had done Bushrod a good turn upstairs; he had told Anna a long-winded anecdote from their University days, and though Anna had blushed a little at the text, she seemed impressed to learn that Bushrod was a bona-fide University man. It was just one more reason for Bushrod to feel better.

Bushrod crossed the gallery and leaned on the balustrade by the Major. "Well," he said, "how you like bein provost, bullyraggin us poor fellows around, scarin the women and children—"

"Hah!" said the Major. "You just better be glad it's me. Say, what was you doin up there anyhow with that *good*-lookin green-eyed cousin?"

Bushrod grinned. "Why, sodierin," he said.

"I have never heard it called that," said the Major. He drew on his pipe. "By the way, all that talk of the University reminds me—did you boys hear that Oxford was burned?"

"No!" said Bushrod. "When?"

"Back in the summer. Late August it was."

"It couldn't of been Uncle Billy, he was chasin us through Georgia then."

"No, 'twas Smith from over in the west somewheres. We was in that campaign, skirmished with him all the month, but he drove us south of town finally and put the torch to it. I mean there was not one brick left atop another."

"Good God," said Bushrod. "The college, too, I reckon?"

"No, I am told old Quinche saved it almost single-handed. Can you imagine?"

Bushrod could easily imagine. He and Major Cross had suffered torments in Latin recitation under the eye of Professor Alexander Quinche.

"Old Quinche. I'll be damned," said Bushrod. Saying the man's name was like opening a trunk and finding something lost. Bushrod's good mood slipped a little.

The Major slapped at a wasp. "Damn these things," he said.

"They was God's plenty of em upstairs," said Bushrod.

"Don't I know it. My daddy once remarked that a wasp is the only creature that's born mad, and dies mad, and never is anything *but* mad his whole life long."

"Yes," said Bushrod, "I believe he was correct."

They pondered that a moment, watching the swatted wasp circle aimlessly at their feet. They watched trance-like, as tired men will do, the struggles of the wasp pushing everything else from their minds. Finally the Major shook himself out of it.

"See here, Carter, let's change the subject. Tell me all about that girl up there, Miss Anna. She is awfully sweet to look at."

"Just never you mind about her, R.K.," said Bushrod.

"Hah!" said the Major. "I'll bet she's tellin her aunt about me right now."

"She don't even *know* you."

"Well, what difference does that make?"

"Listen, Major," said Bushrod, "you have not seen her at charge-bayonet. She is a piece of work, I'll tell you."

"Well, ain't they all?" said the Major.

Bushrod thought they probably were. As the Major began a story about one of his romantic interludes on campaign, Bushrod looked down at his hand and remembered how he'd given Anna the silk handkerchief. Now there was a bold thing, too bold by half. Then there was all that business with the yahoos on the landing, and with Nebo and the pistol. She must think him a damn fool, University man or not.

But then, what difference did it make? In a few days, maybe even tomorrow, he and Jack and Virgil C. would be dodging cavalry patrols, shying for the old Trace road and home. But, no, that wasn't right—Virgil C. wouldn't be dodging any patrols. They would have to bury him here and come back for him later. But then, how would he keep? He wouldn't, of course, not even in the wintertime. They would have to come back and get whatever there was left of him—have to dig him up, dig up old Virgil C. out of the cold ground—

"Oh, Christ," groaned Bushrod.

"What is it?" said the Major. "Are you hurtin?"

"No, no," said Bushrod. "Just thinkin."

"Well, quit thinkin," said the Major. "It ain't good for you."

"Oh, I am so goddamn sick and tired of this business."

"I know, boy. Well, if you got to think, why don't you think on Miss Anna for a while. That ought to right you up."

Yes, it ought to, thought Bushrod, and it did, a little. If he never laid eyes on her again, at least he'd been chosen for a little while, though he'd acted like a fool. Such madness, and in the middle of it all the memory of Anna handing him a cup of coffee, wiping his face—

But tomorrow he would be gone, and there was an end on it. Still, they did have to come back for Virgil C. and maybe he could see her then. They could get a spring wagon from Uncle Relbue and a good strong box from the undertaker, and they would come back next winter when the roads were hard and there wouldn't be so much of Virgil C. left to dig up. He could see the girl then, maybe—she didn't have to know he deserted, he could make up a story. But then, she didn't live here all the time. She said she was from Fayetteville—where the hell was that?

But maybe he would go and talk to Anna again before he left. Yes— he would go and tell her what he meant to do, even put it to her why he was done with soldiering and why he and Jack ought to go home now. What did he have to lose?

The thought of seeing Anna again made him feel better. It would be good to tell her the truth, too—just as soon as he figured out what it was. For now, he would quit thinking about it. He looked around in his mind for other things to worry about, and he found the army there.

With the coming of daylight, the catastrophe that had befallen the Army of Tennessee was apparent to every soldier on the field. Bushrod had not seen the field, but he had seen the wreckage at the great brick house, and he knew that it was all over at last. Bushrod put that down as something he would tell to Anna.

It was so strange, the coming of day in this place. Every field hospital was a shambles after a big fight, but almost always you could feel the army beyond it, pulling itself together, telling itself that tomorrow was another day. This time Bushrod, an old soldier who knew of such things, could not hear the army beyond this yard. There was only a great stillness out there, over the field of Franklin.

"You are thinkin dark thoughts again," said the Major.

"Yes, I suppose I am." Bushrod gestured toward the yard with his pipestem. "Look out there, Major. And I am told we *won* this fight."

The Major laughed, but without humor this time. "Oh, yes. And directly we shall all go up to Nashville and whip them again."

Bushrod looked at his friend in astonishment. "What? You are foolin. This army is—"

"Oh, we shall go up to Nashville, and the gallant Hood, like a pillar of fire, shall lead us." He raised his hand toward the river. "'And I looked, and behold a pale horse: and his name that sat on him was Death, and Hell followed with him.'"

"Yes," said Bushrod. He closed his eyes, trying to remember the words. "'And I beheld, and lo a black horse: and he that sat on him.....had a pair of.....' What?"

"Balances," said the Major. He slid down from the balustrade. "Balances, to weigh all us poor soldier boys against duty and honor and—oh, all the rest. Well, there'll be a reckonin all right, but not here. Last night I thought it surely was, but I was wrong. It'll be up yonder, on the Cumberland."

Bushrod shook his head. "No, Major. It is all over."

"For some," said the Major. He looked out at the yard, and at the dead men arranged on the gallery. "For them it is, but not for us. Unless.....well, I suppose there are some choices left, eh?"

"Yes. Some choices."

"And what do you choose, old pard?"

Bushrod did not answer right away. He thought of not answering at all, or of making up a story, or changing the subject, whatever it took to quit thinking. But he said: "Understand me, Major. I am played out. I been tried in the balances, and that little river just yonder is as far as I mean to go."

"I see," said the Major. He smiled. "Hell of a thing to be tellin the provost officer."

"I'm just glad it's you."

The Major laughed, again without humor. "Well, I'll tell you a thing that is true. Were I not so scared of Bedford Forrest, I would stay here with you. We could fight over Miss Anna instead of Nashville—she's a better prize, by a damn sight."

"I am played out," said Bushrod.

"I know," said the Major. "It is all right with me. But, goin home, see that you don't get captured—they ain't givin paroles anymore. Now, let me trouble you for one of those Lucifers."

Bushrod passed the little box to his friend. "I got them from Jack Bishop. You remember him?"

"Why, I should say so. I recall the time—"

"I ain't seen him since yesterday. Fact is, I am on my way to hunt for him now."

The Major was lighting his pipe. "What happened in the fight?" he asked around the pipestem. "You never told me."

"Damn if I know, R.K.," said Bushrod. He rubbed his forehead. "I don't recall much of it. Seems like we got up on their works though."

"Whose boys were you?"

"Um, Captain Sullivan's company of the Twenty-first. Mississippi, I mean. Adams' Brigade. We was with Loring."

"Adams," mused the Major. "Was there a big cotton gin behind the works, do you remember?"

Bushrod waved his hand. "Somethin, yes. I think we got up on the works there, some of the boys did."

Major Cross took Bushrod by the arm. "Come."

He led Bushrod toward the west end of the gallery, where it jutted out beyond the house. Men were standing there, silent, and in the yard were many others, queued up like mourners at a funeral. They, too, were silent, and held their hats in their hands.

"Make way, lads," said the Major softly to the backs of those on the gallery. "Make way, there."

The men parted, and Major Cross led Bushrod to the front. "There is your General Adams," he said.

Five bodies were laid out on this end of the gallery, heels together, hands crossed on their breasts. They were disheveled, soiled, with that shapelessness that all the war's Departed had, as if they'd been dropped from a great height into the midst of the living.

"Which one?" asked Bushrod, for he honestly didn't know. He had not seen much of General Adams in life.

"There," said the Major, pointing.

Bushrod examined the dead face. "He was our general, he led us away to die, and died himself, and I don't know him. Great God, this is a hard trade."

"He died on the works, I am told," said the Major. "They say his mount is still up there, along with most of your brigade. You all made quite a show, you infantry."

"Perhaps Jack is up there," said Bushrod. "He might be lookin for me up there."

"No doubt," said the Major softly.

"Who is that one?" Bushrod asked. He pointed to a body with an embroidered handkerchief over its face. The man's legs were covered in mud, and he was barefoot.

"Ah," said the Major. "That is Cleburne."

"Impossible!" said Bushrod flatly. "Now you are mistaken."

"No, it is he," said the Major. He gestured toward the men in the yard. "These were his boys. There is no mistake."

"General Cleburne," said Bushrod. He wiped his eyes on the sleeve of his jacket. "My God, Major—I can't....."

"I know," said the Major. "You all were with him once, as I recall."

"Yes, we were his boys, oh, once upon a time. He was brave. He was the bravest, the best of them all, and now he is dead."

"He is among good company," said the Major.

"He came to our fire once. I watched him sittin there, and I thought, 'the royal captain of this ruined band.' That's just what I thought. Now look at him! They didn't even leave him his boots, fuckin sons of bitches. Look at him—and what's the use in it? Tell me that, Major."

Cross took Bushrod's arm and turned him away. "If I could tell you that, would it make a farthin's worth of difference?"

"Maybe. Maybe it would goddammit." Bushrod wanted to look back at the General again, but the men had already closed around him.

"Look here," said the Major. "Why don't you lay up for a while. Then you can find Jack—"

"Jack is not dead!" said Bushrod suddenly.

"I never said he was."

Bushrod began to rub his forehead again. By now he'd rubbed some of the skin off, and his fingers left little smears of blood.

"You *are* played out, ain't you," said Major Cross. "Well, go hunt for our old pard then—but don't you all go runnin off until I see you again. Jack Bishop still owes me three dollars he borrowed off me in Memphis once. We was at the—"

"See you again?" said Bushrod. "Not in Tennessee, we won't."

"Shoot," said the Major. "We'll be back through here in about a week with the whole Yankee nation on our heels, see if we ain't. Probably pass you on the road—mind you don't get trampled."

Bushrod laughed. "*You* mind, and watch your ramblin ass."

"Never fear," said the Major. He smiled his broad smile, the corners of his eyes crinkling. "The day ain't dawned I can't outrun a tribe of cheese-eaters."

The two soldiers, officer and man, shook hands on the gallery. Bushrod went down the steps into the yard, walked a few paces and turned again. "Major!"

"Yes, old boy?"

Bushrod slouched to attention and raised his hand, palm outward, in the nonchalant salute of the Southern infantryman. "The Army of Tennessee," he said.

The Major grinned and raised his hand in return.

Bushrod turned back into the yard. He was dizzy and sick at heart, and the whole littered field of Franklin lay before him. But no matter, for Jack was out there somewhere, and it was still early in the day. In fact, Bushrod needn't have worried; though he didn't know it, he had but a little way to go.

The sun rose and burned away the ghostly mist that clung to the hollows. It promised a fair day, and a cool one.

Anna Hereford stood at the balustrade of the upper gallery and looked toward the trees where she'd glimpsed the battle the day before. Already, she thought, it belonged to yesterday. The Big Thing had happened, and now it was passing away like the cars on the Nashville railroad, leaving them all behind to clean up the shambles, to remember or to forget as they chose.

Major Cross, the provost, had brought order to the upper rooms. The dead were removed, the quick (including Bushrod Carter) shooed downstairs. The badly wounded were laid out in rows to await the attention of the surgeons who were setting up now in the front bedroom, under the windows where the light was fair. Anna had opened the windows herself, flung open all the windows and shutters in the upstairs rooms. It was still bad, and men still suffered, and plenty of blood would soak into the floors yet—but it would not be the smoky purgatory she had feared in the night.

Now Anna stood on the gallery, allowing herself to believe in the simple, faithful coming of the day. She'd washed her face and hair, put on her stockings, changed her dress. The dress she wore now was yellow, a summer dress really, but she had wanted a bright color. So she stood on the gallery in her fresh yellow dress, looking out toward the river and the gray, barren trees, and wondered what she would keep in her heart.

She thought of the battle and tried to fix in her mind what it had been like: the smoke, the demon wail of the Rebels and the hurrahs of the Northern men, the unbroken reverberation of the guns. She would keep that always.

She thought, too, on the long night watches, on the faces and voices and hands suspended in candlelight, and the blood. She thought of the bearded man, the sufferers on the landing, the way her cousin's hands had looked when the dawn first touched them. These things, too, she would keep.

She thought of Bushrod Carter. She took his silk handkerchief from her sleeve, the one he had given her, still crusted with his blood. A memento of the battle, he had said. For the fair, he had said. Anna blushed at the memory. What business did he have saying that? She picked at the dried blood, thought *I will never get this out*. But that was all right, there were plenty of things you couldn't wash blood out of: handkerchiefs, hardwood floors, memory. Still you went on, taking the blood, taking whatever else you could.

The thought of Bushrod made Anna's nerves flutter in a way she would not have expected; she put it off to weariness, to release from the long night, to the knowledge that all her feelings hovered just under the surface on this morning when the world she had known was vanished forever. Yet even as she dismissed her feelings, she knew it was a lie—convenient and practical and safe, but a lie nevertheless. Bushrod Carter spoke to her from behind a door she'd not opened in a long time, and would not have opened by herself. Damn Circumstance then, who had brought him out of the night—him, among all this ragged host—and laid him at the foot of the stairs.

When Major Cross had chased Bushrod downstairs, she had almost stopped him. But then she'd not been ready to admit that there was something unfinished, some words not yet spoken that would send him out of her life as abruptly as he'd entered it. That was the thing, she told herself: she had to close the door, put him away with that other face, that other voice, that dwelt in the darkness there, and fix the lock again. But that, too, was a lie.

The fact was, she wanted to talk to him. She had known so few soldiers really, and none like him—they were all a mystery to her that the events of the night had only deepened. Maybe this boy could explain it all to her: why they had come, how they could do what they did, why they brought ruin in the name of something else. Yet even that was not all, and she smiled at the notion that even she would have to admit it sooner or later, so it might as well be now. She wanted to see if he would call her fair again.

Anna laughed out loud and chided herself for a fool. The boy would be gone tomorrow, most likely was gone already, out looking for his regiment so he could go with them across the river, chasing after the Yankees and whatever it was that drew them on. Gone for good, having closed the door himself whether she was ready or not. And that was all right. It would have to be all right.

Down below, the yard was crowded with soldiers—Anna could hardly imagine it otherwise now. With daylight there was more talk among them, even laughter, as if they were just beginning to understand that the night was over and they were alive. But there were still the suffering ones, and the dying ones, and the bloody-aproned surgeons moving among them. She wondered about the solemn men who stood hats-in-hand staring at the lower gallery—she did not know about the generals laid out there. A movement caught her eye, it was a horseman, walking his mount carefully among the wounded. No one seemed to pay him any mind; he crossed the yard and moved slowly toward the oak grove beyond. He stopped at the edge, looked back, then disappeared into the trees. At the same moment, Anna saw Bushrod.

Damn, she thought. He was not gone after all; there he was, still in reach of her voice. He was crossing the yard, smoking, a lanky boy in a short gray jacket and awful checkered breeches, so much like them all and yet not like them, because he belonged to her in a way none of the others did. The thought shocked her but she let it stand, she might as well admit that, too. She opened her mouth to call his name, but it was too late, he had already entered the grove at the place where the horseman had gone.

She stood for a moment more, pulling the silk handkerchief through her fingers. What business did he have calling her fair? How did he presume to touch her, wipe the blood from her face, speak so kindly? How could he dare to cross the yard under her very eyes when she thought he was gone for good?

"Well, damn," she said aloud, and turned quickly toward the tall open window by which they came and went to the gallery.

Nebo Gloster was still propped against the wall where she had left him, his bony, bloody feet stuck straight out before him. Anna realized that he, too, was looking out toward the grove, though she couldn't imagine what he saw. She did not think of him as a soldier, could not understand how anyone ever had, yet here he was just the same.

"Nebo," she said, "what makes you men do what you do?"

Nebo looked up with an awkward grin and shifted uncomfortably. He had his ramrod across his knees, and now he held it up for Anna to see. "I'd of never tolt it in a hundred years," he said. "Ain't that Bushrod somethin?"

"Oh, he is indeed," said Anna, and smiled, and touched the man's shoulder, and passed quickly into the house.

CHAPTER ELEVEN

When it came to religion, Bushrod Carter tried to keep everything simple. God was in heaven, Christ was the Redeemer, faith was more important than works, the saints looked out for you. He believed, too, that the Almighty took a personal interest in the affairs of men. His life over the past three years had not shaken this belief, though it well might have—Bushrod had pondered the contradictions until his head hurt, but he had never figured out how God could look down on such madness and not take a hand. The best he could do was to remind himself that men made their own troubles mostly, and that God spent a lot of time grieving Himself.

As a Freemason, Bushrod was provided with a useful metaphor: God as the Great Architect, continually nudging the world toward a design He envisioned, while the little entered apprentices scurrying about below could only see what was in front of their noses. As a student of literature, he knew something about the Fates, who seemed to relieve God of a lot of responsibility. Finally, as an Episcopalian, Bushrod believed in the efficacy of prayer. The combination of these various perspectives accommodated nearly every occasion that arose.

Regarding prayer, Bushrod felt it was the petitioner's part to be reasonable. For example, it would be presumptuous of him to ask that Virgil C. or General Cleburne be returned to life, or that the Strangers suddenly lay down their arms and open the gates of Nashville to Major R.K. Cross. However, Bushrod thought it perfectly reasonable to bring up the matter of finding Jack Bishop.

Just within the oak grove, but out of sight of the men in the yard, Bushrod knelt stiffly on one knee and made the sign of the cross. The sun filtered down through the leafless branches, through the weaving smoke of the fires. Crows fretted by the river and somewhere a horse was scuffing the dead leaves. Bushrod looked up into the interlaced canopy above him and tried to put away all the things that were on his mind, so that nothing dwelt there but the pure light he believed God to be. It was, of course, impossible, but he studied the sky and imagined God to be listening from some rampart far beyond, and at last he began to pray.

Through all his life (around forty years—even he didn't know for sure) Nebo Gloster had seen very few women. His mother died borning him; the mulatto midwife, drunk, had squeezed Nebo's head pulling him out, then danced and lit candles while the mother bled to death. His father—goatish, ancient, crazed with corn liquor—killed the mulatto with an axe and threw her to the gars in the Homochitto River. Unfortunately, the full moon burst over the cypress just as the woman's body split the water; moreover, she floated face up, turning and turning in the sluggish current. The old man took these things together as a sign. Shaking with terror, he brought a full jug from the cabin and locked himself in the woodshed; within an hour's time he had emptied the jug, smashed it, and gouged his eyes out with a shard. By daylight he was dead.

So the infant Nebo was raised by his two hulking brothers and a wet nurse they stole from a plantation outside of Woodville. For his first eight years, the nurse—sullen, silent, vicious as a cottonmouth—was the only woman Nebo knew. Finally she made her escape into the Homochitto swamps; the brothers hunted her down with dogs and shot her. They took her fingernails and some of her hair and made a ju-ju bag and hung it on the cabin door so her ghost would stay away.

When he was nine, Nebo went to Woodville for the first time. Then, and on his subsequent yearly visits, he fled from anything, white or black, that resembled a woman. Sometimes, in town, he would watch through the gray shrunken boards of a stable or woodshed while his brothers thrashed and panted over some negro wench. They caught him at it once and, laughing, rubbed his face in the damp, fish-smelling patch between the negro's legs. He never watched again.

In time, the brothers disappeared. One went into the swamp and never came out again; the other cut himself on a piece of rusty tin and died of blood-poisoning, raving (before his jaws locked tight) that the ghost of the old nurse had come after all and was baring its shriveled dugs at the foot of the bed. It was winter when this brother died, and Nebo buried him beside the old man and the long-forgotten mother in the patch of ground where they raised their corn.

So Nebo lived on in the Homochitto bottoms, planting a little corn and cane, trapping muskrats and minding his own business until the roving Rebel cavalry caught him and introduced him to the wide world. Since then, he'd seen more women than he ever thought the world contained.

From most of these—especially the hard-looking trollops who hung around the camps—Nebo kept his distance, not so much from fear as from habit. But as time went on he began to detect a softness, a kindness, about some women to which he responded like a stray dog. He allowed himself to be lured to cabin doors and yard gates where a woman might give him a biscuit or some cornpone or a bit of salt pork; these gifts he would accept with diffidence, hanging his head in awkward silence while the woman spoke kindly to him, calling him brave, wishing him well. He'd gotten along just fine then, and decided that the thing to do was to avoid women when he could, and let them have their way when he couldn't, and maybe he could get back home again without any trouble in that regard. And he might have, too, had not Anna come along.

Anna Hereford hung in the empty, twilit reaches of Nebo's mind like a new star. When, a little while before, she had taken his arm and led him out to the gallery, Nebo had been terrified and speechless. Where she touched him, even through the fabric of the frock coat, the place burned as if a coal had been pressed there. He could still feel it, in fact, and the place on his shoulder where she'd just now laid her hand. Having lived in the woods all his life, Nebo had a rarefied sense of smell, and now the smell of Anna Hereford surrounded him like a cloud of sugar bees: the smell of the glycerin and rosewater she had rubbed on her hands, the smell of her hair, the mysterious essence of the girl herself that made her different from anyone he'd ever known. Her voice, her face, the particular way she moved—all these things illuminated an unused and unprepared chamber of Nebo's heart. He did not recognize the light, nor give it a name, but he could not ignore it.

Clutching his ramrod, Nebo rose from the floor of the gallery and hobbled over to the balustrade. For a moment, he watched the activity in the yard below, trying to comprehend what it all meant, but it made no more sense than anything else he'd seen in the great war. Then he spied Anna.

She looked so small among all the men, and her yellow dress was bright among all the drab grays and browns. She seemed to be moving with a purpose, in the direction of the oak grove that lay beyond the little burying ground. Nebo watched her a moment, tapping the ramrod against the balustrade. Something was pecking at his mind, and it made a sound like the ramrod tapping, and it had to do with the oak grove, the burying ground, the line of trees yonder—all of it seemed to fit together, but in a way Nebo couldn't grasp. It seemed like something bad had happened once, when all these images were together before, and if he wasn't careful something bad would happen here again. Nebo thought about Bushrod shaking and shaking him, saying at him *Do you remember? Do you remember?* and it seemed like he did remember something then—

Trying to think about it was like walking through an empty house. He had done that once, walked through the echoing rooms of a big house that the people had left behind. Things scurried there, just out of sight, and watched him as he wandered lost in the maze of rooms. It scared him badly, and now he was scared in just the same way. He twisted his hands around the ramrod. "Miss Anna?" he whispered. "Miss Anna?" Then, still saying her name, he turned and went through the open window behind him.

In the oak grove, a little distance from where Bushrod knelt to pray, Simon Rope was awakened by the flies swarming on his severed ear. The whole side of his face was covered in them, feeding and laying their eggs in the raw flesh. He brushed them away, and with his little finger dug out those that were trapped down in the ear itself. Then he rose, hawked and spat in the leaves, and looked about him. It promised a fair day for traveling if he wanted to travel—but he didn't really want to. Not yet.

He discovered that he had not slept alone; the corpse of a Federal soldier, killed in yesterday's skirmish, lay an arm's length away. Simon Rope ambled over, went through the man's pockets, found a cheap watch and four dollars. He added this booty to his haversack then, yawning, relieved himself on the corpse.

He was buttoning his breeches when he stopped, listened, turning his good ear to the sound. It was a horse, he thought, moving somewhere in the trees. A horse most likely meant an officer, and Simon Rope didn't want to be caught robbing even the Federal dead. It sounded close, but he could see nothing. Then he remembered how birds scratching in the underbrush could fool a man—they could sound just like a deer or a horse or a man moving. Birds, he decided. It was just birds. He spat again, slung the haversack, and moved cautiously toward the house. In a moment he could see the yard, and his eye was immediately caught by a splash of yellow moving toward him.

"Well, I'll jes be goddamned," he said, and grinned.

Sometime during the night, when it seemed that the yard and house would be overwhelmed with wounded men, one of the McGavock slaves was ordered to remove certain corpses to the privacy of the grove. It was not a job the man relished, so he worked quickly, dragging the appointed corpses out of the circle of firelight, up through the brush to a little glade he knew about. He worked too quickly, in fact; in his haste, he brought along some who were not dead and laid them out with those who were. In the dark and confusion it was not always easy to tell the difference. Now it was morning, and only one of these unfortunates was still alive. He could not move, for he had only one leg remaining, and that was broken. He was propped against the swollen body of a genuine corpse, was glued to the ground by his own congealed blood—yet somehow he lived, and as he passed in and out of awareness, the morning appeared before his eyes in installments, like a serialized novel. He took no interest in what he saw; in fact, it greatly irritated him to be conscious. He preferred to sleep, wanted only to sleep—he did not feel that was asking too much.

Then, during one of his awakenings, he discerned a vague figure in the clearing. He blinked, and at length recognized the visitor as a man he had known once, had been connected to somehow. But it was so much trouble to be connected to anything now, and he wished only for the man to go away and leave him alone. *Go away Bushrod*, he said, though he made no sound.

Bushrod stood on the edge of a grassy clearing six or seven rods in breadth and about that distance from the place where he'd knelt to pray. He had come upon it so suddenly that he startled a flock of crows; the birds rose on flapping, silken wings and settled in the branches overhead, where they croaked and muttered in complaint. Bushrod saw right away what the crows were after.

The little clearing was full of Departed, lying like jackstraws, a blur of sodden uniforms and bare feet and beards and hands, their faces meaningless shapes under the flies. From their positions (nearly all were on their backs, their shoulders hunched as if they were shrugging) they must have been dragged here and left for the crows. That was bad enough, but apparently they had not all been dead; a few had tried to crawl away, back toward the fires and voices in the yard. One of these lay face-down at Bushrod's feet; he had nearly trod on its outstretched hand when he stepped out of the trees.

It hurt him to see these pathetic, lonely creatures, and it scared him a little, too. Every field had its secret charnel places, and to come on one of these suddenly and alone was always a horror—the Departed always seemed to be watching and resentful, as if a living man had no business there. Bushrod shuddered and began to back away when his eye caught a flicker of movement. He froze, watching.

Something had moved. Bushrod knew very well that the Departed were sometimes restless—they moaned, belched, farted, sat upright, did all manner of awful things. So it might only have been that. Or it might have been a crow, made bold by the feast, or even a hog rooting around in the pile. Yet, as much as he wanted to believe it was one of these things, Bushrod knew by instinct that it probably wasn't. Somebody in the clearing was still alive. He swore to himself—he didn't have time to be fooling around, yet he couldn't just leave a man—

There! He watched the hand raise a little way, then drop limply to the ground again. That fellow was alive, though from the look of him, he wouldn't be for long. Bushrod felt sick. He didn't want to go into the clearing with all these Departed, wasn't a thing he could do, he had business of his own—

But what if it was you? he thought, and answered himself: *All right, dammit.*

He moved out into the grass, gritting his teeth, wishing he was someplace else. For an instant, Anna passed through his mind: what if she were to come upon something like this? He shook the thought away, gave a wide berth to the man who had died crawling, and approached the one who still lived.

The crows set up a terrific cawing overhead, somewhere a tree limb groaned in mournful iterance, there was a drone of flies and a first sweet hint of decay. Bushrod moved with infinite care, as if he were stalking game. He could see the man watching him now with heavy, indifferent eyes.

"Hey, podner," said Bushrod.

The mouth in the blackened face moved as if to speak, but no sound came. The hand raised again as if to wave him away.

"I will get you out of here," said Bushrod. "We'll go back to—"

He stopped. In the pale sunlight everything seemed to draw together all at once, draw down to a little bright circle around the man's face, and all at once there was no clearing, no grove, no broad fields, no universe, only Bushrod Carter walking on stiff legs through the grass saying *No, no* then *Aw, no Aw, no* then *Aw, shit Aw, shit*—

Bushrod stumbled across the little way remaining and dropped to his knees beside the dying man. "Aw, shit," he said. He touched the man's face. "Aw, shit, Jack."

Jack Bishop blinked his eyes at Bushrod. "Lemme alone," he said in a hoarse whisper. "Why ain't you dead?"

Bushrod turned his head, vomited bile onto the grass. When he turned again, Bishop pawed weakly at his jacket. Bushrod took his hand, pressed it to his cheek.

"Seen the fellow hit you," said Bishop. "But I got the son bitch, stuck his ass, don't worry—"

"It don't matter, Jack," sobbed Bushrod. "It don't matter."

"Damn flies," said Bishop.

Bushrod waved at the flies.

Bishop coughed, spat blood. "Couldn't stop for you, man, wasn't no stoppin—" He raised his head. "Say, where's that good water, I want some, where's that boy?"

"I ain't got any water," said Bushrod, "but I will get you some."

"Don't go to no trouble."

"Don't worry," said Bushrod, "I'll get you some, Jack." He stood up, too fast again, and moved in a dizzy circle, trying to think of what to do. His chest was hurting now, and his arm burned as if a nail had been driven into the elbow—he cursed and struck his arm with his fist and struck at his bandaged hand and the crows rose all at once from the branches and flapped away toward the river, crying in alarm. Then Bushrod was among the dead.

Always the dead—not the Departed now, but the dead. Like in the murky hall of the great brick house. They were free of everything, released from everything, but still they couldn't let it go. They turned on all they had ever known and mocked it, scorned and belittled it as if they'd been mistaken all along until now. They walked the earth, walked in dreams and in the light of midnight fires, mocking—

Bushrod kicked at them, pulled them over, cursed them. He caught one by its shirt and shook it; the staring eyes regarded him with astonishment. "You think that's funny?" spat Bushrod. "You got somethin to say?" The dead man exhaled a foul breath, and Bushrod flung him away.

Then he saw a blond-haired boy who still had his drum canteen. Bushrod kicked him over, grabbed him by the hair and shook him. "Hey!" he said. He slapped the smooth, rubbery face. "Hey! Get up!" But the boy didn't get up. Bushrod reached in his pocket for his clasp knife, found his good pipe there, broken. He cursed, found the knife, opened it with his teeth. "You give me that," he said, and cut the linen strap of the boy's canteen.

He stumbled out of the tangle of dead, trying to find Jack, turning in a circle while the dead mocked him. They wanted Jack, too. Wanted Bushrod, too. *No goin home now, boys—*

"Jack!" cried Bushrod, and stumbled and fell in the grass. He lay there panting, his bruised cheek pressed to the ground. It hurt, but that was good—let it hurt. Something else was moving in the grove, Bushrod could hear it, a scuffle in the leaves. That was good, too—maybe it was the Strangers rolling over the field of Franklin again, and Death riding with them on his goddamned white horse, hunting for Bushrod Carter that was missed before, and that would be fine, just fine—

And there was Jack. Bushrod crawled to him. "Here. Here's some water, goddammit." He put the tin spout of the canteen to Jack's mouth and watched as the water poured over his chin. Bishop gagged, lifted his head, coughed up a clot of blood that was almost black. He pushed the canteen away.

"That was lovely," Jack said.

Bushrod sat in the bloody grass, the canteen in his lap. He waved at the flies around Bishop's face.

"Hey, Virgil C.," said Jack.

Bushrod took the other's hand again. "Virgil C. ain't here, Jack. Virgil C. is dead, 'member? All the boys are dead."

"Bull shit. Yonder he comes right there."

Bushrod felt a quick shiver crawl up his spine. "Hush, man, don't be sayin that."

"Bushrod?" The voice was a little more than a whisper, and Bushrod bent close to hear. "Bushrod, who all them people over there?"

"Oh, my God," said Bushrod. He was crying now, he couldn't help it. He stroked the boy's hand. "Oh, Jack, it's all right, it's all right.....you are fixin to cross over, it's just the boys you see, waitin for you—"

Bishop shook his head. "No, no."

"Don't worry, pard—it'll be easy, just a little stroll across the grass, I will sit with you—"

"No, no. Virgil C.—"

"That's right, that's right. He is waitin for us, just a little.....a little....," and stopped.

Bushrod was listening now. He could hear it again: a scuffling in the leaves, like somebody dragging his feet. The sound was behind him, moving into the clearing—

That is the way he would come, he couldn't see with the front of his head blowed away—he is lookin for us, he is—

"Who is that, Bushrod?" said Jack.

Bushrod knew then that somebody really was in the clearing. If it was Virgil C.—but Bushrod couldn't make himself look around. It was like a nightmare, where just so long as you didn't turn your head—

Then another sound came, a whimper, like a thing in pain, and Bushrod felt the fear like a galvanic shock, and he thought *Damn you, Virgil C. Johnson* and before he knew what he was doing he turned—

"Great God!" cried Bushrod, and struggled to his feet, his heart pounding.

High clouds raced across the sun, driven by winds aloft. A shadow passed over the yard of the great brick house as Nebo emerged from the back door and collided with Colonel John McGavock on the gallery.

"Beg your pardon," said McGavock, and watched as Nebo passed across the gallery without a word.

The cadaverous figure of Nebo Gloster stalking across the yard—barefoot, in a bloody frock coat and straw hat, carrying a ramrod like a mute's baton—stirred even the jaded imaginations of the soldiers. They turned to watch him, and those in his path shrank away as if confronted by an animated corpse. Nebo took no notice of them. He moved swiftly, gliding along in silence with his eyes fixed on the oak grove. In a moment, he had disappeared among the trees.

The crows were coming back. They wheeled above the trees, cawing impatiently. Some settled in the branches; one, bolder than the rest, lit among the dead men and cocked its eye at Bushrod Carter.

Bushrod was crouched like a pugilist, but his hands were raised, palm outward, as if in surrender.

"Don't," he said. "Don't do that."

"Why, Bushrod," said Simon Rope. "Is that the way to greet a old pard?"

Nebo Gloster, who had lived in the woods all his life, knew how to read sign. He could follow the girl easily through the carpet of leaves—she left a light trail, so delicate and subtle it could be no other's. The sign led him to a big pin oak where it altered radically. Nebo knelt and studied the ground. Something had happened here: an ambush, a struggle. He looked for blood, but there were only the scuffed leaves, their wet undersides gleaming darkly. Nebo raised his eyes and saw a track so clear he could have followed it on a starless night. Two people now, dragging their feet.

Then he heard the crows. He couldn't see them, but he could hear them talking up ahead, telling him how to go. Nebo rose and moved on, silent as a ghost. He didn't need any sign now.

Simon Rope had Anna by the collar, twisting it so that her face was red and her voice a choked, harsh whisper.

"I'm sorry, Bushrod," she said. "I am.....so sorry—"

"Shut up," said Simon Rope, and twisted tighter. Anna clawed at the collar, gagging, her eyes bulging.

"Leave her be!" said Bushrod. "You are killin her, for God's sake!"

"Aw, man," said Simon Rope, but he eased his grip and Anna gasped for breath and the high color drained from her face until there was almost no color at all. Then Simon Rope brought his knife up and laid the blade against Anna's cheek, the point just under the moon-shaped scar. Simon Rope grinned and bit her on the ear. Then he looked at Bushrod.

"Man, I figgered you'd be glad to see me alive after such a hard-fit battle."

"You wasn't in the battle, goddamn you," said Bushrod.

"*Fuck* you," said Simon Rope. "What you know 'bout where I was at?" He shoved Anna further into the clearing, she stumbled over the crawling dead man but Simon Rope jerked her up, shoved her again. Bushrod, still crouching, his hands still raised, took a step toward them.

"That's right, Bushrod," said Simon Rope. "Come on! You just come on, see what happens!"

Bushrod stopped. Anna was watching him now, her eyes wide. She put out her hand, waving it like a blind person would.

Bushrod Carter moved to the side now, his hands still up. When he moved, Jack Bishop spoke behind him: "Shoulda buried you.....shoulda left you in the ground—"

"Is that Jack Bishop there?" said Simon Rope, pointing with the knife.

Bushrod moved back again, slowly, moving his hands now. "That's him—let him be, he's played out."

Simon Rope shook the knife. "Ought not to thowed dirt in my face, you son bitch!"

"Let him be!"

"Ought not to!" Simon Rope was shouting now, spraying spittle. He jammed the knife point into Anna's cheek, shoved her hard and brought them within an arm's length of Bushrod, who was moving again, in the other direction this time, watching.

"Come on, Bushrod!" said Simon Rope, but Bushrod said nothing, he was watching, his eyes flicking toward the edge of the clearing—

"Make you a trade, Bushrod. You wanta hear it?"

"Sure, Simon," said Bushrod, but he was watching past Simon Rope, toward where they had all come out of the woods.

"You *sure* you wanta hear it?"

"Told you I did."

Bushrod could smell the man. He could smell Anna too, the fear on her, but he kept his eyes off her face, didn't want to look at her face. He watched the clearing, heard Simon Rope laugh, heard his voice spilling out as if he'd lost control of it—

"Sure, sure you do, you chicken-shit, shoulda never thowed dirt in my face son bitch you know everthing you think you wanta trade I'll tell you by God trade the cunt for Bishop trade cunt for.....only thing, I get to fuck her first—"

Anna cried out then, tried to twist away, but Simon Rope clapped his hand over her mouth, pressed the knife until it brought a little bead of blood that ran down Anna's cheek and dangled on the point of her chin and Bushrod kept his eyes away, kept them on the clearing—

"You hear me? You can have her after that you can even watch me son bitch then I get Bishop—"

"No," said Bushrod. He was backing up now.

"What?"

"No trade," said Bushrod. He straightened, dropped his hands, kept his eyes off Anna's face. "No trade, Simon. Crows gone get you."

Simon Rope watched him, Anna watched him, the crows and the dead men watched him. Bushrod began to sway, like a man dancing to unheard music.

"Crows gone get you, Simon."

Simon Rope opened his mouth to speak, but no sound came. There was a sound in his head, the words were right there, but he couldn't make them come out. Then he felt it, and looked down. Something was pushing out the front of his shirt.

"Crows'll get you now, Simon," said Bushrod. "Listen to em up yonder."

But Simon Rope wasn't listening. He forgot everything, absorbed in the mystery of what was happening to him. He watched the thing break through the rotten fabric of his shirt and angle out into the light; it was coming out just under his breastbone, gray and greasy, smeared with blood—

He felt the girl break away, but no matter. He didn't care, wanted only to study the thing coming out of him. He recognized it, the threaded end of a steel ramrod, something wet and dark dangling from the tip— impossible, yet there it was—

Then the pain struck him, brought him to his knees. Everything seemed to let go then, he watched his hand open, watched the knife fall slowly, gracefully, into the grass. He saw the girl running. He tried to reach for the knife but his hand wouldn't work—it was right there in front of him but he couldn't pick it up, the damndest thing. Then he let that go too, he couldn't remember what he needed the knife for anyway.

Something black and silky swept across Simon Rope's vision. He clawed at it with his hands, but it slipped away. Then there were more of them, lots more, wheeling around him, but he could handle them all. Never mind—he'd been hurt lots worse than this. Lots worse. He heard voices. *All right*, he said. *Come on you sons of bitches see what happens*. Then he began to crawl.

Bushrod tried to catch her, but Anna twisted away and struck him hard across the face. "No!" she cried. "Don't touch me! Don't any of you—"

"God-*dammit!*" sobbed Bushrod, holding his nose, wanting to smash his fist into the fragile bones of Anna's face.

"Keep away!" she cried. "Keep off me!"

Meanwhile, Nebo Gloster had pulled the bloody ramrod out of Simon Rope. He turned it in his hands, crying, making sounds, then he drew back his arm and hurled the ramrod away; it whistled across the clearing and disappeared in the trees. Nebo began to hop from foot to foot. "Miss Anna!" he sobbed. "Miss Anna!"

Simon Rope was crawling, clawing at the grass. He passed over the knife; Anna saw it, dove on it, scrabbled for it, gasping for breath. Finally she had it. She lurched to her feet and went after Simon Rope, the knife raised—

"No!" cried Bushrod. He grabbed her wrist, wrapped his arm around her waist. She fought him, tried to cut him with the blade.

"Turn loose of me!" Anna sobbed. "I got to kill him! Let me kill him once and for all!"

Bushrod squeezed her wrist as hard as he could, knowing he was hurting her, wanting to hurt her, until her hand opened and the knife dropped away. "Enough!" he cried, his mouth pressed against her ear. "Enough! You will have enough bad dreams as it is!"

He held her, let her fight him, wrapped his arms around her and squeezed tighter until he'd squeezed all the breath out of her. She groaned and Bushrod pushed her face into his shoulder and eased his grip—and as soon as he did, Anna bit him, hard. Bushrod gritted his teeth and held on. He would not let her go, not ever.

Then he felt the girl go limp, and he put his good hand against the back of her neck and stroked her, petted her. "Go ahead," he said. "Go ahead, go ahead." And she was really crying now, she was shrieking, the sound muffled by the stinking wool of his jacket. But that was all right. That was a good thing.....

PART THREE

BANQUO'S RETURN

Mother, you will be glad to know I am no longer afraid of the dark.

—Letter, Bushrod to Jane Pegues Carter
Corinth, Mississippi
April 9, 1862

CHAPTER TWELVE

I n the last hour of his life, Jack Bishop spoke hardly at all. When he did, Bushrod leaned close and listened, but he could never make much out of it. Jack was someplace far away from Franklin, and Bushrod would not have called him back even if he could, not even to say goodbye.

They had not tried to move him; Jack had so little time remaining, and it seemed useless to trouble him. So they stood watch in the clearing: Bushrod and Anna and Nebo, the dead men and the crows.

When Anna had done crying, when the hurricane of fear and anger had passed, Bushrod had expected her to leave, to go back to the house where her folks were, to flee as far from Bushrod Carter as she could. He would not have blamed her. So he was surprised when she asked him to find something she might use to rest on.

"I must sit down before I fall down," she said. Bushrod started to protest, but she waved him silent. "It is all right," she said. "I am worn out with soldierin, is all."

So Bushrod, fearing that if he pressed any harder she really would leave, went once more among the Departed. He found a man who still had his blanket roll. It was an old quilt, actually, made in the double-wedding-ring style. "Beg pardon, I'm sure," said Bushrod, and took the quilt, and spread it upon the ground for Anna. She allowed him to take her hand while she lowered herself to the quilt; she sat, and spread her skirts around her, and looked at Nebo.

"Can you understand how grateful I am to you?" she asked.

Nebo blushed and a painful look crossed his long face and his eyes darted to Bushrod.

"Maybe you could make us a fire," said Bushrod. He pointed. "There's a little blow-down yonder, ought to be some good dry wood."

Nebo limped thankfully away. Bushrod caught Anna's questioning glance and held up his hand for peace. "He knows," Bushrod said. "It's just.....well, he ain't schooled in the social graces."

"Hmmm," said Anna, but she left it alone.

Bushrod tried to get Jack to take some water, but it was no use, it only seemed to hurt him. Bushrod sat back on the edge of the quilt and hung his head.

"He was your good comrade?" said Anna softly.

"Uh-huh. He was."

"Like the other boy? Virgil?"

"Virgil C.," said Bushrod. "Virgil C. Johnson. And this was Jack Bishop. We were all from Cumberland, in Mississippi, a long time ago."

"Oh, me," said Anna. She clutched her silver cross. "I do not believe there is anything I could say that wouldn't sound paltry and empty as a gourd—but I will say it anyway. I am sorry, boy."

"I am obliged to you for stayin. It won't be long, and then....."

"Then what?" said Anna after a moment.

"Well, I don't know," said Bushrod. "I have learned not to plan too far ahead."

"Bushrod?"

"Yes, Anna?"

"I should like to ask you a question, if I may."

"You can ask it."

Anna put her hands together. "If you hadn't seen Nebo comin when you did.....would you have taken the trade?"

Bushrod pondered for a moment. "Well," he said, "let me put it this way. I do not believe old Simon was really in the mood for tradin."

"But would you have taken it?"

Bushrod brushed a fly from his cheek. "No," he said.

Anna gave an abrupt nod of her head. "That was the right answer," she said.

Anna slept after a while, and Bushrod sat close beside Jack, fanning the flies and listening, waiting. He watched the girl, too, in her fitful sleep. She jerked and whimpered at times and once Bushrod tried to pet her but she flinched away, frowning, so he let her alone. Meanwhile, Nebo Gloster sat by his little fire, head bowed, rocking slowly back and forth. Now and then he would talk quietly to himself and look at his hands.

Jesus and Mary, thought Bushrod—*a woeful lot we are indeed*. He tried to imagine what they must look like to the crows lurking in the branches. Bushrod didn't really mind the birds; he liked them for the same reason he liked tom cats, though he couldn't have said what the reason was. No doubt they were enjoying the melodrama unfolding among the mortals below.

No doubt they would peck Simon Rope's eyes out pretty soon.

Simon Rope's body in death was an uncanny mirror of Anna's in sleep. He was curled on his side, knees drawn up, hands tucked under his chin. But he was having no bad dreams, not in this world, anyway.

Simon Rope had not crawled far before he gave up the ghost, and Bushrod wondered why the man had died so quickly. His wound was mortal, probably, but it was not the kind to suck a man's life away in the space of a few moments. It was almost as if there had been nothing at all inside the shell of Simon Rope's flesh to sustain him or linger or prop up the will. Of all the many Departed Bushrod had seen, Simon Rope was the loneliest, the saddest. For a moment, Bushrod allowed himself to mourn for the man. Then, with his good hand, he dug among the grass until he had a handful of rocky dirt. "Hey, Simon," he said aloud, and flung it in Simon Rope's dead face, and was satisfied.

His arm was hurting, and he wondered why, when it was his finger that was shot. He contemplated removing his jacket to take a look, but decided against it. He cradled the arm to his chest. It would quit hurting by and by, tomorrow perhaps, maybe even this afternoon if he could bathe it in the river.

Thinking of the river had comforted him once, but it pressed heavily on him now, for there would be no gathering there. He remembered the vision he had made—was it only yesterday?—and how it had sustained him, but it was gone now, like all those who might have gathered with him. All the old boys, camping this night along a far shore where Bushrod Carter could not follow.

And then, back at the house, he had told himself—even told R.K.—that the river by the village of Franklin was as far as he meant to go. In that, too, he had been mistaken.

As Bushrod sat among the sleeping and the dead, he began to understand. It came as it often did, slowly, like morning coming, when the dark grew transparent and the shadows diluted with something not yet light but not darkness either; then shapes all at once, and lines, and a little color and then a little more, until suddenly the world was back again, fresh and new, looking a little surprised to be here. So it was that Bushrod Carter woke to find himself back at the center again—found Anna, too, and the strange, ragged man who'd saved them—found them all: the broken, the grieving, the dying, the lost. Even Simon Rope was there, working out an irony that the dark birds would appreciate, for it was Simon Rope, more than any other, who had brought him back again.

Jack Bishop groaned and muttered a few disconnected words that had meaning somewhere perhaps. Bushrod felt sorrow nudge at him, but it was not time for sorrow yet. He was too tired, and there was too much death. So he lay down beside his comrade, pillowed his head on the legs of the Departed, and slept for a time.

And dreamed of rivers and calm waters, of all the boys passing down through sunlight and patterns of shade on a slow current that bore them home—

Something woke him, the birds perhaps, or the flies. He had only slept a few moments but his mouth was full of foul cotton and his eye was gaumed shut and he was cold. He found the canteen, cupped some water in his hand and rubbed it over his face. He wanted to be down at the river right then, to shuck his rags and let the river wash him clean, no matter if the water was freezing cold or the woods full of sharpshooters—no matter what. Tomorrow perhaps, or this evening. He looked at Anna, but she was still sleeping. He was about to rise and join Nebo at the fire when he turned to look at Jack.

So there it was, and a long way they'd come to this little clearing in Tennessee. Bushrod watched for a moment, thinking of nothing, feeling nothing, aware of nothing but the memory of quiet waters carrying them home. Then he rose stiffly to his knees and made the sign of the cross.

"Well, old Jack," he said.

Jack Bishop's eyes were open, looking out at the trees. Bushrod closed them, and brushed the greasy hair out of Jack's face. He opened the stiff, bloody jacket and searched the inside pocket, found a blood-soaked letter, a spectacles case, Jack's filthy handkerchief. Bushrod put all these things in his own jacket pocket. Clumsily, he fastened the top button of Bishop's coat, smoothed the front, took the boy's hands, still warm, in his own and held them for a moment, then crossed them on the thin breast.

Jack Bishop, hurrying to catch up with the column.

Bushrod looked up at the paling sky. The sun had disappeared behind the high thin clouds—a bad sign, for it meant cold weather soon. Overhead the trees were empty, the birds had flown. "Too-ra-loo," Bushrod said.

Then he heard his name, and turned. Anna was sitting up on the quilt, rubbing her eyes. He could see her ankle where her skirt was pulled back. She rubbed her arms and shivered and then she looked at him. A moment passed.

"He is gone," she said. It was not a question.

"Yes," he said. "Jack Bishop is dead."

She rose stiffly, awkwardly, like a colt on its unsure legs. Nebo, too, rose stiffly from the ground, and rubbed his hands on the front of his trousers.

"You shouldn't have let me sleep," said Anna.

"It's all right," said Bushrod. "It was only a little while."

She took a step, stumbled, caught herself. Bushrod made to rise, but she waved him down. "I will come to you," she said.

She crossed the little way and knelt beside Bushrod in the grass and together they looked at Jack Bishop.

"He is peaceful now," said Anna.

"Yes," said Bushrod. "It was not hard for him, I didn't even hear him go. I.....I was sleepin myself. Great God, I—"

"Hush, boy," said Anna. "He knew you were there."

"Yes. Yes, I suppose he did. We were pards, and.....and he would know."

Anna lifted her hand. "May I touch him?"

Bushrod felt himself smiling. "I expect he would like that, if you would."

Anna put out her hand, hesitated, then laid it carefully over Bishop's. "There," she said softly. "There now."

For a long moment, Bushrod did not move. When he did, it was to put out his own hand and close it over Anna's.

She did not pull away.

***

Major R.K. Cross stood in the front yard of the great brick house. A lightly-wounded Lieutenant and ten enlisted men were gathered in a semicircle around him. All of them, officer and man, were silent, hollow-eyed, caked with the mud of new-dug graves. The Major regarded them a moment, then pointed with his pipestem toward the south.

"Lieutenant, you must search those woods and the field beyond—Stewart's Corps lost some comin through there. I see one right over yonder, in fact."

He pointed his pipe again, and the men turned their heads. There, barely visible in the grass a hundred yards from the house, was the gray, indefinite shape of a dead man.

"Reckon how we missed him?" said the Lieutenant.

"Hell, they all over the place," said a snaggle-toothed man. "And they gittin so stiff you can't hardly carry em no more. Reckon could we git us a wagon?"

"There ain't any wagons," said the Lieutenant.

"Boys, I hate it," said the Major, "but you will just have to do the best you can. We can't leave those fellows out there for the buzzards. Lieutenant?"

"Yessir," said the officer. "Two ya'll get that feller in the yard, and Wylie, git you down to the barn yonder and see can you find a wheel-b'ar. Rest ya'll come with me."

The Lieutenant saluted and shuffled away with his men. Major Cross watched them go. He watched the Lieutenant's party disappear into the woods, watched the two men struggling with the grotesquely rigid corpse of the soldier who had been killed in the yard. He turned and looked at the house, old and stately and elegant from this elevation, with the autumn morning's sun falling on the brick face. As the Major watched, a man appeared in the open parlor window. He was holding a leg. The leg was naked, starkly white—even from this distance the Major had the impression that it was finely haired with a graceful, almost feminine foot. The man dropped it onto the pile of legs and arms and hands and feet that rose nearly to the window sill. The Major bit off the end of his clay pipestem and spit it out. He turned his back on the house, cupped his hands around his mouth.

"Billy Bevins!"

Across the yard, a man raised his head. "Comin, Major!" In a moment the man came sauntering across the yard leading an enormous brown horse. The man's hat was decorated with a squirrel's tail, from under the brim his eyes glittered merrily and hard. He sported a broad, unruly beard. His jacket was butternut brown, with dingy cuffs that might have been yellow once. "Hey, Major," he said, making a salute.

The Major patted the big horse on its nose. The animal had a "U.S." brand on its rump; the former owner's saddle and gear were still in place. It was the bearded soldier's shotgun, however, that dangled from the pommel by a bit of plow line.

"Listen here, Mister Bevins," said the Major. "In time of war and tumults, what is the role of the light horse?"

The man rolled his eyes elaborately, as if pondering an essential truth. Finally he held up a finger. "In time of war and tumults, the role of the light horse is.....to seek out the enemy, smite him soundly in the ass and ride away rejoicing."

"It's time we were at that again, don't you think?"

"Ah, Christ, Major," said Bevins, "I'd nearly as soon be married again as spend another night in this damnable place—God rest all their souls, by God."

"That's the way I see it, sir," said the Major. "So I want you to get up on this fat, indolent prize and go see if you can find our General Forrest. Present him my compliments, and say that Major Cross requests orders. Mind, now: do *not* say 'Major Cross the Provost' but only 'Major Cross.' He will ask you where this Major Cross thinks he is, and you must tell him only that Major Cross and his detachment are just out of town on the Lewisburg Pike. He will storm and swear—don't pay it any mind—then he will either clap you in irons or send you to some lesser mortal who will tell you how to rendezvous with the main body. This last is the only information I am interested in. It is all I care to know. Understand?"

"Major, I am your man," said Bevins. He put his boot into the hooded stirrup and hoisted himself into the saddle and it seemed to the Major he ought to be able to see into Alabama from up there.

"Forrest is north of the river," said the Major. "And see you don't linger in town." He slapped the big horse on the rump and watched Bevins canter away toward the village and the river he would have to cross.

Suddenly the sun was not as warm as it had been. The Major turned his face toward it, saw that it was climbing into the high clouds. He could feel the weather coming.

When the Major was a boy, there hung in the parlor of his father's house a lurid chromo of Napoleon's retreat from Moscow. Major Cross had not thought of it in years, but he remembered it now: the ragged soldiers leaning into the driving snow, their feet wrapped in rags, the wind whipping the capes of their greatcoats. All their colors were cased, the eagle-tipped staffs rimed with frost. In the foreground a soldier was dying, his anguished face turned to the sky while the column passed behind him. As a boy, Major Cross despised that chromo—it reeked of defeat, end, humiliation, and it made him cold to his very bones. And, because he despised it, he made himself stand before it in long, solitary vigils—especially in winter when the parlor was closed and cold and silent—staring at the soldier who was always dying, hating him, hating the others who did not know they were dying too. The boy swore he would never let himself come to such an end.

And now, here he was.

The Major smiled in appreciation of the joke that Destiny had played on him. He could see himself in the chromo now, one of the mounted officers swaddled against the cold, swept along on the ebb tide of a ruined army. He could also see, as clearly as if it were already a memory, the campaign on which he was about to embark. Ambushes in the icy, death-silent woods. Running fights over frozen roads, the horses slipping, stumbling in the ruts, some of them going down by the head, pitching their riders. Videttes, half-dead from the cold, lifted bodily from their saddles and carried to the fire—if there was a fire. The wind would whip the capes of the troopers' greatcoats, breath freezing in their mustaches, hands raw and red—racking coughs, headaches, sodden blankets, no tents, no forage—and on the retreat, desperate rear-guard actions far from the main body, where men would die to gain a little time for other men they did not know, and who would never know them. Charges and countercharges, the horses' hooves spattering in the ice—a brief uproar of pistols, carbines, shotguns, the clatter of horse artillery—then silence again, the riders vanished, the blood of the dead men freezing in the leaves—

The Major had seen it all before and in a little while would see it all again—only now he'd come full circle from the boy in the parlor who hated the men who lost. Now he was one of them, and in a way he was glad, relieved to have it decided. *Let it commence*, he thought—*let us all cross the river and see what it is to die*—

He turned abruptly, collided with a soldier who had come up behind him. The Major swore and took a step back. Then he recognized the man. "Well," he said softly.

"Beg pardon, R.K.," said Bushrod. "Do you know where I could find a shovel?"

Nebo Gloster dug the grave among the oaks, not far from the clearing where Jack had died. The ground was soft but the roots proved troublesome, and it took him almost all the morning. Meanwhile, Bushrod Carter slept under a sweetgum tree. He had not meant to, but the moment he leaned his head back against the trunk he was asleep. Nebo paid him no mind but went on digging, wide and deep. From time to time soldiers came to watch; they would stand and smoke and talk quietly among themselves, then go away again. Some offered to spell Nebo, but he paid them no mind either.

It was almost noon when the job was finished. Nebo climbed out of the hole, thrust the shovel into the mound of dirt, and put on his frock coat again. It was hard to get the coat on, for he was stiff and sore and could hardly straighten his back. Then he hobbled over to the blanket that lay over Jack and Virgil C. and knelt and pulled the blanket back a little way.

Jack Bishop was peaceful. Anna had cleaned his face and brushed his hair; Bushrod and Nebo had carried him here and laid him out in the usual way. Virgil C. was another matter.

Anna had gone with Bushrod to find his comrade, just as he had hoped she would. When they couldn't find him in the front yard, Bushrod was agitated, but Anna led him around back where they found Virgil C. just as the provost's men had left him: still on his face, arms flung out, rigid as a plank. They found some men to help; Bushrod would not allow him to be turned over, so Virgil C. was carried face-down into the grove, where he was laid beside Jack and the both of them covered with a blanket. Then Bushrod had pointed with the stick he'd been using as a cane. "We must make the grave here," he told Nebo. "Big enough for them both." Now Nebo had dug the grave, and for a moment he squatted on his heels and peered at the men who would fill it.

The tally had been made, somehow. Something was saved, though Nebo could not remember how it all happened. But he didn't care; he felt quiet, peaceful, he felt as if nothing could ever happen to him again.

Then he heard movement and looked up, expecting Miss Anna, who said she would bring their dinner. Instead, an officer was sitting his horse among the trees, watching him. Nebo got to his feet. "What you want now?" he whispered.

The officer was silent.

Without taking his eyes away, Nebo bent and pulled the blanket back over the two dead soldiers. "You seen em," he said, "now let em be."

He began to step backward toward the tree where Bushrod lay. He looked back once to check where it was, and when he turned again the officer was gone.

Nebo sat close to Bushrod and pulled his knees up under his chin. He was sitting there when Anna came.

She had brought biscuits, a little ham, some dried apple slices, all in a lard bucket with a dishrag thrown over it. She brought a boiler of coffee, and under one arm she carried the wooden lid of an ammunition box. She tucked it all between the roots of the gum tree and sat down beside Bushrod.

"Has he been sleepin all the time you been diggin?" she asked Nebo.

"Well, they wa'nt but one shovel anyhow, Miss Anna."

She picked up Bushrod's stick and poked him in the ribs. "Hey, boy—rise and shine!"

Bushrod lurched upright and swore. Anna shook her head. "I do not believe I ever heard that particular word before," she said.

"For God's sake," said Bushrod.

Anna spread the dishrag out and lay the meager rations before them. "Now, go ahead, boys," she said. "I had a bite down at the cookhouse— they had a roast goose and dressin down there—"

"And chicken and sweet corn and collards, too," said Bushrod.

"Yes, and peas, two or three kinds, and barbecue, a whole hog—"

"My lands," said Nebo, his eyes gone wide.

"No, no, no," said Bushrod. "It ain't really true, Nebo. We was dreamin, is all."

So Bushrod and Nebo ate together, ate slowly, making it last, and passed the coffee boiler between them, and Anna watched them, and when they were done she folded the dishrag again.

"We are obliged to you," said Bushrod. "It's not many that fare so well today."

"It is little enough, but you are welcome," Anna said. "I brought you some paint like you asked, it's in the bucket."

So Bushrod looked in the bucket, found a little pot of white paint and a narrow brush. He took these and the lid of the ammunition box and went off a few paces and sat cross-legged on the ground. Nebo followed and watched, fascinated, as Bushrod began to work.

"How you know to do that?" asked Nebo.

"Why, this ain't nothin," said Bushrod. "I am skilled in all the arts."

He winked at Anna, and she blushed and turned away. She walked to the grave, but she didn't look at it, she looked at the sky and the high clouds sailing overhead. In a little while, Bushrod called to her. She walked back slowly, rubbing her arms.

"Look," said Bushrod, and held up the box lid. On it, he had painted:

Jack Bishop
Virgil C. Johnson
21st Miss. Regt.
Kiled Nov. 30 1864

and beneath in very small letters:

Virtute Junxit Mors
Non Separabit.

"What do you think?" asked Bushrod.

"Well, it is very nice," said Anna, "but I believe you left an 'l' out of 'killed'."

Bushrod frowned. "Well, damned if I—" he began, but checked himself and looked up guiltily. Anna waved it away.

"Never mind," she said. "I am growing used to soldier talk."

While Bushrod added the missing letter, Anna read the inscription to Nebo. She skipped the Latin, but Nebo asked her about it anyway, and she had to turn to Bushrod.

"Well, all right—what *does* it mean?"

Bushrod shrugged. "Well, it is imperfectly remembered. What I meant it to mean is, 'What valor has joined, death will not separate'."

"Yes," said Anna. "Of course it would mean something like that."

A temper in her voice made Bushrod look up, but Anna had already risen and turned her face away. "Old Quinche could have done it right, but he ain't here," said Bushrod.

Anna did not ask who Old Quinche was. She walked to the sweet-gum tree and looked off toward the grave.

"Well, all right," said Bushrod. He unlimbered himself from the ground. "Let us do it then, Nebo."

Anna Hereford pressed her back against the tree trunk and watched as Bushrod and Nebo pulled the blanket away from the two dead men. By now the living were almost as stiff as the dead; Anna found that the hardest thing to watch was the slow, painful movements of her companions. But they took up Jack Bishop, and bore him clumsily, and laid him in the grave.

Then there was a problem with Virgil C. "I do not want to see his face," said Bushrod, "but we got to turn him over. He can't be buried like this, I won't have it, I—"

"You go on," said Nebo. "I can fix him."

"No, you ought not to have to do it by yourself. Maybe I could—"

Nebo, gaunt and muddied, swayed against the gray curtain of the trees. He lifted his arm, pointed a bony finger toward Anna. "You go stand over there, old Bushrod. You let me fix him."

"Yes," said Anna. "Come away from there, boy."

"Oh, me," said Bushrod, ashamed of his weakness. He looked down at Virgil C., knowing it was for the last time. The place where Nebo's ball and ramrod had entered was crusted with black blood (there were no flies, for once), the hair around it matted and stiff. The out-flung, rigid arms ended in hands that had clawed at the grass in the last moment of life; one hand was open, the other was still clenched, still holding a tuft of dry grass. Virgil C.'s gray jacket was hunched at the shoulders, pulled up at the waist so Bushrod could see the striped pattern of his shirt. One of the suspender buttons was gone from the trousers, the dry leather tabs of the braces curled up like tongues.

"No," said Bushrod softly. "No, no, no." It was all he could think of to say. Then he raised his eyes to the living man who stood on the edge of the grave.

Nebo caught the look, took a step backward, nearly fell into the hole. "What?" he said. "What, old Bushrod?"

Bushrod moved around Virgil C.'s body and came up to Nebo, put his hand on the man's chest, believed for an instant that he only had to push to set things right: Nebo in the grave, not Virgil C.

Anna's voice came to him from some distant place, but there were no words. There was only the press of his hand against Nebo's chest and the man's face, thin and gray and empty of understanding, and the gaping muddy hole from which Jack Bishop watched with mild disapproval, and then Jack Bishop wagged his finger at Bushrod and his voice crept into Bushrod's head: *Let it be, old pard—there has been enough killin for one day.*

"Bushrod, let it be!" said Anna, her voice hard, asking no argument, like a school bell ringing. "You come away from there and let it be!"

So Bushrod let it be. He dropped his hand. "All right, then Nebo," he said. "You fix him best you can." Then he turned and, without looking back, began to walk across the little way to the sweetgum tree where Anna Hereford waited.

Once, on a grassy hill, in a web of sunlight spun from the blue autumn sky, a boy sat musing.

All around him the long summer was dying. It was still warm for the season, there had been no killing frost, yet the grass was brown and the trees had done their turning just the same: yellow for hickories, purple for the sweetgums, the oaks gone to red and orange, all arrayed to the margins of the world in a glory of farewell. From the town below came the ringing of old Campbell the Smith's hammer; the boy could see the Norman tower of Holy Cross and the ambitious spire of the Presbyterians, the courthouse cupola with its flag waving lazily in the breeze. Down there, too, was the house where the boy had lived all his sixteen years.

The house stood at the end of what had once been a logging road but was now an actual street in the town of Cumberland. A two-storied ell of unpainted cypress, the house looked like a dozen others in the town, right down to the columned portico tacked on the southerly face like an afterthought. The boy's room upstairs was southerly too; in winter the sun slanted through the boy's windows and threw long bright rectangles on the floor. When the house was built, the boy's papa had caused a stand of oaks to be planted around it; these were a generation old now and thrived on the good soil, on the memory of the vanished woods that had preceded them. Year by year the oak trees stretched their limbs closer to the sun, and though twenty years had not sent them high enough to block the sun from the boy's room, now and then in summer a shadow of leaves moved across the windows in quiet prophecy.

There were ghosts in the house down there. His mother and stillborn sister gone together. The elder brother who went to sea with Uncle Jarvis and drowned off the African coast. A man his papa had shot in the yard (he remembered that very well: his papa had been shaving, went out in the yard with his braces dangling, dragged the man off his horse and shot him and broke the man's shotgun across the gatepost, all before the lather dried). The boy had seen all these phantoms, one time or another.

Now the wind stirred on the hill, bringing a swirl of leaves that settled over the broomsage and goldenrod like a flock of yellow birds, bringing the green smell of cedar from the brakes. The courthouse clock began a slow and measured chime: high twelve it was, the watershed of the day. The Smith's hammer had ceased. Pretty soon, the boy's papa would be crossing the square to the Planter's Hotel, where old Doniphan's mute sister would be ringing the dinner bell. Down there, too, Terrible Miss

Chastain would be standing tight-lipped and cross-armed while the schoolhouse mob emptied noisily into the yard.

The boy wished he hadn't thought of that. He ought to be in school right now, and Terrible Miss Chastain would make it warm for him tomorrow. No doubt she would make it even warmer for his cousin Remy Dangerfield, who at this moment was lying on the grass beside him, pillowed in moss, in a cotton shift the color of old daisies. Her arm was flung across her face, her bare feet crossed at the ankles. Under the shift, her small pointed breasts rose and fell in the slow breathing of sleep.

Cousin Remy came to stay every summer when the yellow fever got bad in New Orleans. This year she was staying late and so ought to have been down in the schoolyard on this glorious noon, instead of dreaming on the hillside. The boy wondered what elaborate lie he might concoct to protect his cousin from Miss Chastain's wrath, even though it had been Remy's idea to slip off in the first place. "Hey, Remy Dangerfield," said the boy, and nudged her foot with his own. But his cousin did not wake, only moved her coltish legs and sighed.

The boy sighed too, and watched his cousin sleeping. Before this summer, he could not recall ever wanting to look at her just to be looking. There had not been much to look at anyway: a girl who, had he not known she was a girl, might as well have been a boy. In fact, before this summer she had out-boyed even the rowdy hard-ankles of Cumberland to the point where they were all half afraid of her. But sometime in her last winter's passage she had changed.

This June, when the boy and his papa and old Deacon had gone up to Wyatt's Landing to meet Remy's boat, they discovered she'd brought three trunksful of clothes—two more than she'd ever brought before. Then, at home, when the boy tried to point out things he'd saved up to show her—a fence lizard that would ride on your shoulder, a crow's skull, a water moccasin skin, a big hornet's nest, the new locomotive on the Mississippi Central—she showed no interest. In the case of the snake skin, she refused even to look at it, said it stank and turned on her heel and stalked away. Through the hot summer months she spurned the very boys she'd once bullied into following her, and took up with other girls the secret, unfathomable life that dwelt behind trellises and in parlors bright with afternoon. Toward the end of August, when the sun was beginning to arc toward the south and all the gardens and their once-bright flowers were growing rusty and old, Remy kept to her room nearly all the time. The boy would find her there, sitting by the window, reading or staring out at the blue fall of shadows in the yard, and after a while he understood that wherever she was he could not reach her there. So he went his own way and was strangely lonesome for her.

Then September came and Remy entered Miss Chastain's school, for the fever was still bad down south. The boy hoped that the cold waters of scholarship might shock Remy back to her old free ways, but in this, as in most things, he was mistaken. She actually seemed to enjoy school, and if anything was more distant and reserved than ever. Every morning and evening she walked the half-mile between home and schoolhouse with a cluster of whispering girls whose ranks (this was the boy's own metaphor; his first) were tighter than a British square at Waterloo. At first the boy followed, schoolward then home again, until his cousin began giving him looks over her shoulder that made him feel like a curious insect scuttling in the leaves. Finally he gave it up and returned to the company of his graceless comrades, who slouched to school through backyards and garden patches and who understood completely when he declared that the stuckup Remy Dangerfield could be blasted to hell for all it meant to *him*.

Then, this morning, he had learned for the second time since June that the universe, which he had once assumed to be predictable, in fact made no sense at all. She ambushed him after breakfast. He was feeding the bird dogs, Scotland and France, when he looked up and found her watching him with her green eyes. She stood with her hands folded on the gate of the pen, her short hair pulled back in a ferocious little knot that stretched the skin over her cheekbones, in the black collarless dress that Miss Chastain demanded of her female scholars, as if the only lesson they needed was how to get ready to mourn. Surprised by this apparition, the boy waited awkwardly with the bucket of scraps in his hand and hoped this grim stranger would disappear—and, in a way, that is what happened. One moment there was the stranger, in the next there was Remy Dangerfield again, smiling for the first time that summer in her peculiar way—lips parted, teeth pressed together—that from time immemorial had meant trouble for somebody.

She didn't care to go to school with the other girls this morning, she told him. Not this morning, maybe not ever again. She had made up a lunch pail, she said, and would her cousin dare to meet her in a little while, at the pond down by the cowpens? The boy stammered a reply, his face burning like a stove lid, and when the girl laughed old Scotland the bird dog peed all over himself with joy.

Later, when the boy came out of the willow brakes, he found the pond shining like a polished coin in the morning light. Remy was waiting, her school clothes folded and hidden in the grass, wearing the cotton shift that disguised, but could not hide, every new swell and curve of her young breasts, hips, legs. Her hair—which even this summer she had worn short, like a boy's—was shook loose now, and fell in her eyes and curved around the delicate shells of her ears. The boy stood speechless, seeing in his mind the cicadas that burst out of their old skin and unfolded green and fresh and trembling on the branch.

"Hey, Bushrod," she said, flirting her hair.

"Um, don't the briars hurt your feet?" the boy replied. It was all he could think of to say.

All morning they played in the old familiar woods, in the old purposeless way, Remy chattering on, laughing, causing the boy to take her hand now and then for no apparent reason, and if he thought of school at all it was only as some remote, mildly troublesome thing that had happened to him once. He followed her, watching as she moved through interstices of shadow and light like a creature just come to the world. Everything she touched seemed new all at once, distilled out of the first morning, out of the first sun that crept through the first garden. So it seemed to the boy, who could not know yet that he was no longer a boy at all, that she was leading him from one room to another without knowing it herself.

In time they came to the hill, and she looked around and declared that, of all the many places in the world, this must be her favorite now. She found a patch of white yarrow, and knelt there and wove a chaplet for her hair, and among the small flowers they ate their cold chicken and biscuits and drank cider from a little jug. Then she lay in the grass and quoted poetry from memory in a voice that was drowsy and deep, and her voice and the words she spoke made a strange music that the boy had never heard before. She told him that, without poetry, a person's heart was like an empty glass; to that moment the boy had never thought of the heart as any kind of glass, but as he listened to her voice he told himself he would never again see it in any other way. Strange music indeed.

Then she stretched herself in the grass and slept, and the boy sat close beside and watched her, musing, and the day traveled into afternoon without them and the season spooled away. At last he nudged her again, and spoke her name, and this time she awoke.

Remy stretched and yawned, then propped herself up on her thin elbows and regarded him with her cool, sleepy face. "I had a dream just now," she said.

The boy was silent. A hawk glided over the field, swift and quiet, so low the boy could see its head turning. Presently Remy touched his arm. "What's the oddest dream you ever had?"

It should have been an easy question, the boy had suffered dreams all his life, most of them odd, only now he couldn't think of any. He felt suddenly foolish, searching for words he did not have, and the bright morning seemed all at once to have happened to another, braver, smarter, more worthy than he. He gazed in despair on the empty glass of his heart and felt time moving away like slow water—slow, but you couldn't call it back no matter what—and Remy was moving along it and he was left behind. So he said nothing, and after a moment his cousin lay back again and crossed her arms and said: "Well, I would have told you mine, but now I won't."

"I don't care," he said suddenly, sharper than he meant to, wishing he could make himself stop. "Dreams ain't anything. Just dreams is all." And thinking all the while *Careful. Careful. You are about to lose somethin—*

Time moved away, he could feel it flowing past him. He was outside it now, in some hard, brittle place. He didn't know how long it was before Remy spoke again.

"I dreamed we were on this very hill," she said, "and I woke up and you were watchin me."

"That wasn't any dream," said the boy, hearing his own voice as if it were another's.

"Oh, it must have been," she said. Then, so soft the boy almost didn't hear: "You wouldn't do that but in a dream."

There was a little sound then, no more than a breath but it reached him in the place where he had gone. He stole a glance at his cousin and suddenly he was in time again, floundering in the stream. He had never seen Remy cry, but she was crying now, and not like girls or children cried—no furious rush of anger, no threats, only the first little sound and the quiet run of tears on his cousin's face where it was turned from him, and a widening distance as if she were falling away from him like leaves on the current—

"Oh, Remy," he said, and was frightened by the grief in his voice: *You are about to lose somethin and you didn't even know you had it to lose—*

All at once he could not bear to let it go, whatever it was—he didn't know, he didn't much care, so long as it was saved from losing. "Remy!" he cried, and watched his own hand reach for her, circle her waist and pull her roughly toward him so that her head flew back and her thin, light body arched against him. She came to him with a shocking strength, and she pulled him after her down a long fall of sunlight and grass and the smell of the dying summer, and he knew, as if he'd known all his life, what to do—

And after, for a long time, she would not let him go. She pressed herself to him, spoke fiercely into the hollow of his shoulder. "You will always have me with you now, always, always. You own me, in your soul you own me, no matter how far, how long, whether you want to or not—"

He grasped her hair, pulled her face away and saw her green eyes burning, felt the stream no longer slow that bore them along. "Yes," he said, and then again to the soft line of her mouth: "Yes, I know, always—"

"A long time," she said. She passed her hand over his face, light and hard like a blind person would. "I dreamed that, too. A long time, forever. Do you know that? Do you know?"

"Yes," he said. "I know. Yes."

And he did know. He knew it then, knew it as he watched her a week later standing by the starboard rail of the little steamer growing smaller and smaller until it was swallowed up in the mossy light, vanished around the river bend beyond which he had never been himself. Through all the long winter and spring that followed he knew it, kept it close to him in the shivering nights as he waited for the fever time to come again—

Until one morning in June, the first hot morning when no wind moved in the curtains and he thought it was the blue jays quarreling outside that woke him until he saw his papa sitting on the edge of the bed where the old man had never sat before. "Bushrod, wake up son, and listen careful to what I have to tell you—"

So much time, it seemed—he could not imagine where it all had gone, how the little stream could bear so much. And now he was falling, it was him this time, and there was Remy with her hand stretched toward him, reaching for him over the long distance that was really no distance at all, only a little time, a few days flown like birds—

"Remy Dangerfield," he said.

"That is the second time you called me that," said Anna, and caught him as he fell.

"I am so sorry," he said. "I didn't mean to. I reckon I am give out."

"Well, I can't imagine why," said Anna with her sidewise glance.

They were standing under the sweetgum tree, standing apart, shyly, like children at a country dance.

"I mean—I didn't mean to call you that. I don't know what I was thinkin. I mean, I know who you are. Anna, I know who you are."

"Never mind," said Anna. "Sometimes we remember things."

"Sometimes," said Bushrod.

He was facing away from the grave, but he knew very well what was happening back there. He could see it in Anna's face, too: she could not stop her eyes from watching over his shoulder, watching and pulling back then watching again. Suddenly, from behind, Bushrod heard a sharp *crack* like a dry stick breaking, and Anna's eyes grew wide and unbelieving and her hands moved to the silver cross.

Oh, me, thought Bushrod—*No more fiddle playin in this world*, and before Nebo could break the second arm he turned the girl and led her around to the other side of the tree.

She seemed to be having trouble breathing and had bitten her lip again. There were tears, too—she wasn't crying exactly, the tears just came, as if they had nothing to do with her. Bushrod raised his finger to her lip, almost touched it.

"You are goin to have a bad place there if you don't quit bitin it."

"You must pardon me," she said, and took the silk handkerchief from her sleeve and turned away, and Bushrod stood looking at the woods while she blew her nose in discreet little snorts and tapped her foot in the leaves. At last she spoke, as if to try out her voice: "He had to do that, I suppose. Break his—"

"Oh, yes," said Bushrod quickly. He put out his hand and touched her lightly, just at the base of the neck where the muscles were bunched and knotted like tight little fists. "Sometimes you have to do that, um, to get them to fit, you see. It ain't really so mean as it looks."

She turned then, and all at once they were standing so close she had to tilt up her face to look at him. "Give me your hand," she said. "Please."

So he put out his right hand, palm up, and Anna settled her own in it like a bird alighting. Bushrod thought of when he was a boy and sometimes a chimney swift would come in through the hearth; when that happened, he would always be the one to catch it, he loved to wrap his hand around it and feel the softness and the little hammer of the swift beating heart. Outside he would open his hand; for an instant the bird would lie blinking in his palm, then flicker away so fast he could never find it in the sky. He half-expected Anna's hand to do the same, but it lay still, and he closed his own around it.

They stood a moment, pondering their joined hands as they might a Chinese puzzle.

"Well," said Anna at last. "Here we are."

"Yes. Here we are."

"Um, I suppose polite conversation is out of the question?"

"Well, it would be a challenge," agreed Bushrod.

Anna almost smiled, but her sore lip made her wince. "I suppose it would be," she said, "given the *mise-en-scene.*" Then she did smile.

"The what?" asked Bushrod.

"Never mind," she said. "Still, I wonder what we might have talked about, in other circumstances, I mean. If you'd called on me, say, at home, before the troubles. That is to say—"

She stopped, blushing, and smiled again. Bushrod laughed. "You mean you would let a peckerwood boy call on you?"

"I didn't *say* I would. I meant, if I *had.* Which is, come to think of it, unlikely."

"Well, *if* you had, no doubt we'd of talked on something you like. What do you like?"

Anna thought a moment. "Well, books. You like books, don't you?"

"There you have it," said Bushrod. "I am a deep well of literary wisdom."

"You might think, because I am a girl, that I am ignorant on the subject. The truth is, Papa made sure we all—"

"You are a *girl?*" said Bushrod in astonishment. "Why the nation didn't you tell me before? No wonder you been nothin but trouble since the minute I laid eyes on you. Why, if I'd known that—"

"Bushrod Carter, you are mean and hateful and a damn peckerwood."

"*Now* you're talkin like a old soldier," said Bushrod.

"No wonder," said Anna. "Now I will tell you somethin. I have read *Leaves of Grass.*"

This time Bushrod really was astonished. "*You* have read *Leaves of Grass?*" He almost blushed himself to think about it.

"Oh, Papa was very progressive," she said. "He read nearly the whole thing to sister Bonnie and me, though he would leave out the shockin parts of course—we had to look them up on our own."

"Well," said Bushrod, "I am forevermore laid low. I loved that book, though I am not sure I understood a dern thing in it."

"I didn't say I understood it. You don't always have to understand a thing to love it, especially if it is beautiful."

"Oh, I agree," said Bushrod. "I know a girl, she once said that without poetry a person's heart is an empty glass."

"Indeed she was right," said Anna. She tilted her head. "Is that Remy Dangerfield that you speak of?"

"Oh," said Bushrod. "Well, yes, I reckon it was Remy said that."

"I thought so," said Anna. "No doubt, in the course of polite conversation, you would tell me about her. She is.....?"

"Was," said Bushrod. "My cousin Remy. The Yellow Jack took her, oh, a long time ago."

Anna looked away. A wind prowled through the grove, creaking a branch somewhere; it shifted and brought the smell of death from the field, shifted again and bore the odor of wood-smoke and damp leaves and, for a moment, the sound of a chopping axe. Anna looked down at their hands, still joined, and said: "You were favorin your arm out there, I saw you. Does it hurt much?"

"Ah, well," said Bushrod.

"You may answer the question," said Anna, tilting up her face.

"Well, it hurts some," he admitted.

"Let me look at it. Maybe—"

"No! I mean.....it is only sore a little. It will quit by tomorrow."

"You are a stubborn boy."

"Nevertheless," said Bushrod. He raised his left arm to demonstrate that he could, and with the tip of his little finger touched the scar on Anna's cheek. "How'd you get that?"

"A pony kicked me once," she said. "Don't change the subject."

"All right, then. But what about you? You can't quit cryin, can you?"

Anna reddened, made to pull her hand away but Bushrod held her fast.

"You can't quit, can you?"

"Well, so what if I can't? So what?"

"Well, so it is the same thing," said Bushrod. "It is a hurt from the battle. I have seen it happen before, lots of times, to soldiers even. If you

215

will show me that hurt, then I will show my arm to you. There ain't any shame in it."

"I know that."

"Do you? Do you really know it, or are you just sayin it?"

She pulled her hand away, but gently this time, and this time Bushrod let it go. She half-turned, and when she spoke it did not seem to be to him. "I know all there is to know about shame. I would as soon not talk about it anymore."

Before Bushrod could reply, Nebo was there, silently, as if the smoke had shaped him. "I fixed him, Bushrod," he said.

"I know," said Bushrod. "Um, why don't you keep watch until we come. Will you do that, just for a minute?"

"I'll watch," said Nebo, and he was gone like smoke.

Bushrod took Anna's hand again, and she turned to him and lay just the top of her head against the breast of his gray jacket. "I will tell you a thing," she said.

"All right."

"I came lookin for you. It's what I was doin here when.....when that man—"

"You came lookin for me?"

"Yes. You see, I thought.....oh, it is stupid."

"You can tell it," said Bushrod. "It is not stupid."

She looked up at him. "Part of it was, I thought maybe there was some explanation for all this, all that's happened—some, I don't know, some rule I'd missed, some proclamation, a plan everybody knew about but me—and I thought.....I thought maybe you'd be the one to explain it so I could understand. I'm sorry for thinkin it now—but Bushrod? I am not sorry I came lookin for you."

Bushrod took her hand, pressed it flat against his chest, pulled her to him. He touched her face. "I am not sorry either," he said. "It is about the only thing in the last three years that's made any sense."

Over the top of her head he could see the gray trees, the old citizens of the grove wreathed in tendrils of smoke. He wondered if they really had souls, as the old people said, and if they were listening, and if they would remember. "You said that was part of it," Bushrod whispered. "What was the other part?"

He felt her quick laugh. "Oh, my lands," she said.

"What? You can tell it."

Her fingers traced the square-and-compasses on his jacket. "Well, if you must know, I wanted to see if you really thought.....if you truly thought I was....."

"What, Anna?"

"*Fair*," she blurted, and hid her face.

For Bushrod Carter then, and for Anna, there came a little while when there was no grave, no impatient dead, no ruins. It was a breath's hesitation in time, between the curtain's fall and the moment when it must rise again, but long enough for fragile grace to touch them, and for Anna to find what she had really come seeking in the smoky grove—

Until time nudged them both again and they stepped apart, a little way, and Bushrod said:

"Now I will tell *you* a thing before we go."

"You can tell it."

Bushrod pulled at the front of his jacket and frowned. "We were talkin about shame," he said. "I know, I know—but I got to say this. Back at the house, before we went upstairs, before.....before Simon and all that, when you was gone, I gave up on everything, on soldierin, I mean, thinkin I would just quit and go home, run away, if you will, you know."

Anna waited, searching his face with her green eyes. "And?" she said at last.

"Well, that is what I did. That is what I would tell you."

"And you think there is shame in that?"

"Yes. I am a fool. I wish I wasn't."

"Bushrod Carter," said Anna. She touched lightly the bruised cheek where the musket-butt had struck him, a hundred years ago it seemed. "Do you believe what your cousin said about the heart? Do you believe that?"

Bushrod nodded. "Yes. I always have."

"Then you are not a fool," she said, and smiled for the last time. "Not altogether, anyway."

They turned away then, and it seemed a long way from the sweet-gum tree to the grave, though it was really no distance at all.

Bushrod, Anna, and Nebo stood at the grave's edge, looking down at the blanket-shrouded forms. It might as well have been lumber under there, for all the shape there was. Then, as they watched, the contours of faces, hands, feet seemed to emerge from the anonymous mass—the shape of men.

"Oh, my," said Bushrod. Anna linked her arm in his, gently, for his was the hurt one. With his right hand, Bushrod began to rub his forehead.

"Don't do that, boy," said Anna softly, and pushed the hand away. "See, you have brought blood again."

Bushrod looked at his fingers, then wiped them on his pants. "It don't matter," he said.

Anna squeezed his arm lightly and let it go. "Nebo," she said, "let us you and I go walk in the garden a while."

"Ma'am?" said Nebo.

"Come you hence," said Anna, and took Nebo's arm and led him away.

Bushrod listened to the sound of their going in the leaves. Then, in a moment, and like an old man moving, he eased himself down into the grave.

There was not much room, but he managed to kneel, putting his knee where Jack's leg would have been if he still had it. He made the sign of the cross. He could smell Virgil C. too, a little, but that was all right. *Old Virgil C.*, Bushrod thought.

The Saint Michael medal was attached to Bushrod's watch chain by a tiny gold link. He could hardly see it with his bruised eyes. He fumbled at it, finally jerked it loose. He held the medal in the palm of his hand, rubbed his thumb over the Archangel and the dragon, felt for the last time the old mysterious strength that flowed from the struggling figures. Then he lay it on the blanket where he could see the shape of Jack Bishop's hands.

He drew the gold watch from his waistcoat pocket and opened the case—the delicate hands had stopped. He had no idea what time to set it for, but he wound it and held it to his ear, listening to the fragile wheels move again. He drew the chain through its buttonhole and let it dangle while he watched the second hand make a full revolution. Then he snapped the case shut and lay watch and chain on the blanket over Virgil C.

"Well, boys," he said. "We—"

But his voice failed him, and he wept.

CHAPTER THIRTEEN

By the afternoon of the First of December, the scattered bones of the Army of Tennessee began to draw themselves together. It was an almost supernatural rite the Army had performed time and again, like some mythical beast that refused to die, that writhed up out of its own corpse until it found its shape again. If the shape was diminished, if it had to leave parts of itself rotting in the fields, no matter. All that was important was that it rise, gather its legs beneath it, and totter into the smoke again.

Like his predecessors, General John Bell Hood believed that it was he who must inspire this resurrection. He had ridden up to Franklin that morning through the shambles of his attack, his wooden leg thrust out at a grotesque angle, no longer the gay chevalier who had charmed Sally Preston in the old Richmond days. Blind to the reality of the moment, General Hood saw only the seeds of possibility. He believed he had won a victory: Schofield was gone, the way to Nashville lay open. He had only to pursue, lay siege, draw the Yankees out and defeat them in the open. At his new headquarters in Franklin, the Commanding General smote his fist on the map of Middle Tennessee with eager confidence.

He dictated a General Order congratulating the Army on its hard-won victory. It was read before regiments bled to the size of platoons. He sent his aides and couriers galloping into the countryside with orders for consolidation, assembly, movement, pursuit. Many of the officers to whom these missives were addressed were dead; those who were not dead shook their heads in astonishment and looked about them as if they had missed something.

In the end, it was not the Commanding General—nor any other general, good or bad—who raised the Army from its scattered fragments and made it whole again. Rather it was the corporals, the sergeants suddenly in command of companies, the junior lieutenants and the captains, the field-grade officers who had once been sheriffs and county clerks and cotton planters, the color bearers who planted their battle flags in the rocky fields and sang out the numbers of their regiments: Here is the Fifteenth, here the Forty-third Mississippi..... Here the First Missouri, the Eighth Tennessee, the Sixteenth Alabama, the Seventh Texas..... Here is the old First Arkansas, boys..... All these bullying and pleading and appealing, herding the scattered lambs into a flock once more. And most of all it was the lambs themselves, the riflemen, the privates, who dragged themselves reluctantly out of the night's anonymity and confusion, supressing memory and judgment, hoping for the best, looking for a roll to answer.

So it was that the Army came together, slowly, inexorably, and made ready to resume the campaign.

While larger events were creaking toward Tomorrow, Bushrod Carter stood nursing his wounded arm and watched as Nebo flung the last shovelful of dirt into the grave. Bushrod, who knew something about graves, reflected that, after a few winter rains, the ground here would be sunken and perpetually soggy—that it would still be wet all through the spring while the worms and beetles did their work—that by summertime there would be nothing left of Jack Bishop and Virgil C. Johnson but bones and uniform buttons. Then he remembered that Virgil C. had no buttons left on his coat. Trouser buttons, then.

He was glad that the grave was deep. He had seen too many rooted out by hogs or washed away, so that the occupant's busy corruption was evident to all. The boys would be spared that humiliation at least, and if Bushrod survived the coming campaign.....but he put that thought away once and for all. Whatever happened, the boys would stay here where they could keep each other company.

His arm was hurting really bad now, and it was getting hard to ignore. For a moment Bushrod thought he might take a look, just a peek to reassure himself. But he didn't. Instead, he allowed his tired mind to drift back to the subject of buttons. Virgil C. had pulled every last button off his coat on purpose. Why? For a while, the question assumed a peckish authority in Bushrod's mind. Then another consideration even more troublesome insinuated itself. As Bushrod watched Nebo tamp down the earth, it occurred to him that he did not know how the grave lay on the compass. He turned to Anna, who was sitting on the ground a little distance away.

"Miss Anna, which way is east?"

Anna looked around, pondered a moment, and pointed vaguely. "Well, it might be that way," she said. "But, then again—"

"Oh, it's all right," said Bushrod. "It ain't important." It was a curious thing: not once in all his life had Bushrod met a girl who knew one direction from another.

Nebo was setting the headboard now. "East is over thataway," he said, inclining his head.

Wonderful, thought Bushrod. They had planted Jack and Virgil C. with their heads to the north. He was forced to smile then—he could imagine Jack's reaction on Judgment Day when he rose up facing in the wrong direction. Well, it would have to be all right. There would be plenty of confusion in this country when the final trumpet blew.

The grave was finished, and suddenly Bushrod wanted to be away from it. He wanted to be out of the grove and in the fields again, or better still, on his way to the river. If only he could get there, he would bathe and rest a while and maybe he could think about it all then, about all that had happened since he and Jack first looked across the plain toward Franklin. He saw himself building a little fire, sitting by it on a log and watching the bright cold water. He saw Anna, her yellow dress among the white trunks of sycamores, moving shyly down the bank and speaking his name in the evening—

Now, dammit, there you go again, he thought, and drove the picture from his mind. Whatever else might happen, right now he had to pull himself away from this place. One day he would return, but right now—

One thing more to do, though. He had to say a prayer over the boys, make sure that God, as busy as He was right now, knew that this was a place He should watch over. Better than that, he would ask Anna to speak it. The memory of her voice would be a sweet thing to leave here.

So he turned toward Anna, turned too fast, stumbled dizzily and caught himself and was about to speak when a white streak of lightning lanced through his arm; he looked down in horror, actually expecting it to be shattered like a bolt-struck tree, and in that instant the same white light burst in his head and staggered him again and a sickness blew up from his stomach like a foul wind. The sky, the trees, the fresh-mounded grave, all swirled around the yellow blur of Anna's dress, and Bushrod fought to make it still again thinking *Great God I have been shot—they are comin again and I am shot—oh, not now, not now after all this—*

But in a moment the world came together again and the white light faded and Bushrod knew he wasn't shot. It was his arm, and the pain was so bad he could almost smell it.

Anna! he cried, but the girl only sat there, looking off into the trees.

Anna! He was sure he spoke it, absolutely positive, but again the girl didn't hear. What was the matter with her?

Somethin is happenin, somethin bad, he thought.

He was holding his arm, squeezing it against his side. As if from a great height he saw Nebo approach, the spade over his shoulder.

"Well, they is tucked away," said Nebo.

I know, I know. Listen—

"Won't nothin hardly bother em now."

Bushrod wanted to move, but he couldn't move. He had to get somewhere, needed a place to hide for a while, someplace quiet where he could rest.

I need to get to the river, he told Nebo, but the man only yawned. Then he looked at Bushrod and a puzzled scowl twisted his face.

"What's the matter, old Bushrod?" said the man.

I tol' you, said Bushrod. *I need I need I want—*But he couldn't remember.

"Oh, me," said Nebo, and his face was afraid now. "Miss Anna! Miss Anna!"

She heard then, and rose quickly, and Bushrod saw that her face was afraid as well, though he couldn't understand why. The Strangers were not coming, he was not shot—

Then Anna was there, touching his sleeve. "Bushrod?"

"It's all right," he said. "They ain't comin."

She peered into his face. "Who?" she said. "Who ain't comin? Bushrod?"

But now all he wanted was to be left alone. He heard her voice again, and then she was talking to Nebo and the man said something in return, but Bushrod was not interested, all that had nothing to do with him. He looked toward the grave, Jack Bishop was sitting cross-legged on the fresh dirt, idly shuffling a deck of cards. *What's the matter with you, boy?* said Bishop.

Nothin, said Bushrod. *My head hurts.*

Jack popped a card in his fingers. *Well, hell, I don't doubt it.*

My arm hurts bad, said Bushrod, *but there's nothin wrong with it—'twas my hand that was shot—*

Well, you never know, said Jack.

Virgil C. came strolling up then, swinging a dead possum by its tail. *Hey, Bushrod,* he said. *Look what I got.*

Bushrod squeezed his eyes shut. When he opened them again, Jack and Virgil C. were gone and in their place was the broad landscape of his memory. As far as he could see, there was nothing but death: dead men, washed-out graves, headless torsos bouncing under the wheels of galloping batteries, arms and legs and feet in piles, the swollen bodies of horses, flesh in the trees, raging fires, burning cabins, long lines of infantry swallowed up in the smoke—

He was afraid and began to shiver. He heard his name and turned and there was Anna coming toward him, smiling, with a black flower in her hand. It was like a rose, fresh-picked and beaded with dew. It was beautiful, but he didn't want it.

"No!" he said. "No, I don't want that!"

It was the handkerchief, she was twisting it in her hands and watching him and when she spoke his name he could hear the fear in it.

"Bushrod!"

"No, I got to go. I got to be goin. It is all right."

"No, it's *not* all right," she said. "You are *not* all right. Let us go and have a surgeon—"

"No!" cried Bushrod. He thrust his injured hand inside his jacket. "No, I tell you! They will cut my arm off!"

"No, they won't—what are you talkin about, boy?"

Look at his arm, said Jack Bishop.

"Bushrod," Anna said softly, "let me see your arm."

"No!" said Bushrod, backing away. "Shut up, Jack!"

"Bushrod, Jack is dead, he can't hear you." The girl's voice quivered, but she steadied it. She put out her hand. "Now let me see."

"No!"

"Come on, now," said Anna. Her hand touched his sleeve, moved down it to the wrist. Her fingers closed gently. "Come on, now. I won't hurt you."

"Don't do that," he sobbed. "I am only tryin to do what's right!"

"I know," she said. "Come on, honey. Anna won't hurt you."

She tugged gently at Bushrod's wrist where it was hidden under the jacket, and at last he let her pull his hand out. She held it a moment, stroked it, then began to unwind the bandage. It was black with grime by now, and stuck fast with congealed blood. As Anna peeled the bandage away, Bushrod grimaced and turned his head. He studied the grave—nothing but dirt there, now, and a set of Masonic working tools he recognized as belonging to the Cumberland lodge. "Say," he began, "how did—"

Anna drew a sharp breath. "Oh!" she said. Then, quietly, "Oh, Bushrod."

At first, he told himself he wouldn't look. He shut his eyes tight and tried to call back the picture of the river, but it was no use. He saw nothing but the ghostly image of Anna's face, and that was fading—and so he looked.

Anna had worked his jacket sleeve and shirt cuff halfway up his forearm. She was still holding his hand, and from under her fingers the livid red streaks crawled upward over his arm like poisonous vines and disappeared under his coat sleeve.

Bushrod stared, his heart thumping.

The girl drew a long breath, let it out slow. "Bushrod.....now, boy, I do not want any argument from you. We must take you to a surgeon."

Bushrod drew his sleeve down again and shook his head. "No, no. You see, I don't fancy a surgeon. They are all butchers. There is nothin the matter, I ain't ever been hurt, not in all my battles. You see, my medal—"

He stopped, looked up at Anna. All at once she seemed to be on a far shore, and between them lay a broad, dark water that he knew now he would never cross. "Oh, no," he said. "I give it to Jack."

"No matter," said Anna gently. "Come on, now."

Nebo was kneeling beside him, tugging at his trouser leg. "Come on, old Bushrod," he said.

"I will bring you some coffee," said Anna.

"You will?" said Bushrod. With his free hand he rubbed his forehead. He saw Jack Bishop again, lounging a little way distant. Jack grinned at him, beckoned, then turned and walked into the trees.

"Where is Jack goin?" asked Bushrod.

Anna bit her lip, and her voice was trembling again. "He is goin.....he is goin to my cousin's house. He wants you to follow."

"All right," said Bushrod. "I will go for a little while."

Nebo rose to his feet and made a circle with his thumb and forefinger. "You can look through the glass like we do," he said.

"Come on, now," said Anna. "The both of you."

She took Bushrod's good arm in her own, and the three of them turned away from the grave. Bushrod took a last look and saw that Virgil C. was back; this time he was puzzling over his broken fiddle. Virgil C. looked up. *Say, Bushrod, where you goin now?*

"I don't know, pard," said Bushrod.

"Hush," said Anna. "Hush, now. That's enough."

For a time after they were gone, nothing moved in the silent after-noon. Then, high overhead, a single leaf turned loose its hold and rattled down through the branches. When it broke free of the bottom branch, it spun for an instant, descending. It settled on the fresh-mounded earth of the grave—the first of many to come, autumn after autumn, forever.

Lieutenant Tom Jenkins was, so far as he knew, the sole remaining officer of the Twenty-first Mississippi. He had been hunting for someone senior all morning; he and the regimental Sergeant-Major had traversed the ground between McGavock's and the gin three times, gathered forty-four of the boys, accounted for a handful of the missing—but of the regiment's officers who had gone into the battle, Tom Jenkins seemed to be the only one who came out again. The knowledge weighed on him like a stone. He wanted to believe his survival was an act of Providence; he hoped it was not through any fault of his own.

In a corner of one of McGavock's pastures, the forty-four men of the regiment were gathered under the watchful eye of Mister Julian Bomar, the Sergeant-Major. They were sitting or lying on the ground, sleeping, making coffee, playing cards, smoking, talking things over. Tom Jenkins contemplated his remnant of a command. Forty-four men. No doubt more would come straggling in directly, each anxious to tell his story and prove he had not let the others down. But from the look of things, there would not be many of these. Tom Jenkins was an optimistic man, but he had seen the field.

He felt like he ought to say something to them, though what it might be, he couldn't imagine. The notion of a rousing speech, even if he could have made one, was ludicrous. That morning he and Mister Bomar had stood in a group of men and listened to the surviving captain of one of the Tennessee regiments read General Hood's congratulatory order. They had won a great victory, put the enemy to flight, etc., etc. The officer's voice dripped with irony, and the men hooted. Tom Jenkins had turned gloomily away, embarrassed for General Hood who, after all, was still their commander. Now, alone with his men in the quiet pasture, he tried to imagine what *he* would say if he were the General. But it was no use—all he could think of were empty platitudes, the kind of vacuous phrases offered at a funeral: *My boys, don't the Army look natural—almost like it was sleepin—*

Still, Tom knew he had to say something. He started toward his men, hoping Providence would deliver some suggestions on the way.

When the men saw the Lieutenant approaching, they ceased their talk. Some rose to their feet, others punched their sleeping comrades. Jenkins stopped at the edge of the group. The Sergeant-Major unfolded himself from the ground and came to stand beside his officer.

Tom Jenkins clasped his hands behind his frock coat and looked into each man's face. Without exception, the eyes that looked back at him were unreadable. Whatever the boys were thinking, they were keeping it to themselves for now.

The soldiers gathered around in a half-circle, slouching, hands in their pockets or hooked in their suspenders. Some knelt, some sat upon the ground and plucked at the grass, some fell asleep again almost at once. Tom Jenkins could smell them: their sour breath, their farts, the stink of their wool and sweat, the smell of death. That was one of the things he would carry away from the war: how it stank like death—a rich, sweet smell that festered in the nose and clung to everything but most of all to men. Years later he would smell it on men who had been there. He would smell it on himself in the nights when he would slip from his bed, dress quietly, and leave the house—smell it while he walked the streets and alleys of Cumberland until daybreak. Nothing smelled like that, nothing else in the world. And nothing could wash it away.

The boys closed around. They were filthy, played out, hungry, and dangerous as snakes. Those still awake watched Tom with their empty eyes.

Behind them stood their stacked arms: eleven pyramids cluttered as always with belts and haversacks and cartridge boxes, and draped with their dingy gray jackets. Hats dangled from the tips of bayonets. The stocks of the Enfields were greasy-brown, the brass tarnished, the blueing worn away—but the bores (Tom Jenkins knew) had been swabbed with rags and canteen water and the nipples picked clean. The bayonets gleamed dully; those that had been used in the fight were wiped clean. Across two of the stacks, rolled up on its staff, lay the remains of the regimental flag. It could hardly be called a flag anymore, the fire from the Federal works had burned and shredded it to rags. But they had not lost it—three men had died to save it during the attack at the gin; the fourth man to seize it, and the one who bore it from the field, was Tom Jenkins himself. No doubt he would be proud of that one day, but he did not feel proud now. He felt strangely ashamed, and very tired.

There was the flag. Tom could see it clearly where it lay mute and inert among the bayonets, and he could not seem to nudge his mind beyond it. The sight of the flag stopped him—it was as if he'd gotten right up to the very truth he needed and then couldn't grasp it. *Maybe I am too tired for truth*, he thought. *Especially for truth.*

For the moment, there was no sound in the pasture at all—no wind, no voices, even the crows were silent. Tom went on standing with his hands behind his back; meanwhile, Mister Bomar contemplated the sky, and the men waited. The hands of their watches moved invisibly, crossing an empty place in time that grew broader and deeper with every click of the wheels. Ordinarily men would not have endured such a vacancy for long before the urge to shatter it with a cough or movement grew irresistible. But these men remained silent; most of them had even ceased watching now, their eyes drifting off with their thoughts. So it was with Tom Jenkins as well. He had so completely forgotten his purpose that he was no longer aware there had been anything to forget.

He considered himself, Tom Jenkins, officer of the Army of Tennessee. Here was old Tom, for once wearing his sword and pistol—old Tom Jenkins, erstwhile merchant, whose coat was stiff with the blood and brains of one Tony Beckwith, Private, erstwhile carpenter and father to twelve children whose names the man could never remember without writing them out. Tony Beckwith had been just to his right in the charge, had walked right up to the snout of a gun where it poked through an embrasure, put his hand on it just as the gunner pulled the lanyard. Widow and orphans. Recalling this, Tom Jenkins looked down at his coat, he brushed at it and a little of Tony Beckwith came off on his hand. Suddenly the Lieutenant had the urge to laugh. *All right*, he thought. *That's enough, that's just about enough. Time to go home.*

He looked up at the circle of faces. *All right, boys—time to go home.....let us forget the whole thing, go do something else for a while, I set you free.....*

"Sir?" said Mister Bomar. "Lieutenant?"

"The truth shall make you free," said the Lieutenant.

"Was you goin to say somethin to the men?" asked the Sergeant-Major.

Yes. Tell them they can go home now, tell them it is all over and done with. Tell them I am too tired to—

"Lieutenant!" said Mister Bomar, and Tom nearly leapt into the air.

"Right-o, Sar'nt-Major," he said.

Then, for no apparent reason, a bell began to toll down in the village of Franklin. Every man of the regiment, awake or asleep, began, with some dim portion of his mind, to count the strokes as they fell across the silence, each stroke rising out of the echo of the last so that it was one long, mournful sound—four, five, six—marking the hour perhaps—seven, eight, nine—like the courthouse bell in Cumberland—ten, eleven.....and on the twelfth stroke every mind made a tally, drew a mark, prepared itself for silence again. But not this time. There was a thirteenth stroke, a fourteenth. The bell went on and on, pealing out over the afternoon in its clear, beautiful, melancholy voice. Without knowing why, the men began to grow restless, to stir like a tableau come to life. They moved their hands and feet, pulled up handsful of grass, lit their pipes, tried out their voices on one another. Tom Jenkins shook his head and rubbed his eyes. *Providence*, he thought. *So here is Providence after all.* Then, in a voice so loud it startled even himself, Tom Jenkins shouted:

"Sar'nt-Major Bomar!"

"Right here, your grace," said Mister Bomar, grinning.

The bell had ceased but the echo hung in the air, and out of it rose the familiar fretting of the crows. A little wind stirred up, tilting the broomsage-tops. The voices of the men grew louder, and someone laughed a dry laugh, and Tom looked at the Sergeant-Major, who was chewing a straw and regarding his officer with a curious smile. Suddenly, for the first time in his life, Tom Jenkins believed he was actually communicating with another human being by thought alone:

What do you think we ought to do?

Well, Lieutenant, it is still a regiment, ain't it?

Yes, but—

Well, fuck that, Lieutenant. Nobody has told them they are whipped yet. Just let me go amongst em, see what happens.

You sure?

As the Resurrection.

"Sar'nt-Major!" shouted Tom Jenkins, exactly as he had before, aware too late that he must sound ridiculous.

"Still here," drawled Mister Bomar.

"Ah, yes," said Tom. He pulled himself erect and gestured toward the men. "Look here, Mister Bomar—what is all this? Ain't these fellers ever done no soldierin? Have em fall in straightway. Good God."

"Yes, my liege," grinned the Sergeant-Major, and saluted. Tom Jenkins returned the salute—it felt good, somehow, to do that.

Mister Julian Bomar, incumbent High Sheriff of Cumberland County, was not an Old Army man, but, like all Sergeants-Major, he seemed to have Old Army ways. Sewed them on with the chevrons, Tom Jenkins thought—though strictly in metaphor, for no one in that regiment wore chevrons. In any case, Mister Bomar had that way about him as if he'd never done anything else but soldier, and now he glided among the men, rubbing his hands as if he'd waited all his life for this moment.

"Now then, lads," he said. "You heard the Lieutenant—think you can just stand around like it was election day? Fall in, goddammit!"

He cursed and cajoled, threatened and belittled, evoked strange, militant gods who suddenly loomed with disapproving faces out of the clouds. You call yourselves soldiers, he told them. So many old women, he called them. Old women, standing around with your thumbs up your ass—great God!

He swore to God, to Beelzebub, to the Archangels, the Seraphim and Cherubim. What would their mothers think? Their little sisters? He peopled the broomsage with dead comrades who pointed ghastly fingers in the direction of duty and vengeance—toward an enemy who expected them to cower like dogs. But he—Sergeant-Major Julian Bomar—did not intend to cower, not now, not tomorrow, not in a hundred lifetimes before any goddamned squareheaded sons of bitches. Any you boys want to quit? he asked. Want to go home? Because if you do, that's all right—take your sugar-tit and go. But don't *ever* let me hear you say you went soldierin in the big war—

He called them by name, spun out their generations, reminded them of their marches and battles, their glorious dead and the hardships they'd borne—all the while prowling up and down, before and behind.

Where is your coat, Stuart Bloodworth? Here, put your cap on, cover up those greasy locks. For God's sake, Earl! All them dead blue-bellies and you still got no shoes? Hungry? Shit—you ain't hungry. I'll let you know when you are hungry. Here now, boy, don't put a hand on that musket 'til that officer tells you to—have you just been born? Are your breeches wet? *Dammit* to hell, close it up there—and wake, June Elliot, wake to the glorious morn—I will let you know when you are tired—

The boys shuffled about, groping into their jackets, knocking out their pipes, driven by the Sergeant-Major's voice. They were like thin, ragged, animated scarecrows, hawking and wheezing and complaining. They were all angles, all sharp corners and bristles, lean and wiry like the long-legged horses the cavalry rode. Even the short ones, the squat ones (there were no fat ones) seemed collected for speed, for driving, for long walking down the winter-deep mud, down the fields and barren valleys into the smoke.

Tom Jenkins watched them, and he listened to what the soldiers said:

Oh, Julian, how you do take on! Oh, give it a rest—can't you just let a feller die in peace? Don't prod me, Ike Fentress, and what have you stepped in anyhow?

That's right, said the Sergeant-Major. Ike, go down there by your little brother—great God, his nose is runnin—

Button me, darlin.

See if I ever vote straight Democrat again.

Let me in there, boys—I want to be next to little Teddy 'cause I love him so.

No, thought Tom Jenkins—*it ain't that they don't know they are whipped. They do know. They just don't give a shit.*

The Sergeant-Major was grinning at him then. Tom Jenkins had not noticed before that Mister Bomar's cheek and neck were blackened with a powder burn. Tiny beads of blood glistened where the powder grains lay just under the skin, where they would always lie, where not even the undertaker's cosmetic could hide them on the distant morrow.

"Resurrection Day, Lieutenant," said Mister Bomar, and his teeth shown white in his dark face. He turned, put out his hand, and grasped the color staff. He lifted it clear of the bayonets and planted the butt on the ground and unrolled the ragged, smoke-stained remnant of the flag, shook it loose so that the red field, the stars, the blue saltier and the painted names of their battles broke into the light. Then he lifted it, shook it so that the tatters snapped in the air above him.

"Now, goddammit," he said. "Who wants to be a soldier in the big war?"

In the winter pasture, fallow and brown, the voices rose hooting and catcalling because they were old soldiers and bedamned if they would cheer anymore. Nobody waved a flag at them anymore, not at these boys, not at the Army of Tennessee.

So they mocked and jeered, while the Sergeant-Major grinned and shook the flag at them—

All right, thought Tom Jenkins. *Come on, boys......come on now—*

Then he heard it, what he was waiting for, what he almost hoped he wouldn't hear, but never doubted. It began quietly on one end of the line, like a wind mourning in the grass, then grew in strength and volume as each voice took it up in turn: the old familiar cry again, waking all the ghosts that lay along the road behind, pushing hard against all that the living knew and felt—against grief and regret, defeat and hardship, truth and reason and sense and whatever it was that made a man insist he was important, that he alone stood at the center of the universe. Tom Jenkins drew his sword and held it up and the bright blade gleamed like the bayonets, and as he listened Tom Jenkins felt despair tip over inside him and vanish away, and he knew that from that moment he wouldn't much give a shit either and this was what it came down to and it would have to be enough: a Lieutenant, a Sergeant-Major, and forty-four raggedy-ass privates of the line all lifting their voices, raising a little hell, because the day was passing and the sun was moving down and it was the best they knew to do—

The sound drifted across the afternoon, over ground where men had struggled and died. Anna Hereford heard it, where she stood with Caroline McGavock on the porch of the great brick house. "Listen!" Anna said, and lifted her face, and felt her blood run quick and hot.

The soldiers in the yard heard it and turned their heads to the sound, and the wounded men in the yard and in the house, and the surgeons who worked over them, and the litter bearers struggling over the fields, and the dazed civilians, and Hattie and Winder peering from the door—

Bushrod Carter heard it, where he lay on a blanket in the yard, waiting for Anna to bring the surgeon. At the moment, he did not know that he was waiting; he was deep in a dream about a strange house with many rooms, and all the rooms empty and lit by spears of red sunlight. And the sound reached him from somewhere far outside the house, and he knew right away what the sound was and where it came from and he wanted to be there—

Bushrod rose on one elbow, face glistening with fever, his shirt and hair soaked with sweat. "Listen, Nebo!" he cried. "Listen to the boys! Mississippi—"

"Whoa, now," said Nebo, and made Bushrod lie down again, and bathed his face with the wet rag as Anna had said to do. Nebo heard the men, too, where they were crying off down in the woods, and the sound of it made him tremble.

In a little while, Bushrod was asleep again. This time he dreamed of snow.

In the front yard of McGavock's, Major R.K. Cross was climbing into the saddle of his fractious little gelding. When the sound reached him, he grinned in spite of himself. *Well, go it, boys*, he thought.

The horse shifted nervously under the rider's weight and, as he always did, turned his head to nip ceremonially at the Major's boot. "Quit it, Patch, damn you," said the Major, as he always did. The horse gave him a wry look, and turned his head to the front.

Major Cross adjusted his saber and checked the caps and loads in his revolver. It was so much better up here, on a good horse, where you could see a ways and where you knew pretty soon the ground would be moving fast under you. The Major looked one last time at the brick house—most likely he would never see it again, and that was well, he supposed. He thought of the girl Anna, and wondered how Bushrod would fare with her—old Bushrod, his pard out of the old times. He thought of the strange fellow with the ramrods, and the generals on the porch, and the beautiful Miss Caroline who'd been so kind to him. So much to remember, so much to take with him if he chose. *Ah, well—let it go*, he thought. There was not much time left and it was all fading anyhow, all passing into the twilight where the Major himself must be before long.

The little horse moved restlessly beneath him. It was a hard thing, saying farewell—he could never get used to it. He turned in the saddle and regarded the twelve men, formed up in column-of-twos, who sat their horses behind him. They, too, seemed to be fading before his eyes. He shook his head. *I am just tired*, he thought—*only tired is all*.

The Major looked toward the ford of the river where the dark trees waited. Yonder was tomorrow, and it would come soon enough, and it was all right. He turned again, rose in his stirrups, and lifted his hand. "Forward," he said.

CHAPTER FOURTEEN

The wood behind the McGavock house—behind the quaint kitchen with its chimney-curl of smoke and eternal smell of burnt grease—was not at all like the oak grove. This was a real wood, wild and dark, with great gnarled trees and deep, vine-choked gullies where the stock might have been hidden forever from the eyes of ravenous armies. A remnant of the old forest it was, unchanged since before the oldest McGavock's time, where bobcats lived who squalled on winter nights, and foxes with beady eyes, and delicate, fog-colored deer who often at twilight stood just in the clearing, watching, then vanished with a flick of their tails.

Other creatures lived in the shadows among the twisted branches and vines. These the Negroes told about, down in the Quarters summer nights, when they sat on up-ended oak slabs by a smudge fire. The Wampus-cat, they said, would get you if you went in there, and rip your belly open with his tushes. There was a Great Pig, a hundred years old, that stole bad children and left their bones gnawed and white in the blow-downs. There was the Lord-to-God bird, and a silver dog that came on the full moon before somebody died. There were plat-eyes, too—restless things risen out of the old slave burying-ground. These would make a shape to fool you—a little girl perhaps, or a kitten, or even your mama in a long white gown—and you would go down there and they would have you, and you would wander forlorn all the days of the world.

Winder McGavock sat cross-legged on the sloping grass and considered the wood. He thought about the silver dog and tingled, knowing that, on the full moon just past, the creature must have come and walked this very ground in anticipation of a great harvest. Winder could almost see him trotting along, tongue lolling, glancing back over his shoulder now and then at the moon hung in the sky. The boy shivered and thought about what it meant to be dead. It was a raving and cursing and knocking against the door. It was being stiff with your eyes open and your fists clutched against your chest, and the secret blood that welled up and turned black in the lantern light. Death was Mother weeping sometimes, and little white stones with the names of children you didn't know, and cousin Anna dreaming and talking of dark birds in the trees. Winder did not know how it all happened, but he'd come to learn that the ground between being alive and being dead was no broader than the track of the silver dog, and no harder to cross. It was not something he wanted to think about too much.

In the boy's lap was a soldier's haversack, tarred and threadbare, with a tin cup hanging from the buckled strap. The cup was dented, rusty, smoke-blackened; a filthy strip of rag was wrapped around the handle. The boy touched the haversack and remembered the face of the soldier who owned it: Mister Bushrod Carter, who had come with cousin Anna to the room upstairs, way back at the first light of day. Now it was nearly evening and the early dark was coming on—

Winder heard something flutter in the wood. He looked up sharply, expecting to see the dog sitting on its haunches, watching him. But there was nothing.

He had carried the haversack all day, and a dozen times he'd been tempted to open it, and finally he'd slipped off down here to do it. Just a peek, and he would put everything back like it was, and nobody would know the difference. Still, he watched a while longer. Nothing stirred in the wood, and presently he heard voices drifting down from the yard, and a quick fragment of laughter. These things comforted him—and anyway, Mister Bushrod Carter would not mind if *he* looked in the haversack.

He toyed with the buckle and strap. The buckle had a little roller on it. His hand moved over the tarred linen; tar stuck to his fingers like pine-sap in the summertime.

The soldier's canteen lay in the grass beside him, its brown wool cover speckled with rust. Winder unbuckled the haversack and placed the tin cup carefully with the canteen. He wondered what the rag around the handle was for.

A crow flew overhead, cawing. Winder looked up and saw him against the slate-gray sky. He saw the sun, too: a white disc floating behind the clouds.

Winder opened the haversack and looked inside. He was struck by the odor of rotten vegetables, like the turnip bin at the end of winter, and a rank smell like bacon grease left too long in the pan. Among these were other smells, climbing upward like vines around a fence post: sulphur, lye soap, something like the cistern when it was drained, laundry when it was dirty, straw when it was wet, the feathers of a dead bird. One by one, Winder began to remove the things from the haversack and lay them beside the cup and canteen.

There was a tortoise shell comb, a bone toothbrush, a fragment of soap. A tin of George Hummel's Celebrated Essence of Coffee. A piece of blue ribbon. A dirty rag. Another dirty rag. A stub of candle. Loose minie-ball, rusty tin plate, wooden spoon, a fork with "B.C." carved in the handle. There was some string, a bundle of letters, a deck of playing cards, two clay marbles and a pretty rock. There was a piece of wire with a loop on the end and a thing that looked like a little wrench—one day Winder would learn that these were a nipple pick and an Enfield rifle tool.

There were books. Winder puzzled out the title page of one: *The Book of Common Prayer*. It seemed to be about Sunday school. The other book was hopeless, a clothbound affair crowded with close writing in pencil that Winder couldn't read. The pencil itself was stuck in the binding.

Finally, there was a tintype wrapped in muslin. It showed three soldiers, younger and fatter and cleaner than any soldiers Winder had ever seen. They stood in front of a curtain painted with odd-looking trees, their hands on each other's shoulders, their faces solemn.

That was all there was in the haversack.

Winder peered into the odorous depths of the bag, hoping he'd missed something; nothing was left but a few shreds of tobacco and a dried apple slice. He studied the things laid out in the grass. It was a disappointing, impoverished collection, everything broken, rusty, dirty, bent, tattered. Only the little book with the close writing suggested that there was anything mysterious about being a soldier. He would have to ask Mister Bushrod Carter about it. Perhaps, having entrusted Winder with the haversack to begin with, the soldier would reveal some of the secrets of the book.

A blue jay began to cuss down in the wood. There was a squirrel too, chirring and carrying on—Winder could see his tail flicking in a bare hickory tree. These signs made the boy uneasy. He looked around, saw no one—the grassy rise suddenly seemed a very lonesome place. It was quiet, too, in the way a room is quiet when you look up and find everyone gone. It all had a bad feeling.

Time to go, Winder thought.

He gathered up Mister Bushrod Carter's belongings and stuffed them back into the haversack. He hung the tin cup on the strap and closed the buckle and was about to get up when he saw the tintype still lying in the grass.

He picked it up and looked once more into the soldiers' faces. They gazed back at him in flat, stony silence. Winder had seen so few such images in his life, and all were of people who were dead: Grandfather McGavock in his high collar and cravat; an old aunt, severe of face, her long fingers woven together in her lap; a boy—one of the Dead Children—propped in Mama's bed, clutching a handful of flowers on his way to the little stones—and now here were these soldiers in their short jackets and waistcoats and caps tilted over their eyes, and Winder reasoned that they, as well, must be dead. In the picture their cheeks were tinted like roses and their buttons were gilded—*But they are dead*, Winder thought.

The boy wondered who they were, and why Mister Bushrod Carter carried their image about. *These three are dead*, thought the boy again, and imagined them lying with their chins tilted up and their hands crossed on their breasts and their eyes like clay marbles. Then Winder's thoughts stumbled over the memory of the long night. He saw the door flung open to the little room where the daylight was peering through the shutters— something crying like a calf, knocking at the door—the soldier coming in with a pistol, trying to shoot Nebo, saying mean things to cousin Anna until she slapped the fire out of him. The soldier was Mister Bushrod Carter, and his face was broken, like everything he owned except the tintype of the dead soldiers with rose-tinted cheeks. Winder looked at the image again. It seemed so real, and there was something he knew about it that he couldn't make into words. He stared at it so hard and so long that the men's faces began to move against the painted backdrop as if they, too, were trying to make it into words—trying to tell him what it was that he knew. The boy stared so hard that when he looked up he could see the pale ovals of the dead men's faces against the dark wood, and out of the place where their faces were came the dog.

It was almost as if he'd expected it. *That's what you get*, he thought— *that's what you get for foolin around where you got no business*. Out of the dead men's faces walked the dog, and the boy's blood turned to cold molasses in his veins and all of time narrowed down like the neck of a funnel. He would be taken now, doomed to roam forlorn in the gnarly wood—no doubt he deserved it—his mother would mourn—from somewhere, invisible, he would watch her kneel by the little stones and weep—

He shut his eyes and waited, listening to his own breathing. In his hand the tintype was cold and lifeless, as he himself must be directly. Death was here—the knocking at the door, the flutter of dark wings against the window glass—and soon he would rise out of himself, become a fog or a foxfire or a cold, empty space in the night air—

Waiting. Breathing fast and shallow like a frog. He wondered what it would be like, if he would see the dead men walking in the air, if they would touch him with their cold hands, if he would weave among them like smoke. He wanted to open his eyes, but he knew that, if he did, he would see the dog's face, or a dead soldier's, or the stringy old aunt pointing her finger. So he kept his eyes tight shut, but of course that was no good either, for in the darkness there all the grievous sins of his life paraded, mocking him—

He opened his eyes.

He was surprised at how bright everything was, and how it all looked just as it had before—no dead men, and no slathering, silver-tipped dog loping toward him up the grass. Instead, down by the woodline, there was a thing like a possum shuffling along: squat, bowlegged, not silver at all but a dingy white, as if it spent all its time crawling under greased axles. It was a dog all right, but as a herald of doom it was in a class with the shabby articles in Mister Bushrod Carter's haversack. As the boy watched, the creature lay down in the grass; it did not seem to be interested in the boy, or anything else in particular. It was, evidently, a real, ordinary dog, and not much of one at that.

Winder found his breath again, and felt his blood flow warm in his veins. The thought occurred to him that if he could lure the dog up into the yard with a biscuit, perhaps his mother would let him keep it, though that was unlikely. Still, it was worth a try. He slipped the tintype into the pocket of his roundabout and was about to rise when someone began singing in the wood:

> One morning fair as I did ro-o-oam,
> All in the blew-ming spring—
> I overheard a mai-den, so
> carelessly did—

Then: "Damn the damn briars anyhow!" followed by a thrashing in the brush that sent a blue jay flying overhead in raucous outrage. Again the boy sat transfixed, like a rock in the field, his mouth open and his eyes big and round as the buttons on Nebo Gloster's coat. Presently the voice began to sing again:

> Fain crew-el were my par-ents,
> Who me did sore deny-y-y-y!

237

They would not let me tarry with
My bonny laborin b-hoy!

With the last note, the apparition of a man clad in black from head to toe emerged from the shadows of the wood. An ivory-handled pistol was thrust in his breeches-band, one of his fingers was hooked through the ear of a clay jug.

It's a plat-eye, sure as you're born, thought the boy with renewed interest. Now surely he would be lured to his doom—he would wander forlorn forever, his mother would mourn—

But the plat-eye, like the dog, seemed to take no notice of the boy. It stopped at the edge of the wood and looked about, as if surprised to find itself where it was. Then it raised its arms, the jug dangling, and embraced all the grassy rise. "Jehovah!" it cried. "Delivered out the wilderness, praise God!" It followed this amazing utterance with a long pull at the jug. This accomplished, it wove unsteadily for a space, and then it spied the dog. "Ol' Hunnerd!" it said, but the dog took no notice. "Why, you ungrateful son bitch," said the plat-eye, and raised the jug to throw it. This was poor judgment. The jug spun backward into the trees, and the figure fell flat on its back in the grass. "Well, I'm a son bitch," it said.

In all, Winder thought this unusual behavior for a plat-eye, though he'd been warned never to trust the shape they took.

The figure struggled like a narrow black beetle, using words the boy found unfamiliar. He wondered if they were an incantation of some kind, but soon dismissed the idea—they seemed too common for that. In fact, there was something decidedly soldier-like about them, and the boy had to come to the disappointing conclusion that he was seeing only a man after all.

Finally the man was on his feet again. He hunched his shoulders and shook out the skirt of his frock coat and looked about him. This time he saw the boy. "Aha!" he said, and began to tack up the rise. The dog, with the air of one who has nothing better to do, followed him. In a moment, the boy could see the little red crosses on the collar of the man's coat; then he was looking into the man's face where it swayed against the pallid sky. The face was broad and ashen and the eyes were sunken, but it was not an unkind face.

"Par'n me," said the man. "Mind if I set down?"

"Is that your dog?" asked Winder.

The man whirled about. "Aha!" he said, and drew the pistol. "Where is that scabrous wretch?"

"Please don't shoot him, mister!" said the boy. "He's only just a dog."

The man snorted. "There's some would argue that." He sat down heavily and cradled the pistol in his lap. "Now that's better. The air was gettin a bit thin up there." He fished in his pockets, came out with a cunning clay pipe carved in the likeness of a turbaned head. He stuffed it with tobacco from a leather pouch and lit it with a Lucifer. Clouds of wondrous smoke swirled about them. The boy's eyes were fixed on the pipe.

"Like that, do you?" asked the man.

"It's first-rate," said the boy. "I never seen one like it."

"Ah. Well, it represents a Turk, my lad—one of the heathen tribes. It was give to me by the prominent laity of the Yellow Leaf Methodist Church—you can always tell em, they wear their spectacles on a ribbon 'round their neck. Not the Turks—the others, I mean. Care for a draw?" He held out the stem. Winder shook his head, though he did want to try it.

"As you will," said the man, "though it's never too early to start cultivatin your vices."

Winder wanted to ask about the dog again, but was afraid he might inspire the man to violence, so he said, "That's a dandy pistol, too. I wisht Mother would let me have one—I wouldn't never shoot anybody, just have it, you know. Maybe she would, if it was a nice one." The boy pondered a moment. "Maybe I'd shoot squirrels," he said.

"How 'bout dogs?" said the man. "Would you shoot them?"

The boy winced. "Oh, no—I'd never shoot a dog, 'less he got to killin the chickens the way old Brownie did, or had a fever on him. One day last summer—"

"*Look out!*" shouted the man, and snatched up the pistol.

"What!" said Winder. The dog pricked up its ears and looked interested for the first time.

"Down there!" said the man. He drew back the hammer and aimed the pistol at the trees. "Sons of bitches! See em?"

"No," said the boy, looking fearfully toward the wood.

"Damn woods if full of em," said the man. "Won't let a fellow alone for a minute. Aha!" he pulled the trigger, the hammer snapped on a spent cap. "Damn!" said the man.

"What was it?" asked Winder. "What'd you see?"

But the man didn't answer. Still holding the pistol, he struck another Lucifer and puffed on the Turk's-head pipe. The dog lay its head on its paws and watched them. Presently the man pointed with his pipestem. "That's Ol' Hunnerd there. Boys call him The Marvelous Dog—don't know why. Son bitch stayed with me all night—Holy Jesus, what a time we had of it." The man half-cocked the pistol and twirled the cylinder. "Wonder where I got this?" he said.

"Are you a soldier?"

"Sometimes. Other times, I am not. What'd you say your name was?"

"I am Winder McGavock, my sister's name is Hattie, my papa is Mister McGavock, my mother is Caroline McGavock, cousin Anna is visiting, we live in that house yonder, I know a soldier, his name is—"

"There!" howled the man, and flung up the pistol. Cock, *snap*. Cock, *snap*. On and on, the cylinder turning under the hammer.

"Mister!" said Winder.

The man stopped. He regarded the pistol. "Damn thing's broke," he said. "Wonder where I got it from?"

"What is *your* name?" asked Winder.

"This whole country," said the man vaguely. "Whole damn country, everywhere we been, just a big open grave. Valley of ravens. Jesus."

"Was you in the battle?"

"What?" said the man, startled, as if he'd just discovered there was a boy beside him.

"I say, was you in the battle? Down in Franklin?"

"Oh—the battle." the man thought a moment, then said, "Yes, yes, I suppose I was. Someday you can read my memoirs, learn all about it. I was sober as a monument *then*, all right. Shit." He spat, and wiped his mouth on the sleeve of his coat. "Used to be chaplain of Adams' Brigade, but I am between congregations now."

"What happened?" asked the boy.

The man shook his head sadly. "Whole congregation—gone, skedaddled, taken flight. Never happened before, I'm sure—not to a Methodist."

"Did they run away?"

"After a fashion," said the man. He took the pistol by the barrel and hammered it on the ground. "Damn this thing," he said. "You would think—"

He was interrupted by the flash and bellow of the pistol as it discharged up his sleeve.

"Son of a bitch!" said Winder, and clapped his hands over his ears.

"Goddammit!" said the man. He had dropped the pistol and was flailing at his smoldering coat sleeve; the ball had ripped along inside it, come out at the elbow and plowed a furrow in the dirt. When he had beaten the embers out, the man glared at the boy. "Where'd you learn such language?"

"Why, a soldier—" Winder began, but suddenly the man went into a coughing fit. He grew red in the face, and drew out a handkerchief and coughed into it. When the man took the handkerchief from his face, the boy could see that it was spotted with blood. They looked at it together for a moment, then the man folded the handkerchief and tucked it away.

Old Hundred, wakened by the pistol shot, stood up and stretched and lapped his tongue out in a yawn. He turned around and around in the grass, then settled down with his back to Winder and the Chaplain.

"I think you are drunk," said Winder.

The man nodded. "Yes, yes, I am pretty much pickled—there is a logic to it, though you might not think so."

"A what?" said Winder. But the man ignored him, looking off toward the wood. Presently he began to speak—talking, it seemed, to someone he'd brought with him out of the long night watches, though there was no one but the boy.

"Started too late in the day, like I said, but what the hell? Might as well get it over with, told em that before we ever commenced. No matter. Trouble was, I got lost out there in the dark—Christ! but it was dark. Moses his own self couldn't keep his way out yonder, not on that field. Don't tell *me* about dark."

"What happened then?" asked the boy.

The man shook his head. "Nobody should've lived through that— nobody. But ol' Sam Hook did, oh yes. I found Byron, he said, Well, Sammy, you must look after the boys now, see they all get back to Cumberland. Shit—won't see Cumberland no more, any of us, but I didn't tell him that. I said, Hold on, Byron—but of course it never done any good. It never does once they take a notion to fly. I never saved a single one, you know—not a single one. Maybe you don't believe that, but it's so. And there was so many—I swear to God you could hear em, there was so many. The sky was black with em, they made a sound like birds, like leaves. Well, never mind. I got lost. I said, I wish I'd never come out soldierin, all the good I did. Directly we come on a pool of dark water that was full of dead men, piles of em—don't ask me to tell you what it looked like. Well, I'd give my canteen away, so I said, I'll have a drink of this water. I said to Ol'

Hunnerd, I said, Come take you a drink of this water, but he hung back, all a-tremble, for he knowed what it was. I said, Well, *I* am not too proud, and I dipped my hand in and was just goin to drink when I smelled it— Christ! 'Twasn't water atall. Blood. You understand—a big pool of blood, like standin water."

"My!" said the boy, but the man didn't seem to hear.

"Well, I *had* to find water then. I run toward where I thought the river was—praise God, I found it, come out on a gravel bar peaceful as the day of creation. I washed and washed, laved all the blood away 'til my hands were freezin. Then I just sat down, stared at the water where it was movin along, thought I might pray for the boys but I was too tired, don't you see—nothin would come, no words anyhow, just pictures in my head, so I had to let the pictures stand. I thought, Well, boys, here is the best I can do right now. Pretty soon The Marvelous Dog come along. He said, Come over this way, Sam. You may think I am mad, but that's what he said. He turned around and went a little ways and looked back and said, Well, come on, you ain't doin any good here. So I followed him, we went downriver a ways and come to another gravel bar and he showed me: six, seven men, all Yankees, all dead. Christ Almighty. I could see their faces, white in the starlight—some was men, some boys, come down there to die, I guess. They was stiff already and their eyes wouldn't shut—I tried, but it wasn't any use, so I left em starin. I said, Now boys, you are not of my congregation, but I will bide with you awhile—and I did. All night I stayed with em, stayed with those dead men, and we talked and prayed together. It was a long time, there by the dark water with those boys—it would have drove a lesser man crazy, I'm not too humble to say that, though of course there was angels there too, and they gave me comfort. I could see em standin just across the river, and I said as much. We talked about it a long time, some of the boys said they could see em too, and some couldn't, but never mind. All this time the river sighed and mourned where it slipped along—there was some rocks just there, and it was like somebody talkin in the dark. There was night birds, too, down in the woods—owls and somethin else, I don't know what. Now and then, black things come slidin down the river—I knew what *they* were. One of em got hung up in the rocks, looked at me and said, Well, what is this place? but I didn't know what to tell him. Whole time I never saw another soul, except one time when somebody crossed downstream—must've been a ford there. He sat his horse in the middle of the river, like a statue—somethin, the stars maybe, winked off his spurs. He went on, and it was a long time—but it was peaceful, you know? Then it come daylight after so long a time, and I said, Well, boys, I must leave you now, and they said, Well, we will see you again by and by—so I said, Well, I guess you will, and I went off into the woods. Found the jug somewhere—a cabin, I think. Jesus. Maybe I'll be scared tomorrow—that's always the time for it. Tomorrow and tomorrow. My God."

The man fell silent. He lit his pipe again, and Winder saw that his hands were shaking. They sat without talking for a while. A breeze came and flattened out the kitchen smoke and sent it curling down around them. Old Hundred groaned in his sleep. A flock of geese sailed over, honking mournfully, headed for some secret place in the river bottoms known only to geese. Winder watched them disappear over the trees, and he thought about how he would have done, down by the river in the night with the dead men—

"Maybe I will tell you a story," said the man suddenly.

The boy shifted in the grass, ready to listen.

"What'd you say your name was?"

"I am Winder McGavock, my sister's name is—"

"All right, all right," said the man. "Winder. What kind of name is that?"

The boy shrugged. He had wondered the same thing himself.

"Well, never mind," said the man. "I will tell you a story anyhow."

"All right," said the boy.

"Then again, maybe I won't. I got to find the regiment—been lookin for em all day."

"Please," said Winder.

"Ought to be *some* of em left. The angels told me—"

"What's a angel look like?" asked Winder.

"Look here, you want me to tell you this story or not?" said the man.

"All right," said the boy.

"Well, that's better. I will commence now."

The boy settled himself to listen.

"Once upon a time," said the man, "when I was little like you, I got a pony on Saint John the Baptist Day. He was called Banquo, I don't know why—my daddy named him. He was lazy and mean and not afraid of anything—after the manner of his tribe, don't you know—and the first time I seen him I could tell he had a low opinion of me. Made it plain when I got up on him—throwed me about thirty feet. Daddy laughed. Said there was three ways you could make a animal do your will—you could beat him 'til he had no will of his own, or you could bribe him, or you could be the kind of man he *wanted* to bend his will to—if you understand what I mean."

"Which way'd you try?"

"I bribed him."

"What's bribed?"

"Hmph. I curried that son bitch, combed him, petted him, give him so much feed corn he got wide as a chesterfield—my legs would stick straight out in the stirrups when I rode him."

"Did it work?"

"Oh, yes indeed, if my aim was to get throwed, and stepped on, and bit, and kicked. But as a mollifier, it was all a failure."

"You didn't beat him, did you?"

"It crossed my mind—but no, I didn't. I wasn't made that way, thank God. That left only the one thing: to make myself.....hmmm.....*worthy*, if that's the right word. I asked Daddy how to do it—he said I would have to know myself, that I *would* know when the time came."

"Did you ever?" asked Winder.

The man lit his pipe again, his hands were steady now. "'Twas the fall of the year, around the first frost. One night Banquo broke out of his pen, next mornin Daddy and Uncle Fred and me tracked him up in the woods—Fred had been west, and could do such things. As it turned out, we didn't need to track atall—the buzzards showed us where to go. Found Banquo, down on his belly with his innards trailin behind—a little ways off was a wildcat, dead, his brains was kicked out. Banquo done for him, but too late. Well. I sat down by his head, my heart was broke, I was blubberin like a girl. All the life was leaked out of him except what was left in the eyes—that's always the last to go—and he saw me sittin there bawlin. I thought, Maybe he has waited for me to come so he could die, but the look in his eyes disabused me of *that* notion— 'twas as if he said, I died brave, and all you can do is sit there and wring your hands. Then his eyes was empty, just like that. I will tell you a thing: a man, child, pony, dog— they all die pretty much the same. One minute the eye is quick, next minute it ain't—I been on many a deathwatch since then, and that's my experience. So Banquo was gone, thinkin I was a fool. I think about him sometimes, been thinkin about him today, in fact—"

The man began to cough again. He pulled out his handkerchief and held it over his mouth; when he was done he spread the handkerchief out and he and the boy examined it. There was not so much blood this time.

"Did you bury him?" asked the boy.

"No, the buzzards wouldn't leave us alone, so we piled some brush and burned him and the cat together, up there in the pine woods behind the house. It was fittin, I suppose."

The man was silent then. Winder toyed with the buckle of the haversack, waiting. At last he said, "What happened then?"

"What do you mean, what happened?"

"Well, I mean what happened in the *story*?" said Winder a little pettishly, for he was getting tired.

"Ah," said the man. He dug a pebble out of the grass and threw it at Old Hundred; it made a *thunk* on the dog's back, the dog looked over his shoulder with a malevolent glare. "What was it he expected? I never did know, don't know now. I am still waitin, after all these years. Daddy was right, of course, but he didn't say it would take so long. Maybe I never will know. I always thought, if I could finally be good enough, or brave enough, or whatever it is I need to be, then I would see the son bitch again, like I see those boys in the woods yonder. I thought maybe today, surely today.....but I reckon I never will see him now. Oh, well—that's enough."

The man lay back in the grass and crossed his hands on his breast. The pipe spilled its ashes on his waistcoat and a plume of smoke spiraled up until the man beat it out. He closed his eyes.

"Is that all the story?" asked Winder.

"Ummm," said the man.

"Well, I am sorry about the pony, anyway."

The man did not reply.

"Cousin Anna said there has been enough of killin."

"Did she?" muttered the man. "Good. Splendid."

After a moment the boy said, "Well, are you sleepin?"

"Yes," said the man. "I am give out."

"I have a picture of some soldiers."

The man coughed, once. "That's lovely," he said.

So Winder, too, lay back on the grass. It was cold and damp, and a stone jabbed him in the back, but it felt good anyway to lie there under the moving clouds. The winds aloft were driving them eastward, toward the place where the mountains were. Winder thought he might go and see the mountains some day, but for now he was too sleepy. He could feel it coming: the dense shadow that crept from the place he imagined sleep to live, that lengthened in long fingers until everything was quiet and put away. He often fought it, but he did not fight it now. He, too, was give out, as the man had said.

Even so, he took the tintype out of his pocket and held it up against the opaque sky. The faces of the three soldiers gazed down at him, and it occurred to Winder that he was actually looking backward toward a moment that had passed on some other day—yet it was still here, caught in the little rectangle of tin. The notion moved him, and he wondered if all moments were kept somewhere, to be looked at again whenever you wanted. Probably not. Still, he thought about Banquo the pony. He could easily make a picture of him, nodding along up a green-shadowed road, his halter rope dragging in the dust. The man was there, his hand out, a little corn mounded in the palm—and Winder and Hattie were there, and cousin Anna, and Nebo, and Mister Bushrod Carter sitting in the road with his shoes off..... Maybe that really happened once or, better yet, maybe it was going to. Pretty soon he would wake the man and ask him, and he also wanted to ask if he could hold the pistol for just a minute. And then tomorrow.....

When they found Winder at last, it was nearly dark. Caroline McGavock knelt beside the boy and gave thanks, and she wept a little— not much, but enough. The boy's fists were closed. In his arms he clutched Bushrod Carter's haversack; beside him, in the grass, lay a pistol with ivory grips.

"That's a nice piece," said the soldier who'd come with the women. "Reckon where it came from?"

"I can't imagine," said Caroline. "I don't *want* to imagine." She rose, stumbled, Anna caught her arm.

"Oh, Anna—what if I'd lost him?"

"You didn't lose him, cousin," said Anna. The two women clung to one another for a moment while the evening settled around them. At last, Caroline turned to the soldier. "Will you carry this boy home?" she asked. "I will surely drop him if I try."

"Yes ma'am," said the soldier. "I will carry him."

Anna bent and untangled the haversack from Winder's arms. "This was Bushrod's.....Mister Carter's," she said softly.

Caroline smiled. "The boy has guarded it like the Grail this livelong day. You must keep it now, until the young gentleman—" She stopped, and would have bitten her tongue off if she could.

"Oh, cousin," said Anna.

Caroline slipped her arm around the girl's shoulders. "Well. You must keep it all the same."

"Yes," said Anna. "Another memento of the great Confederate war."

"Let us all go home," said Caroline.

The soldier slipped the pistol in his waistband and gathered up the sleeping boy. Anna put her arm around her cousin's waist, and together they turned back toward the house. A fire was burning in the yard, bright flames already challenging the coming night. They took it as their beacon, and as they moved toward it, Winder twisted in the soldier's arms and cried out. "Whoa, now," said the soldier, and shifted the boy's weight against his breast. None of them saw the tintype drop in the grass.

CHAPTER FIFTEEN

On the moonless, smoky night of the First of December, Bushrod Carter owned more blankets than he had in all his years of soldiering. These included a gum blanket and a wool blanket between him and the cold ground, and for cover two ample McGavock quilts and a brand-new blanket of Federal issue. His head rested on an actual pillow. Moreover, when the temperature began to drop, Nebo Gloster built a fire close beside, not only for warmth but to heat the bricks kept under the blankets by Bushrod's bare feet. Anna Hereford had seen to all of this—she hoped that somewhere in his wandering mind he was enjoying it.

She hoped, but she did not believe.

Bushrod had changed his mind twice during the trip back to McGavock's that afternoon; each time he'd run blindly into the woods, and Nebo had to chase him down. Then, after the second try, his strength left him, and by the time they reached the house Nebo was all but carrying him.

At first, Anna considered bringing Bushrod inside, but quickly saw there was little advantage to it. The house was madness and mayhem, growing worse as more and more men were brought off the field. So they sat Bushrod down in a corner of the yard, and Anna set about gathering up a pallet. She found the wool blankets in a pile set aside for the wounded. The gum blanket was draped over a dead soldier who lay curled up on his side by a green boxwood (Anna lifted the blanket from the body, shook it out, folded it, made herself look in the soldier's face. "I am sorry," she said). She sent Hattie to the cedar chest in the attic for the quilts. Finally she accosted one of the surgeons—the oldest and soberest she could find—and led him to the place where Bushrod sat upon the ground.

"Here he is," she said. "What can you do for him?"

"We must strip his blouse," said the surgeon.

"Oh, my," said Nebo. "He ain't gone like that."

"Do it anyhow," said the surgeon.

It took the three of them to divest Bushrod of his jacket and waistcoat and shirt. "Help!" Bushrod cried. "I am bein murdered! Who will help a widow's son!"

The surgeon, whose patience was long since hammered into a thin blade, took Bushrod roughly by the shoulders. "Look at me!" he said. "Look me in the face, boy!"

Bushrod ceased his struggling. His jaw was slack, and his empty eyes were held by the surgeon's. Then he closed his eyes, and the surgeon let him go. A strand of drool dropped from Bushrod's open mouth. Anna knelt beside him and wiped it away with her hand.

Bushrod's body was white, hairless, frail, etched with grime—it might have been Winder sitting there, waiting for his bath. Anna wondered dully how such a slight frame could be a soldier's.

The surgeon offered only a glance at Bushrod's arm. "It has to come off," he said.

"No!" said Anna.

The surgeon shrugged. "Then he will die. You can see that for yourself."

Anna could, indeed, see that for herself. The arm was beginning to turn the color of blackberries. It was swelling too, and the red streaks coursed through the puffy flesh from the hand to the elbow. It was already beginning to smell.

"It came so fast," said Anna. "It was just.....so fast!"

"It is how it happens," said the surgeon, gentler now. "These boys— they live on parched corn and bacon and coffee, they never sleep, never quit, and when somethin happens to em they got nothin to prop em up. It is a wonder any of em can still put one foot in front of another." The surgeon snorted in disgust. "And now I understand they are goin to Nashville."

"Not this one," said Anna.

"No, not this one," agreed the surgeon. He knelt beside Anna. "This boy is in trouble. There ain't any time left."

"Yesterday I didn't even know him," said Anna. "Now I must choose for him."

"There ain't any choosin," said the surgeon.

"Then let it be done quick, if you can," said Anna.

Anna wanted to go with him, but the surgeon wouldn't hear of it. "Trust me," he said. "You do not want to."

"But I have seen—"

"No," said the surgeon.

Anna watched the surgeon lead Bushrod away. She watched the pale shape of Bushrod Carter stagger across the yard on the surgeon's arm, watched them cross the porch and disappear into the back door of the house, stood staring at the empty rectangle of the door until Nebo came up beside her.

"What they gone do with old Bushrod?" Nebo asked.

Anna shivered. "What they do to all of em," she said.

"Yes'm," said Nebo.

So it was that Bushrod Carter, twenty-six years old and a veteran of all the Army's campaigns, lost his left arm at Franklin.

In the parlor of the great brick house, they held Bushrod down while a rag soaked in chloroform was pressed to his face. The operation was supposed to be performed by a contract surgeon of Featherston's Brigade, Necaise by name, with the old surgeon assisting. Mister Necaise had been working without relief for twelve hours now, and was so far beyond exhaustion, and so drunk on chloroform fumes, that time and the logical progression of events no longer owned any meaning for him. However, he had kept track of the amputations he'd performed by carving a notch for each one in the door he was using as an operating table. He explained this to the old surgeon, remarking that the current subject would be represented by the eighty-seventh notch. "It is simply amazin," said Mister Necaise, "how rapidly these things accumulate. Please notice that each notch is cut at a precise angle of—"

"Orderly!" the old surgeon shouted.

A burly private, detailed from an Alabama regiment, led Mister Necaise away. "Eighty-seven," said the man, who seemed to have forgotten how to walk. "Eighty-seven! Astonishin. Simply amazin."

"There, there," said the Alabama private.

The old surgeon rubbed his eyes and contemplated the patient before him. Number eighty-seven was a handsome boy, and the surgeon wondered vaguely what his connection was to the girl outside. But there was no more time for wondering than there had been for choosing, and the old surgeon selected a knife from the tray beside him. He tested the edge with his thumb; it was dull, of course, and the handle was sticky with blood. For a moment, he considered forgetting the whole thing. A little more chloroform, a few too many grains of morphine, and the soldier and the girl both would be spared a lot of trouble. But, no—once you started doing that.....

The old surgeon sighed. "I am sorry," he said. "I truly am, boy." Then he began to cut.

Now it was evening, and Anna had returned from the search for Winder. Caroline had wanted to come down to the yard, but Anna stopped her.

"You know I want you to come," said Anna. "But—"

"I know," said Caroline. In the lamplight her face was ghostly and drawn, full of shadow. "But what you need I cannot give you, little one. Not now."

"Oh, cousin—"

"No, no," said Caroline smiling. "I am too tired to be of use anyway. I mean to go up and rest awhile, and while I am restin I will think on you, and on that boy—" She stopped and looked away.

"What, cousin?" said Anna softly.

"Huh. Nothin. It's just that.....I never met him. I will always regret—" She stopped again, turned, took Anna's hands. "Never mind. Go to your vigil, and I will think on you, and think how, out of all this madness, you have wrought something good and decent and honorable, and when the time comes.....well, you will know where to find me."

"Yes," said Anna. "I will know."

The two women embraced in the drafty, lamplit hall while men moved and toiled and suffered around them, all traveling into another night, toward another dawn. At last Anna turned to go, and her cousin touched her arm.

"Don't be afraid to grieve," she said. "There is no shame in it."

"I have learned that," said Anna.

"All right. Then I won't worry—not too much, anyhow. Go now, little one."

So Anna went, passed down the hall and through the door and out into the hall. She asked a soldier to bring one of the porch rockers to put beside Bushrod's pallet; there she sat, wrapped in a shawl that Jeanne had made for her long ago, and watched the sullen dusk pass into night.

The soldiers had made a camp of the yard—a haphazard collection of gum blankets and greasy shelter halves and scraps of canvas strung up on bayonetted muskets thrust into the ground. Smoke from dozens of fires threaded its way through the trees. Bushrod would find this all so familiar,

Anna thought, and yet to her it was so very strange. Nothing seemed real—the shelters, the smoke, the strewn accoutrements and jackets, even the men themselves seemed afloat in time as if Anna was not seeing them at all but remembering them. She felt that if she closed her eyes for a minute it would all dissolve, and when she looked again there would be nothing but the empty, muddy yard, the sleeping house, the dark loom of the trees beyond. These things, and perhaps some fleeting shadow that Jeanne would point to and say, "Look, Cherie—do you see them? Do you see the soldiers from the war?"

But, no—Jeanne is gone, run off with the Yankees. You won't see Jeanne any more—

Full dark came, and the bivouac fires winked and glimmered in the woods. From somewhere in the Army's vast encampment, drums began to beat—a signal of some kind, Anna supposed. Bushrod could have told her what the drums meant. *Now, Miss Anna,* he would say, and then he would tell her. She could hear his voice saying it.

A sentry passed like a shadow, his face invisible under the low brim of his hat. He paused and adjusted the musket on his shoulder. "Is everything all right, Missy?" he asked quietly.

"Oh, yes," said Anna. "Thank you kindly."

"You need somethin, you jes call. Say 'Officer of the Guard,' and he will come a-runnin. I promise."

"I am sure of it. Thank you kindly."

The sentry went on. *These boys,* thought Anna—*what will become of them?*

A horse whickered, and a voice rose to quiet him. Somebody was cooking supper; Anna smelled the fatback, heard it sizzling in the pan. Somebody laughed. Nebo Gloster came out of the dark, dragging a limb to put on the fire. Anna remembered an outing on Elk River, on a big gravel bar in low water time. The boys had come out of the woods just like that, dragging limbs, laughing—

So it came then, as it had come to these boys so many times across the crowded years: the night, the end, falling like dark snow over the shapes they had made by day—softening the edges, hiding the dead, turning the blood to water. Soon even the voices would cease, Anna thought, and for a little season there would be some quiet about the earth. Not for long, and not even very quiet—but something saved from death just the same.

Anna leaned forward in the rocker and looked down at Bushrod. For an instant, she thought he was awake, watching her, but it was only his half-open eyes gleaming in the firelight. His lips were moving. *He is talking to somebody, somewhere,* Anna thought, but who it was only Bushrod knew. *Perhaps it is me,* she thought, and wished she knew what to answer.

When they brought Bushrod back from the house that afternoon, Anna was shocked at the sight of him. During all the time she had waited (Nebo sat beside her, watching, telling something about his father and brothers, about tall corn and the moon), she had tried to prepare herself, tried to tell herself that she'd seen enough over the long night before to be ready for anything. But when she saw Bushrod Carter, she found she was not ready at all. His face was pale, almost translucent like beeswax candles, except where the purple and sickly-yellow bruise painted it. His lips were thin and dry, he labored to breathe, his eyes were sunken above cheek-bones so sharp they seemed about to break through the fragile flesh. He appeared actually to have shrunk in the little time since she'd seen him last—in truth, she could hardly recognize him as the boy she had followed up the stairs at dawn, who'd faced Simon Rope only hours before. So quick it all came, like a horseman galloping—but how could she have missed the signs? She remembered the cigar-smoking surgeon: *You might want to wrap up that finger, and put some whiskey on it if you got some.* Good God, that was the best they could do, and now finger and hand and arm were lying in the slippery pile growing outside the parlor window.

The old surgeon had accompanied the litter party. "Well, there he is, Missy," he said as the orderlies lay Bushrod on the pallet. "Whatever he is to you, you got him back now."

"Will he live?" asked Anna.

The surgeon looked at her a moment, then shook his head. "Probably not."

Anna met this news with an icy calm. "I see. Then all this was for nothin?"

"Young lady, I—"

"Never mind," said Anna. "He said you were butchers. He said—"

The old surgeon cut her off. "Now, you listen to me. I have had enough of this—I am tired and old, and I do not mean to be insulted, not by you, not by anybody. I have done the best for him I can—what happens now is up to him and God. You do not care for my advice, but I will give it anyway: look to yourself, and pray, and be ready to accept what comes.

And if you want somebody to blame, go find John Bell Hood. Maybe he can explain about this boy."

"Are you quite finished now?" said Anna.

"With you? Yes, I am finished."

"Then good day to you, sir."

The surgeon shook his head, was about to leave when Anna touched his arm. "Wait."

"What is it?"

"I find that I am not quite finished," said Anna. "I have been rude to you, on.....on purpose. I do not want that to be what you take away from here."

The surgeon almost smiled. He lifted his finger, touched it to her lip. "Come see me when you can," he said. "I got some salve for that." Then he was gone, moving head-bent through the men in the yard.

Now Anna leaned back in the rocker and thought about what the old surgeon had said, about how whatever happened was up to Bushrod and God. She didn't know what Bushrod would think of that, but if he knew his arm was gone, he might not think much of it at all, and then God would be on His own. As for Anna, she couldn't be any help there.

"Nebo?" she said suddenly.

"Yes, Miss Anna?" said Nebo. He was sitting by Bushrod's head with a canteen and a rag. Anna wondered if the man had ever slept in his life.

"Nebo, can you pray?"

Nebo thought a moment. "I don't know, Miss Anna."

"Well, one of us is goin to have to."

"Well, I will take a run at it, if you will tell me how."

"Oh, me," Anna sighed. "Another time, perhaps."

Anna gathered her shawl around her and rocked a while. Somewhere in the camp a man cried out—not in pain, but as one who has wakened from a bad dream. There would be plenty of bad dreams tonight, asleep or awake, no matter. Anna was not sure she could tell the difference between sleep and waking anymore.

Nebo's fire crackled, Bushrod murmured in his fever, the soldiers' quiet voices drifted over the yard. There were many who could not sleep, who walked restlessly through the yard or gathered by their fires and talked incessantly about nothing at all, waiting for tomorrow.

The cane bottom rocker creaked and creaked, a comforting sound. Anna wondered if it would be one of the sounds she carried with her—if on some distant, solitary porch, latticed with the shadows of a moon-vine, she would hear a rocker creak and think of this night, of the starless sky, the soldiers, the boy dying under her cousin's quilts. That morning on the gallery, she had thought of all the things she would keep, but somehow she had not expected this. *I will live to be very old*, she thought—*very old indeed.*

Creak, creak, creak the rocker said. Out of its rhythm rose a song to Anna's mind, the song and the rocker's creak drawing her back to an image she couldn't place at first. When she found it at last, it lay in a quiet place in her heart: Caroline, rocking in firelight, singing Winder to sleep with "Annie Laurie." But that was not all; some other place she'd heard it, and not long before. Then she remembered the army band playing it the afternoon before, in the yard of the house where Bushrod himself had stood waiting to go into the battle, and he was quick and whole then, and she hadn't known him at all, and now here he was—

Oh, my, she thought. *Of all the songs in the world—*

She shook the song out of her mind, tilting her face up to blink away the sudden tears. The fire lit the branches overhead; up there were the sleeping birds, and far beyond was the place where God lived, and He was up there right now making up His mind about Bushrod Carter without so much as a word from her.

What does it take? she asked the high darkness. *Why don't You let me talk to You?* Something good and decent and honorable, her cousin had said— but not enough. "Pay attention!" she said aloud, but there was no answer.

A tree limb creaked above her. She leaned forward and looked at Bushrod again; he lay so still that for an instant she thought he was gone, and her heart nearly left her. But he moved then, just a little, and spoke a single word: "Rain."

Anna sat back and closed her eyes.

Nebo heard the girl snoring softly. It surprised him—he had never considered that a girl might snore. But this was a pleasant sound, not like the braying of sleeping men in camp. Nebo put some more branches on the fire, and when they were going good, he looked at Bushrod.

"Hey, old Bushrod," Nebo said.

There was no answer.

"Whyn't you wake up, Bushrod?"

A wet log sizzled and a jet of blue flame hissed out of it, lighting up Bushrod's face.

He is not goin to wake up, Nebo said to himself.

That thought had been nagging him since nightfall. It was like something already decided, an order come down from the ones (Nebo had never known who they were) who told the soldiers what to do. But it was not like any thought he'd ever had. For one thing, it was not in his head but somewhere under his breastbone. For another, it had a solemn weight to it—no thought had ever *weighed* on him before. It was as if somebody had set an anvil on his chest.

Yet there was plenty going on in his head, too. Thoughts were blundering around in there like a coon in a tow sack, blind and urgent. These had come with the dark as well, and Nebo believed they had something to do with remembering.

He was not much good at remembering. One day, not long after they'd crossed the big river, the man Jack Bishop had shown Nebo his watch. It was the first one he'd ever seen up close. Jack Bishop explained that time moved in a straight line, and that by looking at the watch you could tell where you were on the line. Thinking about it later, Nebo understood for the first time that his life was not, as he had always supposed, spread out behind him like the Homochitto in high water. Rather, it was like the Homochitto in *low* water, snaking along between banks, and if you stood on a high place—like on the top of a pine tree as a hawk might do—you could see the river stretching back and back toward that mysterious place where it was born. That was remembering.

Now, in the dark of the winter night, Nebo looked back down the river and tried to remember. He could pick out a few things: the vicious old nurse, his pappy, burying his brother in the corn patch (He had tried to tell the girl about that while they were waiting for Bushrod to lose his arm—he only wanted to tell her a story, but he got it all mixed up with burying the two soldiers and pretty soon he didn't know which story he was telling—not that it mattered, for Miss Anna wasn't listening anyway.), the cavalry chasing him through the cane, strangers laughing at him—he could even pick out Bushrod Carter telling him something about his musket. But after that there was a long red space, full of smoke and flame and voices in which something had happened, and then he was digging the wide grave in the woods to put the two dead boys in.

He wanted to ask Bushrod what had happened. Bushrod would tell him, maybe even draw it in the dirt for him, like he did one time about something else—but Bushrod was not listening, and ever since dark Nebo had known that he never would.

"Come on, old Bushrod," he said. "Whyn't you wake up?"

But it wasn't any use.

The girl sighed and moved in her sleep. Shyly, Nebo looked at her. Anna's head was tilted on her shoulder; her narrow, scarred face looked serene and youthful, and from somewhere Nebo remembered her laughing. He held to that for a little while, for as long as he could—somewhere she had laughed, and he had heard it.

Quietly Nebo stirred around. He put a fresh warm brick under Bushrod's blanket and lay some more wood on the fire. Then, carefully, shyly, he edged closer to the chair where Anna sat. She was sleeping—dreaming, he hoped, of some pretty thing—but he knew the time must come when she would wake. And when she did, perhaps he could ask her the things he'd wanted to ask Bushrod.

Men were talking in camp. The sentry walked by, a black shape on the edge of the firelight. Somewhere among the trees, a horse was moving. Something, the horse probably, scared up an owl. The great bird swooped over the fire in a flash of wings and disappeared into the dark. Nebo sniffed the air—it was beginning to smell like the deep night.

Nebo Gloster was suddenly very tired. He lay down at Anna's feet, on his side with his legs drawn up. The ground was cold but the fire was good and warm on his back, and it would last a little while. Nebo wondered what he would dream about. Last time, he'd dreamed of a dark and rocky field lit by moving fires, and of a great house where dead men lived. Maybe this time it would be better.

He heard the Homochitto moving, licking at the cypress. He saw the moon on the water. He slept.

There was a quiet space then, when even the most restless took to their blankets, or stared into their fires without speaking. The night pressed down on them, and soon there were only the sentries moving through the firelight. It was always this way in camp: sooner or later the talk must cease, and men must look to themselves or flee into sleep if they were to endure tomorrow.

A deep shadow lay just beyond Nebo's fire, one of those solid black vacancies that men instinctively avoid, as if to enter there were to risk passage through a door they might not find again. Into this shadow the horseman rode, and stopped, and watched a while.

In the tricky, shifting light of the fire, the sleepers—Anna, Bushrod, and Nebo—seemed figures in a very old painting, caught in a vanished moment of repose. It was easy to believe that they might sleep forever, free of pain and grief and confusion, pardoned from all things and especially from tomorrow. They might never change—only the colors around them, already soft, yielding year by year to the benign erosion of time. It was an illusion, of course, for the constellations above were moving ahead of the sun, and the light of day would dissolve the shadows and awaken the sleepers to movement, to life or to death, as it always did. But for now they slept and dreamed, and their peace, for all its deception, was no less real to them.

A long time the horseman watched before he moved away.

Anna Hereford woke shivering. For a moment she could not understand where she was—she seemed caught in a dingy, cloying fog where the only reality was the cold that seized her. Then it struck her: she was somewhere on the battlefield, surrounded by dead men, and the bearded man was coming, turning over the bodies one by one, looking for her. She did not know what direction the house was, nor how far, nor what it was that woke her—a voice, perhaps, or one of the dead men stirring. In a panic she bolted upright, gripping the chair arms. "Bushrod!" she cried.

Her voice roused Nebo, and he sat up stiffly, rubbing his eyes. He might well have been one of the dead, come reluctantly to life again.

"What is it, Miss Anna? Somethin scare you?"

Anna's voice was hoarse, as if she had not spoken in days. "Oh, Nebo, the fire has gone down and I am freezin."

Nebo unfolded himself from the ground like a crane. He looked about him. "Miss Anna, I'll tell you a thing. Somebody—"

"All right," said Anna, "but first stir up the fire yonder."

"Somebody was here," said Nebo, peering into the dark. "I seen him."

For a moment Anna, too, watched the dark and listened, shivering with a chill deeper than cold. Finally she shook it off. "It was just a dream," she said.

"No'm," said Nebo stubbornly.

"All right, all right. But he is gone now. See to the fire, if you please, sir."

"He was right here," muttered Nebo, but he limped to the diminishing woodpile and gathered up limbs and branches and threw them on the coals. A shower of sparks swirled skyward, and in a moment the flames caught and the fire was roaring, sending its light into the deep shadows around and driving them away, flickering on the solemn trunks of trees and the faces of sleeping men and their shabby canopies of blankets and canvas. Nebo leaned over Bushrod then, and peered into his face. "Bushrod? Hey, old Bushrod!"

"What is it Nebo?" said Anna.

Nebo turned to Anna, his face drawn and lined with weariness. "He is mighty still, awful still. I *knowed* somebody was here. It was—"

"Hush!" said Anna. She stood up then, flinging away the shawl—and nearly fell on her face. "Damn!" she said, and clung to the chair. "Now listen—go you down to the kitchen house. Roust that gal out and have her boil some water. Bring it up here, and some rags, too. And some coffee. And don't let her bully you—take a stick to her if you have to."

"I don't want to go out there, Miss Anna," said Nebo, his voice trembling.

Anna looked at the man. After a moment, she let go of the chair and pulled herself erect. "Well, I can't much blame you," she said. Then, moving slowly, stiffly, she lifted the chain and the silver cross over her head and held them out. The firelight winked on the cross. "Take this," she said. "You carry it, and nothin will hurt you."

Nebo took the cross shyly. "Is it magic?"

"Yes," said Anna. "Now, go on. There is nothin in the dark to hurt you—any more than there is in the light, anyway."

"Yes'm," said Nebo, and limped away. In a moment, she could see him no longer.

Bushrod was, indeed, very still. Anna gathered her skirts and knelt beside him, the ground cold beneath her. Bushrod's face (it was bruised and shrunken, but for once it was clean of blood) was turned slightly away; it was beaded with sweat and greasy in the firelight. The stump of his arm lay outside the covers on a scrap cut from the gum blanket. The blood soaking the bandage was pinkish; they'd been keeping it wet as the surgeon had said to do.

Anna touched his hair—it was damp, and coarse with grime, and Anna wondered what it would look like if it was clean and fresh-combed. "Bushrod?" she said.

The stump of Bushrod's arm moved like a blind worm. Anna would not look at it.

"Bushrod? Hey, boy."

This time he turned his face to her and opened his eyes. "Anna," he said.

"Oh, my," she said, and touched his face. "You look awful."

"I knew who you were," said Bushrod. "I did not mistake you this time."

"It would have been all right if you had," Anna lied.

"No it wouldn't. Not now." Bushrod spoke slowly, shaping the words. "Hold out your hand."

Bushrod put up his clenched right hand, and something dropped in Anna's, and she turned to the fire and looked. It was a brass button. She could make out a star on it, and the word MISSISSIPPI spelled out around the edge. She closed her hand on it. "Is it magic?" she whispered.

But Bushrod said no more. Only his eyes moved, as if he were watching something in the dark. Then his eyes closed, and he was asleep again.

Anna held the button tightly and turned her face to the sky. She knew that God was there, beyond the interlaced limbs and the clouds and the hidden stars. And if He was there, surely He could see, and hear, and surely He was grieving too.

"It is time You listened to me," she said aloud, and wakeful men down in the camp turned their heads to the sound of her voice. "I.....I would have loved this boy," she said. "Can't that cancel out the other? Don't it mean anything? Won't You listen to me?"

She shut her eyes and tried to imagine God listening. She searched for an image of Him, found instead the face of General Nathan Bedford Forrest, looking just as he had on the stairs during the battle.

Didn't I tell you there wasn't any shame in it? asked the General.

Oh, why don't you tell Him that? said Anna.

The General laughed. *Him? Why, He already knows it, child. Always has known it. It's you that don't.*

No! He won't forgive—

He did that a long time ago, said the General, grinning through his beard. *It's you that won't.*

"What!" Anna said, and her own voice startled her to waking. She looked around, half-expecting General Forrest to be standing at the edge of the firelight, but there was no one.

Anna pressed her hands against her temples. She was so tired of dreams and of waking and of not being able to tell the difference. "Oh, God in heaven—" she began, and as soon as she heard herself say it, she remembered another voice, Bushrod's out of the afternoon before: *Enough*, he had said. *You will have enough bad dreams as it is.*

"Is it enough?" she said to the darkness. "Tell me! Has all this really been enough?"

There was a sound then, silken and powerful. Anna looked up, and there was the great owl hovering over her, the firelight touching his wings, his eyes gleaming red—only an instant and then he was gone, and Anna could hear him beating his broad wings through the dark, pulling the silence behind him, and the dark birds lifted from the trees and followed him, swirling in their myriads toward the sky. And among the rustle of wings were other voices: the boy who'd betrayed her long ago, and her own voice as she lay in the clover crying of pain and shame and ecstasy, and the voice of the bearded man who'd violated her worse than any.....The birds and the voices rose and swirled and filled the night— *But not for long*, she thought. *Not for long now, because there has been enough of everything, just as Bushrod said*— And it was all right now. The season was changing, the air was drawing them away. They were going away.

Anna Hereford bent again and took Bushrod's face in her hands. "Oh, I don't want you to go," she said. "But it has to be all right. You go on, boy. Go on, now—Jack will find you."

She was crying hard now, and the hot tears dripped from her chin and fell on Bushrod's face. He blinked and smiled at her. "The rain," he said.

"Yes," Anna said. She kissed him then—his forehead, the side of his smashed nose—kissed him finally on his cracked, swollen lips. "Go on," she said. "I will never forget you. I would have loved you. I would have. Go on—quick, now—quick—"

"Some of the boys—" said Bushrod.

"Yes, I know," said Anna. She kissed him again, then pushed the covers down and moved her hand across Bushrod's shoulders—they were strangely smooth, unblemished—and across the smooth, narrow breast. And meanwhile the voices rose in one last desperate swell, and with them now was the army band playing "Annie Laurie"—but fainter and fainter— and the rattle of guns in the windowpanes, the cry of wounded men in their bloody rags and the long cry of the soldiers going into battle, a horse walking in the leaves—fading, all fading as they were drawn away into the night.

Anna lay her cheek on Bushrod's breast. It was warm and hard and fragile, and she could hear the faint drum of his heart.

"Enough," she said softly. "Enough, enough." And she felt the words travel out from her, following the voices into the blowing dark. She could almost see them go, fading like the lamps on the Nashville coach until they drew down into little points and disappeared. She listened then, waiting, but all the voices were gone. There was nothing now but the night, and the distant promise of dawn, and peace at last.

"Go with God, then," Anna said. "This will have to do for goodbye."

Under her cheek, Bushrod's heart fluttered like a moth in a jar. Then that, too, was still.

CHAPTER SIXTEEN

The cold time came, as they had all known it would. A pattering sleet drove down, bearding eaves and fences with ice, covering all the new-mounded graves with their first cold dusting. The ice made fantastic crystal goblets of the trees, and silver lace of the hedges and fence rows. Smoke rose from the chimneys of Franklin and flattened and spread itself through the sleet, crawling over the littered fields, dancing now and then on a vagrant draft. There was a silence, too, as always came under a cold moon, full of sounds that were themselves silence: the creaking of limbs, the query of a snow owl, the distant, solitary barking of a dog.

The Army was gone. In its wake lay a vast ruin of broken things: muskets, gun carriages, ammunition boxes, canteens, clay jugs, spectacles, pocket watches—and men. Especially men. The dead ones filled the ground in backyards and alleys and garden plots, among the woods and low places, among the rocks of the fields. Others who might still be saved overflowed the buildings and houses of the village. All of these suffered, many of them died. Those who were well enough to care awaited news of the Army at Nashville. Win or lose, the Army's fate would decide their own.

Early on this gray and leaden time, on the very afternoon the Army of Tennessee crossed northward over the Harpeth, Nebo Gloster dug a new grave in McGavock's wood. The new grave was next to that of Jack Bishop and Virgil C. Johnson, so close that Nebo had to be careful where he was digging.

He worked in his shirt-sleeves despite the cold. He had broken the ground with a pick, and once had to use an axe on some troublesome roots; otherwise the sound of his shovel was as regular as a ginning machine. The pile of earth by the grave grew higher and higher; not once did Nebo stop to rest, to stretch his muscles, to drink from his canteen. Once begun, he worked until he was finished, just as he had before.

At a little distance, Anna Hereford stood motionless, watching. She was all in deep-mourning, in a dress borrowed from her cousin; imposed on the gray background of trees, she seemed a charcoal figure sketched on slate. She held a black umbrella against the slanting needles of the rain, and against the cold a hooded mourning-cloak wrapped about her. The skirts of the cloak moved in the wind; save that, she was completely still. Not even when Nebo finished the grave did she move.

"I am done, Miss Anna," he said. His voice rang loud in the silent wood. "Do ye want to look?"

Anna shook her head.

The frock coat hung on a limb; Nebo reached it down and pulled himself stiffly into it. For a moment he looked into the grave, then took up the spade and the pick and the axe and limped the little way to where Anna waited.

Anna looked at him. Her face was pale, ashen, but the somber garments had darkened her eyes to the color of cedars. Nebo stood with the tools over his shoulder; his hair, tangled and gray, moved in the wind.

"Then we can bring him now?" Anna said.

"Yes'm. We can bring him now."

Anna put out her gloved hand. Nebo took it shyly, carefully, as if it were glass, and followed Anna toward the house again.

There were no soldiers in the yard now. The wretched little shebangs and the bayonetted muskets were gone, the ashes of their fires were cold and black. The wounded were gone as well, into the house or down into the barns and woodsheds and buildings of the village or, if they were lucky, into other houses where someone could look after them. In the yard of McGavock's house, only the dead remained, little drifts of ice gathering in the folds of their clothing, between their fingers, in the hollows of their eyes.

The generals were long since removed from the gallery, but others waited there: dead men who, by virtue of chance or whim or convenience, had been laid out on the broad pine boards. One of these, shrouded in a blanket, lay just outside the door. At his head, a candle lantern gleamed in the gray twilight, and the flame of this candle moved and winked when Anna knelt beside it.

She knelt, and her skirts' rustling made a sound like birds. Nebo stood behind, his raw, cold-reddened hands clasped before him. Anna removed her gloves, and with her right hand turned down the blanket, turned it down to the waist of the man who lay beneath it.

Bushrod Carter's face was solemn, composed, the face of a sleeper without dreams. He was dressed once again in his gray jacket, brushed and cleaned and buttoned, the empty sleeve pinned up. His right hand lay upon his breast.

"Hey, boy," Anna whispered. She touched his hair; it had been washed and combed, now it glistened with sleet that had crept in under the blanket. Still, it was soft, and fine as cornsilk.

"He looks.....all right, doesn't he?" said Anna.

"Yes'm," said Nebo. "Like a soldier."

"He was that," said Anna.

She rose then, her skirts rustling, and looked out across the gallery to the littered, trampled yard. "Well," she said. "I will tell them it is ready. Nebo, will you come inside?"

"Oh, no, Miss Anna. You go on."

Anna nodded. "Watch with him, then. It won't be long." Then she was gone, and Nebo was left alone on the gallery.

Nebo rubbed his hands, studied them, looked down at the shoes Anna had made him wear in the freezing rain. "Well, well," he said. He walked to the other end of the gallery, stepping carefully among the dead men; he stood there a moment, rocking on his heels, then walked carefully back again. He blew his reddened nose on the skirt of his frock coat, then looked out toward the oak grove. Nothing was moving there. Finally, Nebo sat down, cross-legged, close beside the body of Bushrod Carter.

The patter of sleet made a sound like something walking in the leaves, and away off a dog barked once. There was no other sound. Nebo listened a moment, his head cocked, then he looked at Bushrod's face.

"Well, old Bushrod," he said, "it's mighty quiet now."

He put out his hand and smoothed the blanket over Bushrod's legs. He patted it, and smoothed it again.

"Old Bushrod," he said.

He touched Bushrod's hand. It was cold and stiff, but Nebo closed his own around it anyway. He was sitting like that, still holding Bushrod's hand, when the people came out of the house.

Nebo and one of the McGavock slaves (the same man who'd borne Jack Bishop to the clearing) carried Bushrod to the grave on a Saterlee Patent litter. They moved through the yard in the twilight; behind them, walking close together, were Colonel John McGavock and Caroline, Hattie and Winder, and Anna Hereford. There was no one to watch them pass, only the dead, who kept their own counsel. Into the grove they went, their feet scuffing in the leaves. Overhead, the bare limbs rattled icily in the wind; a little chickadee moved before them, darting from tree to tree like a scout. They followed him to the grave.

Nebo himself lay Bushrod in the ground, and covered him with the blanket, and tucked the edges in. The others watched in silence while Nebo finished his work, watched him rise from the grave, his eyes fixed on something far away. Then they watched him go. He passed among them without a word, without a glance, and walked away in the direction of the river. He never looked back, they could hear him for a little while, then the woods closed over his passing and they could hear him no more.

After a moment, John McGavock cleared his throat. "Well," he said, "if 'twere done, 'twere best done quickly."

He put out his hand to Anna. She hesitated, looked to Caroline, who smiled at her.

"If there are any words," said Caroline, "they ought to be yours."

John McGavock guided Anna with his hand until she stood at the edge of the grave. "It is all right, then?" she said.

He nodded, and bowed his head.

Anna released her cousin's hand. She looked across the grave, thought of Jeanne again and who she might see among the trees yonder: three of them anyway, watching her with faces that would never grow old, waiting for her to speak, and it had to be now because already they were dissolving in the twilight—

Anna lifted her face to the gray sky. "Heavenly Father," she said, and then she began to pray.

EPILOG

One morning in April, Winder McGavock discovered a shaggy pony, his mane and tail full of cockleburs, grazing in the pasture where Mister Bomar had rallied his men.

"Hey there," said Winder.

The pony raised its head and eyed the boy with suspicion. Winder held out his hand. "Come on," he said. "I know where we can get some corn."

The pony seemed to consider this amazing offer. "Come on," said Winder, and turned toward the house. When he looked over his shoulder, he saw that the pony was following.

They moved across the warm, sunlit fields, while the blue jays laughed in the woods.

HOWARD BAHR was born in Meridian, Mississippi. After working for several years at various jobs on the railroads, he received his B.A. and M.A. from the University of Mississippi. From 1982 to 1993 he was curator of Rowan Oak, the William Faulkner homestead and museum in Oxford, Mississippi.